The Jaws of
Turmoil

Best Wishes

Neil

THE JAWS OF TURMOIL

Neil Clift

Text copyright © Neil Clift 2002
Cover Artwork © Lindsay Cole 2003

First published in Great Britain in 2003
by the Self Publishing Network

The right of Neil Clift to be identified as the Author of
the work has been asserted by him in accordance with the
Copyright, Designs and Patents Act 1988

A Catalogue record for this book is available from the
British Library

ISBN 1-90349302-1

To Bahama Momma,
for inspiration...

Rodney Fox,
for courage....

Steve Hindle
for making my dream a reality...

PROLOGUE

Innocent eyes stared up at the screen with a naïve desire for knowledge...

The reporter continued to tell his tale.

"So far, thirteen thousand bodies have been recovered, and only a fraction of the rubble has been cleared... As rescue workers continue to maintain hope, they are working tirelessly around the clock to find survivors of this terrible tragedy..."

"Thomas?"

The young boy ignored the piercing New York accent that emerged from the bathroom, unmistakably that of his mother.

The destruction that stretched from one corner of the wide screen television to the other ensnared the young boy's mind, nothing but rubble, piles of debris and smoke, and frantic people searching the remains for signs of life.

"... The mayor of Tokyo has called this the worst natural disaster on record. From the scenes that I am witnessing, it is easy to see why. I have not seen such tragedy..."

"Thomas!"

Startled, the young boy whirled around, as the slim figure of his mother stormed past his vantage point on the thickly carpeted floor.

In an instant, the image had disappeared.

"Thomas, what have I told you about watching programmes like that..."

"But, Mom, I want to see if they find anyone."

"No 'buts', okay? You are too young to watch the news... I've told you before, there are a lot of terrible things that happen in the news...

It's for grown up people, not you."

The disgruntled child furiously expelled a breath.

"Now, Thomas, you have homework to do. I want it done before you go to bed."

"Okay Mom."

Recognising the limit to which he could push his annoyed mother, Thomas obediently rose from the floor and moved to the table by the window, where a pile of books and a small laptop computer were neatly stacked. As he climbed onto the chair, the Manhattan skyline around their cosy hundred-storey apartment lit up.

Startled, Thomas gazed out of the thick soundproof window that was being continuously pummelled by thick raindrops, which exploded onto the glass as the wind suddenly grew in intensity. Squinting through the distorted image afforded to him by a sudden jagged pattern of lightning in the sky, Thomas could see several skyscrapers below him, light instantaneously dancing over their straight edges.

As the illumination disappeared, something caught Thomas' eye, before being replaced by the hazy image of his own reflection in the window, created by the atmospheric lighting of the apartment. Patiently he waited for the next flash of lightning. When it came he was no longer staring out at the surrounding structures, but beyond them to the sea.

What was that?

Unsure, he waited again. When the lightning came, the image that greeted his eyes was nothing short of surreal. It was as if someone had placed a dark curtain behind the buildings.

Suddenly the sky sparked into dazzling light, once again, but this time it was much closer, and this time Thomas managed to identify the anomaly.

It was water… One huge wall of water!

With the next flash of lightning he was staring at the crest of a huge wave that engulfed the buildings like an abhorrent creation of his darkest nightmares.

"Mommy!"

Hearing the panic in her son's voice, Thomas' mother rushed to his side.

"What is it, dear?"

He was trembling, his gaze transfixed on the window. Suddenly the room began to shake, ornaments leaving their meticulously considered perches and crashing to the floor. As lightning flashed once more, she followed her son's gaze beyond the thick glass to the huge wave rolling over the buildings.

The mega tsunami continued, unforgiving, on a collision course towards them.

Thomas' mother became paralysed like her son.

"Lord help us…"

Chapter 1

Chapter 1

PART 1: PHASE 1

Earth Year: 2081
Project Date: Day 0001 of Year 0001

"So this is the sacred *Eden Treaty*?"

"Yes… In its entirety… Chancellor Conway's words down to the last letter."

A laptop was exchanged between hands that greeted each other from opposite sides of the helicopter cabin.

The elderly figure who had presented the open computer console continued:

"I suggest that you read it carefully, Colonel. We are looking to you to ensure that the Eden Treaty is implemented with extreme efficiency."

The younger man's dishevelled face rose from the laptop to address the elderly man, whose wrinkled features remained partially hidden in the shadows of the cabin.

"I will, Sir…"

Without further hesitation Colonel Tom Simonson opened the portable computer. Reacting instantly to the movement, the screen flickered into life, displaying an immaculately presented document on the screen. The colonel scrolled through its contents:

EARTH DIRECTORATE 234: / 7849: 21/10/2081

BY AUTHORITY OF THE EARTH ALLIANCE:

THE EDEN TREATY:

For the first time in a long and turbulent history, mankind is facing its biggest threat. The threat has come, not from the stars as many have predicted, but from the place that we have affectionately referred to as 'home' for thousands of years - Earth.

The human race has faced many dangers, disease, war and famine, to name a few and we have in the past, walked away from these experiences as a stronger, unified race. Our latest threat, however, weighs heavily upon our shoulders, increasing in mass; the longer that we choose to ignore that it exists.

May I remind you of the quake, in the year 2031, a tragedy that shook every structure to its very foundations, scarring the continent of Europe permanently. More recently, a similar movement hit Tokyo. Barely a year ago, the great storm brought with it a mega tsunami that destroyed the eastern seaboard of the United States, in a swathe of destruction, never before witnessed by human eyes. The salvage operation revealed a death toll amounting to millions. It was the worst natural disaster in the history of our planet.

The storms are now becoming an all too regular part of our lives, and the stability of our safety on this planet has now reached a critical level. Mother nature is reaping vengeance on the race that has taken her gifts, and abused them for selfish gain. Finally, humanity is paying the price for its ignorance. The time has now come to accept that the human race will not survive on Earth - if it chooses to attempt survival in such conditions.

We must enter a new, largely unexplored environment – space!

After years of long searching, intergalactic probes that have been launched from the Alliance Space Station, Aurora, have picked up two planets that upon initial measurements, appear to be suitable to support human existence, with the assistance of state-of-the-art technology.

These planets both reside in the Gamma Quadrant, within the Quaker solar system. Respectively, they have been named Penusia and Coleshia; the former being what appears to be an uninhabited desert, and the latter, a planet covered entirely by water. Even though they have vastly different environments, there has been no evidence of life existing on these planets, despite the existence of high enough levels of oxygen that are conducive to supporting the life to which we are accustomed.

We must now turn our resources towards these goals. We must put aside our differences and make a global effort to make sure that we have the population and the right technology to make these planets suitable for our existence.

In the past, space travel has been restrained by financial constrictions, which as some scientists will argue, has slowed the rate of our progress in exploring the stars. Now our need to reach the far reaches of the vacuum that surrounds us has been made all too clear to everyone on Earth, as each year brings increasingly treacherous conditions and higher death tolls. If we remain on Earth, we face almost certain extinction from the elements, and this is to be our prime motivation towards reaching our destination among the stars.

We must, however, not forget the purpose of this ambition. To propose that it is purely the survival of the human race is to exhibit the same ignorance that we have shown for too long, to too large a degree. Our purpose must encompass the preservation of life. We must recognise that Earth has not just simply changed, evolved to a point where we can no longer feel secure within its environment. We, too, are also to blame, destroying nature's delicate balance, wiping out endangered species and polluting the planet with our waste products. It is not only a time for rebuilding our own lives, but also a time for showing compassion towards the other forms of life that reside on our volatile planet.

In achieving this goal, we must create a new existence for them, as well as ourselves; learn from the mistakes that have marred our past and make sure that we never walk down that destructive path again. Our future must be bathed in glory, rather than destruction. Learning to understand and interact with other forms of life rather than persecuting them must also be among our chief goals. In travelling with them, the future generations will be reminded of the lessons to be learned from our history; as well as being granted the comforting knowledge that, in the long journey ahead, the human race is not alone.

In devising this treaty, I have identified a number of phases in achieving the aim of survival.

Phase 1:
For nations to collaborate in an united effort towards devising the technology that will enable the human race to achieve deep space travel, and sustain a number of forms of life while on the voyage, and upon reaching our destination.

Phase 2:
To collaborate in a united effort to maintain the safety and good care of *all* forms of life, while undertaking the journey to the Quaker solar system.

Phase 3:
Upon reaching our destination, it is the responsibility of the human species to build settlements capable of supporting human existence, and those of our counterparts.

Phase 4:
Once humanity has established the stability of its own existence, it is their responsibility to reintroduce the precious cargo to their new environment, ensuring that they safely acclimatise to their new surroundings.

Chapter 1

These objectives will be collectively referred to as 'The Ark Project'. The project will take hundreds of years to complete in its entirety.

We must learn to live and breathe by these objectives, for our own survival, and the survival of those species that exist around us. If we lose them, we lose a part of ourselves, which, in turn, should raise the question of whether we have the right to exist at all.

High Chancellor Conway.
Chairman of the Earth Alliance.

The colonel slowly closed the machine.

"I guess the tsunami was the final straw?"

"Not just the tsunami. Tokyo was demolished barely a day before, as you well know. Think back to last year, Colonel. England was hit with a force four tornado, an occurrence previously unheard of in that part of the world. El Nino is incensed, Colonel, and we must respond with haste. We can't ignore tragedies that are claiming millions of lives. Remember that the eastern seaboard no longer exists…"

The colonel sat back in his padded seat and exhaled with nervous haste.

"Deep space travel. Just how are we going to manage that?"

"With combined effort, which you are going to assist in co-ordinating."

The colonel's mind began working. He was a military man, not a diplomat. He became wary of the answer that his next question would generate.

"But with so many diverse cultures in the world, how will we get everyone to co-operate?"

The response oozed with clinical disregard.

"We will simply have to take away society's right to choose!"

"Wait a minute – you mean Marshall law?"

"Marshall law, dictatorship, call it what you may; diplomacy is not my concern, and neither shall it be yours, Colonel."

"But…"

"Don't think about it, just listen. This was agreed by the Earth Alliance prior to signing the treaty. Every nation is committed, whether they like it or not. I have also been instructed to inform you that co-operation with the regime will result in special privileges being extended to those families with loved ones involved in instigating the changes."

"And the alternative?"

An icy calm possessed the figure sitting opposite him.

"Remember that you are being given an opportunity here. I would strongly suggest that you take it."

The colonel felt a chill trickle down his spine, before shaking his head. Only hours before he had been flying home to Dallas with his wife and two daughters. There were no options open to him so somewhat defeated he enquired:

"But why the animals? In a race for survival you are going to place the ecosystem above humanity?"

The elderly figure leaned forward, his pointed features bearing down upon the incredulous soldier.

"Although we like to pretend that we live in protected little shells, the truth is that much of our sustenance still comes from the natural world. *Our* survival is determined by *their* survival."

The colonel stared out of the window in the cabin. The sun was beginning to rise over the Atlantic Ocean, sending an orange hue across the sky.

The sinister old man leaned back into his seat.

"Perhaps this will prove the Earth Alliance's argument to you, Colonel. Scientists predict more of these treacherous conditions in the imminent future. Look below you, what do you see?"

Pressing his face to the porthole in the fuselage of the craft, the colonel gazed down at the calm waves.

"The Atlantic Ocean."

The elderly figure cackled.

"I cannot fault your geography, Colonel. Since the tsunami, the ocean has consumed several thousands of miles of healthy land. Do you know where we are?"

The colonel shook his head for one expanse of ocean resembled another to him.

"Below us is what remains of New York!"

Incredulously the colonel looked around. Not one sign of civilisation protruded above the waves. The world had begun to change in more ways than the layout of its continents. Colonel Tom Simonson felt a change occurring in his mind, the shocking realisation that humanity was about to face its greatest challenge.

Chapter 2

Earth Year: 2132
Project Date: Day 125 of Year 0051

Governor Dansun leaned back. His armchair reclined to suit his body position, with a whirring and clicking of small hydraulic gears. He sighed and folded his arms behind his head. The sound of the gears burdened him with a feeling of guilt. This piece of technology was highly advanced, and had required a major use of valuable resources, which could have been put to better use in the daunting project on which the human race currently found itself treading water.

Admittedly, he had a back complaint; a curvature of the spine that often left him in pain, and he had to admit that the hydraulic chair did help his pain to a large degree. Unfortunately, laser surgery had only served to improve his condition to the point that he could bear the pain without screaming. The doctors had told him that he was too old to risk having further surgery. His heart wouldn't take the stress. The pain-killing drugs were only of minor assistance in making his pain bearable. In order to compensate for his constant pain, the Alliance had authorised that he be given the special hydraulic chair. He wouldn't have minded so much if four engineers hadn't been pulled out of commission on the development of the intergalactic star vessels, purely for the 'privilege'. Nothing should detract from the mission. The level of bureaucracy, even in these desperate times amazed him.

Dansun allowed his thoughts to drift beyond the cold confines of his elaborately decorated office. His eyes carefully traced his reflection in the window, taking a thoughtful note of the huge bags that hung beneath his eyes; making it all the more evident to him that he had what amounted to a fairly miserable existence.

Ironically, at this time, he was one of the most pivotal figures in human society, which made the desperation of humankind's situation all the more apparent. For the briefest of moments his mind spared a thought for the millions of citizens aboard the huge space station, going about their routine-driven lives, and for those people who had decided to make the 'choice', as the Earth Alliance put it, to stay on Earth.

There has to be more for these people, for all of us!

His tired eyes changed focus to watch the eerie background, which was the vacuum of space. Small transport shuttles hurried from one corner of his field of vision to the other, no doubt transporting engineers and other staff to and from their allocated roles within the Ark Project hierarchy. This strange sight was complemented by the moon, which hung in a peculiar fashion in the corner of his window; as the centre of hope for humanity, the Aurora, continued its orbit of Earth.

Governor Dansun was glad that he had this office. It allowed him no view of the Earth, whatsoever, constantly staring out at the stars. That would be a perpetual reminder of how things had changed in the past seventy years.

He already had enough memories of those changes, having just turned seventy-eight two weeks before, and now it was important to show strength in the face of adversity. So, he decided that he had to be grateful for small mercies, having somewhere to go where the memories were not forced in his field of vision all the time.

The intercom on his desk suddenly crackled into life, dragging his thoughts kicking and screaming back into reality. The sultry voice of his secretary, Nina, came to his ears. He reminded himself, with a sly grin, that there were still some things in life to be appreciated.

"Governor Dansun?"

"Yes, Nina?"

"Senator McDonald has arrived for his appointment."

Governor Dansun reset his chair to a more upright position, grimacing slightly, as his spinal column once again reminded him of its existence. He turned to face his desk and the door.

"Very well, send him in."

Chapter 3

In another sector of the space station, the result of fifty years of cybernetic research analysed itself in the six-foot mirror inquisitively.

"You are LB-42, the result of fifty years research on the MACU project, or Military Automated Cybernetic Unit. You are a cybernetic organism. Do you understand?"

LB-42 turned to address the owner of the voice, and echoed the statement in a deep, booming voice, completing the monologue with:

"Yes, I understand."

The articulation of the speech was methodical and lacked any sense of emotion.

"Very good," came the reply.

Dr McAllister glanced around at her colleagues, and raised her eyebrows. She returned her attention to LB-42, and walked in admiration around the proud figure that stood rigidly before her.

"You have a purpose... What is your purpose?"

Without blinking, LB-42 replied:

"My purpose is to protect the sanctity of all forms of life encompassed by the directives stated in the Eden Treaty."

"Please enhance on this explanation, LB-42."

"I must protect the safety of humankind at all costs, but with equal consideration and effort towards the other life forms that are accompanying humankind on this mission to the Quaker solar system."

Dr McAllister turned to the assembled group of military generals and doctors.

"You see, already he is beginning to respond to specific scenarios"

One of the assembled group interrupted:

"It is not very convincing, listening to him reiterate your statements like a parrot, Doctor. When will we see him begin to think for himself?"

"Well… Each mental and bodily function is activated in his hard drive at different times. Once activated, LB-42 will learn very quickly, in a matter of seconds, thus, adopting human body movements, thoughts and rationale, so that he will eventually blend in with society entirely. Please remember that he is part human."

Once again, Dr McAllister turned to face LB-42.

"You have a purpose… What is your purpose LB-42?"

"My purpose is to protect the 'Ark Project' in as much as I must uphold the directives set out in the Eden Treaty. I must protect the long-term interests of humankind, and that of the accompanying life forms on the mission, with a consideration for the needs of the mass populous."

"Very good, LB-42."

Dr McAllister noticed that the muscles in the cyborg's chiselled, statuesque physique began to relax from a constantly tense position.

"This is very impressive work, Doctor. Already, he is beginning to show intelligence. He must nearly be ready for Governor Dansun's demonstration."

The doctor was too allured by the figure before her to address the supplier of the compliment directly.

"Mmm, maybe a couple more hours. By then, even *we* may not be able to tell the difference."

"How about the military data files. Have they been downloaded into its database?"

The crude description of her creation as an 'it' stung Dr McAllister, and her reaction was evident through the slightest of frowns on her lightly wrinkled forehead.

"Yes", the Doctor replied. "They will integrate with his bodily functions. All the required knowledge is stored for his mission. You don't have to worry about that."

She cast her mind back to the former stages of LB-42's development. Four decades previously, she had graduated with her Batchelor of Sciences degree, and landed a job as an assistant at a robotics company that had begun turning its head to the development of groundbreaking new technology. ANVIL robotics, by some amazing coincidence, had been approached by certain obscure Alliance military agencies to begin the preparatory stages of a top-secret project that was to prove to be of extreme significance in the future. That was then. The future had become the present, and Doctor McAllister was no longer an assistant.

The result of the involvement of ANVIL robotics and, in turn, herself with the Ark Project was complete. LB-42 was a marvel to behold. His skin had been especially grown to cover an organic muscular and skeletal structure that housed a mechanoid heart and lungs, and other vital organs. It was from these vital organs that his skin would receive the all-important fluids to maintain a healthy complexion and avoid the process of ageing that was a mark of human mortality.

"Doctor, I understand that all his vital organs are artificial. Is that correct?"

Doctor McAllister turned to address her inquisitor before answering:

"Almost correct, Sir, everything except the brain. In that part at least he is human, freshly preserved and clear of any memories from its previous owner."

"Is that wise, Doctor. Surely the brain will die after a normal cycle of human life?"

"Not really, as long as there is a blood supply running through the vital arteries then there will be life in the brain. Technology for artificially sustaining life is almost faultless today, fragments of it anyway. Our concern when making LB-42 was to ensure that he could make conscious decisions – distinguish between right and wrong. An artificial brain would think purely on a logical basis, and, as we surmised in our original designs, an intelligence based purely on logic would not work suitably within the 'harmony' of the Ark Project."

"Why wouldn't it work, Doctor?"

Dr McAllister turned to face the tall, muscular frame of LB-42, her mature features giving way to a warm smile that beamed with pride, before answering:

"Because he would have *no* soul. That is what gives way to the human conscience, and contrary to many an urban myth, it comes from the brain not the heart!"

Teaching LB-42 about life and its complications had been a rewarding experience for her. In many ways he had been childlike in his infancy, while bearing the general appearance of an adult with rigor mortis. Now that his muscles had relaxed he would make more natural physical movements. In one of their private moments together she recalled teaching him to eat, so that he could assume a convincing lifestyle in society.

"LB-42, this is a plate, and this is called cutlery."

Rigidly sitting at the table the cyborg had looked sideways at the plate and the collection of steaming organic substances collected in the centre of the round dish.

"With the fork in your left hand and the knife in your right I want you to eat everything in front of you."

Aiding his mechanical movements to pick up the implements, she had stepped back to watch. While perfunctorily chewing and digesting the meal he'd managed to ask a question.

"LB-42?"

Dr McAllister had smiled at his blank features.

"Yes, your name…"

While the cyborg had carried on putting the food away in his artificial stomach, he looked at the doctor and pointed quizzically at her with his mush-infested knife.

"My name?"

She had thought about using her official title, but somehow she couldn't help feeling like a mad scientist whenever she heard it.

"LB-42, you may call me, Mother!"

"MFFFRRR."

As half-chewed food had tumbled back out of his mouth onto the plate she intervened:

"No, speak when you have swallowed, not while you are chewing."

"Mother…"

"That's better."

She had watched, delighted at LB-42's learning curve. Several minutes later she had been reminding herself to be careful how she phrased instructions, as he began biting into the empty plate. Fortunately, minimal injuries had been incurred by the innocent cyborg…

Doctor McAllister felt a number of stern gazes bearing down upon her. It seemed to last for an eternity before one of the military officials broke the silence.

"Very well then."

One of the figures dressed in an impeccably pressed, navy blue uniform of a high-ranking military official stepped forward and extended a large, calloused hand.

"Welcome to the 'Ark Project', son. I hope you enjoy the trip."

Dr McAllister stared with proud eyes at the fruits of her life's work. She had never had children, and as she began to approach what would inevitably become the twilight quarter of her life she realised that this would be the closest that she ever came to feeling the warmth of the heart that accompanied being a proud parent. In the precarious balance of fate of the human race she concluded that perhaps it had been for the best that she had never conceived…

I hope that the trip is worth taking.

About two hours later, a tall figure emerged from a secret door in one of the Science sector's private corridors.

The door sealed itself magnetically behind the exiting form, with a faint hissing noise; leaving no trace of having ever existed, except to the trained eye.

The figure was a tall man wearing a red uniform, and a cap of matching colour. Both items of clothing bore the Alliance emblem; a blue sphere imposed over a pair of diagonally crossed scrolls, signifying that he was an engineer. This was complemented by a tool belt, which fitted perfectly around the waist of the owner, concealing an impressive array of small, hand-held mechanical devices. He strode to the shuttle bay in a relaxed manner. At the attendant's desk he fumbled in his pockets for his security pass.

The attendant took the pass, and was alarmed at the way in which the man seemed to stare right through him.

"Where are you going?"

"To the admin sector", was the clinical response.

"I see", said the attendant.

Satisfied that the document was in order, he handed it back to the man.

"What's the matter, Engineer Andrews; couldn't you be bothered to walk?"

A smile appeared on the attendant's face, disarming the slight essence of accusation that lurked within the question.

"No, I couldn't deal with having to crowd-surf my way through thousands of Administration staff."

He took the pass and replaced it in his pocket, before tipping his cap and entering the Personnel shuttle.

The journey to the Administration sector was brief, but interesting, none the less. It took him from one side of the space station to the other; a far more scenic and less frantic approach to his destination.

In avoiding much of the space traffic, the Personnel shuttle launched and cruised to nearly two kilometres away from the Space Station, Aurora. It allowed him to take in the spectacular sight, from the tinted window by his seat. He stared out inquisitively. The space station hung in his field of vision, complemented by the glow of

Earth's atmosphere.

The Aurora effortlessly maintained its orbit around the Earth. It resembled a giant mushroom in shape. Huge solar panels dotted the curvature of its top surface, absorbing power from the sun. Beneath, the stem of the space station haphazardly came to a point, which was created in the form of huge communications antennae. All down the stem of the structure bizarre protrusions appeared, in a bold representation of the confrontation between the design considerations of the structure's symmetry and the needs of the human occupants within the huge space station.

From his viewpoint, he could just make out the huge construction bays beneath the structure's umbrella-like solar-powered surface. Within each of them there was a bustling community of movement. This was where the Intergalactic Star Vessels were being assembled. His keen eyesight picked out dozens of smaller vessels scuttling around the larger transport vessels, like worker ants fulfilling the service of the Queen.

Once again, the Aurora became magnified in his field of vision, but through no effort of his own as the shuttle deftly manoeuvred into position in one of the docking bays. Upon landing, the figure readjusted his cap. He moved to the exit hatch.

I have been conceived in a very strange place… Farewell, Mother.

Just as LB-42 left the shuttle bay, blending in with the hurrying crowds of people, a small microcircuit came to life within his hard drive; this was the final working feature of Dr McAllister's cyborg.

For the first time, LB-42 felt the soothing sensation in the eyes, which accompanied blinking.

Chapter 4

"How are the preparations going on the Star Cruisers?"

Senator McDonald carefully placed his glass of orange juice on the immaculately polished table.

"The Utopia and Elysium are almost half completed. The current problem lies with the animal transport vessels. The Super Nova and Mirage have fallen badly behind schedule."

Governor Dansun arched his fingers to a point, locked in thought.

"Is it the same problem as before?"

"Yes", came the reply. "At the moment, the engineers and environmental technicians are struggling to create the right habitat for specific species. The problem lies, not in not having enough space for each animal, but in getting the animals to interact, without interfering with their ways of existing in some way. It destroys the illusion that they are in a natural environment. In the long term, this could be very detrimental to the preservation of their instinctive behaviour. If they survive that long, we could be faced with hundreds of species that don't have the mental capacity to adapt to a new environment."

"I see."

Governor Dansun shakily grabbed his walking stick, and rather painfully, rose from his hydraulic chair.

The development of the Alliance Star Vessels had been a great worry to everyone involved in their construction. Fifty years of global input by Earth's most advanced engineers had allowed for some marvellous discoveries about deep space travel. The thought that most prominently struck the governor was the huge gravity system that would provide the inhabitants of the huge, space vessels with a suitable gravity so that they would not be aimlessly floating around the interstellar, man-made metropolis. This posed particular problems with the aquatic life forms that were to be housed aboard the Super Nova. It would not do to have the most bizarre selection of Earth's creations floating around, hopelessly trying to find water that would be assuming large globular formations in zero gravity, free of the habitats that had been built to support them.

To the engineers the gravity system represented a complex life-support system that would ensure the survival of life in space. To the uneducated the gravity system was simply represented by a series of cylindrical shells that stretched the length of the exteriors of the huge vessels, rotating in opposing directions to create the artificial forces within. Each of the four vessels was to be equipped with a huge database that would keep a record of the life that they housed. These databases would also operate the life-support systems that would control the environments of the inhabitants within.

Although the technology was state-of-the-art, in two hundred years of deep space travel it would be ageing, and many scientists had put forward the idea that without the depth of resources, technology would stagnate, and very little advancement would be made in that time. Thus, by the time that the human settlements were to be established on Coleshia and Penusia, much of the technology implemented would be based on visions created in this time of development and human endeavour.

Governor Dansun shuffled awkwardly to the window and stared out into space.

Senator McDonald quietly watched this painstaking performance. He had learnt from previous experience that Governor Dansun often got annoyed, when assistance was offered in such situations. There was no doubt about it; the man was fiercely independent, even in the face of crippling pain. Recently though, the senator had seen a growing change in the old man. Age had been accompanied by an underlying demeanour of cynicism that only emerged when the two of them had some privacy.

The governor turned to face the senator.

"Transporting a wide variety of different species to two separate planets is quite a mammoth task. At the time that the Eden Treaty was devised, many scientists claimed that it was nigh on impossible to achieve…

"Off the record Ted, I am seriously beginning to agree with them. How *do* you remove, not just one animal, but, for want of a better phrase, a 'custom designed' ecosystem into an environment that is quite obviously false, without mentally disturbing the animals in some way? Like you said, we are suppressing their natural instincts. Can we really take short cuts with something as delicate as the balance of nature?"

These were worrying times indeed, when a respected leader doubted the ability of the potential for success in this endeavour. If the essence of doubt left the confines of this room, the belief of the people would waver. That simply could not happen.

"Oh, come on, Michael."

Senator McDonald shuffled forward in his chair.

"We have to remain optimistic. The new ecosystems were designed with state-of-the-art, virtual reality software. The calculations were made with the precision of machines, not the calculated guesses of some scientist."

"Yes, and the tools for the job were designed by the calculated guesses of scientists!"

The senator puffed his cheeks out in frustration. At times he felt as if the governor was being deliberately obtuse, just to vent some of his frustrations. Nevertheless, Senator McDonald was a compassionate man, and his rapport with the governor was worth investing a little support in when it was required.

"Genetic engineering has advanced so much. The environmental technicians are so close to perfecting 'eco-cloning' now. Soon, all sorts of plant life will be adapted to the new environments. The animals won't know any different."

"In which case, why don't we just take the embryos of different species and grow them when we reach the Alpha Quadrant?"

"Michael, we have covered this ground so many times. Cloning of animal species always produces massive defects. The animals may be physically accurate, but the brain is a highly complex mechanism. None of the animals produced have maternal instincts. They have no parents, and, therefore, learn none of the lessons taught to every living creature in early life."

"With some species, surely, it would be easier to place cloned specimens with non-cloned animals?"

"It may have worked for one or two species, but many species never responded to such experiments. Recreating flesh and bone is one thing, but breeding the animals to interact properly in the ecosystem is something completely different. It has to be this way. Chancellor Conway insisted that this was imperative."

Governor Dansun reluctantly accepted the brutal truth, grimacing in frustration. Every time the 'Ark Project' hit a stumbling block, human obstacles were easily overcome. In the case of transporting the wildlife, the removal of the obstacles required a careful process of planning before they could be excluded from the equation; thus taking up valuable time that the human race didn't have at this critical stage.

"I know you're right", he replied.

Senator McDonald continued:

"Besides, there are massive psychological benefits to the human race."

"How *could* I forget!" came the sarcastic repost.

"The Eden Treaty states that we have an obligation to preserve and support life from Earth in our new homes. Not to mention the fact that approximately two hundred and fifty years, spent isolated in space without any other life forms to interact with, will quite simply, drive the human race mad."

"Is that what you really believe, Ted?"

Governor Dansun began to feel the strain of supporting his own weight. With carefully-measured, shuffled steps he returned to his hydraulic chair, which signalled his presence, with a sequence of meticulous hydraulic adjustments.

"Is this off the record, Mike?" enquired the senator.

"Well, if it isn't, I will soon be receiving my marching orders. Of course, we have been friends for a long time."

Senator McDonald shuffled uneasily in his chair and took a measured sip from his glass of orange juice.

"Well, what I do believe is that twenty-second century propaganda is a weapon not to be messed with."

"*Ah ha*, now we have the crux of the matter", replied the, once again, seated governor, with an air of exclamation.

It was apparent from the relieved expression on his face that removing the weight from his feet served to reduce the pain in his back. He allowed the senator to continue.

"If you think about it, there are some very shrewd public relations personnel within the Alliance. Christ! They need to be. All of a sudden, the remainder of Earth's population are told to ignore everything that they have worked for; to what end? To participate in the 'Ark Project'; a noble effort to rebuild human existence on another planet, with the help of 'Noah and his Arks'. Leading the animals to a safe haven, two by two. I mean, how contrived can you get?"

"You are quite right, Ted. Contrived though it may be, it is necessary. People need to be motivated right now.
For once, this project allows the human race to be part of something positive, building a new life for future generations…"

The governor paused to finish his own drink.

"We are pessimistic, because we have to watch our home planet reject us with increasing intensity. For future generations, however, the objectives set out in the Eden Treaty will be the code by which they will live their lives. Humanity will be educated with environmental awareness, not with the building blocks of adapting to a capitalist way of existence, as has been the case until now. There will be no financial incentives in the future of the human race. The progress of individuals within society will be based upon regular assessments of their performance within the Ark Project hierarchy; the greater the fulfilment of an individual's obligations to the Eden Treaty the greater the reward… For that we must be thankful… Humanity will adapt to a new way of life with familiar company. The animals being there will ease the psychological burden on humanity."

Senator McDonald asserted his agreement with raised eyebrows, detecting the renewed air of sincerity within the governor's voice. With enough effort, they could stifle the feelings of trepidation and convince themselves that they were doing the right thing:

"I hope you are right, Michael. While we strive to preserve nature in all its glory, we struggle to make the human race productive, instead of destructive. I don't know which is the harder task."

"Well, whatever the future holds, the facts remain the same. If we are not fully prepared for intergalactic space travel within thirty years, the latest scientific data predicts that the storm windows will not be big enough for us to return to Earth's surface. We will, effectively, be stranded on the Aurora…"

Governor Dansun was interrupted by the intercom on his desk.

"Governor Dansun?"

"Yes, Nina?"

"Engineer Andrews is here to carry out repairs to your chair."

One of the governor's fingers hovered over the mute button.

"Just a minute."

The brittle digit depressed the plastic key.

"Ted, there was another reason why I summoned you here today."

Senator McDonald frowned in confusion.

"To see how your chair works?"

Governor Dansun laughed.

"No, have you ever heard of the MACU project?"

"Only by the abbreviation. I don't know what it stands for. The last I heard on the subject was that the MACU project was a fabrication created by military 'spin doctors' within the Alliance."

The Governor seemed to become enthused at this statement.

"Well, Ted, I can assure you that it is more than a figment of some exaggerated imagination. What you are about to learn, you must carry with you to your grave. Never tell a soul; do you understand?"

Despite his advanced years, the governor could still summon an overpowering degree of authority. This was one such an occasion when this influence exerted itself.

"I understand", said the inquisitive senator.

The governor raised his finger from the mute button.

"Send him in, Nina."

Some five seconds later, a tall, clean-shaven man entered the governor's office, wearing a red uniform and a cap matching in colour. Governor Dansun waited until the office door had silently sealed behind the newcomer.

"Good afternoon, Engineer Andrews."

"Good afternoon, Governor Dansun. How may I be of assistance?"

Governor Dansun smiled at Engineer Andrews then, wearing the same facial expression, addressed his friend:

"Senator McDonald. Say hello to LB-42…"

Chapter 5

Project Date: Day 52 of Year 0098

Governor Theodore McDonald sat at his desk. He ran his wrinkled hands through his thinning, grey hair, and focused his attention on the object that glistened, unoccupied, in the corner of his room. He had kept the late Governor Dansun's chair as a mark of respect to his friend, feeling that it would have been out of place to make the most of the chair's comfort himself.

Michael, if only you could see what we have achieved...

McDonald was no longer aboard the Alliance Space Station, Aurora. He had been promoted to the governership of the voyage to Coleshia; one of two new homes for the human race, and other forms of life from the planet Earth, now twenty years into their long, tiring journey.

Coleshia represented a huge challenge to the settlers striving to reach this planet. It was covered entirely by water, with a chemical make-up, not unlike that of sea water. Detailed explorations by robotically controlled probes had revealed an unnerving visibility range in the deepest depths of the huge ocean, in some places forty to fifty metres. The visual records that had been received from these voyages made it appear as if the entire ocean was a pool of shimmering spring water.

Upon reaching Coleshia, the colonists would have enough technology and materials to build a settlement on the seabed, piece by piece with the aid of an army of construction submersibles, in one of the shallowest areas of the huge ocean, a mere one thousand metres deep, according to the latest probe readings. The forms of aquatic life taken from Earth's oceans would be adapted to Coleshia's oceans during Phase 4 of the Ark Project; some years after humanity had established a foothold on the planet.

I wonder what it will be like.

He was filled with intrigue, but at the same time a sense of sadness. He would not live to see the journey's end, despite the fact that the status that he now held would require his full attention for the remaining days of his life. Perseverance was simply justified when the fruits of the labour were within grasp. Governor McDonald had long since come to terms with the fact that in his case the seeds were yet to find the soil to bear the fruit. He would be one of several generations of governors, fulfilling the same destiny, watching closely and protecting the precious cargo. Millions of lives were in his hands.

The current leader let his thoughts drag him from his own responsibilities on the Super Nova and the Utopia, in which he now sat, to the occupants of the Elysium and the Mirage, the other half of this pioneering deep space voyage to the Quaker solar system. It was almost a strange irony that they were travelling to the same place for the same reasons, and yet their destination was starkly different.

The planet Penusia was several million miles closer to the star at the centre of the Quaker solar system, and as a consequence, the landscape on which humanity wished to rebuild did not rise and fall gently with the breeze, but was grazed and scarred.

Despite the stark contrast, the regular probe landings, which had been made, had revealed glaring similarities, - the atmosphere contained high levels of oxygen, that the human body could tolerate. Despite this, there had been no reports of any indigenous life. The only signs of life in any form were certain plants, which held no shocking discoveries from initial reports.

If we can adapt to life in an ocean and in a desert, then perhaps our future is more assured than we give ourselves credit for...

That was the beauty of life. Whatever the circumstances life would overcome the changes hurled in its path. Perhaps this was simply the next progressive stage in human development. Maybe a fear of the uncertainty clouded a stronger desire to embrace the challenge. Perhaps the animals on the voyage would adapt to the change with more ease than the humans. Perhaps they would not adapt at all…

With this in his thoughts, Governor McDonald knew that he had a more demanding task than that of the governor of the Penusian voyage. The settlers on Penusia would be able to segregate the various forms of life into huge reserves, until many species had become accustomed to their new environment, allowing the ecosystem an assured period of strength-building.

During Phase 4 of Coleshia's operation, the ecosystem, it was predicted, would have to be pieced together, species by species, like a convoluted jigsaw puzzle, each species nurtured into a strange new environment, and allowed a period of growth before being put at the mercy of a potential predator. In transporting the creatures, a massive allowance also had to be made for the excess supply of ton upon ton of salt water for each creature.

But humanity had no choice…

The freak storms on Earth were a regular occurrence all over the planet. The El Nino phenomenon had claimed the planet for itself, destroying everything as quickly as humanity could rebuild it. For the sake of the journey, Earth's ecosystem had been refined to a group of animals that could exist on each planet - the human race was among that group.

By the time they had departed from their solar system, many species of wildlife common to the planet had either been wiped out by the freak weather or had been reduced to such small numbers by humanity's persecution, to the point where they could not recover.

Governor McDonald's thoughts drifted back to his departed friend; to one of their final meetings. Back then; Senator McDonald was very much the apprentice, at the age of thirty-five. Briefly, and with caution, he thought of LB-42. By now, the cyborg would be an active member of society, hiding his true identity and purpose amidst the human populations of one of the four transport vessels. He did not know which one…

Then, his mind wandered to another amazing feat of human engineering. The huge space cruisers that guided the remainder of the human race; huge, floating cities that stretched for miles, providing valuable life support to Homo sapiens and animals alike.

In the solitude of his office, Governor McDonald thoughtfully rubbed the sleeve of his robe between his finger and thumb. He rejoiced in the fact, that now, in his eighty-second year, he had lived long enough to see humanity overcome the first major obstacle in their titanic struggle for survival. Phase 1 was complete and Phase 2 had begun!

The years passed…

Chapter 6

The Ark Project: Phase 2

A refined evaluation of the first century of the voyage to the Quaker solar system

In writing this report, I have gathered as much data, as humanly possible from the databases aboard the Alliance space vessels. From my extensive research and after careful deliberation, I have been able to establish the following conclusions.

The first century of the human race's voyage across the stars has been arduous. Despite the carefully considered planning that has gone into this project, inevitably, problems have risen. Our initial concerns for the long-term survival of the animal populations appears to have been unnecessary. They are thriving in their new homes, although these domiciles are only temporary. With steadfast, but tactful, monitoring, the maintenance teams aboard the Super Nova and the Mirage are performing a magnificent job in fulfilling the directives insisted upon in Phase 2 of the Ark Project.

In a twisted irony, it is the human race that has struggled to adapt to the claustrophobia and limitations of their new surroundings. Deep space travel has not been the glorious voyage of discovery that many had hoped for. For many, the journey consists of routine, monitoring automated systems, which maintain the myriad of functions necessary to support the life aboard the huge transport vessels. They can no longer bury themselves in family life. Breeding is carefully surveyed and has been restricted due to the confined spaces, by which the human race now has to live. Any couple who wishes to have a child under current legislation has to apply to the administration sectors. Waiting lists are so long that it has not been unheard of for many members of society to lodge their application before finding a compatible partner. Experts have predicted that limited resources will be a factor in birth control even when the planets have been colonised.

People's desire to create has been stifled. Technology has maintained a consistent level throughout the entire journey, due to a lack of resources, which will be needed for the construction of the settlements. Self-indulgence, too, has been restricted. People can go to discotheques or the 'Arena' cinemas. Alternatively, if this does not satisfy the citizens, they can immerse themselves in human culture, within the huge libraries, which contain everything from literature of a factual and fictional nature to film and music archives. Much of the material, however, has been censored due to its detailed depiction of our distant, former home planet. Dwelling on the past is not a characteristic welcomed aboard the Utopia and the Elysium.

The animal occupants of the Mirage, and the Super Nova are proving to be hugely popular with many people. To see independently-thinking creatures, other than human beings, seems to be very rewarding for many. Visits to the enclosures of the variety of species interwoven into the fabric of the Ark Project are always at a maximum level, as it was so predicted in the Eden Treaty.

These forms of recreation, however, do not appear to satiate people's appetite for experience. The isolation and predictability of everyday life are too overbearing for many. To the current generation of citizens who have never seen their home world, the isolation and monotony has led to a new phenomenon. A growing number of the human population have become victims of a condition known as 'Space Trauma'. Victims of this illness become very withdrawn and struggle to deal with reality. As the illness manifests itself and the symptoms progress, the victims begin to have fits and they slowly lose control of their rational thought processes, eventually resulting in an unstable neurosis akin to madness.

The medical sectors have a concerning proportion of sixty per cent of people in their care who suffer from symptoms of this condition. and the statistics are rising. While a cure for this illness has so far eluded scientists, it is estimated that given the current trends of acceleration, 'Space Trauma' will consume one third of the total human population during Phase 2 of the Ark Project. In respect of current population levels, this will mean a number averaging five million should survive the journey to the Quaker solar system.

Another unforeseen circumstance has also arisen on the journey. The human populations of the Utopia and the Elysium have begun to lead very separate existences. To the first generation of this journey, human survival was universally appreciated, and interaction between the two populations was commendable to say the least. As we begin a new century of space travel, a new generation of citizens have been born into the Ark Project and, consequently, an estranged relationship; a growing undertow of rivalry. The thought of potential hostilities is becoming more of a possibility with each passing year.

As a result of this escalating factor, the current governors of the expedition have undertaken a series of visits to each human population. Governor Friedel, leader of the expedition to Coleshia, and Governor Titus, leader of the Penusian expedition, regularly hold conventions to try to unite the two societies of people.

The next century will bring us to our destination. I end this report with the simple, but honest, wish that the suffering that I have witnessed will blossom into high reward for the future, for the sake of the standard of living that we aspire to, and ultimately for our survival...

Professor Hilary Mitchell
Chief Science Officer – Alliance University

Chapter 7

Daniel Davis stood by the porthole, staring into the blue murk of the tank.

"I don't see anything," said the young boy, pressing his face closer to the glass.

"Be patient, Daniel," his mother replied, rubbing an affectionate hand through his short, spiky hair.

She smiled weakly at the form of her son, who stood unaware, transfixed, with both hands pressed against the thick glass. A small patch of mist was beginning to form in front of his face due to his excited exhalation.

It had been a difficult week for the young boy, for all of them in fact. The journey to the Quaker solar system had finally taken its toll on certain sectors of the human population, who had become disenchanted with the ideals that the Ark Project represented. This pressure had culminated in the form of a rebel movement, or the 'Freedom' movement, as they had called themselves.

Daniel's mother shuddered as she recalled the harrowing emotions of the previous seven days. This separatist group had attempted to take over the Utopia. In the depths of the huge, floating metropolis, a violent and tragic confrontation had taken place between the rebel force and the Alliance Military Forces. Thousands of people had died in the bloody confrontation, and the innocent civilians who resided on the huge vessel had been inadvertently dragged into the violent outburst. This was aggravated by the fact that the separatist movement had originated from the Penusia-bound population aboard the Elysium. Now the governors of each vessel were struggling to avoid a full-blooded confrontation between the inhabitants under their leadership. It was going to be a long time before this tragedy was allowed to rest, and the ambassadors of each vessel feared that a permanent division would divide the two parties for many years to follow.

Daniel and his mother were two of the citizens who were lucky to escape with their lives. Briefly, Daniel's mother felt a rapid inflammation of emotion that almost forced its way out of her body, as the sound of explosions and blast rifle fire returned in debilitating waves, seemingly as real now as they had been then. It was a draconian reminder of how large a threat the human race could be to itself. Eventually, as in all physical confrontations, the point of the action was lost in the mire of tragedy and chaos, and yet, even with this level of foresight, Daniel's mother could not repress a burning desire for revenge.

The notion that someone would jeopardise the life of her son angered her tremendously. Life was even more sacred when years of waiting for a childbirth licence had prevented her from having children earlier in life. Daniel's mother managed to summon extreme self-control, steadying her nerves and stalling the tears with a sigh; successfully returning to reality without anyone in the close vicinity realising that she had been away.

All that it had amounted to was terrorism; one of the cynical human traits that the Ark Project had attempted to leave on their distant home planet. Governor Deville had denounced it as the most tragic period in the history of the Ark Project, and one that must never be echoed if long-term survival were to be achieved.

As if this was not enough, young Daniel was fighting his own battle; one that he shared with his mother. The illness that had stolen the lives of so many – Space Trauma - had consumed the life of his father just twelve days previously. Naturally, the boy had been very overwhelmed with grief, and as a result, presently found himself aboard the Super Nova, staring into the huge aquatic complex that housed one of the biggest attractions of the Animal Tours.

Daniel had found himself there at the wish of his mother, who, desperate to take his mind away from the recent events, had followed the advice of a friend, who had advised her that the Animal Tours were a 'most interesting experience', and that 'Daniel would love it'. In this sector of the huge vessel, a varied array of carefully selected life forms had been nurtured, bred and sustained through the long journey to Coleshia. Within his lifetime, Daniel would see and be an active part in the development of the Coleshian settlement. His mother thought that this day would be both entertaining and educational for her son, whatever path of integration he assumed in later life.

Enjoyable, it most certainly had been. Daniel had been immersed in a world more alien to him than any that he had known, from crustaceans to molluscs to the huge fish and oceanic mammals. The colours and shapes would feed his imagination for days to come. He peered closely through the glass at the still depths. How big was the occupant of this enclosure? If any of the others that he had seen were anything to go by, then it must have been gigantic.

As with previous occasions on this trip, the process of viewing the different species began with a detailed monologue by the Aquatic Centre guide, providing a background to each species. The people gathered around her, like children waiting to be told a bedtime story.

"This species has been the most popular on the tour. It has inspired fear and captured the imagination throughout human history…"

As if responding to a cue, seemingly from nowhere, the beast cruised past, eyeing the frozen features of Daniel with an eye as black as death itself, but with a disturbing awareness of the things around it. Daniel was paralysed, rooted to the spot, terrified at the sheer size of it. The guide was unperturbed by the huge monster gliding past the large, transparent window next to the assembled party of parents and children. Some of them didn't share her composure. After calming the cluster of excited souls down, she continued.

"Of course, being such fiercely independent creatures, we had vast problems in creating a suitable environment for them. Originally, we had eight of them, but over the years the numbers were reduced, because of difficulties we experienced in obtaining the right environmental controls to support them. It is rather difficult to discover the secrets of this creature, because they have a tendency to be quite fierce when circumstances do not suit them. We have, however, successfully managed to create a breeding programme. This is why they are together now. Normally they are very solitary creatures. They live for about thirty years, so using basic maths, I am sure that you can deduce that their very presence in the enclosure before you is testament to the success of the programme."

Daniel moved away from the glass, breaking his paralysis through the basic need to continue his own respiratory processes, while a huge set of teeth cruised past from another direction. The triangular incisors were enormous. Daniel estimated that they were each as big as one of his hands, despite the fact that their owner was smaller than the previous specimen that he had seen.

While maintaining a painted grin, the guide continued…

"Human involvement with these creatures has been limited except from the inside of a safety cage. Recently, however, scientists have developed some revolutionary technology that should allow us to interact with these creatures as we have been unable to do in the past."

Holding up a small device between finger and thumb to the crowd huddled around the viewing window, the guide flashed her array of perfect teeth in a broad smile before announcing:

"This is what we call a Protective Aquatic Device!"

As if acknowledging its introduction, the small device began winking at the curious crowd, via a small flashing red light, centrally placed on its black shell.

All this information fell on the deaf ears of young Daniel Davis, who, having returned to the porthole maintained his frozen vigil at the world laid bare before him. Suddenly, he noticed that the creatures seemed to relax slightly. It was as if they felt more unconcerned with the presence of life on the opposite side of the glass.

A voice in the crowd asked the inevitable question:

"What does the device do?"

Daniel wasn't listening to the explanation being awarded by the guide. The only time that he took his attention away from the movement beyond the glass was to give an enthusiastic grin to his mother. His happiness rubbed off onto her, and she returned the gesture. This was the first time that he had smiled in days, and a wave of relief ran through her.

Noticing the boldly printed name plaque next to the porthole, he ingrained the words in his mind. Briefly, he wondered how many animals had the accolade of 'Great' as part of their name. His search revealed that there were not many, and certainly not as many as deserving as this monster.

Today was the start of Daniel's integration into the Ark Project. At this primitive stage of his life, he could not even estimate the impact that sharks would have on the future generations of his family, and none more so than the species before him now - The Great White Shark!

Chapter 8

PART 2: KAUHULU.

Planet Penusia

Project Date: Day 14 of Year 0405

"Hot today, isn't it?"

The tone of the response was blunt.

"Indeed it is..."

Slightly disgruntled at his politeness being rejected, the security guard returned the identity pass somewhat dismissively, and waved the vehicle through. Dominic Strand took it swiftly, and returned it to the pocket in his robe. Personally he found the heat uncomfortable. As the steel gates opened before him he pushed the joystick forward. The eight-wheel drive jeep responded instantly, the electric motor humming away. As he accelerated from the security outpost down the bumpy road, his hat curled up at the front, exposing his nose to the blistering heat of the sun.

On either side of him huge, forty-foot fences bordered the road. He hated this trip. As the smooth dome-like structure that made up several accommodation blocks including his own abode disappeared in his rear view mirror, the monstrous buildings in the centre of the Penusian settlement emerged over the horizon. To either side were two of several immense enclosures that were home to a number of the planet's adopted life forms. Looking to his left, a herd of elephants wandered across the desert, no doubt towards their reservoir. Looking the other way, a small group of zebras hid under the shade of an artificial tree.

This sight was a regular occurrence, day in and day out, every time that he made this trip from his home to the centre of human activity on the planet. Every day the animals would appear at the fences, baffled at the existence of the bars.

Were the bars to keep the animals in, or to keep the human population out?

This was a question that usually crept into his mind at the same point of each day. As a high profile journalist it was his duty to pay attention to such issues, although the Penusian leadership always approved his articles before his words ever appeared in *Penusia's Projection*. It wasn't difficult to determine that such questions would succumb to extreme censorship by the planetary leadership, and Governor Astran was not a man to be crossed. Strand reminded himself to brush such rebellious thoughts to the back of his mind when he met the Penusian leader later that very day.

Besides the depressed looking animals that encroached upon his bad mood, his scheduled meeting was also playing heavily on his mind. Today was the day that he was to assume not one, but two sets of duties within the Ark Project hierarchy; journalist and interplanetary spy.

Suddenly the clear blue sky was tainted with a thundering white streak, as two Penusian military shuttles cruised at high speed overhead. As well as breaking his own train of thought the roaring engines of the speeding craft broke the relaxed demeanour of the zebras, and they galloped out from under the trees into the open.

Looking ahead, the settlement mid-point was becoming clear in his windscreen now. Along the immediate horizon a large wall stretched for miles in either direction. Above, huge, rectangular buildings of different sizes stood proudly in the sky. As the distance decreased Strand could depict the aerial traffic that busily manoeuvred between the buildings. Sighing to himself he predicted that this congestion would be twice as bad on the ground, navigating through the multi-coloured crowds of people and other vehicles, bogged down like himself amongst the masses. Perhaps one day he would upgrade to a small shuttle... On the other hand, perhaps his tendency for vertigo would put an end to that plan.

In less than a day, Dominic Strand would be struggling to acclimatise to another element, for which he had a far greater loathing than wind or fire - water!

"Come in, Mr Strand."

The Penusian journalist entered the luxurious office, deep in the heart of the Penusian Administration Centre; a blast of conditioned air soothing his chubby cheeks that still burned from the extreme heat of Penusia's sun. At the same time he removed his orange hat from his bald head.

"Sit down."

Complying like a dog waiting to fetch the stick, Strand sank into the padded chair, which opposed the desk, on the opposite side of which sat Governor Astran. He was a robustly built man with short, grey curly hair. He was clean-shaven and his dark brown eyes alertly watched the Penusian journalist's every movement.

As rumours had suggested, Strand realised from his attentive stern gaze that this man was very much the control freak that he had heard about through his many contacts in the Penusian Administration Centre.

Despite his many networks of communication this was his first meeting with the leader of his home planet. Somewhat humbled, he nevertheless decided to begin building bridges.

"Good morning, Governor... I would just like to say that it is a pleasure..."

Suddenly the wrecking ball appeared.

"Be sure that it is a pleasure... Don't patronise me with pleasantries, Strand."

The response was efficient and it established the distance of the conversation.

"I'm sorry, Governor…"

"Enough of apologies. I take it that a man of your intuition has already determined why he has been summoned?"

"Yes, Governor, I leave for Coleshia tonight."

The name of the neighbouring planet was pronounced with a sinister overtone, one that Astran acknowledged with the brief trace of a grin.

"I understand that it is your first visit to our Coleshian neighbours. You should feel privileged… Very few Penusians venture to that aquatic place."

Very few Penusians have any desire to visit Coleshia…

Strand's fear of the ocean muted his response.

"Indeed."

"Afraid of the water?"

"I have to declare a certain lack of enthusiasm, Governor."

"Good. I would not consider you to be of true Penusian blood if you were not… Humankind was not born with webbed feet."

"Absolutely, Governor."

The elderly man brusquely rose from the chair and moved sprightly to the window, staring out onto the sun-drenched masses below.

"A man must also realise the delicate nature of interplanetary relations at this time."

"I do indeed, Governor. Sixty-one years is less than a lifetime."

"Very true. A lot has happened though. Humanity has colonised two planets, an achievement in itself… But for many of us who were alive during the Freedom Movement, resentment for our Coleshian accusers still burns very strongly!"

Despite being three generations removed from the Penusian leader, Strand, in this at least managed to find some common ground.

"I would not be a true Penusian were I allowed to forget this fact."

Governor Astran rotated his large frame to face the humbled journalist, the sun silhouetting one half of his contoured features.

"Then you realise why your visit to Coleshia is important… It's not just for an insight into the wildlife in their ocean. This will be the first opportunity in nearly a year that we have been able to infiltrate our aquatic neighbours. Diplomatic relations are few and far between now, and it is important that we grasp any leverage that presents itself."

The governor's aggressive choice of words worried Strand as to just how far he was expected to go beyond the station of roving journalist.

"Leverage… What kind?"

"Anything. Use your journalistic perception. Sniff something out… In the future, should matters get worse, it may prove useful to us."

"Very well, Governor, I shall keep my eyes and ears open."

"Be careful, Strand. I do not want an interplanetary incident here. Use your intuition. I will not go down in history as the second Penusian governor to reside over a reign of bloodshed. That sixty-year-old mistake should remain with the late Governor Deville."

"I will not fail, Governor."

The Penusian leader said nothing. Instead he returned to the window.

A few seconds passed before Strand realised that this was his cue to depart… This was going to be a difficult assignment!

The young boy careered down the corridor on his multicoloured tricycle, imagination fuelling his momentum, legs pedalling furiously. He imagined that he was aboard one of the transport shuttles, skilfully guiding the controls through an asteroid belt.

The incessant din of the shuttle's engines substituted that of the composite plastic wheels grinding over the metal floor. As he left the living quarters of the Aquatic Science Centre, he was returned abruptly to his real surroundings.

A security guard stood up from behind an operations terminal:

"Hey, you there, slow down; you're in a populated area!"

But it was too late. The tricycle and its miniature occupant had blazed around the intersection of the corridor in a blur of technicolour. The security guard depressed one of the many controls on his terminal.

"Bud, we have an unidentified cycling object approaching your sector. Please intercept."

"What, him again!" There was a brief pause, punctuated by what sounded like a lethargic sigh. "Okay, leave it to me."

Some rapidly multiplying distance away the small child saw people going about their business, as the corridor began to become littered with vast numbers of legs and feet - more asteroids to get past...

"*Hey*, watch it!"

"Jesus!"

"Slow down you little urchin!"

The youngster ignored the advice, and took huge pride in the sound of breaking objects and assorted destruction that he left in his wake. As he approached the next security terminal, an obstacle just a little too big to negotiate appeared in his view. The young boy considered playing 'chicken' with this obstacle, but Security Officer Bud White wasn't going to play ball. Reluctantly, recognising that he was not going to subdue this exasperated figure, the young boy began to reduce his speed, the blue front wheel just stopping short of Officer White's polished black boots. He towered over the boy, a giant in a blue uniform. Suddenly, the youth wasn't feeling so brave.

"Just where do you think you are going?"

The voice thundered with authority. With feet spread apart and hands on hips, the boy deduced very rapidly that this was not the body posture of a very pleased security officer. The reply was quiet and timid.

"To see my father, Sir."

"At that speed, I'm surprised that you could clearly see anything at all... You must be Glen."

Officer White had heard of this boy's antics before. His reputation preceded him! In this particular sector of the Aquatic Science Centre, there were only a handful of resident families, thus eliminating potential culprits. Many of the citizens took the recently completed monorail from the main settlement to their pre-ordained daily routines here.

"Yes, Sir."

"If your father hears about this, he won't be very happy, will he?"

"No, Sir."

Officer White leaned down to speak to Glen, who sat squarely aboard the small vehicle, staring, dejectedly at the floor.

"Okay, Glen, leave your bike here, and we will go and find your father… Don't worry, we'll forget about it this time."

The officer felt some sympathy for the children in the Aquatic Science Centre. Apart from the weekends, there was very little for them to do, when they came home from school, while their parents were fulfilling their daily destinies. He took Glen's hand and lifted him off the tricycle.

Wandering back to his operations terminal with the bike in one hand and Glen's small hand in the other, he smiled to himself. Depositing the bike behind his desk, he opened the intercom on his keyboard panel.

"This is Security Officer, Bud White, requesting the current location of Aquatic Science Officer, Daniel Davis."

As Glen was well acquainted with the security officers, it followed that his father was too. There was a brief silence before a response was forthcoming.

"Officer White, he is in the next sector – Zone 10, the Animal Release Zone."

"Thanks."

Switching the intercom back onto standby, he led Glen down the corridor, in the direction of that destination…

When they reached the Animal Release Zone, all manner of people were busy constructing a huge tank, where the species of aquatic life would be held before their release into the wild. Welding torches were sending sparks in all directions. Engineers and technicians were performing all manner of complex electrical surgery, in all areas of the huge science lab, like loyal servants in a hive of bees. Each moment of progress was interspersed by bright sparks and intermittent electrical hisses, which were produced by their unforgiving tools…

Glen stood in awe, wandering what monsters could be big enough to fit in a pool that big. From his viewpoint, in the doorway, he couldn't see the other end of the laboratory. Officer White shouted above the noise to one of the Engineers nearest to him.

"I'm looking for Daniel Davis, do you know where he is?"

"In the pool," the man replied, pointing with the tool that he held in his hand.

"Okay, thanks."

The engineer waved an acknowledgement, before returning to his task. Officer White put his hands on Glen's shoulders, and stared him straight in the face.

"Stay here," he said, firmly.

The young boy nodded, paying close attention to the fact that the authority in his voice had returned. Then Officer White had gone through the doorway, disappearing amongst the hordes of workers.

The minutes went by, and then it happened. A huge explosion resounded around the lab, accompanied by a flash some kilometres down the length of the huge room. Glen was thrown to the floor as the vibrations shook the entire complex. Huge red lights began revolving in the ceiling, accompanied by loud sirens that wailed in warning.

People erupted in panic.

"*Evacuate the area; one of the seals has blown,*" yelled the nearest officer.

From where he lay in a crumpled heap in the doorway, Glen could see water pouring into the laboratory. The seconds seemed to pass like minutes. For a brief moment he could see Officer White, supporting the limp weight of his father, who was covered in blood, stumbling towards the doors that were seconds away from automatically sealing.

"*Dad,*" he yelled.

He got to his feet and bolted through the door. Abruptly, his course was halted by a strong pair of arms, which dragged him back reluctantly, towards the entrance of the huge lab.

"*No, let me go!*" he yelled, kicking and screaming.

Glen's request was ignored, and as he was pulled to safety, he heard another explosion, before beholding his father and Officer White being swept into the pool that was rapidly filling with uncontrolled torrents of water…

He awoke, startled. His breathing was rapid, uncontrolled, and he was sweating profusely. As he became aware of his surroundings his breathing became more regulated. In the darkness he peeled away from his bed and wandered, dazed, into the bathroom.

The light sensors responded to his presence by producing a dull luminescence that afforded just enough light for him to make out where he was going. Washing his face under the cold tap, he stared at himself in the mirror. The dimly lit interior cast shadows on his face, tarnishing his skin in a manner not dissimilar to the way that his past had scarred his mind.

Glen Davis took a deep breath. The memories were still painful…

Chapter 9

Some five hours later, Glen Davis was once again standing in front of his bathroom mirror, adjusting the refined collar of his grey, Aquatic Science Officer's uniform. His shower had not proven to be as refreshing as he would have hoped, and he was still feeling fatigue from his disturbed night's sleep. Upon close inspection, the myriad of red highways surrounding his brown irises emphasised this all too well.

Over the years he had learnt to sleep more deeply, and the nightmares of his past troubled him far less that they used to. He recalled his last meeting with his counsellor. She had told him that there was no need for him to "remain on antidepressant medication". His sleeping difficulties had been reduced to "a level that his body could tolerate". He remembered lacking confidence in this evaluation, and in response, her reply was not what he wanted to hear.

"Glen, you must learn to deal with your problems. Six years old is a very young age to experience the type of trauma that you have been through. Its not pleasant to witness death at any age, especially when it is someone with strong emotional ties with you. Your father died in a tragic accident. Unfortunately, it is the price that you and other first generation Coleshians have had to pay during Phase Three of the Ark Project. Progress is often a painful path, in your case, aggravated all the more by the absence of your mother. I read in your file that she died in one of the last recorded cases of Space Trauma. The symptoms did not manifest themselves until after your birth, when your family were ensconcing into Coleshia's depths."

He found it difficult to admit to himself, even after all this time had elapsed, that events had evolved in such an adverse manner. He couldn't decipher whether he was failing to face up to the reality of the situation, or whether he was coping admirably well in the face of tribulation. His counsellor's 'solution' had been accepted like the final nail in the coffin.

"It has been tough for you… Have you ever considered leaving the Aquatic Science Centre?"

His reply has been a firm, *"No!"*

She suggested to him that leaving the centre might be the answer.

"The fact that you work in the same area as your father did may be triggering off these nightmares."

He had replied that the thought of leaving his life's work was unthinkable. Life had already cost him many of its greatest attributes; he was not going to accept further loss. His closest friends worked at the centre, and he found his responsibilities very rewarding…Working with the sharks had made an indelible impression on his mind, and his body.

Almost instinctively, as he remembered these events, his hand moved down to his left thigh. The scar that was hidden beneath his uniform trousers had not come from a savage set of teeth, but from a fiercely beating tail that had connected sharply with his body. It was the only physical impression that he wore from his numerous encounters with the sharks.

He ran the comb through his black hair, brushing it out of his face. He paid special attention to his appearance because today of all days, he had to be dressed for the occasion. Picking up his security pass as he left, he disappeared through the door of his apartment.

The light sensors in the corner of the room responded to his absence, and the apartment was plunged into darkness, as the door slid silently shut behind him.

Glen Davis arrived at work some thirty minutes later, passing through the same corridors that still plagued his dreams, but this time through the vantage point of a six-foot physique. They looked very different now, having been fully completed, and made operational.

Aquatic Science Centre personnel were busy going about their daily jobs. He greeted various colleagues on his journey, and he soon arrived at the place where he made his relentless contribution to the Ark Project. It was labelled with an illuminated fluorescent sign, situated next to the entrance:

AQUATIC SCIENCE CENTRE – ZONE 10: ANIMAL RELEASE ZONE

The door parted effortlessly as he flashed his security pass through the sensor on the wall. Entering the room beyond, he stopped by the liquid refreshment dispenser, and patiently waited for his drink. Turning towards his office, he was apprehended by a tall, dark-skinned man with close-shaven hair.

"Hey, Glen!"

The enthusiasm was almost overpowering and, as was always the case, Glen reacted to this with sarcasm.

"Hi, Danny. Has someone tried hijacking a Great White?"

"Very funny. That journalist from Penusia is here to see you. He's been asking a lot of questions."

"That's what journalists do, isn't it?"

"Glen, he's driving everyone nuts."

"Where is he now?"

"Waiting in your office. Please take him off our hands," pleaded Aquatic Science Officer, Danny McCormick.

"Okay, give me ten minutes, and assemble the team. Governor Tasken has requested an official approach to this meeting. This journalist will report far more than the Penusians will hear about in tomorrow's news, if he is given half a chance. You know how things are between the two planets."

Danny jogged to the offices, aware of the fact that their team had more to keep quiet about than even the Coleshian authorities knew about.

Chapter 9

Glen, finishing his drink, cast his eye around the huge science lab, checking that nothing looked out of place. The far end of the lab was a tiny speck in the distance. A huge pool that stretched some twelve kilometres occupied his field of vision, carrying the smell of sea water to his nostrils. A wave machine in the adjacent corner of the lab hummed quietly, creating a faint current in the water, mimicking the flow of ocean tides. The water looked undisturbed and Glen smiled to himself, sound in the knowledge of what lurked beneath the waves. Near to where he stood, a metal ladder descended some five feet to a jetty, which ran parallel to the one hundred and fifty foot width of the pool. Small white vehicles - Hover Skis - floated effortlessly above the waves, looking spotlessly clean as they always did.

Satisfied that everything within view was in order, Glen, slightly reluctantly, strolled to the small office complex, sighing to himself. This was the part of his job that he found to be a chore. Public relations were not one of his more desirable priorities.

He entered his office through the automatic sliding door. As he did so, a small, chubby man rose from one of the chairs in the office. It was immediately obvious from the outset that he was an outsider. His skin colour was darker than any Caucasian Coleshian that Glen had ever seen, tanned from years of exposure to sunlight. His bald head reflected the artificial light supplied by the office ceiling. He was wearing a long robe, that hung down to his ankles. It was orange in colour, and by this, Glen could tell that he was a civilian worker. This was in contrast to technical staff, such as himself, who wore body uniforms.

"Good morning," Glen announced, applying a warm smile to his face and extending his hand in greeting.

"Hello, Sir," replied the man, accepting his greeting by shaking hands. "My name is Dominic Strand. As you are no doubt aware, I am from Penusia, and I am here on behalf of the news release, *Penusia's Projection*, to cover your work on the introduction of sharks into Coleshia's environment."

"Glen Davis. I'm head of the ASC, SRT 107. To most people we are known as the 'Elasmobranch' team."

"Elas… Sorry, my ignorance is evident…"

The journalist produced an electronic notepad from his robe, and with a bewildered look on his face said:

"This is all very new to Penusian culture. Can you explain more explicitly what that jargon means?"

Glen chuckled slightly. As suggested by Governor Tasken, he bombarded the man with technical information. This would, with a little luck, steer the journalist away from questions of a political nature.

Remember, Glen, take control of the interview…

"Yes, certainly. Down here, we meet very few civilian staff. Only scientists are fully aware of our standing in the Ark Project. ASC stands for Aquatic Science Centre; SRT is an abbreviation for Shark Release Team. Elasmobranch is simply the name given to the various species that are the focus of our efforts – sharks and rays!"

The plastic pen frantically scribbled over the electronic notepad, as the journalist set about force-feeding the machine with this information.

"What does the number refer to, Mr Davis?"

Glen politely waited for the pen to cease scribbling before divulging any more information.

"107 is simply a way of recognising that we are the one hundred and seventh team to occupy the Animal Release Zone. At the moment we are preparing to release the final species from this stage of the Ark Project."

"Oh yes?"

"Yes, the Great White sharks," replied Glen, sitting behind his desk.

Strand raised his eyebrows in surprise.

"Ah yes, I have heard of these creatures. Very popular as recreational viewing during Phase 2 of the Ark Project."

"That's right. From the logs of the Super Nova and Utopia, this seems to be the case. However, people did seem to complain that they were elusive to spot through the observation ports."

"Is this true, Mr Davis?"

"Certainly, sharks have no owners, and they live on their own terms. The technical staff aboard the Super Nova had great difficulty in creating an environment to support their existence."

"I see… How-"

Strand's next question was cut off in its prime.

"Before we go any further, Mr Strand, perhaps you would like to meet the other members of the team?"

"I have met them briefly."

"Well, maybe your report would benefit from some extra input. The job that we do here is very complex… I can introduce you properly, and then I will be happy to answer any further questions that you may have."

Strand thought briefly, stroking his multiple layers of double chins.

"Well, okay. I'm scheduled to stay here until tomorrow morning. Why not?"

"Excellent," replied Glen, rising from behind his desk.

If the others think that they can wriggle out of this one…

"Mr Davis, would it be possible to see some of the sharks today?"

"Of course, we can take a minisub if you like. Show you how the animals are taking to their new home."

Strand raised his ample form from his chair, the cushions seemingly easing a sigh of relief as they began to inflate. Despite the short distance that had to be negotiated, Glen led the way, before courteously offering to let the Penusian journalist through the doorway first.

The incriminating sound of chattering voices suddenly died away upon their entry…

Chapter 10

Glen Davis and Dominic Strand stood in the doorway of the next office. Glen's surveying eyes were closely examining those of the occupants of the room, who were busily working at computer terminals.

Four desks were located within the sparsely decorated office, which was furnished in a considered series of shades of blue. On each of the desks were computer terminals, accompanied by large hard drive systems. Two men and one woman occupied three of the desks; all were wearing grey body uniforms, like that worn by Glen Davis.

"Mr Strand, meet the other members of the Elasmobranchs."

The three figures raised their heads from their monitor screens in acknowledgement, before returning to their work. Glen led the Penusian to each desk in turn, somewhat vindictively revelling in the knowledge that their attempts to hide away from the journalist's questions had been foiled.

At the first of the approached desks sat Danny McCormick. The most recent addition to the team, he was a very bold character, extremely talkative and from the time that Glen had got to know him, he came across as a very impulsive individual. In his short time with the team, they had realised that this was not detrimental, or even the slightest reflection of his approach to his responsibilities. He was as professional as any of them.

"Hi there… again."

"Danny, I understand that you have already met Dominic Strand from Penusia?"

"Yes, hello again, Danny McCormick at your service," he replied, with an air of sarcasm, grinning at Glen, who responded by glaring at him.

Strand did not seem to notice this, distracted by inserting information into his electronic notepad, which quietly emitted annoying sounds in response to his chosen commands.

"Danny, please tell Mr Strand about your role in the project."

"Well, I am the safety officer in the team. I supervise the diving expeditions with the sharks; check that all the safety measures are followed, such as checking PAD devices, tranquilliser launchers and other safety precautions. Factors such as checking that the air mixture is right and clean-"

The Penusian politely, but firmly, interrupted.

"Excuse me, but what is a PAD device?"

For a moment the eyes of Danny registered astonishment, before he remembered that this man was not from Coleshia. Reaching into a drawer in his desk he produced a small, black device that he extended towards the journalist. The Penusian took the device, and examined its exterior. It was a thin, cylindrical wedge, no bigger than a piece on a draughts board. On one side, it had a small, red light situated directly at the heart of its shell. Above the light were inscribed the words: *Protective Aquatic Device.* Gently tossing the device in the air, Strand felt its density as it landed squarely in the palm of his hand. Despite being small, the contents of the cylindrical wedge were quite weighty:

"How are they used, and what are they protection from?"

Glen, growing slightly impatient, provided an answer.

"On this planet, the species that we release into the oceans are better suited to survival here than we are. It pays to have a few safety measures when we are venturing beyond the settlement limits."

"Believe me, you need eyes in the back of your head to go out there," added Danny, grinning.

"This sounds ominous. Is there something that you are not telling me?"

The Penusian made a respectable attempt at keeping the apprehensiveness from his voice.

"Mr Strand, all this is information that I can give you when we check out the ecosystem. My team work to a strict schedule, and their time is precious."

"I understand, thank you, Danny," said Strand, casting a glance at Glen as a confirmation to move on.

Danny raised his right hand to his forehead in a two-fingered salute. The two men moved on to the next seated member of the team. Strand couldn't help feeling that something important had been glossed over very conveniently by his hosts. He made a mental note to raise this issue again with Glen.

"Mr Strand, this is Mike Cullen."

Upon Glen's introduction, Mike adjusted his round spectacles and smiled warmly at the journalist. Glen regarded Mike as his most trusted friend. They had been friends for years, ever since their days at the Aquatic Science Centre College, and they both shared a strong interest in the repopulation of the sharks to Coleshia's environment.

"Pleased to meet you again, Mr Strand," he said.

He was a very skinny man with a shaved head and a large, hooked nose. He second-guessed the Penusian's next question.

"I'm the team's technical supervisor. In basic terms, this means that I maintain the automated systems, which monitor the sharks' behaviour, checking that the environmental systems are functioning at optimum levels."

The journalist was evidently struggling to assimilate all this information, so Mike simplified his explanation.

"In order to understand how the sharks are behaving we need to have eyes in the water. I provide those eyes!"

"In what way?"

"For close encounters we have a series of cameras set up in our facilities. Even in Coleshia's clear depths, vision in the water is affected by light refraction. Consequently, many of our instruments are complex sonar scanners, assessing the sharks by analysing the information provided by the rebounded signals."

Strand fed this information into his electronic notepad, once again thanking Mike for his time. They moved on to the final member of the team.

Rhona Skallen elevated her head from her terminal. She had long, wavy brown hair, high cheekbones and sparkling dark eyes that were responsible for attracting a lot of attention to her physical features. She stood up to shake Strand's hand, producing a smile that revealed slightly irregular teeth that failed to destroy her obvious elegance. He returned the gesture enthusiastically, giving in to the desire of gazing hungrily up and down her tall, voluptuous, yet athletic, figure.

Glen grinned at her. She was the most single-minded woman that he had ever known. She knew exactly what she wanted from life and she created no illusions about that fact. She was fiercely independent, constantly well presented in her appearance, but always co-operative about doing her share of unpleasant duties for the benefit of the team. In Glen's experience of life this was a breath of fresh air coming from a member of the opposite sex. Perhaps due to sheer bad luck or ill-advised judgement on his part, many of his relationships with women had collapsed when he realised that they were unwilling to tolerate, or incapable of understanding, his chosen path in life.

Deep down, the demons inside him reminded him that this was not the real reason why he was still single after all these years… Here, however, was a woman, willing and capable of accepting the risks that came with working in such close quarters with sharks. He held extreme respect for her, and feelings that he had not yet found the courage to express.

"Mr Strand, this is Rhona Skallen, the team's hygiene expert."

"Pleased to meet you, Ms Skallen, and your role involves what?"

"Well," she replied, annoyed that Strand was choosing elsewhere, other than her face to place his gaze.

"I monitor the sharks' health, checking that they adopt natural behaviour patterns. It is important that the environment we are releasing them into is convincing enough for them to do so."

"How is this possible when they are housed in your release facility, Miss Skallen?"

Strand cast a glance towards the huge lab and the pool.

"The sharks are only in the Animal Release Zone for a short period of time. They were raised in the vast artificial environments of the Super Nova, and we simply keep them in the pool to complete our release procedures. They are in a new scenario here, captivity, and so my role is critical at this stage. We only have a small time window for their release. It is important that they do not show adverse reactions mentally or physically in that time, and that they are adequately prepared for survival on Coleshia."

As she was relating the details of her job, she looked shiftily towards Glen. He was reminded that there were other reasons for the fulfilment of his role in the Ark Project. These thoughts, however, always remained sealed in the profound depths of his mind. He would be glad when this Penusian had gone. It was nothing personal, but past experience had revealed, time and again, that journalists often had more than one agenda on their mind at any one time.

Part of Glen wanted to tell the journalist about the Bodywave Project, to boast about what they had achieved, but he knew that it would have been a foolish manoeuvre. More importantly, he didn't want the sharks being used as pawns in interplanetary politics. He had already decided within himself that this man would learn only what was necessary and no more.

If Isaac were in my position he would have done the same!
Of that Glen was sure…

The Type 3 'Moray' mini-submersible glided out of the Aquatic Science Centre. Within its curvaceous interior, Glen Davis sat at the controls, his attention on the landscape before him. He gazed through the transparent dome encompassing the cockpit. It provided a superb field of vision all around the small craft. To his left, he could see the impressive progress of the monorail making its return journey to the main settlement some kilometres away; the only direct link between the two complexes. The vehicle appeared almost as a silhouette as it charged relentlessly towards its radiant destination.

It was a strange metropolis, illuminated against an eerie background by a powerful lighting system. Buildings of assorted sizes and proportions rose from the ocean bed, positioned around a huge dome-shaped structure in the centre of the complex, which seemed to cast a bold luminescence, originating from its interior and generating throughout the cluster of man-made structures and beyond.

The docking bay doors sealed the huge building from where they had departed. Curiosity forced Dominic Strand into a backwards glance. The shape of the protective shell in which they now sat allowed a good view of the featureless cylindrical structure of the Aquatic Science Centre. Returning his gaze to the bold sight before him, he asked:

"I have to say, Mr Davis, it is amazing how Coleshians have managed to create a settlement in such conditions. Can you explain to me what that dome is? It shines so brightly!"

Glen turned to address his passenger:

"That is the agricultural centre of the settlement. It serves a dual purpose. It not only acts as the growth centre for many of our crops, but also as a valuable source of light for the settlement. I'm sure that you can appreciate that working at these depths can be difficult. Having this much light ensures that traffic within the settlement can move relatively freely without risk of collision."

"I see. How do you manage to generate so much power to create that much light?"

"We have adopted a technique that humans implemented centuries ago on our distant home planet - hydroelectric power! It would be foolish to exist in this aquatic environment, and not make use of its resources. You may not have seen them, but we have a series of generators on the surface that convert the friction of the ocean's movement into electrical energy. This energy is stored in special battery cells that are transported down to the settlement in remote-piloted submersibles. There are hundreds of them dotted around on the surface. Power supply is not an issue."

The Penusian nodded in acknowledgement.

"It is ominous... When I arrived here yesterday, all that I could see was water. On Penusia, we wake up to bright sunshine every day; that is how our power is generated – through solar energy - and we certainly don't have to live with problems such as depressurisation and the risk of drowning, or I may add, *electrocution*. Electricity and water are not best placed together."

With that the Penusian burst into laughter. If he were not witnessing it for himself, he would hardly believe that the human race was defying so many of the natural elements to survive. Glen struggled to see the funny side of his joke. Perhaps his lack of sleep was making him irritable.

"If we wish to see sunshine, we can venture to the surface. The Aquatic Science Centre and the main city complex are situated in the shallowest depths on the planet. As for the issues of safety, our structures are sound in design and fully equipped with fail-safe procedures. We haven't had any major disasters since the settlement was completed."

Strand noticed that, from the withdrawn expression that passed across his face, Glen's statement seemed to conceal more deeply-felt feelings. Perhaps this was stirring memories in this shark specialist that he would rather forget. This thought was short-lived before Glen continued.

"Our technology has overcome the problems of changes in water pressure. Diving equipment allows us to reach depths of up to one thousand feet, without feeling any side effects at all upon swift return to the surface. Not only do our suits allow for non-decompression stop diving at great depths, but all suits are equipped with helmets that allow for greater all around visibility and verbal communication between divers. In the past, divers had to converse via a series of signals, because a mouthpiece had to be worn."

"What about the animals, Mr Davis? Is there not an issue of the sea life causing problems within the city? I imagine that the light from the main settlement attracts a lot of the wildlife in these waters. Surely people will not feel safe to commute amongst sharks, for example?"

The Coleshian scientist frowned. Obviously, the Penusian had not been well versed on their lifestyle before journeying here. Glen had to conclude that this was hardly surprising, as contact between the two planets was scarce to say the least.

"Look around you, Sir," replied Glen. "We are still within the settlement limits. Do you see any threatening forms of life?"

Glen was not enjoying the day so far. Mike, Rhona and Danny had not responded well to the presence of the Penusian. His awkward questions had to be parried for the full hour of interviewing, and he was glad to get this man away from the Great White sharks in the lab. He sensed that Strand was implementing the journalistic technique of looking to make news, rather than reporting news.

"No, I don't see any life forms within the settlement limits, but unlike Penusia, where we keep the animals in large enclosures I have noticed that, on this planet, you do not have the luxury of such measures. There are no barriers around your settlement."

Glen was beginning to struggle with his patience.

"There are two very good reasons for this. Firstly, *all* the different species of animals that have been released during Phase Four have been fitted with special Brainchips."

"What is a Brainchip?"

"The Brainchip is basically a small microchip implanted into the animals not long after birth. As soon as the device is removed beyond the limits for the first time, it activates. If, after that time an animal wearing the device approaches the settlement limits, signals are sent to the animal's brain, warning it of the risk of being in the area. We have special air guns for fitting Brainchips to infant creatures. The procedure is swift and painless, and the microchips are self-targeting, so that no damage is caused to the creature in question."

Strand thought briefly before raising his next question.

"So, you are telling me that every animal, excluding human beings, has received brain surgery. Isn't that somewhat crude, and need

I say interfering with the animals' natural behaviour?"

"Not in the slightest. It is simply a precautionary form of protecting the animals from potential injury in the settlement limits. There are a lot of vehicles travelling to various locations at different times. We do not want unnecessary accidents. We keep the wildlife out, while the purpose of an enclosure, for example, is to keep the animals in, no matter how big it is!"

Again, the journalist was scribbling on his notepad. He pretended not to notice Glen's derogatory remark towards Penusia's adopted habitats for Phase Four of the Ark Project.

"So, if that is the case, Mr Davis, how do you deal with interacting with potentially dangerous predators outside the settlement? I would assume that sharks are the most dangerous animals on your inventory?"

"In a manner of speaking you are correct. Sharks *are* the most potentially dangerous animals on the inventory. As in many cases, the potential is unfulfilled. Just because the capability is there, it does not follow that so too is the desire. However, we have taken precautions to meet the *potential* risks."

"Such as?"

The Penusian's question had a distinct air of venom, but Glen was unperturbed because he was in possession of the antidote.

"The PAD devices that Officer McCormick mentioned are worn by divers and are protection against attack from potentially dangerous predators, such as sharks, which have been released during Phase Four of the Ark Project. This device interacts with shark senses, denying the instinctive reactions that are common in shark attack behaviour. If the shark is afraid then the device will tell it that there is no threat. Likewise, the device will tell the shark that the wearer is not a supply of food before it takes a bite, thus eliminating the possibility of attack on humans completely."

"I see. Are you as confident with the Great White sharks? Ancient historical records show this species to be the most feared out of any species of shark, and the most unpredictable. Maybe that is why we ventured out of the complex, rather than in the oversized swimming pool, which was more conveniently placed in the Animal Release Zone?"

Strand had been doing some homework on sharks. Glen thought quickly, raising his verbal blade to parry the blow.

"Mr Strand, as a first generation Penusian, have you ever been swimming before?"

"On a planet that is being terra-formed from a desert, there is no need to learn to swim," replied the Penusian defensively, folding his arms.

"Well, that is why. The oversized *swimming pool* is designed to mimic the conditions of the open ocean. The waves can be strong, and difficult to dive in, especially for a novice. Not to mention the fact that you would be in the same water as a Great White shark, a creature that existed on our ancient homeland some twenty million years before we did. They outlived the prehistoric reptiles that inhabited our former home planet. I would not allow you to climb in the water with one of these creatures for your own safety. The PAD device may stop you from getting attacked, but believe me, it takes time to learn and understand these creatures. The Great White sharks were not included on the inventory of the Ark Project as a source of entertainment. They were included to sit at the top of the aquatic food chain as extremely effective predators, and they have several assets that have put them there. With no obvious barrier between yourself and them, I think that you would find it rather intimidating, and I don't see you carrying any spare underwear with you…We have a phrase in our team: 'Fear breeds prejudice'. To remove the prejudice we have to dispel the fear, so that is why you have not been given access to the Great White sharks. I think that you would find the experience rather too intense…"

The 'Moray' minisub cruised beyond the settlement limits.

Glen's earlier comments had silenced Dominic Strand for some minutes. In his new found silence he became aware that even without the illumination of the settlement the clarity of colour in Coleshian sea water was surprising. So too was the visibility. He estimated that he must have been able to see clearly about fifty metres in all directions.

The small submersible glided past a school of tuna, swimming in an orderly group, unperturbed by their presence. It took some time before Strand had the courage to ask another question.

"Mr Davis, I am interested to know. How have the Coleshians managed to terraform the ocean, without inducing side effects in the animals?"

That's better, a little more respect...

"During Phase Three of the Ark Project, the Science Division created a chemical, CT-3, that would react with Coleshia's ocean, to complete the chemical make-up of sea water, like that on our ancient home world. By the time the settlement was completed, Coleshia had the basic building blocks to support aquatic life, with plankton being released from the settlement at regulated periods of the year. Although the animals have shown no adverse reaction to their new surroundings, we have noticed that new forms of plant life have appeared on the seabed. These, however, seem to have no harmful qualities – weeds mainly."

"I see," replied Strand, furiously inputting this information into his electronic notepad. "How about reintroducing the animals? Without any divisions or barriers, this must have been more difficult?"

"To a degree, you are correct," replied Glen, adjusting the controls of the submersible to avoid a large school of small, shining silver bullets. Even Glen struggled to make out what they were before they disappeared into the void.

"The main problem with establishing life on this planet has been selecting animals that could survive in the conditions. As there are no shallow waters on Coleshia, there is no coastline. This creates the first problem. For Phase Four, life was selected for its suitability to Coleshia's environment; organisms that were capable of surviving in oceanic waters. Fortunately, the calculations made by the computer simulators hundreds of years ago have prooven to be correct, so far, anyway. The early probes sent here by our ancestors revealed that Coleshia had no polar regions. Therefore, you would have to surmise that it would be impossible to reintroduce Arctic penguins, for example, and other forms of life created for such conditions.

The second problem lies in the fact that the aquatic ecosystem relies on important links to work without our intervention. For example, seals make up a large part of the Great White shark's diet. Seals breathe oxygen, so they need land on which to rest and raise their young. We have overcome this problem by building floating islands for the seal colonies. In this manner, we can overcome primitive obstacles.

We also face problems of climate. For certain species, such as the Great White shark, this is easier to traverse. This species come from a family of sharks, known as Mackerel sharks; noticeable because they have to keep swimming to breathe. This makes them perfect for Coleshia's deep oceans. They are, however, warm-blooded, so their nervous system is protected from rapid changes in water temperature. For many species of animal, it is more difficult to compensate for such changes. At various strategic points of the ocean, we have placed Artificial Temperature Generators. These create changes in temperature at various times of the year, allowing for the migration patterns of many species. It is a small help, but nevertheless, it encourages natural behaviour in the animals.

The final challenge that we have had to cope with, is gauging the right time at which to release the different species from the Animal Release Zone. The Elasmobranch Team has been one of the last to release its species into the ocean, because of the shark's standing in the food chain. For example, it would be impossible to release seals into the ocean, without their diet of fish being established within the ecosystem, and then expect to release the Great White sharks. The seals would suffer from two angles. They would starve and would be hunted to extinction by the sharks. Believe me, Mr Strand, Phase Four has been a real balancing act on Coleshia, but it is worth it to see the animals have their freedom…"

After two hours of watching fragments of the adopted nature of the planet, Glen Davis decided that enough was enough. He had more important things to do than entertain this Penusian journalist, and so he swung the small craft around to return to the settlement. The electric motors at the rear of the vehicle effortlessly adjusted to the new commands.

They were in deep water now, and the sonar detector had picked up a large object some seventy metres in the distance. Visibility had deteriorated slightly at this depth, and the minisub's lights provided a clear path in front of the vehicle. Glen silently hoped that this would turn out to be what his initial thoughts suggested.

As the distance closed between the vehicle and the large object, Strand became uneasy. He shifted nervously in his seat.

"Should we be getting this close? Those sonar readings look pretty large."

"Yes, forty-two feet, that's big all right," replied Glen, grinning.

They remained silent for a minute, looking into the blackness. Then… the submersible's lights picked out a shape through the murky waters. They saw it from a side profile at first, gliding effortlessly through the gloom. As they drew closer, the creature assumed the profile similar to that of a shark. The distance between the sub and the creature began to reduce quickly.

Glen adjusted the controls to reduce the speed, and fall behind the creature, so as not to startle it.

"Behold, Mr Strand. Ever wondered how David felt in the presence of Goliath?"

"My God, its huge!" cried the Penusian, alarmed.

Still, the sub drew closer, revealing the creature to be a gigantic fish. Its blue skin camouflaged it beautifully against the background of the ocean. Across its back was a large formation of white spots, that weaved an enchanting pattern, not unlike that created by the stars.

Glen Davis manoeuvred the vehicle above the creature. It had huge pectoral fins, elegantly allowing it to balance and power through the oceans. Strand could make out five, huge gill slits on either side of the creature's head, which was as broad as the body at its widest point, and which ended in a truncated snout. From their viewpoint, the creature's eyes were completely camouflaged by the patterns adorning its skin.

"What is it?" cried Strand, eyes as wide as saucers.

"Rhincodon Typus... Or more simply, the Whale shark."

"If it is a shark, should we be this close? It looks dangerous, and I don't see any of your PAD devices on board."

"Relax, Mr Strand. It eats plankton, which is released from the Aquatic Science Centre at various stages of the year. We had best move out of its way very soon. The plankton tends to congregate about the surface and it may rise to the surface to eat."

A couple more minutes went by, with Coleshian and Penusian admiring 'Goliath' in all his graceful beauty. In Glen's eyes, this monstrous, angelic beast belonged amongst the stars, with the huge star cruisers that brought them to their respective home planets.

"Seen enough, Mr Strand?"

For a moment silence, then...

"Yes, sorry, I was miles away. How much bigger do they get?"

"Not much, the Whale shark is the largest recorded fish in history."

"How many species of shark have your team released, Mr Davis?"

Glen readjusted the submersible's course and accelerated, before answering. Dominic Strand waited in anticipation, with his electronic notepad at the ready. By this stage the sights that he had just seen had given him a big rush of adrenalin, and he struggled to prevent the plastic computer pen from shaking in his hand.

"Nearly one hundred species. Mainly deep water and oceanic species: Mackerel sharks, such as the Great White, Mako and Thresher sharks, and Requiem sharks, such as Oceanic White Tips and Blue Sharks."

"Most interesting. Why not more? I thought that sharks were not fussy eaters in general."

"That," said Glen, focusing on the chubby face of the Penusian journalist, "is one of the biggest myths surrounding these creatures. Back in the twentieth century, when we still inhabited our home planet, sharks were hunted in extortionate numbers, for various reasons: medicine, bodily fluids, jewellery; even food delicacies and often for fun. It was never a considerate process towards the shark, often barbaric in fact."

Anticipating that Strand's next question would request some explanation for the myth, Glen continued…

"Occasionally, sharks would attack humans. Usually, such attacks were cases of mistaken identity on the part of the shark, thinking that the humans were part of their diet."

"But why?"

"When in the water, humans give off irregular swimming patterns, like that of an injured fish. The shark would sense these vibrations in the water, through sensors in its nose. Homing in, it would take a bite. Sharks are particular in their diet, and have sensitive taste buds. Upon biting they would taste that the flesh was not to their liking, and let go. Most of the deaths occurred through blood loss."

Strand listened on, fascinated, before asserting:

"That would account for such a widespread persecution campaign."

"From our historical records, that would appear to be the case. They were treated as controversial and dangerous, and many species were brought to the brink of extinction… Fortunately, times change. That is why the Elasmobranchs are very keen to ensure that no more excuses for prejudice arise."

Strand nodded in acknowledgement.

"Thanks to the Eden Treaty, that sort of persecution ceased at the start of Phase One. For that, Mr Strand, we must be grateful. You may be interested to know that the elephant on your planet, Penusia, was responsible for more human deaths, statistically than sharks."

For a moment, there was silence before Dominic Strand asked:

Chapter 10

"So, when all the animals are released, what is to be the fate of the Animal Release Teams in the Aquatic Science Centre?"

"To watch and observe!"

"For what exactly?"

"Change, Mr Strand… We call it convergent evolution…"

Chapter 11

The monorail silently came to a standstill within the spacious Aquatic Science Centre docking bay. It was made up of four streamlined carriages, each covered with small, triangulated metal denticles. Only in certain lights could this serrated surface be seen, so fine were the protrusions on the shining hull. This superb design feature was an idea borrowed from the skin of the most effective of oceanic predators, the shark.

At either end of the cockpit carriages, the body converged into a sharp point that, in conjunction with the serrated, white outer shell, allowed the vehicle to travel through the water producing very little drag on its sleek frame. It was powered electrically, but not from the rail, from which it was suspended. The power source came from inside the vehicle itself. Two electrical motors contained at each end allowed the monorail to travel the thirty-kilometre distance in a matter of minutes.

The four members of the Elasmobranch team climbed aboard, and seated themselves on the padded seats that ran parallel to each other down either side of the interior. By this time of the day the majority of the centre's staff had returned to their homes in the main complex, and the cabins were largely deserted. The four occupants of this carriage were no longer dressed in their grey uniforms, but more casually, sporting collarless shirts and loose trousers, which served as a welcome release from the confines of their close-fitting uniforms.

In the affluently decorated carriage, Glen Davis sat facing Danny McCormick and Rhona Skallen, while Mike Cullen was sat next to him, staring out of the cabin window as the monorail began retracing its journey through the ocean. So efficient was this vehicle that the occupants could not feel any sense of movement in the pressurised compartment. As he watched their place of origin disappear into the distance, Mike had to confess to admiration for the level of engineering that had gone into this machine.

"Am I looking forward to this? I haven't felt so much pressure since I took my graduation exams. That Penusian journalist was really beginning to make my head thump," bleated Glen.

Danny McCormick was the first to respond.

"Say, Glen, a few more PR days like that, and you will be running for the Governorship of Coleshia."

"Ha ha," came the sarcastic repost. "Incidentally, thanks for your great support today guys."

His colleagues laughed, and Mike nudged him in the ribs, disturbing Glen from his well-researched position of extreme comfort.

"Well, Glen, Governor Tasken requested that you entertain Strand, not the rest of the team."

"Thanks, Mike."

Rhona decided to bring the conversation to a serious head.

"Did you manage to stop him sniffing around the Great Whites?"

"Eventually. The last thing we want is for the public to find out about the 'Bodywave' Project. We will have the media citizens climbing the walls otherwise."

Danny interjected, "We could always use them as live bait!"

A concerned look came over Glen's face.

"Oh, come on, Glen, it was only a joke!"

The defence in Danny's tone of voice was evident. The poor humour, however, was not playing on Glen's mind.

"No, it's not that. One thing worries me, you know. The Ark Project is supposed to show compassion for all forms of life. I found Strand's ignorance quite disturbing today. He seemed too willing to follow the traditional course of human prejudice towards the sharks."

"Well, you have to see his point of view. This planet must have been quite frightening for him. He's used to good old 'terra firma' between his toes. Penusia isn't renowned for its aquatic life, being largely made up of deserts."

"Christ, the man couldn't even swim properly. Right now, he will probably be thanking his lucky stars that he's on the return shuttle to his home planet," added Mike.

"That isn't the problem so much," replied Glen. "What about the Coleshians? For two hundred years, human kind has observed sharks from observation ports on the Super Nova. Now they are faced with living in the same water as them."

"Glen, you're paranoid," giggled Rhona. "There are plenty of frightening creatures that have been released into Coleshia's oceans. Sharks are no different, and they have Brainchips like all the animals. They won't enter the limits! Besides, the majority of citizens who venture beyond the settlement limits are the patrol teams. It is their responsibility to tolerate all the animals on the inventory of the Ark Project. That includes sharks!"

"That may be true. What about in years to come when *all* the species have been established in the ecosystem?"

The look on Rhona's face was a puzzled frown that signified her reluctance to accept his train of thought.

"By *all*, I assume that you are referring to the Great White sharks?"

"Well, yes!"

Danny contributed his thoughts.

"Glen, you always get jumpy when we enter this phase of releasing a new species into the environment. It must be some mothering instinct that you have or something!"

Now Glen was in a defensive frame of mind.

"Danny, in case you hadn't noticed, our sole reason for existing is to protect the welfare of these creatures. I intend to do just that!"

The monorail began to slow down. From the light cast out from the slender cabin's interior the occupants could just about make out the seabed some twenty feet below them. In the formation of rocks and patches of sand that made up miles of the ocean floor grew strange spindly forms of plant life - seaweed. Once in human history, such a sight would have been called commonplace; but here in the settlement, forms of aquatic life were deliberately kept at a minimum, and sights such as these intrigued people when spotted.

They turned their gazes to the main settlement. The smooth, well-maintained surfaces of the huge man-made structures rose in stark contrast from the jagged landscape, proudly illuminated by the huge agricultural dome at the heart of the bustling complex. The activity within the hive of humanity was salient as the monorail continued to decelerate. Submersibles of various sizes and differing destinations glided past them; some were fitted with various mechanical appendages for lifting and construction, others equipped for a more simple purpose - transport. They hung about navigating via the light of the dome, like flies, mesmerised by the bright light. Buildings of varying proportions began to surround the monorail as it entered the city complex.

Bathed in light from the huge, aquatic structures, the four occupants were momentarily given the impression that they were above the ocean's surface, rather than several hundred feet below it. The docking bay doors parted for the monorail as it concluded its run. Powerful water pumps drained the docking bay of sea water as the huge doors sealed behind the vehicle.

After a couple of minutes the capacious bay flickered into automated life, exhibiting polished steel walls on either side. The reflective sheen of these surfaces was matched only by the gleaming walkways on either side of the vehicle. A fluorescent sign on the wall near the bay exit illuminated a map, detailing the location of different zones within the huge city-like complex.

The monorail's hydraulic doors hissed apart, allowing the four passengers to disembark. They examined the map.

"Hold on to your hats Coleshia, Team 107 is here to enlighten your existence," roared Danny, to assorted groans emitting from his companions.

Outside the docking bay they took a taxi to the adult leisure zone.

The main complex was a cocktail of activity, as the taxi, almost silently, bypassed the children's zone, a juvenile ghost town at this late hour in the Coleshian day, the leisure zone, more respectfully populated, and many others, as it travelled deep into the heart of the complex...

The Clam Buster club was the same experience to which they had grown accustomed during a number of past excursions to get inebriated. The team were limited to alcohol consumption once a month, so that their fitness levels did not suffer. Despite many advances in diving technology, an answer to the basic requirements of good physical health had not been overcome. Consequently, when such occasions rose, they were usually taken as far as their bodily functions would allow.

Glen and Rhona sat on tall stools around a long-legged, circular metal table. Surrounding them were dozens of couples engaged at similarly sized tables. As was obligatory in such places, there was also the large group of 'obviously single' people. They had managed to apprehend enough stools to assemble around a table far too small for such a manoeuvre, so that they could all have a perch on which to sit, while they annihilated more brain cells with various drinking games, in another half-successful attempt to escape reality.

Occasionally, one or both members of the couples would cast a wayward glance in the direction of the large group of people, as their laughing and cheering could be heard over the crescendo of music. One couple had refused to give up their large table for a group of people, despite the fact that there were smaller tables vacant that would have suited them just as well. Glen grinned.

Club culture is a strange phenomenon. Obviously they are reserving seats for their egos as well. Yet more victims of alcoholic over-confidence!

Their attention became distracted by Mike's unco-ordinated and muddled form of dancing, like some puppet on a string, silhouetted by the disco strobe lights. As he manoeuvred around the dance floor, people wearing an assorted variety of a lack of clothing warily cleared a path.

Chapter 11

Glen was reminded of the formative years of their friendship, as he observed this all too familiar ritual. He was privy to the information that Mike's drunken state was not to blame for his exaggerated dancing. The truth was that he had never been blessed with skills in this department! They had become close friends at college, united in a common interest – sharks! Many a drunken night had been spent discussing their plans for the future. It was, as a result, perhaps no coincidence, that they were both working in the Elasmobranchs and both still single. This was a problem that became aggravated by the fact that very few women were willing to spend time with a man who spent his waking hours researching and releasing large oceanic predators into the ocean. Mike's previous relationship had emphasised this point. Glen recalled how, with his own unique rationale, Mike had justified the outcome of this disaster to his friend.

"Women don't like it because they have to accept that we interact with beings with a bigger bite than they have!"

Recalling this moment of philosophical genius, Glen couldn't resist quietly chuckling to himself, before casting a glance across the table at Rhona.

That is what makes her so different!

Glen's thoughts turned to Rhona's first day with the team. She couldn't wait to get into the water with the sharks, and from that point on Glen had been assured that her passion was genuine… Immediately she had been relaxed, interested in the shark's company, and at no point did she expect any privileges or concessions to be made because she was one of very few females in a male dominated sector of society. He admired her for that. It was not an easy thing to control your nerves, especially in the seemingly compromising situations that arose working in close proximity with these creatures. As with many situations in the water, it was another case of mind over matter.

Returning once again to the present, Glen scanned the hordes of people, looking for Danny. A brief gap in the crowds afforded him enough space to discover his location. In stark contrast to Mike, he was relaxing on the sofa, his attention occupied by two curvaceous wavy-haired blondes. He had an arm draped around each of them, and they seemed to be becoming ensnared by his drunken ranting about how great he was.

Danny was the least well known member of the team. He had only been with them for a few months, but he seemed to be a harmless sort of person who worked hard, but also played hard. Glen's latest analysis of the man concluded that interacting with members of the opposite sex was extremely high on his list of priorities. Every time they had socialised as a group since they had all worked together, Danny had not left the Clam Buster alone. Glen was willing to bet that on the current showing, tonight would be no different. Judging by the scene before him, Glen had to conclude that perhaps Officer McCormick had grand designs on his mind tonight.

Glen and Rhona laughed at the evening they had experienced. On many an occasion, they had absorbed drunken comments, and sly facial expressions that roughly translated to, 'how the hell did a guy like Glen manage to get a girl like Rhona?'

If only it were true...

Glen stared into the green depths of his cocktail. He was all too aware that while he felt a sense of pride at these unspoken accusations, Rhona's body language seemed to play the situation down.

Deep down, Rhona hadn't really made up her mind about Glen. He was not uneasy on the eye, with his dark, square-jawed features. His jet-black hair was short and always neatly combed back over his scalp, and his dark brown eyes sparkled with energy. When his features creased with a smile she found that her pulse involuntarily increased, and yet when he wasn't smiling - which was most of the time - his chiselled face looked almost stone-like with a lack of emotion, and his powerful frame looked burdened by an invisible weight.

They were becoming fairly good friends, and there was a certain level of trust emerging between them. He approached his duties well, but there was a lot about him that remained a mystery. He struck her as being someone who succeeded and achieved on a professional attitude. The nature of his role within the Ark Project demanded that in many ways, but occasionally when Rhona had put investigative feelers in his direction, they had always been tactfully and politely diverted. He was very much an enigma to people who did not already know him.

"You are pretty distant this evening," yelled Rhona above the thumping, industrial music.

"Sorry, it's been a long day," replied Glen, sipping his drink.

"Something's troubling you. I can tell when you get like this."

"Are we doing the right thing?"

"In what respect?"

"The Bodywave Project!"

"Yes, I believe so," replied Rhona. "To create communication on an intelligent level with such an independent species can only beneficial. We can learn so much."

"What if it gets into the wrong hands?"

"Why should it? Apart from the team, no one in the settlement knows about the project, and even if they did, who would have the experience of working with the Great White sharks that we have?"

That's what Glen liked about Rhona. She was attractive far beyond the realms of physical beauty; she was reassuring, dimming his moods. Whether she was aware of this influence over his mental patterns, he was unsure, but the more that he got to know this woman, the more he became aware of this effect… The more aware that he became; the more difficult he found it to articulate his feelings towards her.

Once again, the candour in her voice was thick.

"Really, Glen, you worry too much, you *really* do."

This was said with an accompanying smile that proudly displayed her shining teeth.

"I like to think of it as an awareness," he replied.

"Paranoia, more like."

Momentarily, their attention was distracted as Mike inevitably began to lose his battle with extensive alcohol consumption. He crashed into a table, sending empty glasses flying in all directions. He ignored the wall of insults hurled in his direction, fumbling for his spectacles on the floor. Miraculously recovering them, he returned to his hyperactive postulating on the dance floor. On current observations, Mike would last another hour or so. Glen, satisfied that his friend was still in partial control of his body movements, returned to the intriguing conversation at hand,

"Well, I would rather be paranoid than ignorant. With our responsibilities, I don't see any other alternative."

"Possibly, but you should learn to enjoy yourself more."

"My enjoyment comes from what I do."

"Then, maybe you should learn to live a little more, look beyond your chosen lot," retorted Rhona with raised eyebrows.

Considering her point, Glen replied.

"Rhona, my lot is the reason why I get out of bed every morning... Another drink?"

Chapter 12

Glen lay in bed, his mind plagued with thoughts. This was, however, one of the few occasions when his sleep was disturbed for reasons other than memories from his troubled childhood. No matter how hard he tried, he could not get her out of his mind.

Come on Glen... This is almost becoming an obsession. You're assigned with her, for crying out loud!

He began fidgeting around, until he discovered a position on his side that aided the ease of his blood circulation, while continually reminding himself of the brutal facts.

If I pursue this any further, it will end in disaster. Then I would face awkward situations during my daily routine. Especially with my responsibilities, team ethics are of the utmost importance. Personal feelings cannot be allowed to jeopardize the operation... Besides, if life has taught me one lesson it is this... People can't be relied upon. Without the resolve and discipline life can be a killer...

The voice of his counsellor resounded in his mind. These days she was like the voice of his conscience:

"Glen, you have to move on, times change and so do people. We are all bound by the rules of time..."

"Certain things change, but the nature of people remains the same, no matter who we are talking about."

"Oh, come on, Glen, you're an intelligent young man, you know better than to believe that."

"Then why did they leave me?"

A pause that seemed to last a century...

"Life can be cruel sometimes. I can't explain that, Glen. I feel for you, I really do. To lose both parents at such a young age is horrific. Everyone has to concede that… But life is random, senseless sometimes. We all have to move on…"

"Believe me, I am trying, but the thought of losing someone close is unbearable…"

"Because it happened before doesn't mean that history will repeat itself… Your past is your past, and your future is yours to command…"

"Maybe, but we are shaped by events in the past… So surely the past controls the future… Some people are lucky, others are not…"

"No, Glen, you learn from your past, and take what you have learnt into the future."

"If that is true, then I have learnt this… To place your heart in another's hands is a futile risk, which offers nothing but pain…"

Eventually, sheer exhaustion pulled him into a restless slumber…

"Morning all," came the voice from the opening door in the office.

Rhona, Mike and Danny returned their greetings as Glen rushed into the office and sat at the vacant desk, switching on the computer terminal. The machine responded by whirring into life.

"Has everyone enjoyed their day of rest? We have a lot to get through today."

"Couldn't be better," smiled Rhona.

"Fit as a fiddle," cried Danny.

"Mentally, fine, but I have discovered some nasty bruising down the left side of my ribcage," moaned Mike, soothing his ribs with his right hand.

"That will be the table you collided with in the Clam Buster."

Everyone except Mike, burst into laughter at Glen's comments, recalling Mike's drunken antics of the night before last.

"*I* don't remember that!"

"The joys of alcohol consumption, my friend," laughed Danny, rising from his seat to pat Mike on the back.

Mike's reaction was an agonised wince as the connection of Danny's hand on his back sent shock waves through his bruised bones.

"Okay, I think that it is safe to say that you won't be going in the water today," interrupted Glen. "How are our friends today, by the way?"

Examining the complex display of acute sensor readings on his monitor, Mike conjured up an answer.

"All the readouts are indicating that they are stable, no change in the last forty-eight hours."

Glen listened to the feedback with a look of extreme concentration that mutated into a look of relief at Mike's assessment.

"That's good - we need to work quickly. The time allocated to us before releasing the Great Whites into the wild is drawing to an end. We need to wrap up our research *ASAP.* The Bodywave Project must succeed, for the assured establishment of this species onto the planet. We have less than two months before the sharks are due to be released!"

The team worked quickly. Two of the computer terminals were wheeled out into the main laboratory on portable workstations. Mike began booting up the required systems, from where the terminals sat, some feet away from the pool's edge. An array of sensors protruded from the complex instrumentation; sensors designed for the difficult process of monitoring the behaviour of Great White sharks.

Danny climbed into a stationary electric buggy, parked outside the office, and began a circumference of the pool, checking that nothing out of the ordinary had occurred in their absence. This was a regular pre-dive procedure, simply for the peace of mind of those present in the room at the time. Although largely unnecessary due to the complex technology monitoring the environment in the huge laboratory, it always paid to be slightly sceptical about the reliability of the accuracy of the instrumentation.

During this period, Glen and Rhona had disappeared into the prep rooms to climb into their pressure-resisting dry suits. These were thick, grey garments that gave the human body a bloated appearance when worn. Each layer was designed to respond to changes in the water pressure, keeping the body free from the harmful possibility of nitrogen narcosis, and thus completely dry. As the two re-emerged, two hours later, having carried out the preliminary checks to their diving equipment, Danny, having returned from his patrol in the buggy, handed the swaying objects that he carried with him to Glen and Rhona.

"HP–1's checked and ready to go!" he stated.

The safety checks that were required before a dive were numerous, as they had always been. Despite the improved ability of technology, its basic purpose, as a life support system for a human being had not changed. Thus, the traditional paranoia over the fear of equipment failure during a dive was still very strong in diving culture. Even more so considering the unpredictable nature of their aquatic hosts.

Glen and Rhona wrapped the objects around their waists, using the belts attached to each object. Sitting around their right thighs were metal holsters, each concealing what looked like a gun. They produced the objects from the holsters, and checked the ammunition gauges. Glen's digital counter read thirty and Rhona's weapon contained twenty-eight rounds.

"I hope that I never have to use one of these things."

"Relax," replied Rhona, "we've done this before, the sharks are used to us now."

The voice of Danny McCormick encroached upon their concerns.

"Well, if you do have to use it, make sure that it's *in* the water. The explosive tips on those rounds are strictly designed for the purpose. Firing through the air, without water density to cope with, would probably punch a hole through the complex wall!"

"Thanks for the warning," groaned Glen. "I hate guns."

"Well, we won't need to use them, so quit worrying," asserted Rhona.

"Right!" exclaimed Mike. "All systems are normal. The sharks' bio-readouts are regular, and right now they are located roughly in the centre of the pool."

"All of them?"

"That's right, Glen. They seem to be showing that 'community' behaviour again!"

The team had spotted this on a few occasions. Great White sharks were mainly solitary, but there were occasions when the four specimens in the pool seemed to share company as a complete group. To date, this behaviour had been completely docile, and very much against the myth of Great White psychology, hence the team's fascination with it. Glen couldn't help but feel slightly disappointed that their technology would not stretch to reading the minds of the animals, but perhaps that would be too intrusive…

"Let's get suited up," announced Rhona, lifting her air tanks over her shoulders.

Danny assisted her in this task, suspending the streamlined tanks, while Rhona pushed her arms through the straps, and tightened them. He then proceeded to give Glen the same courtesy. Once in place the air tanks resembled giant, silver teardrops suspended in frozen animation across their backs. They lifted their helmets into place, transparent domes encompassing their heads, to allow improved visual awareness and verbal communication under the water.

Mike clicked his microphone into place.

"Okay, can you hear me?"

A thumbs-up signal from the two divers acknowledged this.

"Good, now remember, drop down to ten feet before engaging the motors and your fins."

"Acknowledged," came the reply.

The two divers began the three hundred-yard walk along the width of the pool to reach the jetty, resembling cumbersomely endowed astronauts from humanity's distant past. As with many forms of technology that were designed for aquatic use, the usefulness of their suits on hard terrain was limited.

The hover skis purred across the surface of the water, gliding easily above the artificially generated choppy surface.

"Did you ever read about the astronauts during man's earlier expeditions into space?" Glen asked.

"Yes, I did," replied Rhona.

"In all this gear, perhaps we should have a name. How about the 'Aquanauts'?"

"You pick the strangest occasions for bad jokes."

"Well, it's not every day that you go swimming with the most efficient predator in recorded history."

They felt as if they had the freedom that one only felt when cruising on the open ocean. The horizon, however, did not depict huge expanses of the sea, with land disrupting it in small places, or even the glowing beauty of a sunset. Reality brought with it the clinical steel walls that enclosed the science lab, and high above them, the huge, fluorescent strip lights, which poorly substituted the vibrancy of Coleshia's sun.

Some ten minutes after departing from the jetty, the two 'Aquanauts' reached their destination, designated as the current location of the Great White sharks. As they squatted sidesaddle on the hover skis, they checked their oxygen gauges.

"Two hours left, how about you?"

"The same," replied Glen. "This is the best part. I always get butterflies before entering the water with these beauties."

Mike's voice came over their headset communicators.

"The sharks are located about five hundred yards from your current location. Your presence has scattered them in different trajectories. All readouts are normal. Ready when you are!"

Despite this reassurance, they both double-checked their life sensor gauges and diving instruments. They each had a miniature keyboard attached to their left wrists via a thick strap. The buttons were configured in the qwerty format. Above the keys were illuminated VDU screens, with the printed name BODY-WAVE on each miniature terminal. Next to the wrist-attached keyboards were small, black cylindrical objects – PAD devices. These were built into the diving suits, and each had a small, flashing red light, that winked at its wearer, to signal that it was functioning properly.

Looking deeply into the waves, Glen and Rhona carried out the

Chapter 12

mental conditioning that had become a standard procedure before each dive, regulating their breathing and clearing their minds. They both knew the importance of this skill when staring into the dark eyes of such a marvellous predator. This was the time when fears and reservations were shut away, and the ability to deal with the immediate future was critical. It was the ultimate adrenalin rush...

"Okay, let's do it," said Glen, jumping feet first into the water.

He felt the connection of his body with the waves. Momentarily, rapidly rising clusters of air bubbles clouded his vision. Automatically, his suit began inflating and discovering the natural level of buoyancy to suspend him effortlessly at this shallow depth.

Rhona's feet first landing, close by, disturbed the water.

"Touchdown!" exclaimed Glen.

"Roger that," replied Mike's voice through Glen's hearing aid...

Glen and Rhona allowed themselves to sink down to a depth ten metres below the water's surface, their suits deflating according to the commands of the buoyancy controls, and adjusting the pressure sensors in their ears.

The light produced by the lab's artificial illumination system, gave the couple good visibility. All around them, the water was eerily still, creating a strange sense of exposure and emptiness. Vulnerability was a natural reaction when faced with such a subdued void. They depressed little red buttons on their belts. Looking down at their feet, they could see square points emerging from their boots, rapidly taking the form of diving fins, that moulded themselves around their toes. Knowing the behaviour of their hosts, the two divers engaged miniature jets in their oxygen tanks, which assisted in their descent to a depth of forty feet.

Elsewhere in the huge pool, acute, finely tuned senses picked out an electrical disturbance in the currents that ran through the water. By a powerful instinctive mechanism, four mature and potentially lethal Great White sharks began a curious sojourn from opposing directions towards the source of the electrical disturbance...

Chapter 13

"They are just out of visual range. Should be with you any minute now," echoed Mike's voice in their ears.

Despite the fact that they had engaged with these beasts on numerous occasions, there was a sense of tension floating in the void with them. For a moment nothing… Then, above them a huge form cruised over their heads, almost silhouetted against the light of the lab. It's tail effortlessly swung from side to side, as the first of the Great White sharks came into view.

Two pairs of eyes furiously searched the creature for distinguishing marks. There were no claspers behind the belly, which instantly exposed males. She was huge, about twenty-eight feet long. This was a characteristic common amongst female Great White sharks. Another of the sharks came into view, warily keeping a safe distance. It sporadically appeared from the depths, and then vanished almost as quickly.

Glen furiously tapped away at his keyboard. The message read…
FRIEND

Almost instantly the shark became less reserved, and began to move closer, as if in recognition of the intruders.

Rows of razor-sharp teeth protruded from the beast's powerful lower jaw in an ironic smile. This was perfectly framed by a streamlined head that bulged out into a huge, muscular body and stomach area. This was balanced by a perpendicular, triangular dorsal fin, and curved pectoral fins that protruded from either side of the beast like meagre wings, thus allowing the shark to balance perfectly, but simultaneously providing it with a beautiful symmetry that was bewitching to the human observers. A huge, round eye, as black as the depths of a bottomless pit, regarded the humans, with curiosity and obvious intelligence.

Rhona noticed, with some affinity, a chunk missing from the creature's dorsal fin.

"It's Astra!" she exclaimed.

Rhona had a special understanding with this, the other female specimen of the Great White sharks. She cast her mind back several years to her early days with the Elasmobranch team, and her first encounter with a young, female Great White shark who was still awaiting a suitable name. The docile manner in which Astra had approached still gave her goose pimples. She had flitted in and out of Rhona's field of vision like a ghost, a being from an astral plane, and so the name had seemed appropriate.

With these creatures, respect had to be earned, and much like any other relationship, it took time to break through the barriers of caution that they threw around themselves. Rhona had learnt this, and now had a special relationship with these mighty fish; Astra in particular.

Glen also had a special relationship with these creatures, and he smiled as Astra swam to Rhona and gently nudged her, investigating the familiar human with her perfectly pointed snout, rather than her mouth. It was a form of behaviour perhaps better associated with aquatic mammals, but modern technology and extensive research had provided the best way to draw these emotions from the sharks, to prove that they were not mindless killers. The spearhead of technology, the Bodywave Project, had opened the barriers of communication, freeing this aspect of their behaviour, thus allowing interaction between humans and Great White sharks never before experienced.

By obvious deduction, Glen and Rhona realised that their first visual encounter on this dive must have been with Cleopatra, so named because of her beautiful streamlined physique. She had not shown as much affinity with the humans as Astra to date, but neither did she exhibit fear. Her very presence in the same water was proof enough that she was content.

Suddenly, Rhona let out an ear-splitting shriek. Her body was propelled forward through the water a number of feet, before she managed to stabilise herself. It could only have been *one* of the Great Whites...

With a quality of litheness, Poker Face glided past Glen's floating form. He was the smallest of the four, a mere eighteen feet long. Glen noticed as he cruised past, that he displayed fresh cuts and scars. From historical research, they had known that Great White sharks, above all other species, were very territorial. Glen thought back momentarily, to a strange form of territorial behaviour, known as 'tail slapping', where a dominant shark would spray a subordinate with its tail fin, slapping the surface of the water, that he had observed. The outcome of such behaviour was epitomised in the fresh, small wounds that Poker Face now exhibited. In their current confinements, this form of injury was inevitable. Fortunately, on very few occasions, were the fish severely injured.

Occasionally, hunting could be observed in pairs, but despite the strange congregations that had occurred in the pool, Great White sharks also had a strong craving for personal space!

Rhona typed into her keypad:

HA-HA!

Glen smiled, seeing the words appear on his own keypad. When a communication was made, either by the divers or the sharks, each keypad would display the message, ensuring full communication. The messages were colour-coded to distinguish which shark or diver was communicating the message being sent. He marvelled at the individual personalities of each shark. Poker Face was so named, because of his unpredictable nature – he gave nothing away, and, consequently, never communicated with them. At times, he often thought that Poker Face was trying to scare him, swimming by with his mouth partially open, baring rows of triangular teeth. Perhaps he was taking out his lack of dominance on the humans, frustrated at being the smallest, like the child who is bullied at school.

Chapter 13

Suddenly, without any warning, the three monstrous fish moved to a respectable distance. From previous experience, Glen and Rhona had learnt the meaning of this behaviour. The King was returning…

In the distance, another of the huge fish appeared from the depths, head swinging from side to side, as he powered effortlessly in their direction. He moved extremely close, proudly exposing his twenty-nine feet frame that rippled with strength. As he passed, Glen stroked a hand down the side of his two-tonne body, a shade of misty grey on the upper side and clear white beneath. The stark contrast in skin colour had served his species superbly well as camouflage in the oceanic environment and, as a result, had remained unchanged for millions of years.

As with the other sharks, he had a small microchip protruding from his tough, leathery skin, just behind one of his large black eyes. It was so small that without this detailed view of his features it would have been impossible to see. This was the Brainchip with which every creature in Coleshia's oceans was fitted; the technological link between humanity and nature.

He circled around again. Glen placed an outstretched hand on his nose, as the mighty fish hung momentarily motionless in the water, like a dog waiting for a bone. It was a sight that would have frightened the uneducated, but it did anything but frighten him. Glen knew that if the intent were there he would have stood no chance of defending himself. The intent, however, was not there, and Glen knew that he was safe. The relaxed posture that this huge fish displayed in his presence was enough for his skilled eyes to deduce this. The bond between the two of them was unique, and perhaps too masked in past misconceptions for the majority of people to understand it at all. Most people saw fear when they saw sharks. Glen saw grace and beauty in the animal that proudly occupied the same water as himself.

A message appeared on Glen's VDU display:
FRIEND.

Kauhulu was the youngest and by far the most intelligent of the four Great White sharks. He was also the largest out of the four, a strange phenomenon within White shark reproduction, as the females usually grew to larger proportions than their male counterparts. His size meant that he lost very few conflicts with his kin.

Glen had always sensed that Kauhulu was different. He had witnessed the shark's birth some ten years previous to today's encounter. Even from an early age, he had exhibited unique behaviour, and was extremely susceptible to human contact. None of the other Great White sharks would communicate until they had received confirmation from the divers that they posed no threat. Kauhulu needed no assurance; he was unusually bold in the presence of humans.

Glen recalled Rhona's second day with the team. At that stage Kauhulu was only two metres long; about one third of his current size. This was still a suitable enough size to classify him as being potentially lethal. Glen still remembered the look on Rhona's face at her first close-quarters encounter with a Great White shark. She had been amazed at the close proximity that they could gain with him. It was unusual, even when equipped with a PAD device. He demonstrated less fear than the others, and because of these attributes, Glen had given him the most noble of names - Kauhulu.

In human history, an ancient tribe of natives, the Polynesians, had worshipped a shark deity of the same name.

Ancient myth claimed that this group of humans had a supernaturally strong bond with sharks, unheard of in any other part of the world. This was epitomised by the fact that Polynesian children used to swim very openly with these fish. This, Glen saw as a parallel of his relationship with Kauhulu, and the behaviour that this unique shark undertook towards people.

Two hundred years ago, even entertaining the idea of swimming with Great White sharks, without the protection of a cage, would have been considered an act of reckless stupidity. With the aid of modern technology, the Elasmobranch team had accomplished just that.

Glen laughed out loud.

Convergent evolution was one of nature's greatest wonders!

Chapter 14

Some three hours later, the Elasmobranch team were once again seated in the office, washing down their drinks. In accordance with the procedure, they sat around discussing the events that had just taken place in the pool.

From their position, Mike and Danny had seen everything from the miniature motion cameras that were built into the diving helmets. It was Glen's friend who added his thoughts to the mix.

"Personally, I often think that Danny and I have the best view on these dives – from the comfort of a chair! Checking the instruments is like watching a game of chess, trying to guess what is going to happen next!"

Glen couldn't resist shooting his friend down in flames. He had known Mike for too long to ignore the occasions when he tried to make his position look superior to the other members of the team:

"Only one problem with that, my friend. Watching from the other side of a monitor screen is never the same as being amongst the action. Playing chess is far more fun than watching it! On a more serious note, however, I think that we should all take note of the injuries that Poker Face had today. Although they were not serious, I think that we should acknowledge it as growing frustration on the part of the sharks for a larger environment - freedom!"

Before a response could be articulated they were interrupted by the piercing sound of the intercom buzzing on Glen's desk. He reached forward and depressed the button.

"Team 107 reporting."

"This is Security Officer Andrews at Outpost 17. Senator Phillipoussis is here to see you on urgent business… Subject matter classified!"

Glen cast a surprised look around the assembled team. The bewildered facial expressions were returned. This was a highly irregular procedure. It could only be a matter of the utmost importance for the Senator of the Coleshian High Council to come and address them personally.

"Acknowledge that, send him in."

A moment later the team were gathered around the entrance to the Animal Release Zone, their curiosity heightening the more that they were kept in suspense. The doors silently parted. A tall figure wearing the sombre facial expression and the brown robe of a High Council Ambassador swept into the room, arms crossed with his wrists folded into his sleeves.

Behind him the sound of clinking armour marked the entrance of two armed sentries, holding blast rifles across their chests. They just stared blankly ahead, as if there was no one else in the room. Years of regimented procedure had accustomed their minds to this discipline.

In the peaceful colonisation of Coleshia, there had been no threats of any potential outbreaks of violence, and these armed sentries simply supplied window dressing to the senator's presence, informing the world of his importance. Nevertheless, Coleshian bureaucracy dictated that such security precautions were observed when the senator ventured beyond the Coleshian Administration Centre. No matter how hard the hierarchy tried, the treacherous history of human nature could not afford to be ignored, even in these peaceful times.

The senator stepped forward. The question was asked in a formal and polite manner, as everyone had come to expect from a politician, but the lack of knowledge was surprising all the same.

"Good afternoon, Team 107. I am here on a matter of the utmost urgency. Who is in charge of this operation?"

Glen stepped forward.

"I am, Senator! Glen Davis, how may we be of assistance?"

Chapter 14

Minutes later, the Elasmobranch team were once again in the office, gathered around the senator. At his command the sentries left the room and positioned themselves outside the office door.

It was difficult to distinguish through the robe, but he seemed to be a thin man, judging by the proportions of his face. His long, slim features culminated in a pointed clean-shaven chin that failed to draw the attention away from the Adam's apple, which prominently bobbed up and down like an inflatable beacon on the ocean's surface. Within deep-set sockets were alarming and complex green eyes that made him appear very distinguished. His over all appearance was capped off with short-cropped, black curly hair, which hid under a small skullcap that corresponded to the colour of his robe.

A lot of good things had been said about this man. He had served under Governor Tasken for the better part of Glen's life, despite his youthful appearance, and the Coleshian public had as much faith in him as they did their own governor. Glen wondered if the High Council had found out about the Bodywave Project. Perhaps their security procedures had begun to arouse suspicion, creating the impression of ill deeds being performed behind closed doors. But if that were the case, the High Council would not have sent one of their senior members to confront them. The level of force would have been more evident than the guards who maintained their statuesque vigils outside.

At the end of the day, the Elasmobranch team were not doing anything wrong in keeping quiet about their technological development. Glen had to remind himself that their motivations for secrecy were to protect the sharks from unnecessary attention, not from letting people know of its existence, especially in such a primitive stage of development.

Senator Phillipoussis began relating the reason for his surprise visit.

"This morning, one of the regular patrols beyond the settlement limits came across a strange discovery. One of the sharks that has been introduced into Coleshia's ocean has, how shall we say, been mortally wounded."

"In what respect, Senator?" asked Rhona, rising concern apparent in her voice.

"Well…" He paused briefly, looking around the whole team before continuing. "It would appear as if it was attacked by a creature of some kind. The patrol that brought it in could not verify any probable cause."

"You mean they brought the shark back?" interjected Mike.

"That's correct, Officer Cullen," replied the senator, checking Mike's name tag as he addressed him.

"Where is it now?" asked Glen.

"In Zone Eight. Our scientists have performed an autopsy, but they are baffled. As your team work closely with the sharks, we have requested your assistance in the diagnosis to form a second opinion."

For a moment, silence… Pulling an animal release team off-line for such an exercise was not a standard procedure. The High Council must have had deep concerns about what had happened. The senator continued.

"It might be a freak accident; quite how it happened concerns us considerably, but we are worried that the animals are having adverse reactions to their new home. The last thing we want is for our hard work to be disrupted by any form of genocide amongst the inhabitants of the ecosystem…"

"You think that another shark may have been responsible?"

"Possibly, Officer Davis, at the moment it appears to be our best theory!"

They rushed to Zone Eight of the Aquatic Science Centre. Glen had to admit that he felt very intrigued as to what the cause of death might have been. If Senator Phillipoussis' suggestion were true the wounds would indicate this. Such occurrences were not uncommon, but perhaps a little worrying while the populations were establishing themselves in the ecosystem.

Occasionally, pack feeders such as Prionace Glauca, known more commonly as Blue sharks, would become fatally wounded during feeding. He remembered observing one such 'feeding frenzy'. During the enraged feeding rituals, he saw a young male being bitten by a larger female. Once stimulated by the blood, powerful instincts drove the sharks absolutely crazy, biting and chewing at anything in their path. The young male had swum away with his intestines ripped open. Such was the fury of the 'feeding frenzy', that the male had begun swallowing his own entrails! Although horrific to watch, it was, nevertheless, natural behaviour and such incidents were not uncommon.

Could this be another such scenario? In some ways, Glen hoped that it was. At least it could be classified as natural behaviour. The alternative solution would imply that the animals were struggling to adapt, which would be bad news. In a short time they would know...

Upon arriving at the autopsy lab, Science Officer Matsuo greeted them. Her white robe was stained with bodily fluids that carried a sickening smell to their nostrils. Noses wrinkled in unison.

"You might want these," she said, handing them face masks. "Once these beasts have been out of the water for a couple of hours, they smell bad!"

In all her years as a scientist, she had seen many sights that had caused her some troubled thoughts, but she had to admit to herself that this latest discovery baffled her more than anything that she had encountered before.

"Did you recognise the species?" enquired Glen.

"Yes, Alopias Vulpinus, from the family Alopidae."

"A Thresher shark!"

"That's right, about twenty-five feet in length."

"Surely you know," added Rhona. "it can't be that difficult to obtain accurate measurements of a dead fish!"

Officer Matsuo simply looked at Rhona, before guiding the team to the room that held the answers to many of their questions.

Bang went Glen's theory; Thresher sharks were not pack hunters...

Upon entering the room bearing the corpse, the five figures huddled around the autopsy table. Their immediate queries were easily answered, but these simply created further questions.

Lying on its side was a distorted mess that had once been the embodied form of a female Thresher shark, instantly recognisable by her huge, scythe-like tail, with a short central lobe that now drooped onto the floor. This strange evolutionary development was the fish's chief tool in catching prey, by rounding up schools of fish into groups, thus creating an easier target on which to feed. Her skin was dark grey, and five, fine red lines at various points of the body indicated areas of incision by the autopsy team.

The Elasmobranch team needed no close examination to see the cause of death. From head to tail, the beast should have matched Officer Matsuo's measurements, but she had neglected to tell them one fine detail. The entire ambiguity of her analysis, and that of Senator Phillipoussis' account of the events surrounding this scene were now easy to understand. The shark's head was missing! She had been decapitated cleanly around the gills, just in front of the pectoral fins, displaying large muscles and a cartilaginous skeletal structure. There was no trace of the eyes and mouth.

Glen found the image repulsive. Who or what would be capable of such a barbarous act?

"Any ideas?" asked Officer Matsuo, gazing around the team.

For what seemed like an eternity no one said anything. They just stared at the lifeless remains on display before them.

"It beats me!" stated Danny.

"Me too," affirmed Mike, shaking his head slowly from side to side.

"What on Coleshia could have created such a wound? *Look*, it's almost a perfectly clean cut. There are no teeth marks and the mouth of any animal that could inflict this damage to a shark this size would have to be immense," said Rhona, despairingly.

Glen held his hand to his mouth, his forefinger tapping on his lips thoughtfully.

"I can tell you now, Officer Matsuo, this was no shark attack. I am also one hundred per cent certain that there is no species that has been introduced on this planet, which is capable of inflicting this damage to a fully-grown Thresher shark. This must be one of the largest species of predator currently in the water!"

"What are you suggesting, Officer Davis? An alien being?"

"At this stage, I don't know what to suggest, Officer Matsuo."

"So what do we tell Senator Phillipoussis?" she asked, baffled.

"Maybe this injury was man-made," surmised Danny.

"That would be in direct contradiction to the Eden Treaty. The punishments for such an offence are extremely harsh. If someone deliberately did this, they would have to be extremely determined," stated Mike.

"Or extremely ruthless," replied Rhona. "Glen, that night on the monorail, you were concerned about the Coleshian public's reaction to living amongst the sharks. Could this be a reaction?"

"No, I don't think so. Although the Thresher shark preys on small creatures, such as squid and crustaceans, the uneducated person would not know this. Fear would be motive enough for such a reaction, but it would discourage anyone from coming into close quarters with the shark; which is the only way that such damage could have occurred. An attack of this kind would have been very calculated, and would require close quarters contact, with God knows what as a weapon!"

"Maybe it was an accident. Perhaps the shark was stimulated by the electrical current produced by one of the engines of a patrol submersible. Perhaps she had bitten the motor's propellers," hypothesised Mike.

"The body was discovered outside the settlement limits. The only vehicles that venture that far out are the patrols that check on the animals' progress. It would have been reported."

"Before today, nothing that could be described as strange behaviour has been reported by any of the patrol teams. Not least the sharks. Its just not plausible," asserted Officer Matsuo.

"What if it was an accident, and the perpetrators were afraid to admit to it? Perhaps they were afraid of the consequences," suggested

Danny.

Glen knew that they were clutching at straws, and Rhona knew it too.

"A collision of that kind with the motors of any of our submersibles would damage the engine as much as the shark. The sub would be wrecked, and the cause of death would be obvious."

"In which case we are left with a mystery on our hands," said Glen. "All that I can suggest is that we step up the patrols beyond the limits, and perhaps find a cause for the shark's death by means of observation. Maybe it is something that the patrols have missed."

Something else was bothering Glen... At the back of his mind, a thought kept raising its ugly head, and he was certain that it was most definitely of an unpleasant nature! Was convergent evolution on Coleshia running amok? Was the process of evolution creating changes in the physical make-up of the ecosystem? What changes was this planet inflicting upon the wildlife that it had adopted? Perhaps life was adapting, but not over millions of years, over decades!

Only time would tell...

Chapter 15

PART 3: COLESHIAN EVOLUTION.

Project Date: Day 20 of Year 0405

The 'Manta Ray' cruised through the murky depths, gliding over sinister, jagged rocky protrusions. This 'Ray' differed from the graceful beast that was well recognised for gracing the oceans, seemingly devoid of purpose. The reason for the presence of this monster was all too clear as it clung precariously close to the difficult terrain of the seabed.

It was fluorescent yellow in colour; making it clearly visible from some distance away. The blue tinge of the ocean forced the machine to assume a shade of green. Its curvaceous wings did not show any signs of rippling movement, because they were made of a tough, light-weight metal alloy. Where its tail should have gracefully merged the wings to a point, sat a large prop motor that spun around furiously, propelling the man-made creature through the eerie stillness.

At the front of the vessel was an open cockpit. The protective visor was open, joining almost seamlessly with the streamlined, outer shell. Only one of the seats was occupied. The pilot inside, effortlessly guided the craft through the open ocean, occasionally disrupting his vigil over his instrumentation to cast wary glances from side to side to check for signs of peculiarity within the environment. His finely-tuned reflexes allowed the metal monster to avoid the cruel landscape that would have been all too willing to cause major damage to its soft shell.

Attached via safety lines to the wings were two patrol divers, fully adorned in the pressure resisting dry suits. These bulky garments erupted into rounded peaks in the form of domed helmets, that allowed the divers to gaze around, analysing the seascape via portable torches.

The pilot was glad to see brief terrains of sand that allowed him a short respite from the taxing task of trying to use the craft's navigation lights to outwit the next placement of rocks that assumed perilous locations in their path. Visibility was minimal at this depth, and to attempt this route of patrol at anything greater than their current speed was a course of action recommended by few people.

A nagging thought kept entering the focused mind of one of the machine's human passengers.

"We've been out here for two hours, and we've seen nothing," said the diver who was sitting atop the left wing, frustration in his voice.

"Then that can only be good news," came the reply from the cockpit.

"Look, just stop arguing; we know our jobs, so there is no point in bitching about it," interrupted the diver on the right wing.

Ignoring the resigned statement of his passenger, the pilot continued.

"Well, I don't know about you, Donaldson, but I think that something is most definitely wrong. Didn't you hear? The Coleshian authorities have stepped up the patrols beyond the settlement limits. We're looking for something, man!"

"We're always looking for something. That's our role within the Ark Project. It's what we do as a patrol team. Just give it a rest, Andrews. You'll start hyperventilating if you don't calm down."

The pilot in the cockpit raised his arm, supplying Patrol Officer Donaldson with a single fingered salute.

"Very colourful," replied Donaldson.

Despite often finding himself appointed as peacemaker in the arguments of his colleagues, Patrol Officer Daniels had to admit that the pilot seemed to have stumbled upon a very astute observation.

"Andrews is right," he asserted from the right wing. "For two years now our patrols have been operating twice daily. All of a sudden, for no obvious reason, the patrols are stepped up to three times a day. It doesn't make any sense."

"That doesn't mean a thing, Daniels," retorted Donaldson. "There could be any number of reasons for the increase in our patrols. Our orders have stayed the same – to look for strange behaviour in the animals, and any changes in the environment. The most dangerous creatures out here are the sharks - if, like myself, you *don't* believe what that damned Elasmobranch Team says - and your PAD device will protect you from attack, so stop worrying. Its just another day in the office!"

"Well, I hate to ruin your picnic, Donaldson, but I think that we've already discovered *strange* behaviour amongst the animals," interjected Andrews.

"What do you mean? We haven't seen any!"

For a moment, the two divers on the wings stared at each other through their domed helmets, then at Andrews in the cockpit.

"*Eureka!*" cried Andrews, sensing that the penny had just dropped. "That's the problem, you assholes. We are fifty kilometres beyond the settlement limits, sixty degrees north-west. When was the last time that you saw any fish?"

"He's right," proclaimed Donaldson. "This isn't the behaviour of a natural environment at all. This area is deserted!"

"Hold on one minute. Andrews, did you forget to activate the engine mufflers again? You know that the motors scare the wildlife!"

Daniels prepared himself for an apologetic reply, a smug grin beginning to appear on his face, but his expectations were dampened somewhat.

"They were activated as soon as we left the Aquatic Science Centre! What we have here is a stran-"

Andrews' own analysis of the situation was interrupted by the activation of one of the alarms on his convoluted instrumentation.

"Wait a minute. We've got something on the sonar, and it's big!"

"Where?"

"A kilometre north," replied Andrews. "I don't like this. Maybe we should report it in."

"Report *what* in? We haven't seen anything to report."

Patrol Officer Daniels clenched his hand tight around his torch. His stomach began doing cartwheels. He didn't like this one little bit…

The 'Manta Ray' patrol submersible cruised cautiously through a formation of rocks that rose steeply from the ocean floor to greet them. Long fingers of green kelp stretched towards them - the only immediate sign of organic life in the vicinity.

"At least there are some signs of life around here!"

Officer Daniels' attempt at optimism was destroyed by Andrews' cynical analysis of the environment.

"Only because it's rooted to the seabed!"

Similarly towering formations of rocks erupted in twisted reluctance around them, making the submersible's progress all the more dangerous. As the rocks finally began to cease in their sporadic appearance, the patrol team saw the object from the sonar. At the same time the clusters of rocks seemed to drop away into a bottomless void, as the source of their journey appeared before their astonished eyes.

"*By Coleshia's sun,*" cried Andrews from the cockpit. "What the hell is that?"

"You tell me," replied Donaldson.

"Somehow, I don't think that this was on the inventory of the Ark Project," Daniels interjected.

Before them was a huge object growing from the dark depths of the void. It ascended to heights far beyond their range of visibility, seemingly sprouting towards the ocean's surface. It was an organism, made up of a huge dark purple stalk. Protruding from stems that haphazardly grew from the stalk were several dozen spherical pods that appeared in a kaleidoscope of shades of pink. They swayed in the ocean's current, clearly showing buoyant qualities, thus providing an explanation for the organism's vertical growth towards the surface.

"Okay, I've seen enough," said Andrews, nervously. "Let's get out of here, and report this to the authorities."

"Hold on," said Donaldson. "Let's check it out. It only looks like a plant, like giant seaweed!"

"A *plant*. *Look* at the size of it! How many plants have you seen on this planet that assume the proportions of tall buildings, not to mention the unusual colour scheme of purple and pink?"

Andrews was clearly apprehensive about the situation, but he knew that the patrol team had a responsibility to ascertain more information about this undiscovered life form.

"*Two minutes*, Donaldson; then we're gone."

"Okay. Relax, Andrews."

Patrol Officer Daniels said nothing…

Andrews carefully manoeuvred the left wing of the submersible parallel with one of the larger pods.

Donaldson disconnected his safety line and jumped off the wing. As he began to sink out of his colleagues' field of vision in a cloud of bubbles, he engaged his fins, and used the buoyancy compensator in his suit to ascend to the nearest pod. As he neared it, he began to get some idea of the proportions of the sphere. It was about four metres in diameter. Touching it, he struggled to make out the texture of the smooth surface through his gloves.

"Strange… It feels solid."

Unable to ascertain the strength of the shell, he decided to adopt a different approach, tapping the smooth surface with the knuckles of his clenched fist.

A resounding thump travelled to the hearing aids of his colleagues.

"Be careful, Donaldson!"

The intrigued diver raised his left hand in acknowledgement of Daniels' concern.

"It looks like a shell."

As he stared at the pod, enchanted by the beautiful collage of assorted shades of pink, something stirred within.

Seeing that the colours had moved, he suddenly realised that it was not the shell that glowed incandescently, but the contents within the shell! Startled, Donaldson pushed away from the spherical bud.

Several feet above them, the patrol team had failed to notice that one of the pods had exploded from the inside out, leaving a hollow shell.

"Donaldson, are you all right?" asked Andrews through his headset. "Donaldson?"

"Err… Yeah, I thin…"

The pod in front of him at that moment chose to explode. The pod's contents erupted forth in a shower of fluids towards Donaldson… And then right through him!

The sound of tearing tissue under tremendous pressure could be audibly heard in the hearing aids of the startled divers. The source of the explosion hurtled past the submersible, creating heavy turbulence in the water, causing Daniels to lose his footing on the vehicle's wing. Then, swiftly, it rose to the surface. The crew had no more than a glimpse of it.

"*Donaldson!*"

Andrews, and the recovering form of Daniels struggled to see through the growing cloud of fluids and human blood. Patrol Officer Donaldson's upper torso appeared from the cloud, face staring in frozen horror through his helmet at the stunned crew of the submersible. His lower torso emerged from a different area of the expanding mess. He had been cleaved in two!

"*Andrews, get us the hell out of here!*"

Needing no second invitation, Patrol Officer Andrews swiftly added power to the submersible's prop engine. It squealed in compliance, swinging the machine away from the organism and towards the location of the settlement.

Daniels sunk to his knees to maintain leverage on the wing. He had no time to reach the cockpit. Through the protective dome of his helmet, he could see a shape returning from the surface of the ocean, getting bigger the longer that he looked.

Chapter 15

"Faster, Andrews," warned Daniels' concerned voice.

Andrews glanced in the rear camera monitor of the cockpit. He could see the shape rapidly gaining on them, vertical muscle movements pushing the beast closer and closer still… With his attention momentarily distracted he failed to notice the rock that projected sharply from the seabed. At the speed at which they were travelling, a collision was almost inevitable. The submersible's left wing scraped over the rock, metal screaming against stone.

Andrews struggled for control of the vehicle, causing Daniels to lose his footing on the wing. Daniels' petrified voice screamed in his ear. Andrews once again, looked in the monitor to see Daniels being dragged precariously behind the submersible, attached by three feet of safety line.

Daniels felt extreme pressure being exerted on his suit as his body was forced to take the pressure of the water density, while travelling at high speed. He could feel the garment struggle with the strain. In confirmation of his fears, an alarm sounded in his helmet, warning him that his suit would fold if these conditions were maintained. He had to get back to the cockpit. But how? He was hanging on for dear life as it was.

Terrified, he looked behind him. He could see the huge, razor-sharp beak and the fleshy tongue, with a perimeter of row upon row of razor-sharp teeth. Razor-sharp spikes that extended from the skull and spinal column sliced through the dense water, and the huge fleshy tail powered up and down relentlessly. Large pectoral fins applied balance to this nightmarish monster as it surged towards him.

Daniels drew his HP-1 pistol and fired, leaving one arm clinging onto his safety line. Struggling to compensate as he was dragged helplessly through the water, his aim suffered. His first shot missed badly, exploding into the rocks below. He fired again, almost achieving a direct hit. The exploding round hit a rocky outcrop, causing the beast to slow its relentless chase, but only momentarily.

In what seemed like less than a blink of an eye the hellish creature emerged from the cloud of debris, its vicious beak snapping furiously, and its grotesque bulky body taut as it increased its pace yet again. Were his eyes playing tricks on him, or did the creature's skin change colour? Just seconds previously, he could have sworn that the beast was purple, but now it was bright yellow, mimicking the colour of the submersible. As it charged towards the fleeing vehicle once again, it's colour changed to a furious shade of red.

Patrol Officer Daniels didn't have time to let off another round. With one terrific lunge, aided by a bizarre paddling movement of its pectoral fins, the creature slammed into the back of the submersible, inches from Daniels and regardless of the lethal prop engine that spun furiously, just inches from its head. He screamed, losing possession of his pistol, cowering away from the monster.

In that moment the petrified diver was allowed to note the beast's rippling muscles, bubbling like a flow of larva cascading down a mountainside, which hid under the disgusting moist flesh; then the lifeless yellow eye that showed no sign of intelligence or pain at its violent collision. With his head pounding with adrenalin and fear, Daniels realised that one swipe of the monster's lethal beak would tear him to pieces like shredded paper.

Suddenly, he was no longer staring into the huge, empty yellow eye of the beast. The beast and submersible surged into the distance, the creature brutally hacking away at the metal shell with its beak, while Daniels fumbled for the severed end of his safety line in bewilderment. As he sank to the seabed the alarm in his helmet ceased.

"Daniels, are you okay?" resounded Andrew's petrified voice over the communicator.

"*Get out of the sub, man!*".

Daniels looked on as the vehicle and creature continued to disappear into the distance. The reluctant machine began to shake violently as it struggled to maintain its trajectory while receiving persistent and increasingly violent attacks. Futilely, he could only watch as the beak ripped through the vehicle's shell like a blade through a spider's web, each blow applied with the full weight of the vile creature's writhing body.

Chapter 15

"I'm losing control of... *Help me!*"

Patrol Officer Daniels could hear the sound of the beak tearing through the metal shell of the tortured vehicle.

His breathing was frantic. After a short time, he looked at his navigation dial. In an instant he had worked out his bearings in relation to the settlement. Extending his fins, and ignoring the throbbing pain in his shoulders from the straps of his oxygen tanks, he headed in a south-easterly direction, sticking closely to the seabed.

By this stage of the inexplicable turn of events, he was in a state of traumatic shock. With no torch, he swam on regardless through the murky depths, concentrating only on the settlement, regardless of its distance, and how much oxygen he had left in his tanks. His mind desperately tried to find ways to shut out the wrenching and spine-chilling sounds that continued to be received through his headset. In his claustrophobic surroundings, he found little comfort that could take his mind off the screams of pain and agony that accompanied the end of Patrol Officer Andrews' life...

Chapter 16

The huge space cruiser faithfully hung in Coleshia's orbit. At the end of the vehicle designated as the front there were strange protrusions and antennae that extended from the hull like huge spears, making the titanium nose cone look like a giant pin cushion. Along the length of the vessel the antennae disappeared as the monstrous fuselage distended into the formation of a huge cylinder that rotated in a clockwise direction. This cylindrical shell stretched for several miles, before a huge, cylindrical outer shell that enclosed the clockwise-rotating cylinder continued the length of the vessel, rotating in the opposite direction. These contrasting forces created an artificial gravity within the vessel's interior. The rotating cylinders extended for hundreds of miles before ceasing, almost as abruptly as their formation began.

Two large fins emerged from opposing sides of a large, rectangular-shaped titanium block that continued to increase the length of the monstrous spaceship. These were completed by the huge rocket motors that had remained dormant and unused for decades. The whole vessel bore the appearance of a machine randomly assembled from several million components, and thrown together to create a colossal monstrosity amongst the stars. Its design could never hope to match the symmetry and beauty of the planets and stars with which it shared the vast vacuum of space.

In all truth, necessity compounded by a minimal time allowed for construction had been the predominant factors in the vessel's clumsy appearance. Nevertheless, it had admirably performed its role of providing life support to the human population who had colonised Coleshia.

The Alliance Space Vessel Utopia no longer bore the marks of a civilian transporter. Instead, on the cylindrical outer shell was a blue sphere. Imposed behind the sphere were two crossed blades, stretching on diagonal trajectories. These were the markings of an Alliance Military vessel. Its twin vessel, the Super Nova, on its course of orbit around the opposite side of the planet, bore similar markings.

Aboard the Utopia, Private Ronald Makin was on communication duty. He was whistling to himself, while sifting through classified e-mail transmissions. Communications duty was one of the dreariest jobs that any member of the military personnel could be assigned to do, especially in the peaceful circumstances that existed at this time.

Diplomatic relations between Coleshia and Penusia were bad, but it didn't mean that these e-mails were of any real importance, despite the fact that they contained classified codes. Most likely, many of these transmissions were simply confirmation of mundane procedures and orders, but here he was, checking, shuffling and delegating messages to various military staff. Military policy dictated that matters should be conducted in a secretive manner. The Coleshian officials were suspicious of Penusia's intentions, and no doubt the military personnel of that planet would reciprocate the sentiments.

Delete... What a pile of crap, man!

Private Makin's whistling failed to alleviate his boredom, and as he got on with the task of re-routing irrelevant e-mails, his mind wandered to the neighbouring planet – Penusia. He wondered if his opposite number aboard the Elysium had the similar problems with boredom, and military bureaucracy for that matter!

As he continued to scroll down the endless list, one particular item caught his attention. It was highlighted in bright red, and Private Makin recognised it for what it was – a top priority transmission! Wait a minute; this was addressed for General Miller's attention only. Even if he wanted to view this message he didn't have the password to access it so, disappointed that he couldn't add some excitement to his day by reading it himself, he performed the mundane process of re-routing the message to General Miller's hard drive. In response to this command, complex sequences of circuit boards and switches sent the confidential message into the heart of the vessel. The encrypted message passed through the largely vacant civilian centres, occupied by a handful of military personnel, who were busy constructing machinery in a shower of sparks and industrial noise.

Now that the vessel had offloaded its civilian cargo, it had been converted into a construction centre. Many of the components for vehicles and colony structures were assembled here. Military personnel carried out this vast range of tasks, because they had little else to do. There was no imminent threat of a confrontation of any kind, so the armed forces had to be put to some productive use.

For years, the Alliance military services had been providing the constructive backbone of the colonisation of Coleshia. For all the years that the Utopia remained in use, the Super Nova had been dormant, unused for decades, and the latest information on its future use was to suggest that the huge vessel be turned into a source of scrap, plundered for its raw materials.

General Miller was sitting, isolated in his office. His chair creaked, as he leaned forward to read the confidential e-mail that had been sent to his terminal. After entering the password to access the flashing message, he remained emotionless, absorbed by the text on the screen.

He was a tall, muscular man, wearing the standard camouflage uniform of military personnel. This in itself was a great irony, as the greens and browns that adorned the uniform did not correspond to any existing territory where they could be put to any effective use. His blonde hair was precisely shaven into a crew cut, which suited his chiselled, square-jawed physique.

Momentarily, he paused…

Well, it was simply a matter of time before something like this happened: the Ark Project has been running too smoothly for too long.

He had been trained to deal with scenarios like this. Now it was time to put that training to use! He activated the intercom on his desk.

"Lieutenant Hoffman, prepare the Infiltrator. I'm going down to the Coleshian settlement."

"Affirmative, General," came the reply.

An hour and a half later, the Alliance Military Shuttle departed from its gigantic sanctuary and assumed a course directly in line with the Coleshian settlement. The sleek craft manoeuvred with ease through the intense temperatures of the atmosphere, and it did not slow its progress until it had plunged into the depths of the ocean, all the while faithfully maintaining its trajectory.

Upon docking with the main settlement, the small, streamlined shuttle had drawn a lot of attention from the maintenance teams within docking bay 72. It was a marvel to behold, a craft capable of shuttle missions in the vacuum of space, as well as maintaining full operational capabilities within the ocean. Only a few of these machines had been assembled, and General Miller was one of those fortunate enough to have one at his disposal.

As he departed from the craft, he noticed the looks of astonishment that the assorted technicians and engineers gave him. He analysed the complex maps, illuminated on the wall, ignoring the fact that he stood out like a sore thumb amongst the crowds of people, wearing his camouflage uniform and beret.

Upon locating the High Council Administration Zone, he wasted no time in hailing the nearest taxi.

Governor Tasken was a man who showed the physical strains of leading a huge operation on the scale of colonising a planet. At the age of sixty, he looked at least ten years older. His hair was white, receding very badly, and very thin. His face was a multicontoured pattern of wrinkles that pronounced the responsibility of his position, and his eyes looked tired and strained.

Adorning the purple robe of the governorship, he paced up and down the room, arms folded behind his back, staring at the padded red carpet that sprouted around his bulbous stomach.

"Allow me to elaborate on the e-mail that I sent to you," he said, addressing the general who sat, legs crossed, in the chair, with an emotionless expression on his face.

"Six days ago, Aquatic Patrol Team Five made a disturbing discovery. They returned to the settlement with the decapitated body of an…"

He paused to examine his report briefly, flicking through the pages of his digital display. Finding the information that he required he continued:

"…an Alopius Vulpinus from the breed Alopidae, known commonly as a Thresher shark. Our scientists examined the body, and couldn't find the cause for this bizarre death. I requested that Senator Phillipoussis engage the assistance of the Elasmobranch team in diagnosing a cause of death. It was, after all, an animal that they had established into the ecosystem. They too, were baffled, and upon their recommendation, I had the surveillance beyond the settlement limits increased by an additional patrol per day. Two days later, Aquatic Patrol Team Three stumbled upon a probable cause for the shark's death…"

General Miller remained stonefaced.

"Go on, Governor," he requested.

Was it a trick of his eyes, he couldn't be sure, but he thought that the governor was shaking.

"They discovered a new form of, well, an organism of some kind that appears to have grown from the seabed. According to the report, growing several hundred feet! It had dozens of illuminescent pink pods growing from a purple stem. Upon closer examination, one of the crew of Patrol Team Three was violently killed by the occupant of one of the pods. According to reports, some creature burst from within the pod and sliced him in two."

"Wait a minute, Governor. This organism plays host to living creatures?" asked the general, calmly, a frown of confusion ruffling his brow.

"That's correct, General Miller. The remaining crew members tried to escape. The creature, *of unknown origin*, attacked the submersible killing the pilot as well."

Without trying to react too surprised, the general realised the suggestion that the governor was making. This was an alien creature! For the first time, the human race had discovered life on a different planet!

"What happened to the remaining crew?" asked the general.

"*He* survived, and managed to swim back to the settlement. We cannot verify everything that he has told us, but he is highly traumatised. It was pure luck that a patrol team spotted him as his reserve air supply was exhausted and his suit had almost failed!"

"What happened to the submersible?"

"I'm coming to that, General," snapped the governor, his mottled brow failing to hide the obvious concern that had erupted into his blunt response.

General Miller had noticed that throughout their conversation Tasken continuously fiddled with his hands; a man uncomfortable with the demands of the situation that confronted him.

"May I speak to him?"

"I'm afraid not, General. Patrol Officer Veggard Daniels is a mess. Currently, we have him sedated in the Medical Zone. He's being treated for acute nitrogen narcosis, but the psychoanalysts who examined him doubt that he will be able to function within society again."

"If he is suffering from acute nitrogen narcosis, then couldn't all of this be a hallucination, a fabrication of events in his mind?"

"Unlikely, Aquatic Patrol Officer Daniels has been an active member of the Aquatic Patrol Teams for two years, with no history of illness induced by diving. To the extent that his suit was damaged, it would be almost impossible for the diver to inflict the pressures involved in such damage upon himself."

"Then it must be assumed that his story is to be believed," surmised the general.

For a moment Governor Tasken regarded General Miller, with a hint of fear in his eyes.

"There is just one other detail to corroborate his account. Yesterday, Aquatic Patrol Team Nine discovered the mangled remains of Team Three's submersible, and their report claimed that the vehicle had been torn to shreds, authenticating Officer Daniels' account of events."

"Was there any sign of the creature?"

"No, but I can tell you this, General. I have viewed the images from Team Nine's patrol video, and there is no way that the damage sustained on that sub could have been created by any human means, or by any of the wildlife released by us into Coleshia's oceans! Before we proceed, I shall give you a copy of this disc to view for yourself, I have no desire to see it again."

There was a brief pause. It was enough time for the general to silently acknowledge that the governor was extremely concerned about these events. From what he had heard it was becoming easy to see why.

"So, what's the next step, Governor?"

"The Coleshian High Council has requested that you, as the supreme Coleshian Military Officer, form a team of troops. I want you to return to the location of the organism, and bring back one of the creatures, complete within its pod. We need to know what we are dealing with here, and whether this is an isolated discovery. Lord help us if these creatures are spread over the whole planet."

"It shall be done, Governor."

The Governor felt reassured by the general's calmness, which contrasted starkly to his own neurotic persona. Here was a man who remained professional regardless of the circumstances. He would do what was best for the Coleshian people, no matter how dangerous the situation. Either he was extremely good at hiding his feelings, or he must have been born with nerves of steel. Governor Tasken wished that he could share the general's courage.

"I hope so, General. We have two primary concerns here. Our first lies with the damage that may be sustained amongst Coleshia's adopted ecosystem. If these creatures continue to show a complete disregard for life, many species could die. This ecosystem is not strong enough to cope with such changes! Our second consideration is of even greater concern. Officer Daniels described *dozens* of pods. Judging by the damage on the submersible caused by *one* of those creatures, there is no telling what havoc more of these beasts could wreak, if they find a way into the settlement limits…!"

Chapter 17

Planet Penusia

Project Date: Day 23 of Year 0405

Two, large feline eyes stared at the occupants of the jeep, judging with finely honed instincts the level of the potential threat. After some minutes the lioness became satisfied that a safe enough distance lay between the metal monster and her offspring, and soon the small, wriggling ball of fur that lay at her feet distracted the stare of her sparkling yellow orbs. She settled back down in the long, genetically engineered grass, while her young cub grunted and moaned in a persistent attempt to get her attention.

From the stationary jeep, two figures occupied the front seats of the cockpit, locked in calm and calculated discussion. Out here in the middle of the reserve there was little to disturb or overhear them.

Some kilometres away stood the fence of this preserve, which put a division between the precious animals of the Ark Project, and the surviving pocket of humanity who had accompanied them to this terraformed desert.

The earnest conversation ceased momentarily. The figure in the passenger seat ran his fingers over the metal handle and trigger, locked in thought. As his mind regressed further, his hand slid down the length of the barrel, and the cross hairs that sat neatly atop the weapon.

Sergeant Nakata looked warily in the direction of his weapon-bearing passenger.

"Sir, may I enquire the purpose of the presence of a HP-7 blast rifle? That is rather a heavy precaution for this meeting. We have rendez-voused in this quadrant before and have never been threatened by anything warranting the use of such a weapon."

For a moment, the contemplative figure sitting next to him said nothing, and then, while maintaining the focus of his gaze he replied:

"What's the matter, Sergeant, is it making you nervous? If so, then you are the first soldier that I have met who has been reluctant to be in the close proximity of a gun."

"I'm sorry, Sir, I thought that something might be amiss…"

"Something *is* amiss, Sergeant!"

Sergeant Nakata frowned in concern, and cast wary glances around the large open plain. He squinted through the dazzling sunlight that made the distant horizon shimmer, trying to see any possible cause for concern.

"Relax, Sergeant. Look behind you. What do you see?"

The officer obligingly strained his head from the driver's seat, the padded springs beneath him creaking in compliance, as he cast his eyes around the counterfeit landscape behind him. In the distance was a large group of trees, genetically grown, as was much of the forestation on this planet. This was the direction from which they had driven. Beyond those trees stood the reserve fence, and beyond the fence, the proud, tall structures of the Penusian settlement. They were an array of buildings, some tall, some dome-shaped while others could barely be seen above the trees.

Sergeant Nakata recalled the sight that had greeted their entrance to the huge enclosure. The gazelles had congregated there, staring at the jeep enviously as it passed through the gate that they could not traverse.

It was a fact that could not be escaped. The 'welcoming committee' as they had been named, were a strong reminder of the contradictions of the regime under which the Penusians existed. Several pairs of large dark eyes had stared hungrily at the expanses of land beyond the enclosure - at freedom!

All these miles of open land for the animals to roam, and it still amounts to no more than a grandiose prison!

As if reading the sergeant's thoughts, the figure seated next to him suggested that he look in the opposite direction. The sight that greeted Sergeant Nakata was the golden figure of the lioness, licking and grooming the reluctant, hyperactive form of her cub. Nakata frowned again, unable to grasp the logic.

"You see, Sergeant, we have two choices. Humanity is on one side and the animals on the other. This is the crossroads at which we find ourselves!"

Suddenly the penny dropped; Sergeant Nakata's thoughts had arrived on the same mental plane as those of his superior officer. The officer grinned at his subordinate. The sergeant was a loyal soldier, and a smart one who would develop well under his leadership.

The 'Freedom' movement that had occurred several decades earlier, on humanity's journey to the Quaker solar system had been 'amateurish'. It had not had the benefit of military precision and organisation behind it. This time it would be different, and every member of the Ark Project would be forced to sit up and acknowledge the intentions of their movement and the sincerity of their motives. He had given his life to the Ark Project, and, as a result, bore both the mental and physical scars. Whenever he looked in the mirror, he was reminded of that fact, and the lioness before him reminded him of how those scars had been obtained.

When he was a young officer, he too had believed in the vision of the Ark Project. A standard animal release procedure into this very quadrant that had gone disastrously wrong, leaving him in intensive care struggling for his life, had sewn the seeds of doubt in his mind. He felt reassured by the presence of the blast rifle, and without realising; he reasserted his grip on the weapon, his knuckles turning white. This suffering – what was the purpose of it? For the purpose of building a suitable home for the animals, so that they could coexist with humanity.

For him, as for a growing number of Penusians, of whom Sergeant

Nakata was one, the reality was different. The two did not coexist. Humanity still stood on one side of the bars and the animals on the other. What was worse was that the 'welcoming committee' knew it too, staring pathetically through the bars every day.

How many more human lives could have been saved if the animals had not been given a priority?

Even their Coleshian neighbours lived by these constraints, but whereas water prevented the use of bars, the animals were implanted with Brainchips – using technology as a barrier, rather than steel. Unfortunately they were too naïve to realise the truth. Everything on their planet was manufactured, right down to the air they breathed. They lived in closed little boxes, their horizons the doors at the end of corridors.

On Penusia the horizons were blistering sunsets that lit up the galaxy around them, and made their prison-like existence all too apparent. Recreation advertised as cinemas, museums and discotheques were nothing more than patronising rewards for an unrewarding existence. This was not about anything as basic as materialism. People had functioned within society for years without currency, and performed their duties. Everything was exchanged with no demands in return, but it was not enough anymore.

When questions had arisen before, the answers had arrived in the form of a violent quelling. Now the Ark Project hierarchy would not be able to ignore those questions anymore!

Chapter 18

General Miller paced slowly up and down the mission-briefing hall, his heavy footsteps resounding around the large room. His fierce blue eyes scrutinised the assembled party of Alliance Space Troops seated before the raised platform on which he stood. The look that he cast around the room was of a challenging nature, deliberately so in an attempt to evoke a response from the small army.

For a brief moment he allowed the soldiers to digest what he had just told them. There were looks of amazement, fear and even smiles, in response to the mission brief that they had just been given. They hadn't seen active duty for some years. For many, it was their first operation of major importance. The mixture of apprehension and exhilaration amongst the small army was evident, despite the lack of vocal response.

"Does anyone have any questions?"

For a moment, silence, then one of the soldiers seated three rows from the front stood up in an awkward, hesitant fashion. He was a young, thin, dark-skinned man, who fidgeted with his dog tags nervously. In a slightly nervous voice he enquired:

"How much do we know about these… creatures?"

Before returning to a seated position, he swallowed nervously.

It was hardly the fierce, resolute courageous response that the general had desired. Somehow, the general could not find it in his heart to chastise this man for showing fear on the back of this particular briefing.

"Very little, other than the fact that this form of life was not traceable when the planet was initially explored for resident life forms. The patrol officer who survived the incident was psychologically damaged. We are unsure of the clarity of his account, but we have managed to get a detailed description of the characteristics of the creatures' physiology. This species would appear to reach lengths of up to three metres. It resembles an aquatic mollusc in many respects, but with an armoured hide, serrated with bony spikes. It also has a horizontal tail at one end, complemented by large pectoral fins; and yellow eyes with a large aquiline beak, lined with sharp teeth.

The creature also has the 'cute' characteristic of changing colour to suit its mood, somewhat like the cuttlefish.

From these characteristics, we can only assume that the animal relies heavily on visual acuity, perhaps using colour as a mode of communication. The teeth would strongly suggest that the creature is carnivorous in diet.

Judging by what this species did to the Thresher shark and the Patrol submersible, we must also assume that the beast is highly territorial, and that it is only a matter of time before Coleshia's ecosystem is damaged beyond repair, with eventual devastating consequences to the settlement. Unlike much of Coleshia's wildlife, human technology does not seem to deter these creatures."

Once again, General Miller paused. During this explanation, his facial expression remained unchanged, his voice unwavering and clear. He recognised the need for strong leadership; to show his own fear would have been disastrous for morale.

In the broad scale of things, it made no difference. No one alive, including the general himself, had ever been involved in an encounter with an alien life form before. There was only so much preparation that could be done, and everyone present in that room was smart enough to know it.

During the short space of another pause, he thought of some assuring words to finish the mission briefing.

"This is a new encounter for all of us, but you have been trained to deal with situations such as these. At this stage we are not engaged in war. Our mission is specific. Capture one of these beasts, so that we can determine its physical and mental characteristics – if we can avoid conflict, then we will. Knowledge is the key to all power. If we can obtain that knowledge we will have the advantage in this situation. We must succeed for the sake of the Ark Project, for the sake of The Eden Treaty and the aquatic and human inhabitants of Coleshia… That is all… Dismissed!"

Five 'Beluga' submersible craft cruised through the ocean, bathed in an aura of light, created by the navigation beams of the craft and the searchlights of the armed troops that knelt atop the sleek vehicles' exterior. The beams cut deeply through the murky depths like long, neat tears in the darkest coloured fabric, giving some comfort to the troops in their claustrophobic surroundings.

General Miller gripped his blast rifle firmly, his keen eyes scanning the seascape for signs of movement. They had an ample number of troops for this mission, but the general could not help doubting that their safety lay in numbers. A voice resounded in his ears, breaking the silence.

"General, we have the location on sonar."

"Affirmative, Lieutenant. Okay, people; remember your briefing, keep your wits sharp and the mission smooth."

As the assembled teams approached the sight of the bizarre host organism, the general barked out another order.

"Maintain a level two hundred feet above the seabed. We want clear visibility in case of contact."

Through the gloom, the searchlights of the vehicles picked out the strange growth, the spherical luminescent pink pods swaying in the current, like large dewdrops, hanging on the leaves of a tree. The host organism looked totally alien in this environment, a tumourous growth infecting the healthy flesh of the landscape.

The throng of troops drew closer, and upon another of the general's orders, one of the submersibles broke the formation and descended to the ocean floor to inspect the base of the organism. It was a matter of minutes before the team that had departed made a startling discovery.

"Sir, the organism appears to be growing from a concave basin, about twenty metres wide. Sir, it's a meteorite crash site!"

Some twenty yards away from the growth, General Miller gave the order to hold their position, and he received this information with a clinical rationale, before issuing his commands.

"Team One, move in and rendezvous. Take one of the smaller pods... Team two, return to our depth and maintain patrol of the immediate area with Teams Three, Four and Five."

In response to his orders, one of the submersible craft cruised to a position parallel to one of the nearest pods. Through coincidence, this happened to be one of the smallest. The divers atop its metal shell readied themselves with cutting gear and circular saws.

The general looked down the full length of the organism. A number of the pods had now exploded, giving birth to their vile contents within. He could see at least twelve empty shells suspended in the water on purple stalks, connected to the large purple stem.

"Keep your eyes open, more of these things have hatched!"

Some four minutes laboriously passed. The sound of the furiously whirring blades of the cutting saws was occasionally interspersed with the sound of the prop engines of the submersibles jerking into life spasmodically, as the pilot of each vehicle struggled to hold their craft in a constant position against the strong current of the ocean. In the density of the water, these sounds reached the hearing sensors of the troops four times quicker than they would have done in the air. The process was interrupted by a cry of alarm from a member of Team One.

"*What is it, Private?*" barked the general, the concern hidden deep within his voice.

"Sir... There is pink fluid coming out of the stems when we make the cuts. Oh Jesus, man. It's disgusting."

As the general began to see the pink fluid permeate the water surrounding Team One, it confirmed his suspicions. The host organism was the life support for each creature, as well as the place where each creature gestated and grew before their birth.

Briefly, the soldiers cast concerned looks at one another, hands clenching tightly around their blast rifles, jittery index fingers tensing around the trigger mechanisms.

Sensing the unease within the group, the general intervened.

"Calm down, troops… Maintain your position and proceed as planned…"

Some thirty minutes later, the assembled teams of troops withdrew from the strange alien creation, much to the relief of the members of Team One, who now had the dismembered pod, complete with its contents, wrapped in a titanium laced net, trailing some yards behind them.

The remaining four submersibles formed a square perimeter around Team One and their precious cargo, with a member of each remaining team pointing their weapons at the pod, while the remaining troops formed an outwards facing perimeter, weapons ready.

General Miller noticed that nothing stirred in this part of the sea. It was as if a gigantic hand had swooped down and scooped every form of sentient life from the ocean. He found it very disturbing.

"General, our sonar has detected an object approaching swiftly from the east. God… It's closing fast!"

Before anyone could react, a multicoloured blur rushed past the assembled submersibles, scattering the outer perimeter of troops.

"What the…?"

Alerted by cries of alarm over his headset, General Miller barked his orders.

"*Use your diving suits, and fall back into formation. We must hold the perimeter… Now!*"

But it was too late. The creature returned from above, a red and green emissary of death, its razor-sharp beak extended wide, dagger like teeth waiting to inflict lethal damage.

General Miller could clearly see what made this creature a likely cause for the death of the Thresher shark. The beak looked extremely powerful and sharp, capable of destroying any organic life that was unfortunate enough to get in its way. Without any fear, the creature crashed into the perimeter craft of Team Four in a violent blur, a writhing mass of armoured flesh and spikes that tore the floundering divers to pieces, scattering their battered bodies like pins on a bowling alley. The impact sent violent waves of shock and sound throughout the water, as the submersible veered out of control, fortunately enough for the rest of the group, away from the perimeter.

Repulsed at such a tempestuous onslaught, the response was swift.

"*Open fire!*" roared the general.

Blast rifle shots resounded and lit up the perimeter of troops. Explosive shells thudded into the creature's body, as it attempted to reel away from the onslaught. Some of the shells impacted with the tough hide of the beast, creating small craters in its armour. Many of the shots, however, thudded into its soft belly, exploding within the fleshy interior. The creature's bodily fluids began leaking in repulsive pink clouds, and in the haze that was being created, its skin began to change colour, adopting reds, blues and yellows, creating a strobe effect as it convulsed in agony. As the stomach was punctured, the general noticed air bubbles rising to the surface.

Eventually, the squirming beast became inert, its skin adopting a pasty grey texture, like that of a stone statue. Even in death its yellow eyes seemed to see everything and react to nothing, emotion an alien presence in its visual senses.

The general was reminded of an ancient legend from humankind's home planet, about a beast that could turn any living being to stone, if they dared to look into her eyes. The blast rifles had cast their stare and had taken this creature's life. He watched as the inert, lifeless form began to spiral into the darkest depths.

"General, we have lost Team Four. Attempts to hail them are negative, Sir."

"Nothing would have survived that impact," replied the general. "Hold the formation. Team Three; move more centrally, we can do nothing for our comrades now. Return to the settlement as planned."

The cloud of alien blood became intermingled with that of human beings, and it now made visual observation of the surrounding ocean very difficult.

A whole sub team wiped out by one creature!

The general was certain, by this point, that this alien species represented a larger threat than was originally anticipated. Governor Taskens's caution had been well placed. There was no ambiguity in the situation now… The threat was clear…

These creatures represent a true nemesis to the Ark Project. I must ensure that they are not allowed to interfere with my directives…

Chapter 19

The creature of unknown origin lay, belly down on the autopsy table, its head drooping towards the floor. On another table rested the transparent pod that had been cut open by very precise hands. Neat incisions had split the sphere almost in two, and its interior lay exposed and bare.

With the benefit of strong artificial lights, Science Officer Matsuo and General Miller, both wearing sealed bacterial contamination suits, realised that the glowing nature of the pods in the water was caused by the contents inside. Sticking out awkwardly from one half of the shell was the severed stem that the Alliance Space Troops had neatly cut away from the host organism. The stem, upon examination, was made up of a complex series of tubes that led to the pod's interior.

Officer Matsuo fumbled around inside the pod, and rose from the smelly interior displaying a fleshy pink umbilical cord, entwined around itself, which had now been severed from the inert creature on the opposing autopsy table.

"Most interesting," she said to the general, who like her was engrossed in the autopsy; too much so to grant her an acknowledgement.

Two armed guards stood by the door, also dressed in contamination suits, clutching their blast rifles across their chests. No chances had been taken during this procedure, despite the fact that the alien creature had already been pronounced dead.

Officer Matsuo turned her attention away from the empty pod, and shuffled awkwardly in her white body suit to the table supporting the limp weight of the creepy body. General Miller followed her. She began fumbling around the creature's inert form. She opened its lifeless beak, checking inside its mouth, taking great care not to tear her suit on the sharp teeth. She let the beak drop. It slammed shut, the creature's tongue hanging pathetically to one side in an almost comical fashion. Feeling around the skull, she inserted two fingers into what appeared to be nostrils on the bony forehead.

With each part of the painstaking analysis of the dead beast's grey body, Science Officer Matsuo put fresh information into her electronic keypad. Briefly turning her attention to the complex machinery suspended above the autopsy table she activated the laser, allowing the ray gun time to warm up. While she was waiting for this to happen, with a piece of chalk, she drew considered incision lines in the armoured shell, contemplating how she was going to negotiate the landscape of sharp, white bony spikes on the creature's back, some of which were nearly a foot tall.

Governor Tasken finished reading the document. Saving the confidential report in his terminal hard drive, he also took the care to place a confidential password on the controversial information.

He was seated behind his desk, his purple robe cascading down the arms of his chair. Standing beside him was Senator Phillipoussis, wearing the brown robe of his position as Tasken's right-hand man. This was the position where he had loyally stayed for many years. It was his loyalty that had enabled him to view the document over the governor's shoulder; and now he was among only a handful of people allotted with the details of this delicate matter. The remainder of that small pocket of individuals were Governor Tasken, and the sincere figure sitting opposite them, who had produced the report.

"Well, General Miller," said Governor Tasken, cynicism clearly audible in his voice, "it would appear that the Ark Project has adopted Phase Five."

In many respects the Coleshian leader seemed to be a much more confident character in the presence of his subordinate – Phillipoussis.

He was far more relaxed than he had been during their previous meeting. Perhaps the shocking circumstances surrounding the Coleshian administration at this time had finally digested in the neurotic governor's stomach.

For a moment the general allowed confusion to alter his stern features. To his knowledge, Phase Five had never existed.

"Which is, Governor?"

"The establishment of confirmed contact with a race of alien beings."

"Yes, Governor."

"Our worst fears have been established – first contact has proven to be *hostile*."

Over the years, the governor had listened to many theories about the possibility of discovering resident life in the Quaker solar system. With a somewhat twisted sense of humour, he found it ironic that this discovery had manifested itself as such a threat right under their noses.

Of all the planets in the galaxy, it had to be theirs!

"If you'll forgive me for asking, Governor, but how are we going to break this news to the Coleshian public?" enquired Senator Phillipoussis, somewhat hesitantly.

"For the moment we will say nothing… God, the Penusians will love this!" claimed the leader before rolling his eyes, then he laboriously rubbed his hands over the wrinkled landscape that was his face.

Such was the bitter feeling between the two planets that an incident such as this would only induce a shrug of the shoulders from their Penusian neighbours… The hatred born in the aftermath of the Freedom Movement burnt fiercely in many Penusian hearts. They still felt an injustice for being branded terrorists – no help would be extended from them.

"The Coleshian public know all that they need to know for now. We will mention that Aquatic Patrol Team Three, during a routine patrol, lost electrical power on the submersible, and while steering blind, crashed into a collection of rocks."

"What about the increased military presence?" asked Phillipoussis, casting a glance in the direction of General Miller.

"With the Aquatic Patrols being put on hold for an indefinite period, and regular patrols being made by Alliance Space Troops, people will become suspicious. Tongues are already wagging."

As always, the governor paid close heed to the words of his trusted aide before answering.

"Let them wag, my friend. Release a statement, relating that the regular APT missions have ceased for the convenience of a military training operation."

General Miller listened intently to the words of the governor, becoming increasingly concerned by the course that this meeting was taking:

"Governor, is it wise to keep the Coleshian people in the dark? What if the creatures infiltrate the settlement *soon,* and the citizens find out the hard way. That might only serve to build resentment towards the High Council, not to mention the loss of life that will be inflicted if the people are not prepared!"

In an instant, the weariness had drained from the governor's face, to be momentarily replaced by a stern glare.

"I appreciate your sentiments, General, but the way I see it, we have no choice. The last thing that this settlement needs right now, is panic arising amongst its citizens. Can you imagine what news of this magnitude would do to an installation of this kind? We will release all the information *only* when we *have* a solution. Senator, release the statement as planned."

"Very well, Governor," said the senator, gliding almost silently out of the room, like a ghostly spirit.

Chapter 20

Project Date: Day 24 of Year 0405

The clock read twelve hours past midday, Coleshian time. The monorail began its final journey from the Aquatic Science Centre to the main city complex. On the planet's surface, the sun had gone down, and darkness had blanketed the sky. At the depths of the monorail link, this made no difference for it was dark all the time. The only light to be seen came from the large underwater structures on the seabed at either end of the monorail line.

Some two kilometres away, one of several Alliance Space Troop Patrols was cruising within the settlement limits, checking for signs of disturbance.

"Wait a minute, there's something moving on the sonar," stated one diver.

"Where?" replied the other diver cautiously, averting his gaze from the sea to his instrumentation.

"Oh, it's okay, it's just the monorail making its final trip."

"Jesus, Smith, don't scare me like that."

Satisfied that nothing was out of the ordinary, they continued their patrol, unaware of the fact that if they had been in their current location twenty minutes earlier, their sensors might have picked up a large form blending into its surroundings beautifully, the skin colour mimicking that of the surrounding rock formations that created the terrain of the seabed. The only way to see it would have been to watch the vertical muscle movements, forcing the tail up and down; propelling the beast through the settlement limits, mere feet above the ocean floor.

As it was, the patrol team were not there, and neither their own eyes nor the enhanced, but still limited vision created by their surveillance equipment, spotted the penetration of the camouflaged beast into their domain.

Nathan Bradley sat in the empty carriage, lost in his thoughts. His eyes were trying to pick out the landscape in the sea beyond the window, but all that he could see was the reflection of the carriage's lit interior. Suddenly a bright flash flew past the window. Bradley blinked, and rubbed his eyes. Peering through the window again, he saw nothing. It had been a long day and he was tired. He had heard the report that the Alliance Military Forces were training in the area. It was probably nothing.

As a Hygiene Porter in the Aquatic Science Centre, he was required to work long hours, cleaning up the waste left by the other staff, long after they had retired to their own private activities. At last it seemed as if the long shifts were beginning to pay off. Just days before, his quarterly assessment had been very good. Soon he would be allowed to move farther up the administration hierarchy. It would be a blessed relief to be free from cleaning up other people's rubbish.

He promised himself that he would attempt to unwind, with what was left of the night. Perhaps he could go for a few drinks in the Adult Leisure Zone. He particularly enjoyed the Clam Buster discotheque. At the moment this represented his best opportunity to find a partner to begin a family. Or maybe he would relax in the Human Culture Zone and take in an ancient motion picture from the human race's distant past at the Historical Cinema. He looked forward to having the choice. Sometimes, in these oppressive, claustrophobic surroundings, escapism was of the utmost importance to the human psyche.

His thoughts were violently interrupted as the monorail began shaking. The tremors became increasingly brutal, shaking the carriage until he was thrown to the floor. The vehicle came to a halt, and almost as abruptly as it had begun, the shaking ceased.

Lying on the floor in terror, Nathan noticed the distinct absence of a particular sound, the comforting low hum of the vehicle's engine. What had happened; had the monorail been derailed? As he struggled to regain his footing, he could see seawater pouring into the next carriage, the water level rising up past the windows in the pressure door separating the carriage he occupied and the leaking carriage.

Panicking, he ran down to the far end of the empty carriage, and sat in the corner, near the opposite pressure door. He prayed that his carriage would not leak; he prayed that someone would come and rescue him. Breathing erratically, fear gripped him in a tight embrace.

Nathan Bradley did not get the opportunity to unwind that evening. A moment later, the window next to him exploded from the outside in. In the split second that this happened, he didn't have time to react.

The large open jaws of a huge beak headed incisively towards his head. He had just enough time to make out a fleshy pink tongue, surrounded by rows of razor-sharp teeth...

Chapter 21

Project Date: Day 25 of Year 0405

It burst from the calm, surface waters. Thrusting rocket boosters hurtled the projectile into the atmosphere in a matter of minutes. As it left the gravitational pull of Coleshia, the rocket boosters died down, and the long, sleek projectile allowed its forward momentum to propel it to a pre-programmed destination.

It cruised past the Utopia. The vessel's surveillance crews were oblivious to its presence, despite the complex radar sensors that protruded from the monstrous spaceship's bulk. Boldly, the ultimate result in stealth design continued on an unwavering trajectory, until it activated reverse stabilizing thrusters that brought the shining, sleek shape to a halt within the endless realm of space.

For some minutes it remained motionless, and then cracks began to appear over its silver shell, disturbing the shining, polished cylindrical surface. As the minutes passed, the metal casing began to fall apart, jagged fragments jettisoning away from the contents inside. Some minutes passed again, before a small, black cube was left, barely a foot in diameter.

Through the assistance of automated timer switches, the cube began a transformation, morphing from one shape to another. From seemingly impossible arrears of its form, large arms emerged, eight in all; making the limbed cube resemble some bizarre mechanical arachnid. Then, metal plates, seemingly from nowhere, began to form between the arms, eventually creating the concave shape of a dish.

Through an identical process, a dish appeared on the opposite side of the cube. The cube then split down the middle, so that one dish was pointing at Coleshia, and the other at its neighbouring planet.

The dish began acting as a relay between two points of contact. One on either planet...

Radar Jammer Activated. Transmission 3452...
UPLINK ESTABLISHED.
PASSWORD ENGAGED.
GALACTIC E-MAIL RECEIVED.
UPLINK COMPLETED...

LEGION@1:
Good day, my friend. I must inform you of the latest development. The Coleshian leadership are becoming concerned about an issue of growing concern. The authorities have discovered an alien life form that is posing a considerable threat to the settlement and the ecosystem.

LEGION@2:
I see. Could this potential threat be in danger of contravening our plans?

LEGION@1:
On the contrary! One of the creatures attacked the monorail link that runs between the Aquatic Science Centre and the main city complex, killing three civilians yesterday.
Coleshian citizens were unaware of this organism's existence up until this point. The authorities wanted to keep it a secret to avoid panic, masquerading under the guise of a military training operation. The attack on the monorail has swung events in our favour. The High Council will have to be honest with the public now, in order to avoid a backlash of public opinion, and perhaps worse.
To add to their problems, the High Council's worst fears have been realised. The species knows the location of the settlement, thus turn-

ing the screws on the leadership to act swiftly.

LEGION@2:
This is extremely promising news. We have been waiting for the time when it would be suitable to strike. At last a crack has appeared in the Coleshian administration.
Wavering belief amongst the Coleshian public might be just what we need to topple the powers that be.
The time is drawing closer…

LEGION@1:
I would suggest that we commence with our plans as soon as possible. The opportunity to act has never been more available than the present time. The people of Coleshia will turn to any leader who offers them freedom from this madness. Are the foundations in place for Phase One?

LEGION@2:
It is in hand. Very soon, Penusia will be forced to realise that our ultimate survival lies in only one course of action.

LEGION@1:
Excellent. I have to express my fears as to the security of the jamming filters on this line. It is risky to maintain this conversation. I trust that I will be made aware upon completion of Phase One?

LEGION@2:
I can assure you that *all* Coleshia will be made aware upon completion of Phase One. I shall contact you in due course…

LEGION@1:
Acknowledged… Farewell, and good luck.

TRANSMISSION ENDED
UPLINK SEVERED…

Chapter 22

PART 4: A NEW FOE.

Darkness. Everywhere! It was an abundance of nothing!

Nothing, in contradiction with itself, had a texture. It was not like that of air, but thicker. It had a similar density to that of...

He couldn't quite gauge it... That was it. Water! He began swimming, arms and legs powering through the aqueous fluid, but everywhere he turned revealed more emptiness. Several seconds passed before blind logic struck him hard. Suddenly, he began to panic. If this was water, how the hell was he breathing?

For a moment he began thrashing about wildly, and then it dawned on him that he was still alive and not suffocating. He was breathing the liquid like a child in the womb. He hung, bobbing around weightless, suspended amongst the great expanse that was nothing.

As his eyes became more accustomed to nothing, he could make out a blue tinge to the never-ending blackness. It was almost as if he was thousands of feet down in Coleshia's oceans, but without the body-crushing pressure, and with the curious ability to breathe sea water. Despite this, his taste buds could not detect any salt.

Suddenly, he saw movement in the distance. A large object, drawing closer, appeared just within the range of his eyesight. It maintained a straight course, and its size and shape became apparent, as it headed on a trajectory below him. It was a huge, cylindrical object, rounded at one end, and forming a blunt point at the other, where a gigantic prop motor sat. Two, large, rectangular horizontally positioned fins that protruded from the sides of its body helped the ancient machine to balance. Ominously, it reminded him of the pectoral fins of a fish.

Suddenly, before his eyes, the monstrous machine began to mutate. The rounded nose became a sinister and sharp point, like that of a missile head. The huge rectangular fins became triangular, and angled down beneath the submersible's sides. Ripples of movement began to pulse down the vehicle's body, like the horizontal body movements of a large fish, as the fuselage seemed to change into flesh. The machine began moving like a living organism with independent thought, not a man-made, clumsy machine.

He turned in panic, swimming furiously to try and escape the huge monster that now had the sinister shape of a huge shark. Daring to look around he saw the mechanical beast heading in his direction, the horizontal thrashing of the tail propelling it closer to him. A crescent moon-shaped mouth appeared, exhibiting rows of metallic teeth. Its progress was relentless.

As the futility of the situation became clear, he ceased thrashing about. He opened his mouth to scream, but no sound was forthcoming. He was stranded, helpless, as the mechanical monster closed in on him, jaws wide open, waiting to tear through his flesh…

He awoke, sweat beaded across his forehead and huge droplets adorning his shaking frame, allowing the bed sheets to form a tight mould around his body.

Glen Davis sat up, and in the semi-darkness of his bedroom, struggled to decipher this nightmare. The previous morning, he had found out the cause of death of the Thresher shark, during an emergency High Council meeting. It was worse than he had suspected.

It was *Coleshian evolution*, not convergent evolution that had been responsible for the shark's death, a creature born out of the control of the detailed inventories of the Ark Project. As he had also suspected, Aquatic Patrol Team Three had not been the victims of electrical failure on their submersible, as the public announcement had stated. As an Aquatic Science Officer, deep down he had known that something out of the ordinary was responsible for their deaths.

Now, the attack on the monorail had put the Coleshian High Council in a difficult situation. The public would soon demand answers. The High Council were hoping that tomorrow's emergency meeting would provide those answers and prevent panic from taking over the settlement. It was good to see that in the face of possible human extinction, the Coleshian Administration were no longer taking the matter lightly.

Glen lay awake, pondering his latest nightmare. This was different from his other introspective dreams. Somehow, although painful to experience, he sensed that this particular dream was not about him… What was his mind telling him?

Chapter 23

Project Date: Day 27 of Year 0405

Glen rose early that morning, still troubled by his thoughts. He left the accommodation zone where his living quarters were located, and wandered down to the docking bay where a series of manually piloted passenger submersibles had been arranged to transport personnel to the main settlement in the absence of the monorail.

A steady queue of people had formed in anticipation of the same event, and it was almost an hour before Glen was allowed to enter the neatly upholstered interior of one of the submersibles. The luxuriously padded red walls and seats were kept spotlessly clean, in an attempt to disguise the fact that their current means of transport was by no means as efficient, or as comfortable as the monorail had been.

Red, perhaps not the most tasteful colour for such a purpose, in the light of recent events.

As the submersible laboriously left the docking bay, Glen stared out of the round window located next to his seat. He had never been afraid of the sea; why should he? After all, he had spent the best years of his life diving with the most efficient and feared predator ever to swim in the oceans.

Perhaps this is no longer the case…

Today, Coleshia's murky depths assumed a sinister perspective in his mind. The sight of the Alliance Military Patrol submersible, which now occupied his field of vision, did not aid this emotion. The crew's constant fidgeting was evident sign of their fear and lack of willingness to be in the ocean, despite the fact that the troops riding the vessel were armed with enough weaponry to destroy an Alliance Space Ship.

Following the attack on the monorail, these military escorts had become a mandatory requirement for traffic between the main settlement and the Aquatic Science Centre, and, as the submersible passed the wrecked carriages of the monorail, clinging futilely to the rail by only one of the traction motors like the empty husk of a cocoon, it was easy to see why.

The wreckage was beginning to attract a growing number of divers and technicians, hovering around the redundant machine like scavenging fish around a carcass. The sight of the twisted carriage created a series of shocked reactions from the passengers aboard the submersible.

Glen had to admit that he was surprised by the designated course of the sub:

A less scenic route might have been in order... Perhaps the pilot was satiating his own curiosity...

Staring out into the murk, Glen found his thoughts being drawn to the alien creature. He wondered what it would look like in its element. The captured specimen had assumed an abject, almost comical appearance out of the water. It reminded Glen of the appearance of a shark out of the water; a useless mass of flesh that became distorted under the force of gravity. Although rendered ineffective out of the water, in its own element the alien species had proven to be every bit as comfortable as a shark. Strong, and judging by the latest piece of destruction - lethal!

It sent a shiver down the spine of Glen Davis, the scientist who had clocked up more hours in the water with the most unpredictable of predators than any other living human being...

Glen entered the library and walked through the many aisles of storage disks that adorned the shelves. Selecting the item for which he was looking, he found a vacated terminal and inserted the mini-disk into the machine. The title flashed boldly on the screen in red letters:

Chapter 23

A DETAILED HISTORY OF AQUATIC WEAPONS AND MACHINES

It was his dream that led him to this building, to this text. Why had the ancient machine appeared in his dream the previous night, and what was the connection with the sharks? He felt that it was necessary to alleviate his curiosity before attending this afternoon's meeting with the Coleshian High Council. He started with a text that had been among his favourites as a child.

He had a feeling what the machine might have been. Submersible technology had not changed that greatly since it's invention. More powerful, sleeker design, but the fins and motors served the same function…

As he scrolled through the images of ancient submersibles, one image in particular caught his attention. The machine in question was, according to the information displayed neatly beside it, from the twentieth century – from mankind's distant home planet. It almost identically matched the one in his dream… *A nuclear submarine!* These monstrosities were, according to the information listed beside the picture, the most powerful weapons of war at one point in the history of humankind…

Suddenly, it hit him. How could he have been so slow in deciphering its meaning? It made sense to him now.

Glen could envisage how his counsellor would have responded in this situation:

"Mr Davis, the reason why this image has manifested itself in your mind in such a violent manner, is because your mind does not want to accept the conclusions that it is establishing…"

Unfortunately, his counsellor would have been correct…

It was still very early in the day. Glen took the return trip to the Aquatic Science Centre, in the hope that its inhabitants might help him to find some answers.

Glen spent some two hours in the Animal Release Zone, sitting on the jetty in the corner of the huge pool. He often found it to be quite therapeutic to mull over his thoughts by the water. In the distance, occasional disturbances would appear on the calm surface, as dark fins cut through the water like a knife through butter.

This time the therapy did not work. The same conclusion kept rising from the mire of confusion.

Suddenly, his concentration was distracted by the presence of another life form near the jetty. Cleopatra glided beneath the waves, past the jetty. Glen dipped his hand under the waves, stroking her back as she moved effortlessly past him. As always, she was remarkably relaxed. Then, for nearly two minutes, the water was still, until Poker Face stealthily rose from the depths, inquisitively darting around the jetty. Glen, with a supreme knowledge of this fish, wisely withdrew from the edge of the small platform. Unfortunately, Poker Face still had to be approached with the full protection of a PAD device, as always living up to his name.

Eventually, the excited fish tired of investigating this area of the huge pool, and disappeared into the depths with a terrific swish of his large tail. Glen sat on the jetty covered with water. He stood up, dripping, and on his portable keypad he typed in a statement:

VERY FUNNY.

He would have to change before he went to the High Council meeting, but he still had plenty of time for that. Besides, he didn't really want to be here when the rest of the team arrived later in the day. This morning was going to be difficult enough without explaining his decision to them, especially Rhona. He was dreading her reaction. He knew that she wouldn't like the idea, but as he saw it, in the light of the current situation he didn't have any choice. *He* didn't like the idea, but if the survival of all life on Coleshia was at stake, including humanity, no matter how much he disagreed with it personally, how could he ignore it?

This problem went beyond his feelings plus those of his team and he knew it. It was this concrete fact that forced him constantly down the same alley of decision.

Chapter 23

Glen returned his attention to his keypad.

KAUHULU?

For some thirty seconds there was silence. A fin sliced through the surface water, about one half of a kilometre away, and then disappeared. Glen was looking around eagerly, and then, as if he had literally just appeared there, he saw the huge, white under belly of Kauhulu. He could see the powerful jaws lined with triangulated white teeth, as the beast cruised past him on his side.

Humankind used to refer to Great White sharks as 'White Death'. Glen knew how this reputation had been acquired. He had read the reports of how recreational bathers known as 'surfers' were attacked, seemingly from nowhere, mistaken for food. He had also watched the sharks during feeding time. To keep their instincts finely honed, the four Great White sharks were fed live food. It was one of nature's cruel side effects that such beautiful fish could be so fearsome. During this once-weekly ritual, however, Glen had marvelled at the ease with which the sharks would take the seals, their preferred meal: quickly, effortlessly and relatively painlessly for their prey, unless the predators were spotted upon their stealthy approach.

A large black eye that had once signified the visual aid of an instinctive killer in the eyes of humankind, now took on a mysterious intelligence that peered deeply into Glen's soul, asking him many questions. He was reminded of how humanity's relationship with the Great White shark had improved during Phase Two; of how much the human race had learnt about these sharks. Kauhulu's tolerance of Glen at all times was proof of how much this ferocious species had learnt about the human race!

This was a friendship that Glen found easy to tolerate. The shark never made any demands of him. He… They…were pure, honest in their motivations, not conceited. Perhaps this was why Glen returned to this domain that held so many bad memories every day. Perhaps this was the reason why he worked so hard to give these animals a good start in their new home…

His respect for these creatures of the deep was paramount, and it steered his determined desire to succeed…

The light reflected off the surface of Kauhulu's back, creating strange patterns that danced around on his tough grey skin.

Then his thoughts were drawn to how technology had allowed sharks and humans to progress in their troubled relationship. Firstly, the PAD devices that assured a human's safety from attack, and the Bodywave Project. The Great Whites were the 'guinea pigs' and they were responding superbly well. Not only could the human race swim freely with these predators, but also now an intelligent relationship was being established between the species. Great White sharks and the human race were learning to move freely in the same environment. The positive consequences of this transcendence could only be imagined. And now… Unforeseen circumstances were going to twist the highest peak of Glen's life against both himself and the sharks.

The Elasmobranch Team had designed the Bodywave Project so that sharks and humans could interact together. Now the technology would be used to make the sharks work for humans. Glen stroked Kauhulu's back as he glided past. This was one of those situations that life had a nasty habit of throwing into his face. Whichever way he turned, he couldn't win… He had felt the same way when his counsellor had told him to leave the Aquatic Science Centre to deal with his father's death. There was always a price to pay for striving for happiness.

Glen stood up, totally convinced of the decision that he had to make, and, as a result, was thoroughly depressed. As he left the Animal Release Zone, one message was transmitted from his keypad to the delicate sensors of the Brainchips worn by each of the sharks:

FORGIVE ME…

Chapter 24

Eventually the afternoon arrived and Glen Davis found himself amongst the gathering of Science Officers in the cylindrically shaped High Council conference hall, in the heart of the Coleshian Administration Zone. Eight rows of seats were tiered around the hall, surrounding a huge presentation platform set on an invisible mechanism designed to rotate to address the seated delegates; one half of whom were Aquatic Science Officers. Glen was amongst this assembly, whose responsibilities like his were to release groups of species into Coleshia's oceans.

All the teams had completed Phase Four of their respective programmes and had now graduated to monitoring the progress of the animals, with the exception of the Elasmobranch Team who were scheduled to release the Great White sharks mere weeks after this meeting.

The other half of the room was filled with members of the High Council who among their numbers boasted the presence of Senator Phillipoussis wearing a brown robe. On the revolving platform stood Governor Tasken dressed in the customary purple garments of his position. Accompanying him was a big man, wearing the uniform of the Alliance Military Forces. He stood clearly in advance of six feet, complemented by a muscular frame and hands that could have been no smaller than shovels. His disciplined, emotionless features were complemented by a blonde crew cut. To Glen he epitomised the archetypal soldier, and the purple beret, sitting awkwardly atop his head signified to all that he was a senior member of military staff. It also allowed the people present to put a face to the heavy military presence around the settlement.

All around the room, there was a level of noise and chatter. People knew the purpose of this congregation! The lights around the edge of the room dimmed, shrouding the audience in darkness. The chatter ceased almost as quickly as the light disappeared. Correspondingly, a huge centrally-positioned dome in the ceiling of the conference hall dimmed until only the two figures on the speaking platform were illuminated.

For a moment there was silence, then Governor Tasken shuffled forwards to the microphone.

"People of Coleshia, you have been summoned here today for a grave and crucial reason. During our time on this planet, we have developed our environment to create a new home, not only for humankind, but for the aquatic forms of life taken from our ancient home planet centuries ago. We have nurtured and taken every step to ease the wildlife into their new home, as was set out in The Eden Treaty.

Since High Chancellor Conway's vision of man and nature leaving a shattered Earth to survive together amongst the stars was realised when we touched down here, we have survived in relative peace, as have our Penusian neighbours. We have endeared the concept that all life is sacred; lived and died to fulfil this ideal as the driving purpose of our existence, but now a weight hangs on *our* shoulders, threatening to destroy *our* way of life! A threat that could eclipse Coleshia's adopted ecosystem and threaten the safety of the settlement limits.

Today, I have with me, General Miller from the Alliance Military Forces. He will bring you all up to date with our situation, and the new enemy that thwarts the progress of life on Coleshia... General?"

General Miller silently walked up to the microphone. He inserted a small disc into the computer terminal, expertly moulded from the revolving base of the platform, before addressing the assembled committee...

Chapter 24

The huge alien creature cut through the air, with purpose, vertical body movements pushing the fifteen foot body towards a group of Aquatic Science Officers seated three rows from the back of the huge conference room. The startled looks on their faces were testament to the realism of the image.

"As many of you are, by now aware, this, ladies and gentlemen, is the crux of the problem. The holographic image that you now see is one to one in scale. From visual verification this is the largest specimen observed to date."

General Miller stared around the room, steely blue eyes piercing through the darkness. He could make out the rustling sound of fidgeting bodies, suddenly confronted with a lifelike hologram of the alien creature. A faint murmur went up from some corners of the room, as several imaginations violently collided with the harsh reality before their eyes.

"Believe me, these beasts are more menacing in real life. Feast on this, people, and while you do, I shall indulge you with the facts and latest theories on these… aliens."

For a moment the general paused.

"We have been at pains to give this species a name. For the record, these beasts shall be referred to as Carcinomas!"

How fitting that the general should choose the name of a cancer. Just like a tumour the aliens were destroying the living tissue surrounding them.

Glen Davis almost managed a smile at the swiftness of his observation. His thoughts, however, were abruptly interrupted by the booming voice of General Miller.

"This is what we know about the Carcinoma. It is a hostile organism that seems to have a number of distinctive characteristics. It has a large beak lined with layers of teeth. From this we have been able to deduce that it is carnivorous in diet. It knows no fear, and is unafraid of attacking objects and organisms larger than itself. The attacks on the submersible and the monorail have been proof enough of this theory, not to mention the hideous demise of the Thresher shark.

We believe that it is very territorial. In capturing one of these specimens, just one creature destroyed one of my submersibles and took out ten of my best soldiers in one fell swoop. The Carcinoma possesses huge strength, and its armoured beak is more than capable of tearing through thick layered steel.

The autopsy of the captured specimen revealed a number of other factors. Its large yellow eyes have a series of layered plates called Tapitus Lucidum. Some of the science officers will be familiar with this phenomenon. These reflective plates in the eyes allow for powerful visibility in the darkness of water. We believe this is the Carcinoma's strongest sense, and we have also surmised that the creature uses visual awareness to communicate."

Almost instantly, the vile holographic body began changing colour far more obligingly than it would have done in real life.

"Notice the changes in colour, similar to the common cuttlefish. As far as we can tell, the creature probably uses a series of colours to communicate, and these colours change with the creature's moods. Please also pay attention to the pectoral fins and the armour plating across the creature's back and head. This is a strange characteristic unseen to human eyes. Such evolutionary developments have not occurred since the time when ancient marine reptiles swam in the oceans of our distant home planet millions of years ago. The spikes make it impossible to attack the creature from above. It is most vulnerable on its soft underbelly.

Also note the four nostrils located on its forehead. Our autopsy revealed that the beast has large lungs that can expand to hold huge quantities of oxygen. Therefore, we know that the Carcinoma breathes air. These lungs act like air sacks that provide buoyancy under the water.

Our analysis showed no evidence of any reproductive organs. We have been able to deduce that Carcinomas are born in reproductive pods, that have grown from a host organism situated some fifty kilometres beyond the settlement limits."

The General paused again. This, the most detailed analysis of the alien species had to be absorbed by everyone in the room if there was any hope of finding a solution. The holographic image changed from that of one of the alien creatures, to a scaled down version of the strange host organism, with all of its pods intact. When the silence became too much to bear he continued.

"The Carcinomas grow in the pink pods. Each pod is a womb, and as you can see, worryingly there are well over one hundred pods. The thick stem is basically a huge umbilical cord for each organism. How the organism originated is unknown, but it is located in a crater on the seabed, which is now believed to be a meteorite crash site. We have hypothesised that the meteorite brought with it some strange bacteria that had been dormant for countless years. Perhaps the bacteria were waiting for a kick-start, which we may have provided when the chemical formula, CT-3 was released into the oceans upon our settlement here. In creating the conditions for our life to exist, we may have inadvertently begun the evolutionary process of an alien species.

This theory would appear to be corroborated by the fact that there have been no additional sightings of other Carcinoma host organisms. Current evidence would suggest that this life form has only appeared in this specific location, especially in the light of the hypothesis regarding the bacteria from the meteorite, which brings us to the conclusion that this life form does not descend from Coleshia.

This leads us to the goal of this meeting. Every point of contact between humanity and the Carcinomas has resulted in human death. They pose a serious threat to the wildlife in the oceans, seemingly killing anything that moves, and if another specimen strays into the settlement limits, who can guess at the cost to humanity? On their own, they are a lethal threat. Once the majority have hatched, the Coleshian population will be confined to the settlement limits. Eventually, more of these creatures will discover the settlement, and with current advances in technology we will not stand a chance. They are quicker and stronger than us. To put it bluntly, they are more adapted to life in the ocean than we are!

The human race is not numerous, and mass confrontation against the Carcinomas may prove very costly. Make no mistake, they are strong and aggressive, and we may be facing the extinction of human life on this planet if we fail to act!"

The awful truth of the situation hit everyone hard. Like many of the delegates in the room, Glen Davis shuffled awkwardly in his seat in an attempt to remove the chill from his spine.

"We *do not* want mass hysteria breaking out in the settlement. We need a solution and we need it fast. This meeting will adjourn for three hours in the hope that we may find one."

It almost seemed paradoxical that a man of the general's physique could appear so forlorn.

"We hope that your knowledge of oceanic life will help us to find the answers…"

Chapter 25

During the intermission the collection of the most knowledgeable minds on the planet filtered out of the huge conference hall into a refreshment room. The food laid out for them served little more than a decorative purpose. They had enough trouble digesting the facts of their predicament, let alone the expanse of snacks that stretched out before their eyes. This was a time of facing up to the dangers that now faced the Coleshians, and how they were going to deal with these dangers.

Unlike many of the High Council members and Science Officers around him, who chattered away like flocks of manic birds, Glen spent his time in isolated thought propped up at the bar, sipping an orange juice. An entire life's work was slowly being destroyed, and every single person in that room knew that a disturbance to the eco-system might destroy it completely, not to mention the obvious threat to humankind. The video images that he had seen of the patrol sub-mersible wreckage and the remaining sections of the monorail, had not put the Carcinomas in a positive light.

Deep down, like everyone else there, Glen knew that the human race was in no fit state to start fighting wars, especially the violent contents of over one hundred of those psychedelic coloured pods. The population level was low, and their defences were primitive. Be-fore, the only threat had been a neighbouring planet with an axe to grind, but like themselves, with primitive tools with which to do anything. For this reason alone no conflict had been forthcoming. It would take decades for engineers to develop the technology that could manoeuvre through the sea as well as the Carcinomas. By that time it would be too late. Soldiers provided much of Coleshia's skilled workmanship. If heavy casualties were sustained, it would take even longer to retrain the required number of people to carry on with the task of building machinery and components for their vehicles.

Glen finished his drink. He didn't feel like socialising with his peers. He knew the solution to this threat; he had known it since his visit to the library that morning.

"The time has come, ladies and gentlemen of Coleshia. Have you any suggestions to offer the committee?" enquired Governor Tasken, failing to hide a look of futility behind his weathered features.

A tall, dark haired Science Officer rose to her full height amongst the wave of daunted people. In Glen's estimation, she was approaching the middle era of her life, and she handled herself with the maturity of someone approaching such a milestone. She appeared unperturbed by the attention of so many people.

There was hope! Perhaps Glen would not be forced to play his hand after all. Perhaps the burden of nurturing a difficult solution would not be his.

"Governor, I am Aquatic Science Officer, Anita Welkins. We have heard a great deal today about the Carcinomas. We have heard how they pose a serious threat to us, not just our values and the way we live, but our very existence! You present us with hell and then ask us to smother the flames with a glass of water! I am sure that I am not alone when I say that the best minds in the galaxy could not think of a quick solution in the time given to us."

It was evident at this point that Officer Welkins was struggling to keep anger from her voice. She looked around the room, to see several masked nods of agreement. It fuelled her momentum.

"That we are in grave danger is not under dispute, but let me tell you this. With two Alliance Space Vessels at our disposal in orbit why do we not consider the possibility of fleeing this planet? Surely in the face of certain death that would propose to force itself upon us it is the only option?"

Governor Tasken looked indifferent to her questions.

"Officer Welkins, it shocks me to hear an Officer of Aquatic Science, such as yourself talk this way. Do you not remember the oath that you took upon your eighteenth birthday?"

He shifted his attention to the population of the whole room.

"I ask all of you to look deep inside yourselves. As Science Officers your oath was to protect the life forms that made the journey with us to Coleshia. That not only includes yourselves, but the animals out there, beyond the settlement limits, that play a deadly game with the Carcinomas. Would you give them a new home to watch them perish?"

Officer Welkins' response was swift.

"It is not our desire to leave them. With two vessels in space why do we not try to resurrect them as permanent homes for the animals and ourselves? We talk of confronting these monsters. Why not capture our own species and move to another planet? Out of all the millions of worlds in the galaxy, there must be at least one that can support our existence. A slim chance it may be, but surely one worth risking under the circumstances?"

Governor Tasken breathed deeply. He realised that what he now faced was a true test to his people's belief in the Ark Project. As he replied, he made sure that his insecurities were deeply masked in his voice:

"When our voyage began, long before any of us were born the human race was under enormous pressure. We left Earth with a slim chance of success. Time was not on our side. Our resources, fuel and raw materials, would only stretch to a one-way trip. We may be able to re-enter space, but for how long could we survive? What if we never find a new planet to call home? It is a reality I would rather not face if there is any chance that Coleshia can be saved. Do we sacrifice everything that we live for? Do we compromise the preservation of life that the Ark Project has taught us for our own immediate survival? What is the good in buying a brief moment of time if we die knowing that we have betrayed ourselves and our ancestors?"

It was a brutal truth that everyone in the hall understood. To leave Coleshia would be to betray the Ark Project.

Officer Welkins bowed her head briefly before adding:

"I do not wish to appear disrespectful to the Ark Project, or the hiatus from selfish gain that has hung around the neck of humanity for several centuries now. If we must stay, and if we cannot fight the alien threat alone, then we must turn to our Penusian neighbours for help. Like us they recognise the sanctity of the Ark Project."

Governor Tasken smiled weakly at Officer Welkins.

"Plans are underway to employ the help of our neighbours. My trusted Senator Phillipoussis will shortly embark upon a mercy mission to Penusia for that very purpose. Interplanetary politics must be cast aside in these difficult times."

It was a hollow statement, and one that Tasken felt foolish for even entertaining. Everyone in that delegation knew that Penusia would not extend helping hands towards Coleshia, and even if by some miracle they did, what could they offer? Most Penusians had never seen an ocean, let alone travelled to the darkest depths of one.

So that left one option - relocating the human population to Penusia. Again the impracticalities were all too apparent, because searing heat and miles of deserts were as alien to Coleshians as oceans were to Penusians.

It was doubtful that they would cope with such a harsh change in the environment. Hope was a foolish emotion…

Glen Davis sat in silence, observing the stalemate at which Officer Welkins had arrived. It was obvious to him that the governor's words were a feeble attempt at providing hope to the committee. Recalling his testing interview with Dominic Strand twelve days earlier, it was clear that the Penusian condition did not allow for military assistance in the oceans of Coleshia. If water gave them pause for thought, the nightmare under the waves would do little to change their mindset!

Come on, Glen. Find your nerve. There is no choice for the Coleshian people other than what you can offer them.

Glen knew that there was no hand better than the one that he had clutched feverishly to his chest all day! He reluctantly rose from his chair. He wished that the soft furnishings would engulf him and prevent him from performing his duty as a Coleshian citizen.

"Governor Tasken. May I be permitted to address the assembled committee?"

"Certainly, Mr Davis," replied the governor, verifying the speaker's name on his computer terminal. It was clear that the tired old man welcomed the brief respite from clutching at straws.

"Please, step forward and speak your mind."

Glen left his seat, filing past the seated Science Officers, suddenly feeling extremely naked. As he made his approach to the speaking platform, he recalled how much he hated the public relations side of his job. The butterflies began to stir in his stomach, and he nervously took his place behind the microphone, swapping the disk in the terminal with one of his own.

"Ladies and gentlemen, my name is Glen Davis. I am the head of the Elasmobranch Team. Some of you will know me from my active release project with the sharks."

Glen paused for a moment.

Why are you waiting, man, for God's sake get on with it.

Glen forced the words into his larynx and upon the expectant committee.

"Governor Tasken, I believe that I may have the answer to Coleshia's threat."

Before any one could say a thing he flicked a switch on the terminal, and a hologram flickered into life, five feet above his head. A couple of amazed gasps emerged from the council members. It was strange how Glen's reluctance now dissolved as he began to share his thoughts with the stunned occupants of the room. He began to speak with authority, as if he were meant to speak these words:

"This holographic image is also on a one to one scale. As you will notice, it is some ten feet larger than the alien creature."

Looking above him, Glen admired the streamlined muscle movements that slithered down the hologram's body, as it swam through the air, cruising around the conference hall.

"I'm sure most of you will recognise him. Carcharodon Carcharias, otherwise known as the Great White shark.

Before I continue, allow me to provide you with some information on this species, so that you can compare it with your knowledge of the alien creature. It is this comparison that has led me to certain conclusions. The Great White shark dates back some twenty-five million years, which as you are aware, was the time of prehistoric reptiles upon Earth. At the time this fish was not the dominant aquatic predator on the planet, but it survived that age, and rose to the mantle of a top predator because of one brutal truth - it was the best hunter. This is why the environmental computer calculations stated that in Coleshia's ecosystem the most efficient predator would be a Great White shark!"

Glen's eyes tried to pierce the dimness, as he looked around the encompassing committee. He tried very hard to appear sincere; despite a swelling feeling within himself. His own love for the sharks left him with undeniable guilt for what he was doing.

"Let me tell you why I feel that this shark is superior to this alien creature. You see, we are not dealing with a Thresher shark, an organism designed by evolutionary processes to catch relatively small organisms. The Great White shark was designed to take on far bigger prey. General Miller, you stated that this being relied on a visual acuity as its primary sense, whence the changes in skin colour as a mode of communication. Great White sharks can see from a distance of seventy-five feet. When approaching the surface, the shark employs a dark-adapted visual system. Like the alien creature, they have a layer of Tapitus Lucidum in their eyes, similar to many nocturnal creatures from our home planet. In addition to this, the Great White shark navigates through the ocean using the most complex of radar guidance systems. Sensors in its nose can pick up electrical currents in the water that are given off by every living creature. It doesn't need to see its prey. It can feel their location. I believe that taking advantage of these senses will allow us to realistically combat the Carcinomas."

Glen allowed his audience to digest what he had said. Suddenly a voice boomed out of the darkness. It belonged to General Miller.

"Point proven, Mr Davis, but how do you intend to use these evolutionary skills?"

"Being, in my opinion, far more intelligent than the Carcinoma, the Great White shark is highly territorial, using various patterns to attack prey and rival organisms that are perceived to be a threat. The one that I believe can be the most dangerous to the alien creature is what we call the 'sneak attack'. Great Whites are oceanic predators, which means that they hunt near the surface. As the alien creature breathes oxygen, it has to rise to the surface to breathe. This makes it a prime target for a creature like a Great White shark, which can rise from a great depth to attack an organism on the surface."

As if commanded by his descriptions, the nose of the holographic shark began rising as if on course to helpless prey that lurked near the surface, providing an unnecessary, but effective visual aid to the descriptions of Glen.

"From below, the creature will take a debilitating bite, which in the case of the alien creature is its vulnerable spot, under the belly... Whereas the Carcinoma is relentless the Great White is calculating!"

The penny dropped as if it were a ten-tonne boulder, as it became clear to everyone in the conference hall precisely what Aquatic Science Officer Glen Davis was proposing...

The silence seemed to last for an eternity. The lights in the room came back into existence. Glen glanced around at the astounded faces.

A voice from behind him spoke first.

"Officer Davis, I am Aquatic Science Officer, Van-Velden. I have listened to every point that you have raised today, and I have to admit that I have my doubts about this course of action. Using the Great White sharks as offensive killing machines against the Carcinomas. How preposterous! What are you going to do, dangle seal meat in front of them to steer them in the right direction?"

While making his statement, Officer Van-Velden, a short stocky man, boasting dark hair and a bushy beard held his hands outstretched, gesturing for some response to his challenge. Before Glen could find the words to parry his inquisitor, another question was fired in his direction.

"Mr Davis. Is it wise to release another predator into Coleshia's oceans, especially if it is as 'superior' as you claim?"

General Miller was regarding Glen with a fierce blue-eyed stare, the next voice of scepticism.

"More to the point, Mr Davis, how can you possibly guess the sharks' reaction in this scenario?"

Glen held the challenge of the general's cold stare. He couldn't figure out why, but this man gave him the creeps.

"Quite simple, General. All I have to do is ask them!"

The meeting had been moved from the conference hall to Governor Tasken's office.

Accompanying Glen and Governor Tasken were General Miller and Senator Phillipoussis. They stood around the desk, regarding the small portable keypad that Glen had produced from his pocket. The label above the VDU display said: BODY-WAVE.

"Why wasn't I made aware of this development before?" said the governor, incredulously.

"My apologies, Governor, but we kept this project very quiet for good reason. The last thing that the team wanted was the media hounding around the Animal Release Zone. A project with this significance would draw a lot of attention."

His words made good sense.

"So let me recap, Mr Davis," interjected General Miller. "Sharks communicate through a language of postures. This device allows us to communicate with the sharks through special receivers built into their Brainchips, and vice versa."

"That's correct, General. These receivers translate the words on the keypad into body movement signals that register with the sharks' senses. Likewise, the keypad translates the sharks' movements to decipher the thoughts that are being conveyed! Over the years quite a relationship has developed, while humans and sharks have been confined to similar spaces. It is simply the next evolutionary step that Great White sharks become conditioned to human interaction. For so many centuries they have been shrouded in mystery. Only now are we beginning to unlock the doors to these secrets, and we are only managing to do this by breaking through the biggest of all barriers - communication!"

"It really is incredible," said Governor Tasken, examining the small keypad. He was like a child examining a new toy. The glimmer of hope wavered with enthusiasm in his voice. "Exactly how do you intend to develop this project?"

"Well…" Glen paused with unease. "Initially, Bodywave was designed to form a better understanding of Great White sharks, so that humans could interact with them with greater success. The security of PAD devices does not seem to be enough assurance as far as these predators are concerned. With this technology we can dispel the myth, once and for all, that they are simply mindless predators."

"Now your technology is going to be used to emphasise the killing instincts of this species; not very conducive to a positive image. This must have been a difficult decision to make, coming forward as you have to aid the Coleshian cause."

General Miller's comments struck a poignant chord in Glen's mind. He did his best to hide his torment.

"I can assure you that I have battled my demons over this, General."

It was clear through the lack of eye contact that Glen had not won the battle.

"Assuming that we can regain control of the planet's ecosystem, then the project could be expanded to different species of life. It could draw humanity and nature a huge step closer. The trick is to work out how different species communicate. Once we have achieved this we can adjust the fitted Brainchips to access the relevant receptors of an organism's brain."

"Just how many of these fish do you have at your disposal?"

Glen was hesitant in responding.

"Four."

General Miller laughed out loud.

"Officer Davis, when you suggested this initiative I perceived an army of Great Whites to battle army of Carcinomas… Oh dear…"

"It can work with military assistance, I *know* it can."

"How reliable is the technology?" interjected Senator Phillipoussis.

"The technology is entirely reliable. Unfortunately, although we can translate the sharks' thoughts, we cannot read their minds. They will only communicate with us if they desire to do so. That is why it is important to have a good bond with the sharks. Trust is a key issue."

"Trust, with a *Great White shark*?" General Miller couldn't hide the mocking tone in his voice.

"Simply having big teeth does not mean that they are not afraid of the unknown!"

The general said nothing, but raised his eyebrows in acknowledgement of Glen's sharp retort.

"A very noble idea, Mr Davis," replied the senator, "but in all honesty sharks have carried a fearsome reputation with them throughout history. It can be, shall we say, difficult to shake off."

"Didn't the Eden Treaty talk about learning to interact with 'sentient life'? Each shark has different characteristics and a personality to match. They respond to the team, and are learning friendship and trust, and one particular individual is learning our names. The reason that sharks have a bad reputation is because humanity has never been able to control them."

Somehow, the weight of guilt upon Glen's shoulders increased as he began to wonder whether or not silence would have been a better policy on this historic day…

At this point in time, Glen considered her persona reminiscent of an active volcano that was near to erupting.

"So what happened next?" Rhona asked, frowning.

Mike and Danny were staring intently at Glen, as he unravelled the day's events.

"Well, Governor Tasken and General Miller agreed that there was potential for using the Great White sharks in an initiative beyond the settlement limits. They want us to complete the Bodywave Project as swiftly as possible."

"You mean that we are going to turn the sharks into weapons?" said Rhona, with a level of disgust.

"It looks that way," sighed Glen.

Wait for it, here it comes…Mount Rhona is about to blow…

"Oh, Jesus, Glen. *How could you?*" yelled Rhona.

Glen began to open his mouth in defence, but his speech was cut off in its prime.

"After all we have done to create a positive image for the sharks, you want to destroy that by putting our most valuable species at the *forefront* of Coleshia's arsenal?"

"Rhona, sooner or later the Great Whites would have to face the Carcinomas. I would rather that they were equipped to deal with the situation…Do you think that I haven't deliberated over this?"

"What I think is that you are too obsessed with your own feelings to consult your team. This goes against everything we have aimed for… I might have guessed that you would try to improve your own standing in the administrative system at the expense-"

Glen had reached his limit. Exhausted from the mental strain of the day and in no state to reason with Rhona's wrath he retreated to a bureaucratic approach.

"Officer Skallen, *I am* the senior officer in this team. Continue your tone and attitude and you can be dismissed for questioning *my* authority!"

It was a low blow, and one that Glen instantly regretted. Rhona said nothing. Her shocked eyes searched his face, and as the tears began to form she turned and ran from the office. Shocked by his own actions Glen could only watch in paralysis as she stormed from the Animal Release Zone.

For a moment there was silence. Glen turned to the silent figures of Mike Cullen and Danny McCormick. He had a tremor in his voice.

"I've requested four weeks, so that we can develop the level of communication with the sharks as much as possible before the initiative commences. A shorter time window could result in major lapses in their training."

The two silent figures simply nodded before turning to leave Glen alone, once again. As Glen buried his head in his hands Mike made one final statement to his friend.

"She was right you know… You *should* have talked to us first!"

The slightly wounded tone in his voice was condemnation enough.

As his colleagues drifted from the huge laboratory, Glen, for the second time that day went down to the jetty. Only this time, he was not worried about what he could do; he was left worrying about what he had done. It had been worse than he had suspected - disapproval from all corners!

The graceful bodies in the pool had always been there to steer his judgement in the right direction. Right now there was nothing but an endless expanse of water with no sign of life at all. Glen remembered how much he had admired convergent evolution. Today he hated it, as life, once again twisted out of his grasp.

Chapter 26

Convergent evolution…

The phrase kept running through his mind.

When nature adopts a form that is perfectly suited to the environment that encompasses it…

Glen Davis reclined in his chair. It creaked, reminding him that there were limits to its flexibility, as he leant back and stared at the ceiling. In the past, the term had come to apply simply to physical changes within the anatomy of a species to suit it's environment. Since the beginning of the Ark Project's second phase, every species of shark aboard the Super Nova had been thrown into a new environment. Although the enclosures were realistically built up to resemble natural habitats as much as possible, there was one change in the lifestyle of the sharks that couldn't be disguised - their attitudes to the presence of humans…

This was a factor particularly true of the species that had been scarcely acquainted with an existence in captivity. For them in particular, technology had been pushed to its very limit to provide appropriate life-supporting conditions. Technology, without inspirational people like Isaac Slater, would never have been developed, and, consequently, would have made the possibility of sharks traversing deep space impossible.

Ultimately, without the sharks, the food chain would have become unbalanced, and this would have jeopardised the entire operation on Coleshia.

For hundreds of years humanity and sharks have been in direct contact.

Glen sighed.

I guess that it is inevitable that changes will take place.

In the case of the Great White sharks the changes had manifested themselves on a mental level. Perhaps these characteristics had always been evident, and only through two hundred years of research had scientists begun to uncover the truth about these elusive creatures; that they were intelligent life forms with individual characteristics - personalities! How many times had Glen seen the proof of this discovery? How many times had he seen the bold intelligence and leadership of Kauhulu, the docile, timid approaches of Astra; not to mention the seemingly teenage aggression of Poker Face?

Isaac Slater recognised this intelligence long before the technology that he helped to develop had allowed official confirmation of the fact. Maybe humanity rationalised its own ignorance by announcing it as a 'discovery', giving it a name and describing it as a change.

The Great White sharks had adapted to close contact with human beings. As time passed, their fears and defences dropped, and since the instigation of compulsory safety measures, such as the use of PAD devices, humans had enjoyed decades of close contact with these magnificent fish that had once been described as 'maneaters'. The research of others had pushed the Elasmobranch Team to a summit where they were now overcoming the most arduous of barriers - communication!

Now, centuries of research would be wasted in the fulfilment of the belief that sharks were ruthless machines of destruction. That would be the image conveyed to the Coleshian people, fuelling the prejudice that had damaged *all* species of sharks in the past!

Glen tried to smile at the irony of the situation, but his facial muscles were reluctant to provide a positive response. He knew all too well that the perverseness of the circumstances was nothing short of tragic…

"*I don't care, Mike!*" screamed Rhona, from the medical office.

She was fast approaching tears, while furiously slamming small medicine bottles into a case.

"Rhona, slow down for crying out loud. You'll cut yourself," soothed Mike, rubbing a hand over his shaven skull.

He had often been the middleman in heated debates between Rhona and Glen. Both had enough adherence to professionalism to make such occurrences infrequent, but none the less highly volatile when allowed to escalate.

He found it very difficult at times. Glen was his closest friend. They had been close since their days at college, but he also professed a fondness towards Rhona that was strictly platonic. She was very head-strong, but amazingly caring and it was at times such as this that her passion showed.

Mike was also aware of Glen's feelings towards Rhona. As a close confidant to both of them he recognised the nuances in attitude that they showed towards one another, and despite Glen's silence over the subject, Mike knew that his friend's feelings extended beyond professional intentions. He recalled when the two of them had argued before with regard to medication that had to be administered to Astra.

"Rhona, look… I have the final say in this issue, and as your ranking officer…"

"Don't you pull that bureaucratic nonsense with me, Glen. You know that I have a point, and it bothers you that I haven't been in the team as long as you…"

"Rubbish, all that I am saying is that we should wait a little longer…"

"For what, Astra to drop dead?"

"Hey, that's not fair, I'm only thinking about her welfare you know."

At this point Rhona had been towering over Glen, hands on hips, while Glen, on the retreat, backed his chair into an operations terminal.

"You already know what the medication will do."

"Well…er, in such instances I find that it is beneficial to wait for the test results…"

"Glen, you know as well as I do what the diagnosis is!"

And so it continued, irrational and intense…

The strange irony was that they both had the same goals at heart –

the welfare of the sharks and the ecosystem. The difference was that in this particular situation they had opposing views on how to achieve that goal. They were like quarrelling lovers, blissfully unaware that they belonged together.

"*How could he?* Doesn't he realise what he is doing? Mike, we can't allow this to happen. It's *immoral*, that's what it is. *Four* Great White sharks in existence, and that moron is going to send them out as… As *bloody* soldiers of *war*."

"Listen, Rhona, just think it through for a moment."

"*I'm tired of thinking, Mike*… Look, you know as well as I do that Great White sharks adopt the 'K' lifestyle to breeding, like humans. They have very few offspring, and they devote their time into developing these offspring, like human beings. If we lose even one Great White to the Carcinomas, it could destroy any chance of producing future generations. They could become *extinct*!"

"I know that, Rhona… Glen knows that too. He's *thinking* in the long term. Right now, the Carcinomas are destroying the ecosystem that teams like ours have created. If the Great Whites are released, where will they live and for *how* long? As it stands, there are no natural predators to the Carcinomas. You saw what one of those creatures did to a shark nearly three times its size. Christ, even the Coleshian people are on the endangered list. Manpower and technology are not enough in this fight. By working with the Great White sharks we have another solution, for the ecosystem *and* for us! Either way, to keep the Whites in captivity for longer than necessary could be detrimental to their ability to survive in the wild. Eventually we will have no choice but to release them. Surely it is better that they are prepared for what's out there, don't you think?"

Rhona slammed the lid shut on the medicine bottle case. It was confirmation enough to Mike that he was getting somewhere.

"I guess so. How can Glen live with himself? He seemed so emotionless when he *eventually* told us. Doesn't he feel any guilt for *sentencing* them to death?"

"Okay, Rhona, he should have told us, but he knows that. I can assure you that no one in the team feels more guilt about this than Glen. He's a good man, and he loves the sharks as much as anyone. He also knows, from an objective frame of thought, as we all do, that a Great White shark is possibly the most superbly evolved predator that the human race has ever known. We are not talking about a helpless fish; we are talking about a cunning predator with a *superb* territorial instinct. That was his basis for selection. He believes that they *can* survive out there, and maybe save all our asses at the same time! What chance do we stand against these aliens, with our primitive metal cans? Very little! Glen is only trying to fulfil his obligations to the Ark Project, by ensuring that nature has a chance of survival against the Carcinomas. We must *not* blame him for that."

Rhona's beautiful face wore a sombre expression. With dissipating anger, she knew that ultimately, Glen had chosen the right path, arriving at the only option available to him. It was difficult to stomach all the same. As the realisation hit her, she became overwhelmed by powerful thoughts.

"You know, I will always remember the visual documentary that I saw once years ago, before I joined the team. I remember being profoundly struck by it. Thinking about it, it was the main reason why I joined the team.

Dozens of sharks brutally heaved onto boats, via hooks that dug deeply into their mouths. I remember how vulnerable they looked out of the water, mouths opening and closing in desperation for breath. They weren't granted release from their misery… The fishermen chopped their fins off, and then threw them back into the water. Several species just recklessly thrown back like valueless refuse…"

Mike recalled with a high level of disgust the same documentaries that had educated him to the distasteful treatment of sharks in the distant past. Needless to say the conclusions did not need to be stated. Such a sight would have disgusted any human being with an ounce of compassion, let alone devoted scientists. Nevertheless, Mike felt that it was appropriate to let Rhona know that he understood her point.

"Valueless refuse that was still alive! No longer capable of anything, even the most basic of functions. Condemned to die through starvation and suffocation. Somewhat like asking a human being to climb a ladder without the aid of arms or legs. I know the video, we all do. As you work with these creatures you realise the true cruelty of labelling them as 'killers', when the human race has been guilty of the worst atrocities known - and for what? So called culinary delicacies…"

Mike smiled at Rhona.

"Believe me, Rhona. We are all on the same wavelength as far as the sharks are concerned. Although it is difficult to accept what we are doing, we must have faith in the fact that if we succeed, all will benefit from our endeavours."

There was a brief period of silence, before the focus of the conversation changed.

"You've known him a long time, haven't you, Mike?"

Mike frowned, his mental patterns playing catch-up to the tangential direction of Rhona's question.

"Yes, Glen is one of the best. We took our Aquatic Science Centre exams together."

"Don't you find him to be, well… removed, quiet, even distant a lot of the time?" enquired Rhona, confusion on her face.

"Yes, but there is nothing wrong with being quiet. You know Glen, he speaks when he has something to say."

"But he never seems to let go. He lives for his work, and nothing else."

"Not true, Rhona; when you get to know the man, you just have to know which locks to pick to find the real person underneath. And there is nothing wrong with being fulfilled by your job. Would you dive with Great White sharks if you didn't find it fulfilling?"

"I guess not."

"Why the sudden interest in Glen?" Mike asked, wearing a grin that hinted to Rhona at knowing more than it revealed.

"Well… He's just so mysterious. Never talks about his past."

"I don't blame him for that."

Mike's features clouded over, as if he were going through some internal conflict. Alarmed, Rhona responded.

"Mike, are you all right? I shouldn't ask too many questions."

Sighing, Mike, removing his spectacles and cleaning them with his sleeve had resolved his mental tangle.

"No, its not you. Perhaps I shouldn't be telling you this, but it may help you to understand him a little better. I'm sure that Glen will understand in the circumstances... He loves the sharks more than you could ever realise!"

"How do you mean?"

Mike paused again. How would his friend react? Glen had sworn Mike to secrecy with regard to his past. Mike put it down to the fact that Glen wanted the past to stay firmly behind him, and the less people who knew about it, the easier it was for Glen to look forward, and move on from those painful memories. He hoped that Glen would not be too offended by his actions.

"We are all first generation Coleshians aren't we?"

"Yes."

"Well, when Glen was a boy, his father was part of the construction team that built the Animal Release Zone. At the age of six, Glen witnessed a dreadful accident. One of the seals in the lab ruptured, creating a nasty leak. Several hundred people died... Glen was dragged from the scene while he watched his father perish... He's been battling the demons ever since."

Rhona listened intently. When, eventually she found the words to speak, it was with an incredulous tone of voice that she found difficult to mask.

"He works in the place where his father died? Surely the Coleshian administration would question his ability to fulfil his responsibilities under that sort of ... distraction?"

She was dumbstruck by the fact that for so long she had assumed that she had Glen well and truly plotted out in her head. Her measurements had been wrong...

Before responding to her question, a smile broke the surface of Mike's face.

"The Coleshian Administration chose to ignore those questions on the back of the first *ever* recorded ninety-nine per cent score on the ASC exams! When probed as to which area of expertise he would wish to enter, Glen replied that the Elasmobranch Team was the only choice for him. Since then, Glen has avoided those sort of questions with good results. The team has had no fatalities since he has been in charge of the release project. He bears the scar from the *only* human injury himself, obtained from the tail of an animated Thresher pup while installing it with a Brainchip. I think even you, Rhona, would have to agree that with this knowledge you *cannot* question Glen's devotion to all things Elasmobranch!"

Chapter 27

"Would you look at this!" exclaimed Danny, in what could only be described as near astonishment. They huddled around the video monitor, inquisitively watching the events unravelling before them.

"This is incredible," Rhona enthused. "I never thought that I would get the chance to see this before they were released into the wild."

She spared a fleeting glance in the direction of Glen, who appeared to be doing his best to avoid her gaze. Since the previous day, following Glen's meeting with the Coleshian administration, events had unravelled this way, and now the tension in the lab was undeniable. Mike and Danny chose to ignore what was happening by immersing themselves in their studies.

"Well, sweetheart, you better believe it," replied Danny, with pompous overtones, while maintaining his vigil of the events displayed on the screen.

From concealed housings on the sides of the pool, powerful cameras were picking up the events taking place in the Animal Release Zone. Cleopatra and Kauhulu were swimming extremely closely together, cruising along a parallel trajectory in a relaxed, unfrenzied manner. This lazy type of behaviour could signify one thing only. To the untrained eye, the first signs of courtship would pass unnoticed. To four Elasmobranch Scientists this was a major development in shark behaviour that provided a number of clues as to the status of the Great White sharks. Mike was the first to hypothesise.

"This is extremely positive. I never thought that they would mate under such a disrupted lifestyle, especially with all the training we have been giving them!"

"Where's the saxophone…? I feel like a peeping tom in the cupboard!"

Danny's audience cast a curt glance in his direction. He gave an apologetic glance to his colleagues.

"Sorry, I was just trying to inject some humour into the proceedings."

"Humour is only funny if it is tastefully applied," replied Glen. "The reason that this is happening is *because* of the training that we have given them… They are planning ahead!"

"Planning ahead! Are you serious, Glen?" asked Mike, shocked.

"Strong proof of intelligence isn't it. They understand the implications of combating the Carcinomas. In the event of the death of the males, survival probability will be increased if the females are impregnated before the offensive begins."

Glen's comments hit each of them, numbing the group into silent observation. Cleopatra was releasing pheromones into the water, a course of action that had drawn Kauhulu close to her. Now he found himself traversing the path of Great White conception. By now he was swimming almost on top of Cleopatra, his stomach pressing on to her dorsal fin, until it bent over to the side. The pair became entwined. Kauhulu bit down on her left pectoral fin, as the pair began to slowly spiral into the deeper and murkier depths of the pool. The wonderful process of conception continued, as the magnificent beasts disappeared out of the range of the cameras…

"It has been one week, Mr Davis. Before I venture to Penusia for their assistance in our plight, I would like an update on proceedings."

The green orbs peered deep into those of Glen Davis. He found Senator Phillipoussis' presence somewhat awkward at this time. The Bodywave Project was entering its most frenetic phase and pressure on their available time was great. Nevertheless, Glen had to remind himself that the release of the Great White sharks had a huge significance now to the entire settlement, and the concern of the Coleshian authorities was to be expected in the current circumstances.

Once again, Phillipoussis had insisted on flamboyance in the face of necessity, the two sentinels following him around like lobotomised slaves. Glen was unsure whether it was the senator's presence, or that of his protectors that irritated him more.

"Senator, in the first of our remaining weeks, substantial progress has been made. The Great White sharks are showing superb territorial awareness that seems to improve on a daily basis. In addition to this, the sharks are responding as well as ever to human contact. We feel that they are beginning to show an understanding of our cause."

"Excellent news, Mr Davis. Tell me, what problems have you encountered?" asked the senator, ruffling his brown robe, and dismissing the guards to the entrance of the huge laboratory.

With an increasing distance between Glen and the sentries, he decided that it was the guards who made him feel uneasy. Recalling his dislike of the HP-1 pistol that he had to wear as a safety precaution in the pool, Glen put his minor phobia down to the huge blast rifles that each sentry proudly displayed. The other benefit of this action was that without the combined presence, the senator was forced to look rather ordinary, which served to remove some of Glen's nerves when addressing the Coleshian official.

"I regret to admit that there are difficulties, Senator. The first is gauging how the sharks will react to the alien presence. Although territorial awareness has improved, short of dropping a live Carcinoma into the pool, a precise account of the Great Whites' reactions to this species will be impossible to determine before the initial confrontation. With a little luck, the sharks will engage the creatures as invaders to their territory."

The senator nodded.

"I am concerned about the lack of solid fact that surrounds this strategy, Mr Davis."

"I understand, Senator, but think of it this way. You have heard about what an aggressive Carcinoma can do. How do you think an aggressive Great White shark behaves? All animals are most dangerous when they feel threatened, particularly predators. These fears arise from territorial awareness, from an instinctive desire to protect their space. As long as the Great White sharks interpret the Coleshian Ocean to be their domain, then they will oppose the Carcinomas!"

"I see…"

"This leads to our second problem: guaranteeing that the Great White sharks adopt an attack pattern that will kill the Carcinoma in one blow."

"Please explain."

"During the test of the alien's flesh, it was recorded in the autopsy report that the creatures have a chemical make-up not unlike that of marine molluscs. Their flesh may not be poisonous as such, but *all* sharks are fussy eaters. If a shark doesn't like the taste of what it has bitten, then it will spit it out. Such a lacklustre form of attack would leave the Great Whites exposed to what would most likely be a largely active Carcinoma. If it is still active it is dangerous."

"So how do you propose to solve this problem?" asked the senator, peering at Glen, down the length of his nose, with a tone of voice that matched the sincerity of his facial expression.

Ignoring the importance that the senator placed in his question, Glen replied:

"We intend to adopt the approach of the Great White's preferred form of attack. As I stated in the High Council meeting, from below and behind, the sneak attack. I suspect that many of the Carcinomas will be quite vulnerable to this form of attack, especially when returning to the surface to breathe! This is how the sharks catch seals. Sharks only attack via the sneak attack when looking for a meal, which is why we need to merge the territorial instincts with the feeding instincts. We have to make the Great Whites attack the Carcinomas with no motive other than to remove them as threats to their territory."

Senator Phillipoussis was staring at the miniature Bodywave keypad.

"How do you manage to teach the sharks these… lessons?"

"It's not a case of teaching; more a case of tinkering with their emotional reactions. As my previous point about the shark attack patterns illustrated, rather than teaching the Great White sharks something radical, we are simply juxtaposing some of their behaviour patterns."

"The sharks must be clever fish to understand this."

"Indeed they are, Senator."

While pointing at the keyboard, Senator Phillipoussis investigated further.

"I'm not sure that I understood at the previous meeting. So this device acts as a two-way dictionary, so that sharks can understand humans and humans can understand sharks?"

Glen's face wrinkled at the poor attempt to grasp the Bodywave concept.

"Not quite. Sharks communicate through postures. Despite having wonderful bodies, they are not contortionists. Their language is limited to a certain number of 'words' if you like. To get a point across concisely, you have to use the appropriate word, such as …"

Glen showed the senator an example. His fingers worked rapidly over the keys of the small device.

GLEN… FRIEND OF KAUHULU.

After typing this phrase on the illuminescent VDU display, the two men stared at the screen. Barely a few seconds later a reply appeared:

KAUHULU, GLEN… FRIENDS.

"Did one of the sharks say that?" asked the senator, alarmed.

"He certainly did," beamed Glen, proudly.

The senator was almost frozen in disbelief. Enjoying the reaction, Glen decided to eliminate further routes of pessimistic inquisition.

"Allow me to demonstrate their understanding of our plight."

Once again, his fingers skilfully manoeuvred around the keyboard:

KAUHULU, UNDERSTAND THREAT?

A few seconds of inaction passed, before the VDU display scrolled a response before watchful eyes:

YES… GLEN IN DANGER… KAUHULU IN DANGER… LIFE IN DANGER… WE PROTECT YOU… WE PROTECT

US… WE PROTECT LIFE…

"Different levels of thought. Do you see the pattern? He recognises the threat to all life, and he has not even entered the ocean yet!"

"Well, Mr Davis, I have to admit, during the Council Assembly I was sceptical about your proposal. Now, I see that you have these… fish, well under control."

"Senator, we did not develop the Bodywave Project to 'control' the sharks like robots. It was developed to bridge the gap in communication, so that each species could learn from each other."

"Of course, Mr Davis, no offence intended, but being humane about the situation will not ensure our survival or that of the ecosystem. These are desperate times."

To address the governor or his right-hand man in a rude manner would have been disrespectful, but the senator's lack of respect for the sharks appalled Glen.

"Senator Phillipoussis, if what you said were true, why would you be about to embark on a 'mercy' mission to Penusia? Why would I be breaking my back to complete a project, which despite the best of intentions, looks to be serving anything but a humane purpose? We could all just sit here and let the Carcinomas wreck the ecosystem that we have built, and then take our chances when their only obstacle is the settlement, and they come for us. This *entire* settlement is about humane endeavour! What about the people who have donated their lives for over two hundred years to the Ark Project, an ideal in itself, based on humane beliefs – conservation and preservation? If we stop being humane, then we will lose our ecosystem, and far more besides that."

Senator Phillipoussis was emotionless. Sharp, staring eyes regarded Glen like the points of daggers. Beneath those dark orbs, Glen could see rage bubbling away, with the imminent threat of exploding. It was several seconds before the senator made a response that was spoken with a good deal of forced restraint.

"I have neither the time nor the compulsion to discuss politics with you, Mr Davis. Good day, Sir, I shall leave you to continue your studies. My shuttle awaits. *Be* sure to update Governor Tasken on your progress."

Senator Phillipoussis folded each arm into the opposing sleeve of his robe, and silently glided from the Animal Release Zone lab, collecting his sentries upon exiting.

The angered reaction of the senator threw Glen's thoughts into disarray. How could he have offended the High Council by stating the fundamental beliefs of the Ark Project? The thought stayed with him only a short while as he noticed that another hour had passed on the clock that hung above the lab's exit… Another hour of preparation lost…

Chapter 28

Project Date: Day 41 of Year 0405

The Elysium continued on an unfaltering circuit of the Planet Penusia.

Viewed from the stars, the blue sheen of Coleshia's surface differed greatly from the terrain of its larger neighbour. A misty yellow engulfed the visible areas of the planet, amongst which small patches of green could be seen congregated in an isolated plain of the huge, revolving desert. The forestation highlighted how little of the planet's open space had been utilised in the development of the huge wildlife preserves, and towards the centre of the green clump lurked a misty grey smudge that was the hive of all human activity on the largely unoccupied ball of dust.

The Penusian settlement was nothing more than a blemish amongst the organic walls of trees that surrounded it and yet one half of the human race lived in this colonised landscape. From space the several thousands of kilometres of terraformed world appeared no more significant than an anthill, and the monstrous bulk of the Elysium was dwarfed by the sheer magnitude of the planet... Much of the daily life for the people of Penusia consisted of routine. There were no obstacles, such as huge oceans to work around, and no signs of hostile alien creatures threatening the environment.

In a small pocket of life aboard the Elysium, Officer Gallen piloted the Perimeter Module slowly over the surface of the huge vessel, its sensors scanning the outer structure for abnormalities. Unexpectedly these sensors began to chime, and the image that had been received so clearly on Officer Gallen's terminal began to break up.

That's odd, he thought, squinting at the hazy image received from the small robotic vehicle's camera. Intricately, Officer Gallen used his controls to direct the small craft to the source of the disturbance, motivated by curiosity and caution. Irregularities in the environment were not uncommon. Occasionally, these painstaking checks would reveal space debris causing minor damage to the ship's hull.

As the tiny vehicle drew closer to the source of the disturbance the image on Officer Gallen's monitor became almost impossible to decipher. A strangely glowing hemispherical orb appeared to be protruding abruptly from the hull. With all the interference, it was difficult to describe the anomaly as anything else.

"What the hell-"

Officer Gallen never had the chance to complete his exclamation of alarm. In an instant a blinding light filled his monitor screen as the glowing orb exploded…

Throughout every zone of the Coleshian settlement, people ceased whatever they were doing. The gravity of their duties dwindled as the announcement resounded through the loudspeakers. The metallic overtones gave no hint as to the seriousness of the message.

"Please head towards your nearest communal area. An urgent news bulletin has been received from our Penusian neighbours."

Such interruptions in the daily lives of the Coleshians were rare, and because of the infrequency of such announcements an instant wave of cynicism began to generate among the population. The negativity of the Coleshian people was well founded as the female newsreader described the catastrophe that appeared before their eyes.

"The mysterious explosion of the Elysium has been causing chaos on Penusia. Lethal shards of debris from the ship, having been dragged into the planet's gravitational field, continue to violently beat down on the helpless inhabitants. As these images taken from the Penusian settlement network show, they have been pummelling the planet's surface, destroying the settlement structures and the wildlife enclosures. Mass panic has ensued as the wildlife and citizens alike struggle to find cover from the deadly storm. As yet, there has been no word as to the safety of the Coleshian envoy, Senator Phillipoussis, currently on an official visit to Penusia. With communications on the planet disabled, it may be several more hours before we have any details of his condition."

With the announcement of his name, a small image of the senator appeared, neatly bordered in gold, in the bottom right-hand corner of the larger image that depicted man-made Armageddon. From the left of the screen the newsreader reappeared, superimposed over the vision of mass destruction.

"What caused this tragedy remains unknown at this stage. We will keep you informed as this tragic and devastating event unfolds."

All around the settlement, looks of horror became the shared reaction of several thousand Coleshian people.

From his office, Governor Tasken watched in terror, as the steel rain smashed into the Penusian settlement. With each impact and explosion the governor's concern grew for the safety of his friend, Senator Phillipoussis.

Aboard the Utopia, General Miller watched the horrific display from a monitor in his quarters. His straight-faced features did not echo the stunned astonishment of the Coleshian audience, as the wreckage of the Elysium continued to indiscriminately destroy life on Penusia…

Chapter 29

For those souls fortunate enough to find shelter, the images of the cataclysm on Penusia's surface was truly nauseating. Even with the knowledge that several hundred feet separated the protective bunker they were in and the torn and twisted surface, the assembled party of Penusian Council Statesmen could not help but look on, frozen with fear and disbelief at the sights to which the surveillance cameras were drawing their attention. It was now becoming apparent to them how lucky they had been to find shelter before the effects of the explosion had hit the planet's surface. Each and every one of those present in the bunker silently prayed in thanks that they had been a part of the Penusian High Council and, therefore, considered important enough to be granted this means of escape.

Cameras located on the outskirts of the perimeter limits looked inwards, as huge pieces of flaming wreckage that had not been consumed by the intense heat of the planet's atmosphere, came crashing to the surface, regardless of the man-made structures that were destroyed in their wake.

At intermittent periods, several pairs of eyes would look at the low ceiling of the bunker, as if their frightened minds had convinced them that the several feet of soundproof materials around their protective hive could not muffle the apocalyptic sound waves that permeated the soil around them.

Alternate scenes from the same tragic script sporadically substituted the images of destruction on the screen. Showers of debris provided a kaleidoscope of colour; a searing red background on which madness and chaos reigned.

In the huge wildlife enclosures, the tranquillity of nature became permanently disrupted as terrified animals found themselves at the mercy of the destroyed, Elysium. In their attempt to find safety from the shower of smashed and charred wreckage that sporadically fell about them, a mass stampede led by a terrified group of elephants broke through the weakened perimeter fences of the enclosures. Self-preservation became the dominant instinct of every living creature, as the heads of frightened giraffes bobbed frantically past the remains of collapsed buildings and the gazelles, ignoring the fleeing lions, leapt majestically past craters of flame. To be exposed in the open spelled almost certain death.

Elsewhere, within the Penusian settlement, huge riots broke out. Panic-stricken citizens fought for their lives. The ground became littered with hats of assorted colours that normally served to protect the Penusian people from the sun's rays. Desperate in their fight for shelter from the deadly storm, screaming hordes scrambling past each other ignoring the fleeing parties of terrified animals that hurtled past them, and occasionally through them.

The human race and nature had been united in a way that even the architects of the Ark Project could not have envisaged… The fear of death!

All the while, the burning wreckage continued to rain down…

"That's it, we're finished!"

Silence…

No one in the bunker could offer any positive contributions to refute the claims of this statement. The dying flame of hope had been extinguished…

"Senator Phillipoussis, I believe you have just witnessed the end of Penusian civilisation!"

Senator Phillipoussis looked on, bewildered. The regret in his voice was clearly evident.

"I wish that I could offer some words of consolation in these dark times, but I am as powerless as you."

Governor Astran looked destroyed. He was a pale imitation of the strict, manipulative politician he once was; a king without his empire. His grey curly hair was dishevelled. As did his companions in the dark confines of the room, he wore a growth of stubble, gained from two shattering days in the claustrophobic confines of the protective bunker. The destruction that they had witnessed had been of the worst kind, indiscriminate and meaningless! It was an event that that was etched into their memories forever...

At that moment, the doors to the bunker opened. A figure dressed in a long, brown robe swept into the room.

Senator Phillipoussis recognised the man as Senator Varden, an ambassador of equivalent status in Penusian terms as his status on Coleshia. The Penusian senator wrinkled his nose in repugnance at the smell of stale breath and body odour that now filled the room and then swiftly glided over to the Penusian governor, an air of urgency in his stride.

"Governor, the protracted fall of debris from the Elysium has significantly eased off. Colonel Conran's forces have moved to the surface level. The recovery operation has begun."

"What is the situation at present?" asked the governor, negatively.

The senator paused, nervously trying to formulate the correct words in his head. Like the Penusian officials who gathered around him, he too wore a thick growth of stubble that made him look out of place in the well-maintained robe. It was a juxtaposition of images that could be likened to a homeless person wearing a smart suit.

"Come on, spit it out, man!" pleaded the impatient governor.

"It's not good, Governor. Huge structural damage has been caused to the settlement. Dead bodies are scattered everywhere. At this stage, the full extent of the damage is difficult to predict. It would also appear that the animals lucky enough to survive the storm have broken free of the enclosures!"

Governor Astran sighed wearily, and rubbed his hands over his face, in an attempt to fight off growing feelings of fatigue and exhaustion, gained from two days of ample worry and little sleep.

"Yes, we saw some of the stampede on the monitor here. Very well, proceed as planned. We must salvage whatever and whoever is left from this nightmare."

"Yes, Governor." Senator Varden bowed before hurrying from the room.

As the doors obligingly hissed shut behind the departing senator, Phillipoussis realised that even the nature of his mission had become rather insignificant compared to the current itinerary of Senator Varden. He was not yet at the stage of having to mop up an entire civilisation, but with the Carcinomas still very much in the back of his mind, he refrained from attempting to predict how long it might be before he too was faced with such responsibilities.

Governor Astran, feeling the effects of nausea, addressed Senator Phillipoussis, seemingly struggling to come to terms with the debilitating crisis that he had fought so hard to avoid on this planet.

"I am afraid your problems with hostile extraterrestrials has been somewhat overshadowed over the past two days. My God, what a *bloody* mess!"

"I understand, Governor," replied Phillipoussis, humbly. "The Coleshian people will help the Penusians in whatever way is deemed possible."

"Judging by your account of events at the Coleshian settlement, you are in no position to assist us. It appears that the Ark Project has entered its darkest phase…"

The convoy of vehicles slowly made its way over the scattered remains of the Penusian settlement, their huge rubber tyres struggling to gain leverage over the piles of rubble that had once been tall and proud structures. The six-wheeled monsters growled as they relentlessly negotiated the difficult terrain, occasionally pausing for the occupants inside to scan the tortured landscape. The electric engines furiously emitted a range of high-pitched wails, as they struggled to cope with the range of rubble and debris that ominously protruded in their path. Fires haphazardly lit up the area for miles around, where the debris stubbornly continued to burn. The vehicles came to a halt once again, the crescendo of their screeching engines dying down to little more than a dim hum.

Along the convoy of Alliance Mobile Transport Vehicles, partitions and openings appeared in the sides and roofs of their bulky shells. Armed troops poured out, adorned in full body armour. Many were carrying blast rifles and assorted projectiles, as they emerged, alert, cautiously finding footholds in the precarious terrain beneath their feet. Each also wore bulbous head protection in the form of a helmet that reflected the blinding rays of Penusia's furious day cycle.

At the front of the convoy stood a small, but stockily-built, soldier, scanning the horizon through his tele-lenses. Removing the eyepieces from his field of vision, his brown eyes fiercely followed the same path of observation, as if he didn't trust the magnified image of the telescopic equipment. It was hard to imagine any creature surviving this mess...

A deep scar adorned this soldier's left cheek, adding a fearsome perspective to crude features, contorting his face into a permanent grimace. Suddenly, his observations were interrupted.

"Colonel Conran?"

The man turned and barked his retort.

"What is it, Sergeant?"

"Sir, the first survivors have been discovered by Team A. Some are delirious, others just in a state of shock."

"Have you given them the news?"

"Yes, Sir."

"And their response was?"

"They refuse to believe it, Sir. They claim allegiance to Governor Astran and the Ark Project."

For a moment the Colonel digested this information. Reaching these people would be a tough task. Nodding, he replied:

"Sergeant, any man, woman or child who still has their head in the clouds, and refuses to accept the new order, will have to suffer the consequences."

"Which are, Sir?"

A twisted grin emerged on the colonel's face, the scar struggling to abide by the movement of his facial muscles.

"Shoot them!"

Sergeant Nakata left Colonel Conran with his thoughts. He distributed the colonel's orders around the armed force without question or doubt, as any man professing to be a soldier would have done. He had served under the colonel for a long time, and time had taught him to trust in his seemingly harsh conclusions of situations. He was a strong leader, and in these difficult times, the qualities of such an individual were imperative to restoring order.

For the greater good, tough decisions had to be made. With Penusia in a state of chaos, compassion was a secondary concern for a soldier. The new order would allow the human race to stride forward at a great pace. To breach the most obsolete parts of the galaxy, and allow humanity to stamp its authority on the next frontier. That was the rightful destiny of humankind.

Sergeant Nakata, like many others under the colonel's leadership had decided that the Penusian leadership's claims of having too little resources to guarantee survival in such an endeavour was simply an excuse for not taking the risk. The way that he and many like him saw things, the Ark Project had seen many risks undertaken. What difference would another risk make? It was so much more appealing than the constrictive 'holier than thou' policies of the Ark Project that had controlled the destiny of the human race for so long.

The Alliance was a fractured ideal. The Coleshians and Penusians were divided, had been for centuries; two governments, two planets, two races and now two ideologies. Penusia, in the eyes of Sergeant Nakata and others of a like mind, was a hellhole, a desert struggling to support the life that had been imposed upon its dry surface.

Throughout this miserable existence, the human race was constantly force fed reminders of a distant home planet that to many seemed more a work of legend than a part of humanity's historical past. Rec-

Chapter 29

reation was designed to tantalise people with a way of life that could no longer be fulfilled. Films, library files and museums were things to be seen not touched. Without even realising it, the hierarchy had loaded the gun with images of a life richer and more exciting than what they had. Personally – he would be glad to leave.

The sound of static on his communicator returned Sergeant Nakata to the real world.

"Sergeant, we have discovered some of the animal survivors – feline, big cats. What are your orders, Sir?"

It was time to bring down the old order. In time suffering would be replaced with glory.

"Shoot them. We may be glad of the food in the coming weeks…"

It penetrated the clear skies, moving with more control and poise than any of the debris that littered the atmosphere of Penusia. Unperturbed, the object swiftly began its descent to the planet's surface. A series of invisible radar shields prevented its detection from the ground, in the event of any machine still being in operation to perform such a task.

There was certainly minimal chance of being detected from space. The remaining vessel in orbit of Penusia, the Mirage, was currently more concerned with avoiding the wreckage of its twin ship, the small crew almost breaking their backs in working to achieve a safe distance from the hazardous atmosphere of the planet. The tiny, streamlined object that had successfully negotiated the perilous atmosphere closed in on a designated target.

The Infiltrator descended rapidly. Within its interior, General Miller skilfully guided the craft's controls, paying special heed to maintain a respectable distance from the remains of the Penusian settlement. Even when forced to view the devastation with his own eyes the horrifying sights that greeted him did not perplex the general.

Chapter 30

Project Date: Day 44 of Year 0405

The shuttle carefully navigated between the debris, cautiously swinging wide of sections of the destroyed, Elysium. Its precious cargo included Senator Phillipoussis, accompanied by his armed guard and Senator Varden, also accompanied by a modest armed force.

They began their ascent in silence, bewildered by the destruction that had occurred over the previous three days. Staring out into space, entire compartments and rooms could be seen that had once formed part of a mighty star cruiser… It was still hard to comprehend what had transpired as the shuttle climbed away from the destruction below.

"Senator Phillipoussis, as my opposite number, you must be able to appreciate the severity of our situation. At this time, neither I, nor the Penusian people can offer you assistance in your hour of need. I fear that this visit will prove to be no more than a repayment of the courtesy of your visit to Penusia. It will be some time before we can regain any control of the situation, if at all."

Even at a time of such disaster, interplanetary politics still managed to find its way into the conversation. From his chair opposite Senator Varden, Phillipoussis smiled weakly in response.

"I believe your problem somewhat outweighs ours. When your engineers managed to reboot the communication modules, I received some positive news. It would appear that we are close to a potential solution to our problems."

Senator Varden coldly received this information. It made his visit to the settlement on Coleshia all the more pointless and painful given his own planet's plight. His planet needed his services, and Governor Astran had expressed slight disdain at having to acknowledge interplanetary custom in the face of such a huge disaster. Penusia was crippled at this time. Pleasantries were rather low on the list of priorities. Nevertheless, he also recognised the need to maintain good relations with Coleshia, especially in Penusia's time of need. Patience had to be observed.

"What is your news?" enquired Senator Varden, dismissing his grievances, elbows resting on the arms of his chair, while his hands formed a peak.

"One of our scientific research teams has been working on a project that has neared completion. It will prove itself to be of invaluable worth in the forthcoming confrontation."

"And what is this project?"

Senator Phillipoussis smiled weakly at Senator Varden. He tapped his right temple with his index finger. It was a gesture that the Penusian ambassador found intensely patronising.

"Classified at this time, but it will be unveiled to you when it is unveiled to the Coleshian public tomorrow… It promises to be quite spectacular…"

"If you want me to be honest, Governor, I would strongly suggest that you reconsider this course of action."

Glen was trying very hard to dissuade the Coleshian leader. He had not responded well to the news of a public demonstration involving the Great White sharks, and he didn't appreciate the fact that his first one-to-one interaction with the Coleshian leader was in opposition to this request.

"Officer Davis, the only way for the people to have faith in this solution is for them to see with their own eyes that it can work. Your research with the Great White sharks has been kept largely anonymous for so long that many people know nothing of the Bodywave Project. We must demonstrate to the Coleshian citizens that the sharks are our allies in this hour of need. Although you are privy to a more detailed insight, many people still regard these fish as crude killers. What concerns you so? You have assured me that there will be no risk of being attacked if I am in possession of a PAD device. My entering the water with them will be the ultimate leap of faith, and it will help to dispel the public's fears. With the disaster on Penusia, it is *doubly* important that we offer the Coleshians some security on their own planet."

Glen noticed that Tasken's personality seemed very different without an audience. When conversing with an individual he seemed apprehensive, his eyes darted around the room nervously, and this did not fill Glen with any confidence at all.

"Governor, there is a potential health risk to yourself. No disrespect intended, but your age could cause potential problems."

"Officer Davis, do you honestly think that I have spent my years on this planet without ever putting on a diving suit?"

Glen didn't have time to form a reply...

"The Coleshian administration are not purely equipped to create ill-informed judgements and press buttons... I will have you know that I used to be a rather competent diver in my youth. That said, I do not intend to be entering deep water. The pool in the Animal Release Zone should be tame enough to cause little stress to my heart, which has received a clean bill of health in the last *seven* of my health reports, despite the advanced stage of my years..."

"Governor, I accept that, but I doubt that even you have entered the water with a Great White shark before. It will, to say the least, stimulate your adrenalin, and these fish are very sensitive to their surroundings. They do sense fear, Governor, and it would not be advisable for you to freeze up in their company."

For an instant his words almost pierced through the governor's psyche, the elderly man casting a brief glance down to his feet. Glen's last attempt to change the governor's mind had fallen flat on its face.

"Officer Davis, I appreciate your concerns, but we are talking about the survival of the Coleshian way of life, not one or two individuals. I feel that your concerns are worth overlooking in this instance. These tragic circumstances have given us all cause to think about many things, and I doubt that you are happy to be involving your Great White sharks in any of this, but circumstances have taken away the choice in this matter. We must all pursue tasks designed from necessity, not desire…"

Glen knew that it was futile to pursue this course of argument anymore. Nevertheless, he could not help reaching a profound conclusion:

This situation is getting worse by the hour… The last thing that the Bodywave Project needs is preferential attention from the Coleshian media. It is inviting trouble, especially as the project is being advertised as a weapon rather than a device for communication. We are turning the sharks into monsters!

General Miller moved stealthily amongst the barely recognisable remains of the Penusian settlement. While passing a huge concrete and steel overhang, something caught his attention. Closer inspection revealed the object to be a dead body. In the current circumstances, this was not an odd sight. The orange robe draped awkwardly over the rotund body. General Miller rifled through the pockets of the man, retrieving his identity tag.

STRAND, DOMINIC. No 483297. OCCUPATION: JOURNALIST – **PENUSIA'S PROJECTION**

What had drawn the general's attention had not been the sight of another dead human - there were hundreds scattered everywhere. It was the precise blast wound in the back of the deceased man's bald head, the fourth such injury he had seen. From experience, he knew that this type of precision required organisation, skill and discipline; the qualities gained from military training…

"Of course, we must consider the possibility of sabotage," interjected Senator Varden.

Senator Phillipoussis readjusted his position in his chair, his eyebrows raised in an arch of surprise.

"By stating that, I hope that you don't mean to insinuate that it was Coleshian in origin and design."

This form of verbal jousting had been continuing for almost an hour. Once again the Penusian ambassador attacked.

"Does it not strike you as strange that a vessel that has travelled for some two hundred years across the stars without malfunction should choose to explode when it is only partially operative? I do not see that our planet has anything to gain from such atrocity. Our operations have been crippled. With a current death toll of one hundred thousand, which is steadily rising each time that I consult the statistics, it also appears that we may never have the manpower to resurrect any semblance of a self-sufficient society again!"

"I can only offer my sympathies," replied Phillipoussis, humbly. "Once we have managed to curb our own problems, then Coleshians will be happy to co-operate with Penusia. I *also* see that Coleshia has nothing to gain from sabotaging your operations, seeing as we were relying on your assistance to overcome the threat of the Carcinomas. There are any number of possible explanations as to why the Elysium exploded. It could simply be a horrific accident. It is not uncommon for space debris to penetrate the hulls of vessels and cause severe damage to the sensitive areas of those spacecraft. With a minimal crew, it is a possibility that such damage could have been overlooked. So let's not jump to conclusions, Senator. We just don't know at this stage. The citizens of both planets will look for our governments to be strong in these circumstances, not paranoid and insecure."

Senator Varden, listening to Phillipoussis' words, had to admit defeat. The human populations on each planet were under threat. Both ecosystems were under threat. Was it just a tragic coincidence? Coleshia, however, still had time to avert disaster. Penusia was ruined, turned into a wasteland in just a few days. It would be difficult to resurrect the Ark Project in such circumstances.

Penusia was an open target for interplanetary politics, and Senator Varden did not like it one little bit...

Chapter 31

A profuse number of Coleshian eyes centred on one event. The news of the Carcinomas existence and the damage that they were causing to the planet had drawn a huge audience to this broadcast that had promised to shed some positive light on what was a very severe situation.

As the Coleshian administration had predicted, a general state of alarm had been raised throughout the settlement, and as Governor Tasken had stipulated, the leadership's response to the desperation of the people in this time was also swift. Only a few hours had been allowed for the Coleshian people to assimilate the shocking news before this bulletin had been broadcast, in an attempt to quell the people's fears.

Now every Coleshian eagerly watched, via a network of huge screens, the huge pool situated in the Animal Release Zone of the Aquatic Science Centre. Although the initial shots of the huge laboratory were filmed too far away for distinguishable details, the Coleshian people could distinguish the presence of High Council members, Aquatic Science Officers and of course the inevitable presence of the military, through the colour of their uniforms.

Senator Varden was among those people who formed a blurred pattern around the sides of the huge pool from behind the enforced safety measure of specially constructed barriers. He wore a bemused look on his face. Being privy to Coleshia's 'saviour', while his own planet sunk deeper into the abyss of chaos, did little to lighten his mood, even if Coleshia's support had been promised upon completion of the eradication of the Carcinomas. What good was that help now? Nevertheless, he could not hide his curiosity, but he did his best to mask this from Senator Phillipoussis who stood in close proximity to him.

The purple-robed figure of Governor Tasken shuffled awkwardly to a microphone, thoughtfully placed some four feet in front of a camera, one of many in the lab, which was broadcasting the events to the settlement. The tired governor cleared his throat in announcement of his intention to speak, his neurosis well disguised before sternly addressing the camera lens.

"Citizens of Coleshia, yesterday, I announced to you that the abnormality in Coleshian procedures that many of you had begun to notice, was as a result of an unpleasant discovery - h*ostile* alien life. Throughout every phase of the Ark Project, we have risen to every challenge, but now we are faced with a crisis that is not within our control… Suddenly, we discover that our new home has been put under threat by a sinister foe; an alien being that becomes violent and aggressive to any living creature that it encounters. In recent times it has also become clear that the settlement limits offer no safe haven to you, the Coleshian people, while this threat exists. Our technology has been too primitive to protect us from the Carcinomas. With the news of the disaster on Penusia, it now appears that the entire human race could be under threat.

As we are all aware, the Ark Project has entered its darkest phase. With hope, I can now present a solution in our bleakest hour. When the Ark Project began hundreds of years ago, it was with the intention of showing compassion and goodwill to our fellow life forms, to build a future for them as well as ourselves. This close interaction has led to the blossoming of a wonderful relationship with a species of creature that outlived the prehistoric reptiles that once dominated the home of our ancestors. A creature that once was so despised by humanity, as to be hunted to near extinction…"

He paused.

"Citizens of Coleshia, our hopes rest on the supreme predatory shoulders of the *Great White shark*!"

The cameras pivoted to the pool, as if in expectation of some dramatic occurrence. It was a comical sight. Nothing stirred near the surface. An orchestra of applause emerged from a meagre group of council members assembled amongst the audience. The pool remained still… The sharks remained elusive, aware of a heavy human presence on the surface; strange life forms that were not the individuals with whom they were familiar.

Throughout the settlement people were flummoxed. There seemed little to clap about. Nothing could be seen from the pool's surface. It remained quiet and still.

Senator Varden smirked slightly, and raised a quizzical eyebrow towards Senator Phillipoussis, who was standing some five yards away, with his armed guard forming a protective shield around a table, adorned with strange technological gadgets that Varden had not been acquainted with before. Somewhat curious as to their nature he began looking for clues in the laboratory. The use of these devices became clear, as Varden could make out what appeared to be identical instruments worn by two Science Officers. They were diving instruments!

Governor Tasken hastily continued.

"The Elasmobranch Team has spent many years interacting with these creatures. Their research and work with the release of sharks has provided them with vital information that has led to a number of discoveries about their behaviour and intelligence. These discoveries have culminated in the Bodywave Project; a revolutionary system of communication developed to bridge the gulf between humanity and the shark species. With the aid of this project, we can now utilise the predatory skills of the Great White shark, combined with the firepower of the Alliance Military Forces, to rid our home of the Carcinomas once and for all. These magnificent beasts will give us the edge in this struggle, and to prove this fact to *you*, the Coleshian people, as a symbol of our unity I will swim with the Great White sharks!"

Once again, applause rang around the huge lab. This sentiment was echoed in the settlement. The Coleshian High Council's propaganda campaign was working, as fading hopes once again became ignited.

Somehow the mathematical dilemma of the survival prospects of four Great White sharks against the masses of Carcinomas became lost in the furore of the occasion.

As the team approached the jetty, Governor Tasken lagged behind, escorted by his personal staff. The cameras captured this deliberate manoeuvre of pronounced visibility, tracking the governor's movements as his purple robe was removed, revealing a tight, black diving suit that had been pre-prepared for this public charade.

Glen Davis and Rhona Skallen adorned their domed diving helmets and climbed into the water, floating by the jetty to assist the governor in his entry. After detailed checks of the governor's equipment by Danny McCormick, the Coleshian leader was assisted in adorning the cumbersome instruments before being lowered into the water like a baby. Satisfied that the governor's suit was properly inflated, the party of three drifted out into the pool on the current created by the wave machine. The governor was nervously treading water, holding tight to the extended arms of his companions.

The Coleshian public watched, engrossed in the events taking place.

A voice resounded in Glen's ear. It was that of Mike from his cleverly concealed position out of the view of the cameras:

"Glen, they are three kilometres away. They've responded to your presence, approaching from opposite directions. Be careful, they are jumpy at all the activity on the surface."

"Acknowledged," replied Glen.

His right hand worked quickly over the keyboard on his keypad, while Rhona maintained a firm grip on Governor Tasken.

FRIENDS…

From the murk, three forms entered their field of vision. Cruising through the water like torpedoes, Cleopatra, Astra and Kauhulu approached from opposite directions, sharp and alert. Intermittently they passed the floating party, inquisitively.

The governor fidgeted nervously, somewhat alarmed by the fearsome appearance of these beautiful monsters, and the ease with which they negotiated an environment that was so alien to him. He remembered Glen's warning, and he had to concede that he felt rather intimidated at this stage of the proceedings. It was easy to see why Officer Davis had attributed so much predatory prowess to these creatures. Every ounce of their perfectly designed bodies looked unbelievably strong and capable of disabling a Carcinoma with ease.

"Glen, they're very wary," said Rhona.

"I know. They don't know the governor. I think it concerns them that there are three of us now... Governor, try to relax a little. They are accustomed to the presence of Rhona and myself usually. Remember, they are simply inquisitive!"

Governor Tasken flashed a concerned look at Glen through his helmet before nodding in compliance and silently steeling himself against the knots that were forming in his stomach. Each shark cruised by, keeping a respectful distance from the newcomer. Large, triangular fins sliced through the swell on the surface.

Transfixed, the Coleshian public watched the beautiful symmetry of each of the fish, as they glided near the surface, seemingly unbothered by the presence of the divers. The governor was right - perhaps the Coleshians did have a new ally.

Suddenly, the smaller, but more agile form of Poker Face burst into the scene. His swimming patterns were agitated and erratic. Mike's panicked voice reverberated through the earpieces of Glen and Rhona.

"Something's wrong with the governor's PAD device. My terminal readouts indicate a malfunction!"

Almost at that instant the water became deserted. The governor looked at Glen, alarmed.

"Am I in danger, why have they gone?"

"Nothing to worry about, Governor, a technical problem with the equipment. Okay, we are abandoning the demonstration. Let's get back to the jetty," said Glen, looking at Rhona, and speaking with unwavering composure.

Suddenly, Poker Face reappeared from the shadows at tremendous speed. He began to hunch his body, his back arching up and his pectoral fins protruding vertically beneath him. Increasing his speed, and protruding his upper jaws, the agitated beast circled the divers menacingly. The two scientists knew this to be unmistakably aggressive shark behaviour.

Glen and Rhona responded with urgency, while above the surface, the onlookers continued to watch, oblivious that any peculiarities were taking place. Glen glanced at his keypad. The VDU display showed one word - FOE…

Recognising that there might not be time to type a message to the startled beast Glen spoke quickly:

"Quickly, huddle around the governor, we'll form a protective circle around him. Perhaps Poker Face will calm down when he senses our PAD devices."

They formed a tight circle under the now frightened governor's arms, and began to paddle back to the jetty. Governor Tasken did not question their unusual actions. As they paddled on the surface, the dorsal fin of Poker Face continued to circle around them, with sinister purpose.

"It's not working, Danny, prepare the tranquilliser. We've got a situation here," said Glen, between breaths. He looked to the side of the pool to see Danny already loading a large weapon.

The actions of the Science Officer had not gone unnoticed by the crowds of people standing in his vicinity. People cast concerned looks in his direction. He had already spotted the dangerous shark behaviour, which had been confirmed by the huddling formation of the divers. Being one step ahead of the game had drawn a lot of attention in his direction, and a murmur went up around the large science lab.

In an instant it happened. Glen and Rhona felt a heavy impact, as Poker face's sharp snout wedged it's way between them, dismantling their protective circle. They each let out a cry of alarm, as the one tonne monster insistently continued to inspect the anonymous and helpless organism that was, Governor Tasken. By this point, Glen and Rhona had realised that a spooked Great White shark had outsmarted them. Simultaneously they reached for their HP-1 pistols, but it was too late…

The governor thrashed wildly, confronted with the realisation of one of his worst nightmares. He closed his eyes, as powerful jaws closed around his helpless form, and razor-sharp teeth tore through his diving suit. Almost as quickly as he felt the impact, the antagonised shark let go, and swam away, in a frenzy that was related in clear detail on the broadcast to the Coleshian public…

Where Poker Face had left an unmistakable impression, red clouds began to appear in the water - *blood*. Screams erupted around the room.

"Quickly," panicked Glen.

The two divers held the inert governor on the water's surface. Through the helmet they could see that he was severely wounded, a trickle of blood emanating from the side of his lips and dripping down his chin. With some haste, they dragged him back to the jetty, arms tightly locked around his limp body.

"Mike, get the medics!" screamed Rhona into her communicator.

As the three figures approached, people crowded around the jetty, arms extended, to lift the governor from the water. The medics were on the scene, almost instantly, carrying cases of assorted medicines. The shock was evident on the faces of all those present and all those who looked on via the huge screens situated throughout the settlement.

As it became increasingly obvious that the governor was badly injured, panic surged in waves amongst the crowds. Armed guards ran to the edge of the pool, and began firing their blast rifles blindly into its depths. In a flash, Danny had discarded the tranquilliser, and hurtled himself into the pack of troops, bundling as many to the ground as he could, mimicking the pattern of falling dominoes. What the cameras now saw was chaos; concerned and alarmed faces and the medics frantically trying to stop the governor bleeding, as his suit was cut away.

In the panic no one was paying attention to Security Officer Khaled, who was close to despair in his attempt to gain Senator Varden's attention, who himself wore an expression akin to a look of amusement at the chaos on show before him. At that point, one thought was running through the mind of Officer Khaled as he looked at the lifeless, torn body of Governor Tasken. Who would believe the communication that had just been relayed from Penusia?

And they said that lightning could not strike in the same place twice...

Chapter 32

PART 5: FEAR

Project Date: Day 48 of Year 0405

The Elasmobranch Team recollected the events from the previous two days. The irony was sickening. From being the potential 'saviour' of the human settlement on Coleshia, circumstances had cruelly inverted, so that now one of their most valued sharks had been responsible for the death of the most prominent human being in Coleshian society.

The public backlash was shattering. None of the team had been approached with regard to the events, but despite the absence of their input, judgements were being made by the public and the media. On debate programmes, High Council Statesmen and spin doctors wielded catchphrases as if they were weapons:

'The sharks are monsters, if the Carcinomas don't get us the sharks will...'

'How can we place our hopes on such unpredictable and volatile shoulders? It's insane...'

'You know, I thought that the threat came from outside the settlement, not from within it.'

The agonised viewing of these debates became more tortuous with each passing hour.

Rhona spoke forlornly, running her hands through her long brunette locks.

"Glen, you were right. The Ark Project has changed very little in human society. The prejudice has been there all along."

"All it took were the right conditions for that prejudice to arise," added Mike, with resignation in his voice.

"I don't understand it," interjected Danny. "That PAD device was working fine when I checked it."

"I can confirm that," added Mike. "All my systems were in the green, until moments before Poker Face attacked."

"There has *never* been a case of a PAD device malfunctioning like that before. They have always had a reputation for reliability," continued Danny.

"A malfunction, however, would account for Poker Face's aggressive behaviour," surmised Mike.

"Perhaps it was more than *just* an accident," said Rhona, defiantly.

Silence embraced them as they stared at her incredulously.

"What are you implying – that the governor was murdered?" Mike blurted out.

"Well, why not?"

"Why would anyone wish to do that?" asked Danny.

"Who knows? One thing, however, is certain. A lot of events that have never occurred before are forcing us into very new territory," she replied.

Glen wore a confused frown.

"If it was murder then that would imply that the late governor's PAD device was sabotaged… If that is the case then the authorities will look for someone who was close to the equipment."

Danny's thoughts were wholeheartedly defensive.

"Wait a minute, do you realise what you are saying? *I* was the last person to check that device, and it was working fine."

Glen put his arm out in front of Danny, in a gesture for him to calm down.

"You have to think carefully. Who else might have looked at the equipment – security guards maybe?"

Danny shook his head.

"Well, did anyone see you carry out the check?"

"No, not to my knowledge."

Anxious to change the course of the debate, Danny attempted to broaden the scope for suspicion.

"Mike, you said that the device was working on your systems-"

"Wait a minute, just hold on. I said that my systems were in the green just before the attack. Check the software for yourself if you don't believe me... I did *not* see you check the PAD device... There were hundreds of people in that lab for Christ's sake. The last thing that I am going to be doing at a time like that is observing the actions of someone who is supposed to know what they are doing."

Danny backed away from the group

"This is nuts... Are you accusing me of murder? Oh, that's great... Terrific... Your Honour, I believe that the foul deed was committed with a thousand pound fish... Well, that's not something you see every day..."

Rhona grabbed his shoulders.

"Calm down, we are not accusing you of anything, okay? As Mike said, there were hundreds of people in that lab. If it was murder, it could have been anyone. Anyway, what possible motivation could you have to inspire you to such action? We may not have known you for very long, but I am pretty sure that you would not be capable of this."

Despite her assurances she cast a wary glance at Mike and Glen.

How well do we really know this man? Could he really be capable of such a deed, if so why?

Trying to free herself from such thoughts, she continued:

"Just look at the situation. After a so-called 'malfunction', a frightened and aggressive Poker Face bites Governor Tasken. He dies from the resulting blood loss, not the nature of the wound itself. Perhaps a younger man with a stronger body would withstand such trauma, but for someone of the governor's age, such a wound would certainly invoke a fatal response. It's classic Great White shark behaviour; to investigate an object, by first bumping it with its nose, and then biting."

They all nodded their agreement.

"Almost simultaneously, the news arrives from Penusia. Governor Astran is murdered by a group of rebel Penusians who infiltrate the High Council, in some attempt to capitalise on their current state of chaos and seize power. Now take a step back from this mess. Problems have arisen in pairs. First, the discovery of the Carcinomas, followed by the explosion of the Elysium, mere days later."

Rhona paused to take a breath before completing her hypothesis, but her final words were stolen before she could utter them.

"Then, the almost simultaneous deaths of the leaders of the two planets," finished Glen. "I think that Rhona is right. There is a connection there somewhere, involving whom and what is anyone's guess. One thing's for sure. It's much bigger than *any* of us!"

"In what respect?" quizzed Mike.

"Assuming that the events are associated then it had to be someone with the relevant connections to make it happen."

"Okay, who?"

Mike's second question was very crucial to the entire theory, because it was the reason why the whole premise fell to pieces, and Glen knew this.

"Maybe it was someone in the High Council, either on Penusia or in our own administration!"

"Surely not, Glen! If that is true then it would be a conspiracy on an unimaginable scale."

"Mike's right, Glen," added Rhona, "not to mention the fact that such accusations could place those people voicing them in very high contempt!"

Glen continued his train of thought, ignoring Rhona's concerns.

"Let's break it down piece by piece. The discovery of the Carcinomas could have been used as a window of opportunity. While the Coleshians were busy worrying about this threat, the unexplained explosion of the Elysium took place, which as far as we know could well have been premeditated. So we have two unconnected events that sent waves of disruption throughout each planet."

"We already know this, Glen, where are you going with this?" Rhona's question was laced with impatience.

"Then we have the death of the two planetary leaders. Governor Astran, apparently murdered by desperate rebels in an attempt to seize control of Penusia, coinciding with the death of our own leader, who seemingly suffered at the receiving end of an agitated Great White shark, owing to equipment failure during a propaganda demonstration aimed at easing Coleshian fears over the Carcinomas."

Mike wore the look of someone who had totally lost the train of thought.

"But why does this point to a conspiracy, Glen?"

"At the very worst where can the accusations lead? We may never know if the Elysium were deliberately destroyed, probability would suggest 'yes' despite the absence of fact. Nevertheless, Governor Astran's murder could be viewed as opportunistic in the circumstances. Then the death of Governor Tasken; the tragic result of spiralling circumstances originating from the discovery of hostile alien life on this planet, where beyond accidental death, the only obvious perpetrators are a Great White shark and... us!"

The harsh truth connected with all of them... As a group they could all be blamed for the late governor's death. Glen continued his point.

"As it stands there are two obvious conclusions to be gained from this. Firstly, that Tasken's death was a tragic accident, which we could be accountable for on the grounds of negligence, and secondly, that we engineered his death, which implicates us for murder. Whether or not Danny was the last person to check the PAD device could become irrelevant."

Rhona's voice almost contained a hint of despair, as she realised the horrifying conclusions to which her initial hypothesis had led them...

"The only hope that we have is that the evidence is not tampered with in this investigation. All these events would serve to cover up the obvious truth... That the Carcinomas' discovery and the tragedy of the Elysium were simply decoys disguising a darker chain of events…Overthrowing the leaders of each planet! The real question should be why would someone be willing to risk the survival of the human race for such a gain? The truth is that we are in sinister hands, and we are powerless to do anything about it…"

For the first time in years, unaccustomed human emotions raised their ugly heads – fear and paranoia…

Chapter 33

Project Date: Day 50 of Year 0405

"I have called this meeting with you to discuss our *current* situation."

Governor Phillipoussis sat rigidly in the chair that had once held the form of the late Governor Tasken. The new governor was adorning the official purple robe of the Coleshian leadership. From the other side of the desk, in their grey uniforms, with their arms behind their backs stood the Elasmobranch Team.

The governor, immaculately presented, regarded each of them with eyes that bore little beyond anger. It seemed evident in his body language that he took on his latest appointment with a certain amount of reluctance. He had not envisaged that he would have replaced Governor Tasken so soon, or in such tragic circumstances. Glen had dreaded this moment. Phillipoussis' grief had been well documented in the media, and he suspected that the new Coleshian leader would not have much empathy for them now. The governor made his feelings on this matter plain.

"Before I go any further, I want you all to know that it does not please me to be seated in this office in these circumstances."

"No, Governor," replied Glen, feeling somewhat like the schoolboy awaiting punishment from the teacher.

Here it comes...

"The Coleshian High Council is facing a very precarious situation. I need not say how furious they are as well as the Coleshian civilians and myself at the governor's death. Following these events, I have to consider the validity of your sharks as a suitable saviour to the problems on this planet. Perhaps it is not wise to release one indiscriminate killer to eliminate another."

"The Great White sharks are not indiscriminate killers, Governor."

The defiance on the face of Rhona was evident.

"Well, if that is the case, why are we discussing yet another statistic, Miss Skallen? The demonstration was set up to prove that the Great White shark could be a suitable ally to the human race in its struggle against the alien threat. That demonstration failed miserably."

Governor Phillipoussis was in no mood to entertain compassion, and, consequently, the four science officers before him began to feel the burden of pressure.

"Perhaps the Great White sharks are a waste of our resources and time. I most certainly feel that the individual in question should be considered for extermination. He has demonstrated that he is too unpredictable."

"That's not fair."

"Isn't it? Perhaps you do not understand. From many sections of the settlement, there are cries for 'heads to roll'. Would you rather that your precious fish are blamed or yourselves?"

Enough was enough.

"Governor Phillipoussis, with all due respect, you can not hold us, or the sharks accountable for Governor Tasken's death. I expressed my concerns personally to the governor before-"

"*Be quiet*, Mr Davis," interrupted the new governor.

Glen could see where this was going, and despite himself, he could feel buttons being pushed. He clamped his jaw shut.

"If it were not imperative for the Coleshian settlement's survival, I would have you and your fish removed from the settlement and blasted into space! Your concerns are not important. What is important is that in the past two days, two planetary leaders have been murdered."

Glen picked up on the governor's words.

Murder – then it was sabotage. This could be trouble…

"We could do little to help the situation on Penusia, sadly... Nevertheless, I am sure that the late Governor Astran's replacement, Governor Varden, will work to the height of his capabilities to put Penusia back into a civilised order. Governor Tasken's death, *however*, was little short of bloodcurdling. It could have been avoided."

"Governor," pleaded Rhona, "his PAD device failed and, as a result, he was attacked. The shark was not to blame. He was only instinctively responding to what he thought was a hostile situation. We checked everything before the demonstration. The technology failed, not the sharks."

"The question, Miss Skallen, is why did it fail?"

Glen took over, recalling the manner in which the governor's diving equipment had been immediately removed from the scene before any examination could take place, forcing him to recollect the discussion that he had shared with his colleagues about the potential for sabotage.

"We cannot answer that at this stage. The late governor's diving suit was confiscated before we could examine the equipment for faults. All that we know is that his PAD device went off-line during the demonstration. This caused the shark to attack. An instinctive reactio-"

The new governor cut Glen off.

"Mr Davis, the Coleshian authorities are handling this investigation. If there were any 'faults' in the PAD device, then they will be found."

Already it appeared as if the governor was alluding to their guilt...

"Governor, doesn't it strike you as somewhat dubious that such a reliable piece of technology should malfunction at such a critical time? If you check the history of the PAD device, you will see that it has an unblemished record with regard to malfunctions. Not *even* one while in active service!" Not to mention the fact that Governor Astran *was* murdered, almost simultaneously. It's a rather strange coincidence!"

The trace of sarcasm was evident in Glen's final statement.

"Mr Davis, be careful what you are insinuating. An operation on this scale would take the involvement of senior staff, and making allegations against Council members is a serious business, especially if you have no proof."

"I am implying nothing," Glen replied, forcefully. "However, I find it strange that in a time that is supposed to be remembered for being compassionate to all living beings, that the compassion can be forgotten to satiate human ignorance."

Governor Phillipoussis laughed out loud.

"Mr Davis, I find it highly unlikely that your sharks hold any political viewpoints on these matters. If, as you are *not* suggesting, there is a conspiracy wrapped up in all this, I can assure you that fingers will not be pointed on an interplanetary level. The events, although equally tragic, are unrelated I'm sure. There is no evidence to prove any of what you are implying. What I am able to guarantee, however, is this. That in the event of sabotage being diagnosed as the cause of Governor Tasken's death, you may find yourselves being asked one or two exacting questions!"

The four science officers looked at each other.

"That is *ludicrous*," cried Glen.

"Is it? See how it looks from an outsider's point of view. The animals that you work with are being assigned to almost certain death against the Carcinomas. Admittedly, Mr Davis, you proposed the idea, but in the circumstances, and I sympathise, you had no choice. Nevertheless, it provides you with a motive for sabotaging the demonstration. If the Bodywave Project proved ineffective then the sharks would not be utilised in a defence initiative, and thus their lives would be preserved from almost certain death. You make no secret of your affection for these animals, so that adds plausibility to the claim!"

Glen became angry, his face turning a shade of red in frustration.

"And a conspiracy on a higher level would *also* have a motive; for example – power!"

Governor Phillipoussis' features remained unchanged, as if they had been etched in rock. Glen was facing a brick wall!

"Mr Davis, let's pretend that your last comment remained unspoken. I have done some checking in your data banks and you have had a rather turbulent life. I see that your father died tragically when you were six, ironically enough, in the very room where you do most of your research, the Animal Release Zone. Perhaps you have enough motive to exact revenge on the people who allowed your father to die? What better way to make this point than engineer the grisly death of Governor Tasken before the very eyes of Coleshian society?"

Glen was unable to respond, paralysed in amazement. Each counter blow to the governor's claims resulted in the development of fresh wounds. The governor continued to hack away at Glen's mind.

"Of course, it is understandable. With no mother to care for you, confined to the fostering facilities that the settlement offers, you must have had a lot on your mind. Very difficult to deal with at such a tender age."

Glen felt something snap inside him. The buttons had been pressed, striking at the sensitive core of his emotional psyche.

"How dare you, you son of a…"

He rushed forward, arms extended in a torrent of rage. Suddenly, six pairs of arms had grabbed him around the waist and arms.

"Glen, calm down!" yelled Mike.

"Think about it," said Danny in his ear. "It is what he wants you to do. Think it through, man. Don't let him get to you."

Governor Phillipoussis rose from his chair, unmoved by these events.

"Of course, there is also the possibility that more personnel could have been involved in taking the late governor's life."

All of the team stared at the governor. Glen ceased struggling.

"As Mr Davis is the commanding officer, he has the final say in everything, but you are all open-minded people, capable of thinking for yourselves. Maybe you were all in it to save your beloved pets from being killed in battle."

The governor stared cruelly at Danny, who stared back, dumbfounded.

"Exemplified by you, Mr MrCormick."

Beads of sweat adorned Danny's dark-skinned forehead, while

Phillipoussis continued.

"As the Safety Officer in the team, you checked the equipment before it was used. You, Sir, risked the lives of a dozen troops, reacting to their opening fire as you did. None of them was wearing a PAD device. They could have been seriously injured. Surely this impetuous action is not the desired conduct of a safety officer observing the requirements of his duties?"

"Governor," retorted Danny, angrily. "The troops were firing on the sharks. I didn't want one of them to get shot, especially considering how important they are to us…"

The fact was that the governor had every reason to believe that they had committed the crime… As he had so efficiently noted they had the motive, but somehow Glen felt that there was more to this meeting than just threats…

"Danny, cool it," interrupted Glen. "Okay, we get your point. What do you want?"

Governor Phillipoussis breathed deeply and stared at the ceiling, before proclaiming:

"*Eureka!*"

He addressed the team again.

"The people are afraid. Just yesterday, two more Carcinomas were killed entering the settlement limits, with the loss of twenty more troops. Time is ticking away. I want your team to continue your operation, and prepare the sharks for the battle, under surveillance of course, and I do not want any of you to speak publicly about what happened. There must be no ripples in the water. The last thing that any of you need right now is undue attention."

Glen felt the thickness of the irony as he recalled expressing the same feeling for the need for confidentiality to the man who now lay dead in the morgue. What a tragic way in which to be proven right.

"If the Coleshian authorities discover anything during their investigation, I'm sure that you will be contacted in due course. Now go home, and think about your priorities as citizens of the Ark Project. You had better start praying that you can rectify this mess!"

Chapter 33

With that, the governor's armed guard entered the room, and escorted the Elasmobranch Team out of the governor's office.

Upon reflection, it was clear that Governor Phillipoussis was not making hollow threats. If blame was to be allocated for Governor Tasken's death they were obvious culprits. Their only course of action was to maintain their preparations for the planned offensive against the Carcinomas in the hope of the truth coming to the surface. It was apparent, however, that they were now quite firmly in the pocket of Governor Phillipoussis, and they were powerless to do anything about it.

"Well, what do we do now?" quizzed Mike.

"You heard the man. Do your jobs. If we deliver the goods, then perhaps the authorities will look more favourably upon us," replied Danny.

"Where are you going?" said Rhona, in frustration, as Glen stormed down the corridor.

Before answering, his balled fist thumped the wall.

"Well, you heard the man, Rhona. I'm going to assess my priorities…"

With that, Glen disappeared around the corner leaving his colleagues to ponder what exactly he viewed his priorities as being…

Chapter 34

First there was anger, adrenalin pulsing through his body, with no obvious target at which to exert his frustrations.

Space Trauma...

It had been years since anyone had uttered those words to him. Before today the last person had been his counsellor during one of their meetings... He had been three years old when his mother finally succumbed to that horrific illness... He barely knew who she was...

From the other side of the glass Glen had mentally recorded every detail of that visit. What had struck the young child most profoundly was the tender way in which his father had held her frail hand. It was one of the few occasions that he had seen his father cry, tears that unstoppably flowed as she stared at his face with a lack of recognition, the symptoms of the trauma having seized control over her body and mind. Glen would have liked to have remembered his mother as having endured a peaceful end to her life, but Space Trauma was a violent illness. When the fit began, her body wracked in agony, her arms flailed throwing Glen's father to the white, polished tiled floor of the room - the cries of anguish could be heard through the thick glass. Glen couldn't recall her face clearly - her hair and the soft pillows that supported her head had masked her features.

As Glen was led away from the window fear and confusion clouded his young mind, the symphony of her anguish haunting his ears... It was not long after that day that her body and mind gave up the struggle for life... As time dragged by, painfully, slowly, anger was replaced with a more inflamed emotion - guilt...

Chapter 34

Is it because of what I have done to the sharks, the governor's death, or because she thought I was doing the wrong thing?

It returned in powerful waves, growing in intensity, and yet he failed to isolate its source. Right now there seemed to be so many explanations as to why it wracked him so. As a direct consequence of his idea, the Ark Project was poised to lose a unique species of creature, the Great White shark, in defending another endangered species, the human race. Glen tried very hard to ignore the fact that he might have inadvertently ignited a hate campaign against the creatures that he loved so much. If this wasn't serious enough, the death of the Coleshian leader posed a more complex mental battle.

With laboured movements he made his way to a cabinet tucked away in the corner of his living quarters. Opening a blue, panelled door, he retrieved a pyramid-shaped bottle that was rarely given the opportunity to escape the confines of the blandly constructed, slender unit. He poured some of the brown, transparent liquid into a small glass, and lazily fell into the padded sofa that was tucked neatly into another corner of the living room.

It just didn't make any sense… Coincidence was too nice a word to describe the recent events that had resulted in the deaths of two planetary leaders on an almost simultaneous timescale. Sabotage seemed far more appropriate, but who was implicated?

Glen sipped his drink thoughtfully, savouring the taste of the artificial whisky. The more he thought about it the more it seemed less likely that one of his team could have instigated this tragedy. When Governor Phillipoussis threatened Danny, it was a strong suggestion that the Coleshian authorities did not suspect one individual for the death… Despite everything that had transpired, he found it very hard to believe that one of his friends could ever have found it in their soul to engineer such a tragedy. He knew from his own grounded sense of reality that this was impossible, despite the wavering finger of accusation from the Coleshian administration.

The events of recent weeks had begun to exact their price on a mental level. He felt exhausted, but not surprisingly sleep evaded him.

Power!

The Ark Project may have cured certain human frailties, but corruption may not have been one of them. Phillipoussis was a man who liked to flaunt his position, striding around with the exaggerated decoration of an armed escort. Perhaps he was involved. If he were responsible he would have an ideal scapegoat - them! While they were under his control they would be able to do nothing to refute the charges of murder… But that too would be most unlikely. Firstly, because he was universally recognised as a trusted friend of the late governor, and if he were motivated by power, it would be too obvious a method of disposing of his mentor… The alternative reason for Phillipoussis' intimidation tactics could be far nobler, and this was the more likely of the two scenarios. Perhaps in his own mind he was doing what he believed to be right for the Coleshian people, ensuring that the mission for eradicating the Carcinomas from the ocean using their sharks was completed regardless of other circumstances.

Maybe Glen was climbing the wrong tree altogether. Perhaps he was being paranoid… Perhaps the Ark Project was the swan song of the human race. Maybe it was just a strange mixture of coincidences, and humanity was doomed to extinction, after relying on the support of technology for too long, just a tiny blemish in the history of the universe. Perhaps the suspicion was simply a reluctant response from a species that refused to accept that the cruel nature of survival had inflicted defeat upon it.

Maybe the Coleshian authorities would find some answers, or maybe, as Phillipoussis had rather bluntly threatened, their findings would conveniently point to members of the Elasmobranch Team. But no! It was just too difficult to accept that coincidence had caused so much damage to an entire culture. Perhaps Glen was fishing in the wrong direction. If the powers involved were strong enough to cause such devastation, then fixing the evidence was easily within their capabilities.

Then a thought entered his mind.

Organisation! That is what the culprit(s) would need. That was the key. Precision. The man at the conference – General Miller! He had close involvement with capturing a specimen of the Carcinoma, and ever since that day he had been conspicuous by his absence. Perhaps the capture of a specimen was his way of assessing the threat for himself, before instigating other plans. It was since his departure from the planet that things had been going disastrously wrong.

As he began to think about the possibilities it all made sense. Little was known about the mysterious military man, but Glen knew that certain assumptions fell well within the realms of credibility. The general had access to the technology to blow up the Elysium. A man with that much power could also manufacture the death of Governor Tasken.

Glen recalled how sceptical the general had been to his idea, opposing his suggestion to implement the sharks in a defence initiative. Could this have been his way of trying to obscure the shark's involvement, to prevent the threat from the Carcinoma being neutralised, but why? And why cause such havoc on Penusia?

Glen hopelessly found himself clutching at straws, once again…

A knock resounded. Could it be the Coleshian authorities with more questions?

Through a disorientating haze generated by the artificial whisky, Glen groggily made his way to his door, from where the knocking sound originated. Pressing a button on the wall, the door slid back…

"Rhona!"

"Hello, Glen."

Her clothes were of a casual nature; a collection of shades of blue, but Glen couldn't help noticing that she looked astounding. It was an annoying habit that she had of assuming natural beauty regardless of her attire. Annoying to Glen because he always succumbed to it. Her long brunette locks were tied back in a ponytail, enhancing the ease with which Glen's eyes greeted the beauty of her angelic face.

Her brown eyes stared at him, full of life, sparkling in a manner that he knew his own tired and weary visual aids could never mimic.

In her right hand, she carried a long, cylindrical object wrapped carefully in thin white paper.

"I've brought some wine. We were worried that you might do something silly. You looked really upset today."

"Glen, Mike told me about your past."

She waited for a reaction.

Glen frowned, and staring into his glass replied:

"So now you understand why I am... so distant... Funny how circumstance can change so much of your expectations of the people that you meet later in life."

"Understandable in the circumstances."

Her attentiveness to what he was saying indicated that she was concerned about the way he felt. It was an expression that he had never seen imprinted on the face of a woman who had been such a big part of his life before. Her sincerity was extremely touching, and not offensive to his machismo.

The level of the conversation changed...

"It's hard to explain... When my father died, I had nothing. I felt as if I no longer had any identity. Growing up on your own can be awkward, to say the least. I went through life like a ball in a pinball game, randomly rebounding off obstacles in my path. There was no guidance, no one to turn to for advice, just the wardens at the fostering facility over in the main complex."

"Couldn't they help?"

"Not really... They seemed to show the same passive love for everyone in their care. The whole set-up was obviously a fake. Just being at school made it obvious. While I sat in the corner, insecure and lonely, they would be chattering away about the things that they had done with their parents, and what their parents had given them... The saddest thing of all is that as I got older, the things that I was hearing became more alien to me. I didn't even understand what they were talking about!"

For a moment, silence transpired between the two of them, before

Rhona gently laid another question onto Glen. At last she was finally beginning to find the man inside the enigma.

"How did you discover the sharks?"

Glen's eyebrows raised in response and a look of colour washed across his face at the thought of the sharks.

"During the early stages of Phase Four, the school that I was attending sent us on a field trip. Due to the infancy of the Animal Release Procedures many species were still aboard the star cruisers awaiting transfer to the Animal Release Zone. We were escorted around the huge vessel, watching several aquatic forms of life. Many species we couldn't see, because their enclosures were so huge and the animals couldn't be coaxed to the viewing ports, but in some cases the wardens of the enclosures managed to entice the animals closer.

Great White sharks were among the more co-operative species, mainly because of the consistent use of PAD devices at that time. They were not apprehensive. As they cruised before our eyes, most of my classmates recoiled, consoled by the teachers, but not me… I moved right up to the glass, and waited for them to come close. I just couldn't get enough of them."

Glen's voice was full of passion as he continued.

"I remember a surreal moment when a diver appeared at the viewing port, perfectly buoyant and unperturbed by the company that he was keeping. He waved to me from the other side of the glass, seemingly careless of the prowling Great Whites. At that point I realised that this was my future. I wanted to know everything about these beasts. Why their teeth were so big, why they themselves were bigger than many other fish, but most importantly, I wanted to know how a human being could be so relaxed in their environment, and how the people on the outside looking in could be so afraid? I wanted to understand them. So when it came to my chosen sector of duties I decided to study the sharks. I wanted to be that diver in the water!"

Glen paused to take a sip of his drink. It felt good talking to Rhona.

"It gave me some focus and taught me that life was about much more than my own circumstances. An animal that demanding of my attention had to be there for a reason… Have you ever heard of Isaac Slater, Rhona?"

Rhona had to admit that the wine was beginning to obscure the clarity of her mental archives.

"The name is familiar, but…"

Glen waved a hand in a dismissive manner before expanding on his question.

"He was one of the pioneers of shark research in the Ark Project before the days of the Eden Treaty. More importantly he was a shining example of human courage!"

"Why is he so significant?"

"Centuries ago, Isaac Slater was a fisherman on our home planet. He used to fish with a crude weapon and primitive breathing apparatus – a snorkel. I believe people in his profession were called 'spear fishermen'."

"I remember reading about them years ago. It was an occupation not without danger from what I understood."

"That's right, Rhona. Isaac was significant because he caught the sharp end of the danger! A six-meter Great White shark appeared while he was in ten metres of water. Those were the days before PAD devices and true to the form of many interactions between humanity and Great Whites, he was attacked. The shark took his right arm and his left leg before deciding that he didn't like the taste. Isaac floated on the surface for several minutes before being spotted by a passing vehicle – a boat I believe."

"Did he survive?"

"Oh, yes. It was *after* his attack that he became involved in shark research, and he was one of the most proactive researchers around. Despite requiring the use of primitive artificial limbs for mobility, he saw through the anger of his attack. The rest of his active life was spent taking people on expeditions around the oceans searching for the Great White shark, trying to unlock the secrets of their behaviour. That was courage, Rhona. The man barely escaped with his life, and the Great White shark had taken much of it away from him, but he used his experiences to a positive end. Without him, little would have been known about these fish and we certainly would have found it impossible to include them in the Ark Project!"

"So you thought that if someone like Isaac could have their life shattered and turn it around you could as well?"

"That's exactly the point. Isaac was a mature man when he fought against his demons. I was very young – impressionable, but I am grateful that I had the opportunity to effect a change. In the shark's world, all humanity's problems make no sense, at least that was true until the Bodywave Project was initiated. It was like the greatest release I could ever have. What had gone before made no difference to the present. Working with the sharks, I regained some of my identity. I love getting to know them, their personalities. It allows me to feel as if I have a relationship that is my own. Sharks are so misunderstood that most people don't believe that one shark can behave differently from another."

"What about your father?" asked Rhona, delicately.

His eyes became glazed and his concentration drifted before he answered.

"At first it was difficult. Do you know, my counsellor told me to leave the Aquatic Science Centre, to build a life in the main settlement? It was unthinkable to me. So I learned to rationalise the situation."

"How? Working where your father died must have been terrible."

"It came down to a simple choice. I could run away, and live in the main complex, while losing the one thing in my life that made any sense… Or I could carry on working with the sharks. Watching Coleshia's environment grow, it was satisfying to have been part of it. Working in the Animal Release Zone allowed me to feel that my father hadn't died for nothing, that at least his efforts had not been a waste of time."

There was a brief silence for a moment before Rhona said the only thing that came to her mind.

"Your father would have been proud of you…"

Glen smiled, staring into his glass of wine. It was more satisfying to hear those words from her, not some therapist who said it purely through compulsion.

"I like to think so."

Looking up he stared into her eyes.

"What about you?" Glen enquired.

Rhona thought for a moment, pleased that an interest in the past of another had been reciprocated.

"When I was young my mother used to tell me not to waste the time that I had… She used to come home to the living quarters every day depressed and unfulfilled. At the time I never understood. One day she told me that working in Coleshian Administration had never satisfied her, and that if I was to find happiness in later life, to be honest and pursue my dreams."

"Sharks?"

Rhona nodded before continuing:

"One of the modules that I studied at school focused on aquatic predators. I remember being horrified at the way in which sharks were used and slaughtered… It was so sad, so brutal. Nothing I had seen had ever touched me in such a profound way. So I followed my mother's advice and took my Aquatic Science Centre exams in shark biology. Not long after that I graduated. I figured that perhaps the most fulfilling experience this life could offer me would be to help misunderstood species to settle into a new home… It is also quite exciting too…"

Glen smiled warmly at her, taking in the smooth contours of her face.

"You never talk about your parents… Do you mind me asking where they are?"

She smiled before placing her stare firmly in her half-empty glass.

"Departed…"

"I'm sorry, I didn't mean to pry…"

"No, its okay. It was some years ago… My father was a member of the High Council. He never figured in many of the big debates, he sat behind the scenes, pulling the strings at the top of the administration… That was how he met my mother, while in communication with her admin department. He died very peacefully when I was twenty. Full of grief and at a loose end my mother lost the will to live when she could see that I was on track… I guess she felt redundant… A couple of years later she passed away…"

In all this time Glen had not known about her parents.

Perhaps this is why she tries to understand…

"What about companionship? Do you have any affections for anyone?"

She stared him squarely in the face.

"Yes, there is someone."

Glen couldn't help himself, and blurted out the inevitable question:

"Who?"

Rhona giggled at him.

"What interest is it of yours?"

"Well, I er…"

"It could be someone you know."

Attempting to read her features, his lack of experience could not tell him whether she was toying with him or telling him something. There was silence for a moment, before Glen refilled their glasses with wine. By this stage he was feeling rather inebriated.

Just say something…

"You were right, involving the Great Whites in this mess is possibly the worst thing that I could have done."

"No – you did the right thing."

"All that I have done is jeopardise my friends, and succeed in creating prejudice against the sharks."

She saw the pained expression on his face, and then she realised. His decision to use the Great White sharks had not been an easy one. It was clear to her now that Glen weighed the value of a shark's life equally to that of a human being. Mike was quite obviously a good judge of his friend's character.

"Funny, isn't it," Glen said, with a false smile on his face.

"What?"

"Human nature killed our leaders. Human nature was responsible for the explosion of the Elysium, I'm certain of it. Sharks are not the monsters, the human race are the monsters!"

Silence again…

"We don't talk like this normally, do we?"

"In what respect?"

"Well, you know, about us…"

Glen shook his head, staring into Rhona's dark brown eyes, wishing that he could disappear into the depths of her dark orbs. At the moment they offered comfort in a world that dealt out so much pain.

Then it happened.

First a kiss…

Quickly, they pulled away from each other, then hesitantly their lips joined again, and the chaos that surrounded their lives was dissolved by new emotions… Right now, the world didn't matter…

Chapter 35

Darkness encroached upon Penusia's horizon, smothering the landscape. The still of the night was punctuated by the call of a distressed animal. It howled in the distance, calling to any living being that cared to listen. There was no response from the crippled planet.

The settlement that had once been a bustling centre of activity was now a scattered collection of human relics, smashed and distorted beyond repair. Huge twisted lumps of metal that had not been consumed in Penusia's blistering atmosphere still smouldered. Once they had been part of an intergalactic life support system. Now redundant of that responsibility, they served as the tombstones of a mass grave that had all but consumed life on Penusia. Dead bodies had been left where they had fallen, and the effect of exposure to the elements was beginning to take its toll.

Amongst the wreckage of the Penusian settlement, General Miller hid amid the remains of a collapsed building, trying extremely hard to ignore the smell that was beginning to permeate the air. His nostrils flared, attempting to draw the oxygen from the rankness of smoke and decay.

The Penusian Administration Centre miraculously rose from the wreckage, almost completely unscathed from the fiery deluge, and among the many lit windows, dim light emitted from the governor's quarters. As the general patiently waited, small teams of soldiers entered the largely deserted area, clearly displayed before him.

Dressed in dark uniforms to shield them against the night, the two groups of half a dozen troops swiftly wound their way through the remains, until they stood on opposite sides of the entrance door.

After brief, silent signals that defeated the focus of the general's vision, ten of the troops entered the huge building, and from the open doorway there was a brief flash. The two soldiers guarding the entrance scanned the horizon, in a deliberately cautious manner. Blast rifles! From his well-concealed position, General Miller continued to watch. Through the windows flashes could be seen in sweeping patterns across the building, dazzling, even against the aura of the dimly lit rooms.

Some time passed and the flashes could still be seen in sporadic bursts as the troops double-checked the structure before a six-wheeled Transport Vehicle pulled up in front of the building. A small, stockily-built man emerged wearing the uniform of an Alliance Colonel.

As the general struggled to see through the darkness, he made out a strange robe that covered the man's back, and formed a peak around his head. Squinting through the blackness, he deciphered the nature of the golden covering - lion fur! On the man's head was the skull of the dead feline. This garment spoke a thousand intentions, none of which were pleasant on the back of the apparent massacre of what remained of the Penusian High Council. The man entered the building.

Stealthily, General Miller began the careful process of picking his way through the treacherous terrain. Most buildings had more that one entrance. He set about finding the alternative way into this one. He drew his blast pistol, fully aware of his own responsibilities… He *had* to reach the governor's quarters…

Governor Varden stared at the ceiling. He concentrated intently on the elaborate patterns that formed hypnotic shapes in a blaze of colour. He had finally achieved his ambition; his dream. All of his life he had loyally worked towards one goal - to be the governor of his home settlement. The tragic circumstances in which he had achieved the pinnacle of his ambition gave him no satisfaction. He had managed it by default at the expense of the human population of Penusia, and he couldn't help feeling that he had been cheated.

He looked to his left and saw the sleeping form of Claire. She snored gently as she lay on her back, the duvet rising and falling in time with her breathing. At least someone could sleep… Now his dreams and plans were destroyed. He was the governor of a planet with no purpose, the population were all dead, and the chances for long-term survival had been all but destroyed.

Suddenly the door to his quarters slid open. Governor Varden sat up in alarm, squinting at the silhouetted figure in the doorway. A number of questions came to his mind, but a flash and the sudden convulsions of his companion halted them all. Shock waves rippled down her body as life reluctantly left her.

The heat of the impact singed the governor, and he recoiled in pain. Before he had time to react to the cold-blooded murder of his partner, the aim of the blast pistol was altered to a new trajectory, and Governor Varden found eternal sleep…

Chapter 36

General Miller sat patiently at the controls of his shuttle. After hours of searching the communication frequencies, he discovered the channel that had been the focus of his examination.

A deep, male voice broke the silence occasionally interspersed with static interference.

"All teams prepare for take-off. Maintain radio silence throughout the duration of our journey to the ASV Utopia."

It was several minutes before four military shuttles left Penusia's orbit. Manoeuvring through the debris with extreme caution, they set a course for Coleshia.

Some two hours passed before General Miller engaged the engines of his craft. Once again, with the powerful stealth instrumentation initiated, he carefully navigated through the debris that had concealed his location, before adopting coordinates almost identical to the small convoy that had preceded his ship...

"Colonel, we are approaching the A.S.V. Utopia, Sir."

"Very good, open the communication channels. Get their attention before we feel obliged to knock."

On the bridge of the leading shuttle, Colonel Conran sat in the captain's chair.

At last, humanity will be free of the shackles of the Ark Project. People may think that I am a terrorist now, but history will recognise me as a hero – the unrecognised saviour of the human race.

The skin that had once so beautifully complemented a lioness, now added to the fearsome appearance of the colonel, the scar on his cheek standing out in shades of crimson.

The Communications Officer carried out the command.

"ASV Utopia, this is the Military Personnel Shuttle, Mantis, do you copy?"

There was a static pause before a response was received.

"Acknowledged, Mantis, what is the purpose of your presence in the area?"

"The Penusian United Front is ordering the remaining crew of the Utopia to stand down from their stations and to prepare to be boarded."

Silence…

"Negative, Mantis. Our orders are to await instructions from our commanding officer."

"Crew of the ASV Utopia," the Officer reiterated, with a greater depth of command, "stand down from your stations and prepare to be boarded. We are armed and will destroy the Utopia, if necessary. We know that your defences are limited. If you do not wish to end up like the Elysium, you will comply with our demands."

Nearly a minute passed, a minute of escalating tension that could be felt throughout the bridge of the shuttle, before an answer was offered.

"Acknowledged, Mantis, you may enter on docking bay five."

Colonel Conran grinned.

So far, everything is proceeding as planned. If the Coleshian people are sensible, then further suffering will be averted. Now we shall see how precious human survival is to the Coleshian authorities. We will test the very fabric of the Ark Project and then humanity will see that our destiny lies beyond the Quaker solar system… They will see, they will see…

The shuttles landed in an organised formation in the huge docking bay.

"Release the troops," ordered the colonel.

On each of the shuttles, huge cargo doors opened. Row upon row of armed soldiers poured from the interior, armour clattering noisily with each purposeful step. Their weapons shone in the well-lit docking bay, loaded with lethal intent. In liberally-sized teams they spread out into different sectors of the huge vessel.

The process of assuming command of this monstrous ship had begun. The sound of blast rifle fire echoed throughout the gigantic docking bay as the intruders discovered a pocket of individuals from the maintenance crew...

In the pandemonium that followed, no one noticed the undetectable sleek form of the Infiltrator approaching the Utopia, with a purpose of its own design...

Chapter 37

Project Date: Day 51 of Year 0405

It had been a race against time, a race that the Penusian United Front had efficiently won. By the time the broadcast was made, the Utopia was no longer under Coleshian control. Despite an ill-fated attempt by her maintenance crew to alert the authorities as to what was happening, the first official transmission by the United Front was the definitive moment when the deep blue planet became aware of any disturbance on the gargantuan spacecraft.

Governor Phillipoussis watched the determined face that glared at him from the screen in the confines of his office. He wondered if General Miller had been apprehended or killed... Time would tell... The face that occupied his screen now was definitely not that of General Miller, but the scarred, disturbed visage of Colonel Conran, callously framed by the head and fur of the dead lioness.

He was a fearsome sight; where the lower jaw of the deceased feline should have been, there was the fierce stare of the colonel's brown eyes. Beneath that he wore a healthy growth of stubble that failed to cover the scar tissue on his cheek. The upper fangs of the disgraced creature hung down upon his forehead, the eye sockets closed in an expression, which suggested that the big cat had suffered extreme pain before dying.

"I am Colonel Conran, leader of Penusia's United Front. I order you to open *all* communication channels. What I have to say is relevant to every living being on that excuse of a planet that you call home. If you fail to comply, my troops will have no qualms about destroying the Utopia from where we now confer with you."

"You leave me little choice," replied the Coleshian governor, obediently.

A moment later, internal communications had been interrupted, and every loudspeaker and video monitor was flooded with the presence of the colonel.

"People of Coleshia, I am Colonel Conran, leader of Penusia's United Front. No doubt, by now you are all aware of the devastation that has been caused to our planet. Penusia is no more than a wasteland. Arising from a basic need for survival, I have taken control of what remains of her armed forces, and anyone else who has managed to survive this tragedy. Governor Varden is dead. The Penusian High Council is no more. My troops and I are the *only* survivors! That is why we are aboard the ASV Utopia. Changes in our circumstances have also given way to a change in priorities. We, the United Front, have come to your planet to inform you of these changes…

For centuries the human race has conformed to the regulations, or perhaps I should say, *restrictions* of the Ark Project. Everything that has been achieved has been done with a consideration for the other forms of life that accompanied us on the long journey from our distant home planet – Earth. Times change, and with that change we must accept that the objectives that are important in our lives also change. For a time, the Ark Project served us well. Now that the final steps have been made, it is time to strive towards a new goal – survival!

The human race does not belong in this solar system, struggling to maintain the relics of an existence that belonged to a planet that was dying when we deserted her. We belong among the stars, spreading our knowledge and wisdom to new life that we may encounter; driving forward and conquering new, unknown territories. Were it not for the restrictions imposed by the Ark Project we could be striving to meet that goal. For the sake of other forms of life, I cannot, and will not stand idly by, while you decide on the best way to defeat an alien threat and preserve your precious ecosystem, while we, the Penusian people try to gather together the remains of a lost society.

Chapter 37

The Ark Project is history, therefore, we have taken the necessary steps to return the natural order to the way it was. Our surroundings are there to be taken advantage of, not to be wrapped up and protected from elements beyond our control. It is the survival of the Ark Project, *or* that of the human race! Your refusal to acknowledge this fact has brought us here with the following demands..."

Briefly, the colonel readjusted the lioness' skull, thrusting his chin forward in an authoritative fashion.

"We ask *you*, the Coleshian people, that first, you will swear allegiance to the new order, and abandon the Ark Project. Secondly, that you all co-operate with us in a united effort to leave this lost cause and continue our search throughout the stars for a brighter future for the whole of humankind. With the remaining space cruisers we have enough recyclable materials to make this dream a reality. We can survive for centuries more in search of a realistic home planet for the human race. Do you really believe that you can coexist with animals that live and breathe salt water? Is not the source of your nemesis at home in that environment?

I am not a completely unreasonable man, and so I propose this. That we, the United Front hold negotiations with the Coleshian High Council to iron out our proposals and discuss the plans for the disbanding of your settlement. To ensure that you conform to our proposals, we have taken the following measures. The remaining crew members of this ship are in our custody. If you refuse to entertain our proposals, we will destroy the Utopia. You have already seen one example of the devastation caused by the explosion of such a craft. We recognise that as your settlement is located in Coleshia's oceans, the construction facilities aboard this vessel are vital for your continued survival. Without her facilities, the Coleshian settlement would surely become crippled. So, I urge you to think carefully about what I am proposing. We await your response..."

With those final words, the communications channels were cut, once again, and the Coleshian people were left to contemplate the fragile thread from which their way of life precariously dangled...

Chapter 38

The Infiltrator touched down on the hull of the Utopia, like the speck of dust that had found purchase on a freshly polished surface. A retractable landing mechanism emerged from a hatch in the belly of the small craft and connected with the hull of the huge star cruiser, magnetically locking the ship into position like a limpet to a rock.

An opening appeared through the seamless hull of the sleek craft, and a tall figure emerged, dressed in a white spacesuit. As he began to walk with somewhat awkward and considered movements from the shuttle, he could feel the magnets in his boots rooting his feet to the tough metal shell beneath him. It was a reassuring feeling when he looked out into the emptiness that engulfed him.

In glaring contrast to the silent vacuum of space, Coleshia protruded from behind the huge hull of the Utopia, a blue sphere striking in its symmetry. He had to stare down the entire length of the Utopia to admire it. Sporadically, protrusions from the ship's hull would disrupt the symmetry of the sight before him, like large obstacles obstructing a driver's vision on the highway, stretching for miles into the distance. It was a most profound optical illusion, as if he was standing on the barrel of a huge gun, pointing at the aquatic planet. Momentarily, he felt that he could walk down the length of the hull, and at its end would be the huge, blue mass, within touching distance, smooth and round, like a ball on a snooker table. When he looked the other way the huge cylindrical outer shell of the vessel's gravity generator obscured his view. It continued to rotate in a clockwise direction, while the layers beneath rotated in the opposing direction to one another.

This was the focus of General Miller's attentions, and he began to make his slow, laborious progress across the vessel's surface. By the rotating structure, he located a personnel hatch, highlighted by its red and yellow markings. He continued his slow walk to this entrance, like some small parasite, searching the flesh for the crucial artery. It was only when faced with a view such as this that the proportions of the vessel could be appreciated. He was in one tiny section, and yet when he looked around he could not see where the hull ceased to exist, such was the magnitude of the Utopia's size.

Eventually, he found the door, and inputting the code in the keypad, he floated into the air lock. As he had done on Penusia, he had successfully discovered an alternative way into a huge structure that appeared to have few entrances.

The door slid shut behind him, and he used his magnetic boots to gain a secure foothold.

When he reached the inner hatch, he used the touch sensitive function on the monitor screen to restore pressure and oxygen to the airlock. Within minutes he had removed his helmet, and drawing his blast pistol he braced himself for a possible encounter before venturing deeper into the constructed hive that he knew so well.

Several minutes passed before the general was satisfied that this sector of the Utopia was unoccupied. It was the best indication that he had of having achieved a successful entrance into the ship undetected.

They would have already been around me like flies around faeces if they knew that I was here...

Finding a ventilation hatch, he climbed awkwardly into it, and in its confined space, he climbed out of the spacesuit. Leaving it in the shaft, he crawled along the confined ducts, towards the command centre of the ship...

"We await your response..."

Colonel Conran stood up from the communication module, and

removing the lioness' fur, he began preparations for his impending trip to Coleshia. Scratching his bald head, he paused in a contemplative pose momentarily before giving his next order.

"Shoot the remaining Coleshian troops – we don't need them."

The order was given without a trace of emotion or compassion.

"Yes, Sir."

The soldier left the command centre, while Colonel Conran swiftly manoeuvred around the room, barking instructions to his troops, who were operating terminals.

From the ventilation shaft in the ceiling, a steely pair of eyes watched the events unfolding below. There was only one thing left for him to do. Silently, General Miller crawled away from the command centre.

From another sector of the ship the massacre of several confused soldiers took place to the cacophony of multiple blast rifle fire… The sound reverberated around the ventilation ducts, booming in the general's ears, the anthem for hundreds of extinguished souls…

The Ark Project is all but a memory now. I must act quickly…

When he was satisfied that no one was within earshot, the general produced a small communicator from his uniform pocket, and switched it to a specialised frequency.

"Sergeant Scott, do you copy?"

The tone of voice in the reply consisted only of expectation. The Sergeant was not surprised to hear from the general.

"Yes, General?"

The general slowly whispered a series of instructions to the officer, conclusions that he had derived calculated on the basis of information far more informative than that which he had seen in recent days.

The sergeant does not know about the massacre yet… It must stay that way, at least for now… I am a soldier, and I must follow the objectives of my training… Balance where there is chaos…

"Yes, Sir…"

Sergeant Scott was a loyal soldier. He had always followed the general and that was why he now found himself in the confidence of his elusive superior officer. The events of recent times had given rise to doubts about many things, but Sergeant Scott was a soldier by profession, and he knew that the chain of command should always be adhered to, whatever the moral implications. A good soldier always justified his actions by the very nature of the chain of command. Nevertheless, the abnormality of the situation gave rise to many feelings and Sergeant Scott could not resist asking the general a question – he had to know at least something about his significance.

"What about you, Sir? People have noticed your absence. They are accusing you of being involved in the terror that has taken over their lives. The Coleshian authorities are requesting your presence in the High Council to explain your actions…"

The general paused thoughtfully before answering.

"What do you want to know, Sergeant? Why do they accuse me so?"

Again there was a period of silence.

"Forgive me, Sir."

It was clear that Sergeant Scott would only be satisfied with an honest answer. In this time of uncertainty certain truths needed to be acknowledged. The general concluded that through continued loyalty perhaps he deserved one.

"The answer is simple… They accuse me because I am involved, Sergeant!"

Chapter 39

When Glen Davis and Rhona Skallen saw the broadcast, they were still together. Both were feeling more buoyant and vibrant since they had discovered a new depth to their relationship. Only after making love had it become apparent that their bond was about much more than the relief of sexual tension. There was the ever-growing feeling of companionship that alleviated the loneliness, perhaps one of the greatest burdens that anyone could bear. The mutual respect and trust between them was strong. Only now did they both know how deeply their feelings went. They had what many couples longed for and referred to as 'chemistry'.

The tranquillity of their privacy was suddenly cast to one side as the sinister visage of Colonel Conran framed by the skull of the dead lioness appeared on their video monitor. It was as if the creature had swallowed something disagreeable and had regurgitated it in the form of Conran's scarred features. They watched in disbelief and horror, struggling to find the words to summarise the transmission. Afterwards they simply stared at the blank screen; unable to comprehend that the stranglehold around the human race could increase further… But it had.

"Doesn't that man realise he could kill us all? We would crumble without the Utopia," cried Rhona.

"That's exactly what he realises, Rhona. He is banking on the fact that the Coleshian people don't want that to happen. Give up the Ark Project or give up your lives!"

"What do we do now, Glen? Did you see what he did to that

lioness? It's barbaric!"

Glen frantically dressed into his grey uniform with a determination that Rhona knew all too well. Sensing her concern he enlightened her to his thoughts.

"Quite frankly, I'm not prepared to sit around with my thumb up my backside, waiting for the High Council to act. They won't, they have no choice at this point. My guess is that they will call off the assault on the Carcinomas, because they believe that it will contravene Conran's wishes. They will see angering him as highly risky."

Maybe Conran is not the only military officer in this mess… It is about time General Miller accounted for his actions in recent days…

"I'm already a suspect in Governor Tasken's death. I can't sit idly by while the authorities look for a scapegoat. And to cap it all off, Conran's maniacal beliefs would suggest that there is a strong likelihood that the 'new order', as he puts it, will have shark fin soup on the menu."

"What are you going to do?" asked Rhona, dressing quickly. "Conran has placed a lot of self-importance on the human race. If we are forced to leave Coleshia, no one will care about the survival of the animals."

"Well *that* is what's important to me. It means too much. Damn Conran and his terrorism!"

"Are you sending out the Great Whites?" asked Rhona, alarmed.

Glen looked her straight in the eyes before replying:

"Yes, and I am going with them!"

She stared at him, a look of complete horror on her face… Glen was the first man for many years that she had let into her privacy, and now she could lose him.

It took two panicked intercom calls before she was united with Mike and Danny, and all three of them were struggling to keep pace with an extremely determined Glen Davis, who stormed through the Aquatic Science Centre towards the Animal Release Zone.

"You can't come in here. Governor Phillipoussis has ordered a halt to the operation, while the negotiations take place," said the guard, adamantly.

"Negotiations? That's an interesting choice of word to describe it," replied Glen.

In a moment the guard was laying on the floor, in a state of unconsciousness, a steady stream of blood pouring from his nose. Glen picked up the guard's blast rifle and adjusted the settings to stun.

He flashed his security pass through the sensor and the door obligingly opened. Inside the huge lab, two more security guards were alerted, bursting from the offices.

"Hey, you can't-"

Glen cut the first guard off in mid sentence. There was a flash, and the guard was thrown back into the wall with a thump. As his inert body slid to the floor the remaining guard began to draw his blast pistol, but with an accuracy that he never realised was in his possession, Glen shot the man in the chest, the pistol thrown from his hand and arcing into the pool.

Glen began to busy himself with the preparations…

"Glen, this is crazy. You'll be killed out there. We can't succeed without military assistance. There are too many of those creatures. The provisions that were made for the offensive require considerable military support, and we were not expected to enter the water ourselves. The operation can't work like this, its complete suicide."

Glen, with some difficulty, began to ease himself into his diving suit, paying no heed to Mike's pleas for him to reconsider. It was quite apparent to all present from the driven expression that he wore, that he had made up his mind, and the prospect of facing imminent death was not going to change that.

"Do you think that I was ever going to enter the Great White sharks into this without my expertise as well? I wouldn't trust anyone beyond this room to operate a Bodywave keypad."

"So you planned this all along. When were you going to inform us?" enquired Rhona, temper simmering in her voice.

"Look, all of you. I don't expect any of you to come. It was never my intention to put any of you in harm's way. I feel that I have already inflicted enough damage."

He gazed around the concerned faces of his friends.

"This is something that I have to do. *I* caused this mess, *I* put the sharks in jeopardy, and I also involved you as well… It was unfair of me to demand this of you all. You are my friends, and I should have consulted you before I took any action on the matter."

"But why, Glen? We could be risking more than the fate of the ecosystem if we ignore Conran's demands, and I think that this course of action could easily be construed as doing just that!"

"This operation is all about saving the wildlife on Coleshia, not exactly high on Conran's wish list! I know what you are thinking. Conran has the human race over a barrel, but do you think that he is going to care about the death of four Great White sharks? You heard him. The only way that he views wildlife is as a source of food. Taking advantage of the resources around us. I cannot subscribe to that way of thinking. Under his leadership that is the way that it will end, with the sharks on a dinner plate! I would rather die knowing that they had fought for their freedom than die at the whim of a terrorist. Don't be fooled by his words. All that Conran wants is power, and he is willing to use tyranny to get it. Do you wish to live under that regime? I certainly don't!"

They listened to the words of their friend. It was a harsh point of view, but silently they all had to concur that it was extremely observant.

"So how do you propose to succeed, Glen?" asked Mike. "How can you conceivably expect to communicate with four sharks from one keypad? It is a logistical nightmare!"

Glen continued to pull the suit over his body. The absence of an immediate response indicated the inadequacy of a suitable answer.

"Don't try and stop me, Mike, I have come to terms with the risks-"

Rhona cut Glen off.

"And what about us, Glen, have you thought about that? Jesus, man, *what about you and me?*"

"Rhona, I…"

"Now listen to me, Glen Davis. It hurts me, as it does us all, that you could consider throwing your life away like that. You never talked about this and you must have known it all this time. For God's sake, man, we are your friends, and you propose to leave us all, shut us out and condemn yourself. We all love the sharks, Glen, but there must be an alternative way, please just stop and think…"

There was desperation in her voice now, and all of a sudden Glen ceased pulling the suit over himself. His body went limp. With the garment still hanging from one shoulder, he looked around at all three of them.

"I'm sorry. The world is going mad around me, and all that I know is what I know to be right. The Ark Project may be crumbling about us, but there are still ideals that I believe in. The truth is that I am not doing this for the Ark Project. Lord knows, I have enough reason to resent it. Firstly, it took away my family, and now it proposes to destroy my credibility and denounce me as some traitor. Phillipoussis will make good his threats to me, simply to have a scapegoat for Governor Tasken's death. The loss of their leader is still very much in the minds of the Coleshian public, even more so when confronted with the demands of Conran. I have to do this for myself as much as anyone or anything. If it means that I lose you as well that is a price that I will have to pay…"

The startled Science Officers looked at Glen as he finished suiting up. They saw how determined he was, how angry he was. They cast concerned glances around one another.

"Well, maybe it's a price that we are not willing to let you pay alone," said Rhona.

Frowning in confusion Glen stared at her again, pausing momentarily from the careful deliberation of putting on his diver's suit. A wave of feelings rose within him. He opened his mouth to speak, but he couldn't find the words to say.

"We are going with you," she said.

"*No*… You could be killed."

"We know that… Right?"

Mike and Danny nodded their agreement.

"Just wait for us, Glen," said Mike, rushing to get three more diving suits from the storage room…

An hour later the Animal Release Zone was deserted. The entrance door slid open, and Sergeant Scott rushed into the huge laboratory. The first things to come to his attention were the now stirring bodies of three security guards, who groaned as consciousness began to return to them in painful waves. He noticed that one of them seemed to be in possession of a rather smartly broken nose, blood caked around his mouth. He struggled to see down the far end of the huge pool, but he could make out no signs of movement.

Quickly he ran into the offices. A flashing screen on one of the computer terminals caught his attention. He raced to it. The message that he had least wanted to see flashed before his eyes:

LIFEFORMS RELEASED…

The Elasmobranch Team had already gone. General Miller was right. With some urgency, he activated his communicator.

"They have already left. Teams One, Three, and Five, get out there. Proceed with vigilance and caution…"

Chapter 40

The Mantis shuttle surged from the Utopia, and became a burning streak as it entered Coleshia's atmosphere, on course for the aquatic settlement.

General Miller remained aboard the Utopia, stealthily concealed in the ventilation shaft, and once again, fully dressed in his spacesuit. He found it awkward to see through the grid in the shaft, with the bulk of his suit enclosing his body. The sound of his own breathing rang heavily in his ears. At one point, it almost seemed deafening.

"Colonel Conran has left for Coleshia. I can't wait to see those animal scientists squirm," said one officer to another in the command centre.

"Yes, we have waited a long time for this opportunity. Now we can strike, and make our lives our own again."

Timing will be a crucial factor, but then again, timing is crucial to everything...

General Miller counted the number of men in the room. It would be risky, but he had to take the chance...

Three, I've handled worse...

He drew his blast pistol and silently rose on his haunches. One of the officers walked directly beneath him... With a crash he burst through the access grid. An astonished officer looked up to see two heavy magnetic plated boots land in his face. The guard was killed instantly, and the two bodies landed together in a crumpled heap.

The wind was knocked from the general's body. The other two officers were alerted by the noise and commotion behind them, and rose from their terminals, hastily drawing their weapons. Simultaneously, the general was back on his feet, blast pistol in his right hand, while his left held the inert body of the dead officer in front of him as a human shield. There was a series of thuds as the dead body took the full force of the fired weapons, spraying blood in all directions.

Timing is always the deciding factor!

The general returned fire. Two successive blasts caught both officers in the chest, the force of the impact launching their weapons in the air and catapulting their bodies back over the operations terminals from where they had risen.

The general acted quickly. Struggling to manoeuvre in his constrictive spacesuit, he advanced to one of the terminals. Then, once again activating his magnetic boots he became rooted to the floor. He knew that there was little time before the disturbance would alert other troops. Hastily, he began adjusting controls on the operations terminal with knowledge and precision that revealed that he had occupied the vessel for some years. He prayed that no one would enter while he was in this vulnerable position.

Balance where there is chaos...But am I the agent of chaos, or has my training allowed me to pursue the correct course of action, even though it appears to be the incorrect course of action?

Only now, did his facial expression give any indication of the action that he was about to take, the frown on his forehead depicting an inner conflict within his mind. His breathing became erratic and heavy.

I hear the voice from my past. She speaks to me, telling me the way that life is. She was the closest individual to a mother that I ever had. Oh, Mother, tell me that I am right now, give me reassurance...

Her face came to his mind.

'At the time, it will be intense. At the crossroads of sacrifice you will need more than obvious reward to justify the action. I gave you a good heart. Use it to good effect. Let it guide you, when doubt clouds the path upon which you tread...'

By now the general was nearly hyperventilating, his breathing becoming so uncontrolled that his body was shaking.

Military life allows me to reach beyond the limitations of my conscience – my soul! I have killed before, but now I feel the knife entering my mind, destroying my emotional outcry at my actions… I must fulfil my mission…

Hundreds of lives, all wasted. Damn you all for forcing me into this…. •

The final combination code was entered into the terminal. The procedure was complete. Flashing red lights erupted into visual brilliance throughout the vessel, accompanied by a cacophony of sound as sirens began to wail, sending their warnings.

A metallic voice, lacking in repentance interrupted the call of the sirens.

WARNING, ATMOSPHERE DRAINAGE PROCESS ACTIVATED. YOU HAVE ONE MINUTE TO ENTER YOUR SPACESUITS…

The command was repeated, and the countdown had begun.

59, 58, 57, 56…

The general once again retreated to his haunches, nestling below the operations terminal, while all over the Utopia interior hatches to every room and corridor slid open in response to the command.

In a vacuum, it will be painless, over in seconds, as it sweeps through the ship…

38, 37, 36, 35…

The general clung on to the terminal, exhaling heavily into his helmet, body heat steaming up his visor, perspiration dripping onto the thick glass. He followed the countdown in his mind, as the adrenalin coursed through his veins.

26, 25, 24, 23, 22…

I am the agent of chaos… Please forgive me…

General Miller walked back to the airlock. Occasionally, he passed light fittings that hung precariously, suspended in zero gravity from their sockets, displaced by flying debris that had smashed its way through the vessel in an attempt to exit into the vacuum. Other equipment too, had also suffered in an attempt to stay rooted to the interior of the vessel in the force of the vacuum. Debris floated about him, aimlessly drifting like dead leaves on a body of water.

His mind feverishly tried to ignore the mangled forms of flesh and bone that his torch repeatedly insisted on bringing to his attention. They were twisted and distorted beyond any recognition, battered and crushed from the titanic power of space. The effects of a space vacuum had boiled their blood in seconds.

He struggled against nausea as he picked his way through fleshy and bloody globules. Walking through another mass grave, a vision of death and destruction, the sensation in his toes as his magnetic boots made contact with the floor, resounded within him, like the unrelenting thump of the drums on a funeral march. He struggled to justify his actions to himself, but all the time, his bodily functions were overwhelmed with a numb, tingling sensation.

The general removed his helmet. He gratefully took in the oxygen from a fresh air supply in a series of deep breaths, before walking in a fatigued fashion to the locker in the cockpit of his small shuttle. It was a blessed relief to be free from that oppressive tomb, a tomb that he had created.

His crew cut, blond hair was now dishevelled, and swamped in perspiration, from the claustrophobic confines of his spacesuit. He ran his shaking hands back through his hair, in an attempt to stop the sweat from stinging his eyes.

Can the sanctity of life be justified by so much death? Have I been treading the wrong path all these years, should I have been asking questions of others, as Sergeant Scott asked of me?

From his locker he withdrew a large, heavy metal suitcase, which he placed on the floor, before opening the lid. Kneeling down, he pulled out a black wetsuit. It was equipped with all the standard gadgets, including a PAD device. Lifting the domed helmet and air tanks from the case, a new layer of clothing was revealed beneath.

The general was feeling nostalgic… He lifted the neatly folded garment from the case, running his finger over the name label. A slight smile pierced the corners of his lips, and his eyes became clouded as he became lachrymose. He clenched his fists in an attempt to stop his hands shaking.

It used to make sense. When you told me, Mother, it all made sense... now the path that I tread burns my feet... Nothing makes sense any more...

He needed a stabilising influence, a reminder of why he had done what he had done. He held the folded garment close to his chest, crushing it against his body, as if it could alleviate the guilt that afflicted him so...

Turning his attention back to the diving suit and equipment, he focused on his next course of action...

How ironic that the Ark Project should end just as it began - in complete chaos!

Chapter 41

PART 6: CONFRONTED!

Four perfectly designed bodies cruised through the depths, scything through the murky ocean as if the water were misty air. Attached to the dorsal fins of these graceful beasts by an extended arm, were four divers.

Their breathing respirators sent up a recurrent stream of air bubbles that was rhythmically timed with the exhalation of their breathing.

They were wearing extremely large air tanks to allow for a prolonged period spent in the water. The curved shapes gave the cumbersomely endowed divers the appearance of having wings. Underwater lamps were mounted on their shoulders, which moved simultaneously in the direction of their head movements, piercing the darkness, and revealing more of the deserted expanse of water.

"This is creepy." We passed the settlement limits over twenty minutes ago," said Mike, squinting at his instrumentation.

"I know. No life anywhere," added Danny.

"The Carcinomas have driven the wildlife away," asserted Glen.

The sharks swam in an abnormal formation, slowly accustoming themselves to their new surroundings, each of the fish swimming in close proximity to the other. It was as the team had trained them to do, to offer the best protection in the event of attack.

It was this knowledge that forced culpability onto the shoulders of the Elasmobranch Team. The unthinkable had happened. They had interfered with the Great White sharks' natural behaviour. Their guilt was epitomised by the miniature Bodywave keypads that each member of the team now wore on their left wrist, as if the creatures were connected to each diver by electronic connections, like helpless bodies on puppet strings.

All four of the sharks now responded to their names, and communication could be isolated through the use of names by any of the keypad operators.

Glen stared in constant awe at the majestic way in which the mighty fish cut through the depths, seemingly unbothered by the additional weight that the divers added to their two-tonne bodies. He wondered if they felt any resentment at the fact they were being used for such a purpose.

Rhona hung on tightly to the large dorsal fin of Cleopatra. Deep down, she was very concerned. Cleopatra was pregnant. Allowing for their survival would the unborn pups suffer as a result of such frantic activity? In all probability, allowing for her survival, the number of pups that she gave birth to would be of minimal importance, as the strongest of the litter would very quickly establish dominance over the others and kill them. Suddenly she realised that the sharks were accustomed to living under the threat of death. From the moment of their birth they were taught that to survive they had to play by the most perilous rules! She looked across to Astra, who simply stared back with an emotionless black eye, gliding through the ocean with effortless ease.

What are you thinking right now?

With some affection she watched the graceful form of the female Great White shark cruise parallel with her. Danny McCormick was hitching a ride via the monstrous beast's dorsal fin that was missing a chunk of cartilage.

Since Governor Phillipoussis had placed a surveillance team in the Animal Release Zone, they had been robbed of the joys of observing the natural behaviour of these magnificent beasts at their own leisure. It was just a pleasure to be near to them again.

With Conran's 'proposed' changes for the human population, would this course of action be recognised for any long-term good for the human race at all? They could all die for nothing.

Suddenly the sharks' relaxed cruising became more agitated. Each diver looked at their miniature VDU display, while struggling to maintain a grip on the fins of their guardians. They had sensed something…

DEATH… was the response.

"This may be the time. Get ready," warned Glen.

A beeping sound resounded in the earpieces of the divers. Frantically they checked their sonar scanners hanging from their belts, which alerted them to the new presence disturbingly later than the superior senses of the sharks. An object was descending from the surface at a gradual rate.

"It's about two hundred feet above us," stated Rhona.

From the lighter surface haze that struggled to penetrate the depths, the team could make out the silhouette of a large creature – a fish. As it sank deeper, huge lumps of flesh could be seen to be missing from its mutilated body, savagely torn away. The formation of sharks separated as the dead fish sank further. White markings were visible across its back - sporadically placed spots, like a spray of white ink. Huge cuts and scratches were visible across its body. They were not the wounds inflicted by any beast that the human race had come to know as natural. Unlike the shark that aimed to kill swiftly, these wounds indicated that the Carcinoma was not born with such a compassionate approach to survival.

"A dead Whale shark!" exclaimed Glen, horror creeping out in his voice.

It was clear that size was no deterrent for these creatures.

"It must have returned to feed on the plankton, released by the settlement."

"Those things are close," said Danny, his eyes furiously inspecting the sea, a tremor of fear in his voice.

"Chances are that now the Carcinomas have discovered the settlement, they will pinpoint it as one of the largest threats to their territorial conquest," added Glen, wincing at the extent of the wounds that his shoulder lamp highlighted on the butchered fish.

The sight of such destruction gave rise to feelings of self-preservation. Suddenly it occurred to Glen that it would be almost impossible to communicate with Kauhulu, while using his HP-1 pistol to defend himself. His free hand would be holding the weapon. Their lack of numbers threw up a massive flaw in their defences.

"Glen, we're not far from the settlement limits. Maybe they are attacking it now," stated Mike.

"We can't help them if they are. The sharks' Brainchips will prevent them from re-entering the settlement perimeter. The Alliance Military Forces will have to deal with it," Glen retorted.

As the dead body sank further into the dark, still waters, the sharks reformed their protective swimming formation. He didn't know if it was his imagination, but they had seemed all too willing to huddle together again. Kauhulu's sudden movements almost wrenched Glen's arm from its socket. He felt no need to consult his keypad to guess what they were feeling. They were afraid!

From the far side of the settlement a sleek object cut through the water. It halted and settled just within the invisible boundary recognised as the settlement limits, landing in a gully of kelp.

General Miller emerged from the Infiltrator's hull, wearing full diving gear. Scrambling through the thick kelp that caressed his suit he headed for the main complex, a combination of controlled finning and propulsion from the tiny air jets on his teardrop-shaped tanks steering him towards his goal. He was in full knowledge that his presence had to remain undetected from humans and Carcinomas alike if he were to ensure survival… Not least, his own at this dangerous time! But one thought kept driving him on through fear and exhaustion.

I must ensure that the next phase is completed…

Chapter 42

The submersible rendezvoused with the Mantis shuttle, on the ocean's surface.

Colonel Conran and his small-armed force carefully disembarked and descended down to the main settlement via a considerable military escort. Shortly after reaching the complex they emerged from the vessel into the heart of the docking bay, where Governor Phillipoussis and assorted council members were waiting to receive the new arrivals.

It had not gone undetected by the colonel that there was also a considerable military presence lingering at the rear of the assembled party of officials. Taking in the air, he struggled against a twinge of fear at the sight of high, enclosed walls and a brightly-lit ceiling. Remaining expressionless he steeled himself against the slight emergence of claustrophobia that struck his body. Nervous whispers behind him strongly suggested that his troops were also suffering after a life spent in vast, open spaces. This merely served to make the visiting party twitchy, adding further tension to a meeting that was difficult enough before it even began.

He addressed the assembled group of people, breaking the ice with a sledgehammer.

"I see that you have arranged quite a welcoming committee to greet us. You may outnumber us down here, but I can assure you that I am unwavering in my decision to destroy the Utopia… If the circumstances should arise!"

Colonel Conran forced a smile that had all the warmth of a polar region.

"We do not doubt your sincerity, Colonel," replied the governor, "but you must understand that there are still many people within this community who have a strong affection towards the Ark Project."

Raising his stern gaze to the hideous headdress of the murdered feline, the governor continued:

"In order to improve the diplomacy of our 'negotiations', and perhaps to make my people more willing to entertain your proposals, may I suggest that you remove your - head garment?"

The colonel continued to smile, and he let out a brief chuckle.

"Governor, in case you hadn't noticed, *I* am in control of this situation. The Coleshians have no right to make *any* demands of me. I will continue to wear this garment because it is a statement of intention and necessity. We must throw away naive feelings of compassion and respect for other life forms. They are relics of the Ark Project, a resource to be plundered and used. The human race must accept that and move on. Survival is a harsh business, and the human race must take harsh action to progress… Now then, I must speak to you alone, Governor. We can take the time to address your spin doctors at a later date."

"Governor, is this wise? You can't trust this man," stated one of the assembled group.

Governor Phillipoussis raised his hands to silence the official, and gazing levelly, with an air of defiance at the decadent colonel replied:

"We must show strength, regardless of this man's actions and threats. I do not believe that he will kill me. At this stage it will not benefit him to do so, but for the sake of the Coleshian people, we must comply with his wishes."

This statement was carried with an air of diplomacy that the Coleshian administration had not seen from their newly appointed leader before. Their concern for his safety rose…

Governor Phillipoussis and Colonel Conran entered the governor's office. Two armed guards waited outside the room. Their blast rifles were drawn across their chests, a symbol of their intention, should the circumstances arise.

With the furore that had arisen with the arrival of Colonel Conran, no one noticed a diver entering the docking bay, discarding his diving gear in a maintenance shaft and disappearing without trace into the confusion of the settlement. Free of his diving suit and air tanks, he was now dressed in the red uniform of an engineer. General Miller had successfully re-entered the Coleshian settlement unnoticed!

Two zones distant from the Coleshian Administration Zone where Governor Phillipoussis' office was located, the general, once again, entered the confined space of a ventilation shaft, fully intent on avoiding unnecessary encounters with security guards. Silently he crawled the huge distance to the governor's office, bypassing the guards situated outside the door, who remained unaware of his presence.

The general reached the metal grid in the ceiling. Peering into the room below, he could see the seated forms of Governor Phillipoussis and Colonel Conran, facing each other from opposing sides of the governor's desk.

Silently, he listened to the conversation, taking place beneath him, resting his right hand on his blast pistol. It would soon be time to complete the next phase...

Chapter 43

As the carcass of the Whale shark departed into the murky depths of the ocean, the eerie stillness of the sea returned. With death so vivid in their minds it was hard not to be afraid of what the darkness held in store for them. The Whale shark had paid the price for being so bold, for being desperate enough to risk returning to the settlement to feed. What price would they have to pay? With such a rapid impact on the ecosystem, it occurred to Glen that perhaps the Carcinomas would resort to genocide when their current sources of food were extinguished.

Suddenly the sharks once again detected movement in the water. So much about a shark's behaviour was instinctive, and, consequently, their response to the change in the environment around them was instantaneous as they began to display agitated behaviour.

The Elasmobranch Team checked their sonar scanners.

"There are four creatures resting on the surface," declared Rhona. "It could be Carcinomas."

"It would seem likely," affirmed Glen. "Nothing else would be brave enough to rest on the surface of these waters."

They returned their attention to their Bodywave keypads. The sharks already knew...

FOE...

Their judgement was clear. Quite how they knew the nature of the presence on the surface was unclear to the divers as they obligingly let go of the pectoral fins of their hosts. Even after centuries of study it was apparent that only thin layers of the Great White shark's psyche had been unveiled to probing minds. So much about these creatures remained shrouded in mystery, and yet here they were, the deciding factor in the biggest gamble ever taken by humanity in allowing nature to dictate its destiny. Their adapted territorial instincts took hold, and all four sharks took off in separate directions, like savagely trained guard dogs set free of the leash.

"I hope that we can call them back," said Mike, feeling somewhat naked without the benefit of a two-tonne predator as protection.

Danny tapped his miniature keypad.

"These things have a long range, and there is nothing out here to provide any interference…"

"You know that is not what I mean!"

The cumbersome bodies bobbed up and down on Coleshia's surface, floating with the current. Rows of serrated bone-textured spikes towered menacingly from the water. A razor-sharp beak appeared from the waves, and a jet of water emitting from the beast's nostrils shot several feet into the air.

The Carcinomas were relaxing, tails lazily slapping the surf as they allowed themselves to drift with the waves. Their skin colour was blue, mimicking that of the water's sun-enhanced surface. They had fed well on the carcass of the Whale shark, and their efforts had reduced them to a dozy slumber on the surface. They were at ease. Nothing in their new home brought any fear… But they had not encountered everything that Coleshia had to reveal…

They were unaware of the fact that they were being observed from deeper water. Ignorant of this, they continued their relaxed posturing, pectoral fins spreadeagled in indolence. How could they know? They had not encountered this form of life in their brief occupation of the aquatic planet. Stealthy movement and a cunning form of attack, prevented the Carcinomas' visual awareness from being alerted to another presence within their immediate vicinity.

From some one hundred feet below, their nemesis surged towards them, with frightening speed. Suddenly, the creatures were hit by a sickening blow in their soft, vulnerable bellies, two tonnes of aggression that connected with the force of a speeding missile.

The synchronisation of the attacks was unprecedented. Rows of razor-sharp teeth pierced alien flesh, assuming a hold, while powerful upper jaws crunched down. The force of each blow threw the creatures into the air, their helpless bodies fleetingly leaving the waves in a frenzied spray of water. The sharks held fast as the creatures thrashed wildly, beaks opening in pain, but uttering no sound, before gravity returned predator and victim to the depths of Coleshia's oceans.

Moments later the swell died down and the only evidence of any life having been present were slowly dissipating clouds of pink alien blood that dispersed into the water. The sea returned to the relative calmness of the gentle rise and fall of the waves…

"I was unable to prevent the Elasmobranch Team from leaving the facility. They disobeyed my orders."

"Will they pose a threat?"

"Ultimately they will be dead before they realise it. The Carcinomas patrolling the oceans will ensure that."

"And what of this man, General Miller? Troops on the Utopia claimed that they were awaiting his orders. What threat does he pose?"

"He's a very mysterious man. I have checked his history on the database, but very little information was recorded on him. General Arran Miller… He has served the Alliance Military Forces for nearly three decades, but that is about all I know. I can, however, tell you this… If anyone shows a more clinical approach to the sanctity of life than you, it is he! He went out with a team of troops and captured a live specimen of the alien species without breaking a sweat. I am concerned as to his whereabouts at this stage. He has not been located since the explosion of the Elysium."

There was a thoughtful pause before a reply was uttered.

"Well, I consider myself to be very dangerous, Governor. So I can only deduce that he must be one lethal son of a bitch! I will advise my troops to be aware of his arrival. He certainly is not aboard the Utopia.

We would have found him. That leaves one likely possibility. He must be near the action, in the settlement somewhere. I want him found!"

General Miller continued his silent vigil from his vantage point in the ventilation shaft, unperturbed by the mention of his name. He tapped the handle of his blast pistol in silent contemplation of the next phase....

Chapter 44

The sharks did not return, and the four scientists struggled against a tremendous urge to recall them back. This, however, would have been wrong, and they knew it. The Great Whites had just entered their new home, and they had been trained to defend it with their lives if necessary. The sooner they became acquainted with their new habitat, the better chance it would spell for their survival.

As it was, the divers themselves were in a dangerously exposed area of the sea, and a large proportion of this desire rose from the protection that the mighty predators offered them. They were totally vulnerable to attack...

"Stay close," warned Glen. "We can use our shoulder lamps to check around us."

The divers huddled together, and as if by fate their sonar scanners began to chime in simultaneous acknowledgement of a presence beyond their tiny entourage. Multicoloured flashes darted around in the distance, evading the alert eyes of all but one of the group.

"The light from our lamps must have drawn their attention," stammered Mike.

"Either way they will find us. At least this way we can see them," reasoned Glen.

"How many did you see?"

"Maybe half a dozen, it's hard to tell down here," came the terrified response.

"Looks like we're outnumbered," interjected Rhona, with a clear texture of resignation in her voice.

258

For what seemed like an eternity, the water seemed ominously empty. The only sound was the rising stream of bubbles from four breathing respirators, and the gentle hum of the air jets that allowed the divers to maintain their depth without wasting valuable energy finning. Each diver scanned the surrounding seascape. Darkness, nothing! The absence of aquatic combat training showed in their defences. There was one trajectory that they neglected to check, and it was from this direction that the attack came.

Suddenly, from beneath their searching eyes a huge force slammed into the huddled party, embedding itself right down their centre, scattering the startled divers. A blood-curdling scream was heard through their earpieces, and as they turned, the team saw an unmistakable beak impaled through the helpless body of Danny McCormick. Air was escaping rapidly from his tank, mixing with the blood that was beginning to erupt from the deadly wound in his stomach.

The creature began savagely shaking its head, its spiked back writhing, as Danny's torn body was rapidly drained by death.

"*No…*"

Glen screamed, and all his anger was transferred to the rounds that erupted from the barrel of his drawn weapon, the machine's deadly venom spewing forth and puncturing the creature's body, sending convulsions of pain through its powerful frame.

Red and pink blood became intermingled in a clouded haze, and with the creature's throes of death there was conspicuous dissipation in the colour of its skin. It assumed a pasty grey texture, and the lifeless beast sank into deeper water, with the dead body of Science Officer Danny McCormick impaled on its' beak, arms spreadeagled. He looked as if his last moments had been spent pleading with life to release him from the suffering.

"*Danny!*"

More flashes returned Glen to his senses, as Rhona expertly disabled another of the Carcinomas, the explosive shells condemning it to death almost instantaneously. It didn't take a genius to deduce that if two had been killed, and Mike's sighting had been correct, then they were outnumbered by one. In this predicament it was enough to spell certain death. With skilful movements of his fingers he reacted quickly…

HELP US… FOE

"Danny!"

Mike panicked and began powering frantically after the body of his colleague that was fading into the depths beneath them. Glen intercepted him, grabbing him by the shoulders and levelling their domed helmets, his hands shaking with adrenalin. It was clear that Mike was beginning to crack under the pressure.

"Glen, he's dead… We're *all* gonna die!"

Glen shut his eyes, the shock of the horrific death hitting home.

"Listen to me, Mike…Listen. He's gone. There is nothing that we can do for him now, Let's make sure that he didn't die for nothing… Come on, Mike, get it together!"

They resumed their protective, huddled position, pistols ready. Suddenly, one of the creatures surged past, as if it had just appeared in some bizarre act of magic.

Rhona fired.

"Missed!"

It was a perfectly timed cue. Each of the stricken divers found themselves staring squarely into the fearsome mouth of a Carcinoma! With an unbelievable agility they danced around the condemned group, dodging the rapid fire from the spitting blast pistols. Aimless shells flew past them surging away in the dimness beyond the monstrous aliens, exploding into nothing. Like some rehearsed performance the colourful creatures turned blood red, like the water around them and surged towards the stranded divers, beaks snapping violently. So intent were they on their prey that they failed to realise that they too were being hunted…

In a display of aggression, far more controlled and instinctive than their own, the Carcinomas suddenly found themselves helplessly trapped in powerful jaws that erupted from the red clouds, like Angels of Death. The divers watched, shocked and transfixed, as the creatures that they regarded with so much respect assumed the guise of mindless killers. They were horrified. Never before had they been so exposed to the ferocious power of an attacking Great White shark. With eyes lifelessly rolled back into their sockets, they savagely shook the life out of their victims, bodies twisting and heads shaking furiously. Their monstrous tails swayed from side to side countering the thrashing of their jaws. Razor-sharp teeth tore through alien flesh, as the creatures were thrown around like soft, cuddly toys in the arms of demonic children.

Of all the gambles that the Elasmobranch Team had taken, this was the greatest. Their training had paid off. The sharks' accurate sense of taste ignored the disagreeable texture that now permeated their mouths, and they continued to erase the life from the Carcinomas until they remained still.

Seconds seemed like hours before the divers could balance themselves against the turbulence, and each shark obligingly let go of the battered and twisted bodies that retreated to the seabed in clouds of pink blood.

The fish returned to the divers. Poker Face darted around, sensing the absence of one of their party.

FRIEND?

Glen, struggling to hold back waves of nausea answered the curious creature's question.

FRIEND GONE...

Glen stroked Kauhulu's nose, as the huge fish resumed its place beside him. It was years of experience that allowed the scientists to derive reassurance from the huge fish, rather than trepidation in the face of such an efficient display of killing.

Once again, the sharks became agitated, and instantly swam away. Their senses were more finely tuned than the crude technology of the divers. Fearing the worst, the divers drew their weapons again, gazing intently around them.

A short time passed before a voice broke the sound created by their heavy breathing. It was not one that they recognised.

"Team 107 do you copy, over?"

Glen, Rhona and Mike looked at each other, awaiting some spark of recognition towards the new presence from one another. It did not appear… Should they answer? It could be a patrol, sent out on Conran's orders. If so would they try and stop their mission? Upon reflection, Glen concluded that Conran would not waste troops on aiding the demise of a mission, with an exceptionally high probability of fatality. There was little in the man's character to admire, but stupidity was not one of the qualities that appeared to be on show… No doubt the Coleshian High Council would acquaint the colonel with the perils represented by the Carcinomas…

"Team 107. Do you copy?"

Someone, however, was out here… Who was it, and on whose authority were they here? It was this curiosity that forced Glen into a response.

"This is Aquatic Science Officer, Glen Davis. I am the senior officer of Team 107, the Elasmobranch Team. Who are you and what is your purpose?"

"I am Sergeant Scott of the Alliance Military Forces. I am under orders from General Miller to assist you on this mission."

It was the first time that Glen had heard that name uttered in several days.

"The mission seems to mutate by the day, Sergeant… What is *your* interpretation of our objectives?"

"Short of attempting grandiose suicide, by venturing beyond the settlement limits by yourselves, my interpretation of this mission is the same as yours - to eradicate the Carcinomas from the ocean! The only difference is that I intend to use high explosive charges to destroy the host organism, rather than gambling with angry fish to pick the aliens off as they appear. Did you really expect to succeed by yourselves?"

Glen answered a question with a question.

"Does Conran know that you are here, Sergeant?"

"No, as I have stated, I am under orders from General Miller. Conran's agenda is a separate issue…"

Satisfied that the officer was telling the truth, Glen allowed an explanation.

"Well, I can only assume that you are telling the truth if you have risked your own lives to get here. Let's just say that not everybody agrees with Conran's demands. This is our way of life, and we will not let the unreasonable demands of a terrorist alter that, no matter what price we have to pay!"

"Officer Davis, are you aware of the political implications that your actions could have on the Coleshian people?"

"As much as you do, Sergeant… Besides, survival should precede politics, although I have to confess to seeing the opposite reaction occurring in recent times! By the way, your presence in this area would not have anything to do with our involvement in Governor Tasken's death would it? Just how much importance do *you* place on politics, Sergeant?"

"I am a soldier, Officer Davis, not a politician. I will not lie to you. If we should survive, it is an issue that requires a resolution… I would not be doing my duty if I pretended that we could ignore what has occurred! However, rest assured that my purpose here is singular in its design."

"I will hold you to that… How many men do you have?"

"I managed to gather thirty-two without drawing unnecessary attention."

"How do they feel about sharks, Sergeant?"

The long silence that preceded the answer needed no words to punctuate the general level of feeling.

"We are trained to deal with these situations. Why?"

"You might wish to advise your troops to be careful with their trigger fingers. My Great Whites are in this area, and I don't want any confusion between them and the Carcinomas."

"Understood, Davis. What the… I think I've just seen one of them. I thought that the Carcinomas were frightening enough… They are big fish, Officer Davis!"

"Just make sure that you show a respectful distance. As long as your

PAD devices are activated your troops should be fine."

"Affirmative… Now that we are together in this, I propose that we use your sharks as a decoy when we approach the host organism. That is if we can get close to it. Right now, there is no telling how many of those things have hatched."

"Well for all our sakes, Sergeant, I hope that we live long enough to get close to the host organism… By the way, what's the story with General Miller…?"

Glen had finally discovered a question to which the mysterious sergeant had no answer…

As the three divers awaited the return of the Great Whites and the appearance of the soldiers, they could only hope that the Carcinomas presented the only immediate threat to them…

The resistance hatch in the ventilation shaft slid back, grinding against the ceiling. With a high level of agility, the red uniformed body of General Miller dropped to the corridor floor, landing with a muffled thump. It was with some trepidation that he left the secrecy of the air conditioning system… He needed to find a power point and soon. His radio was dead. Not only did it prevent him from communicating, it prevented him from picking up the conversations of others. The last that he had been able to deduce from the movements of Conran's troops was that they had orders to shoot him on sight.

A visual description of the general had already been circulated around the settlement. Alliance troops and those serving under Conran now patrolled every inch of the Coleshian settlement. In this curfew-enforced sector of the complex, without the aid of his communicator eavesdropping on the conversations of others, he could find himself trapped in a very short space of time.

The general quickly ran down the barren corridor. Locating another ventilation shaft that looked more fruitful in providing a hopeful route to a power supply, he removed the grid guarding the access port. Time was running out… As he was about to jump up, he was stopped.

"*General Miller?*"

The booming voice was male, dripping with venom, and by now he recognised it. It resounded from behind him.

"Turn around, General. Slowly. Don't do anything stupid."

Acknowledging the command, the general was greeted by the sight of a squat figure hanging out of an open doorway, a blast pistol extended from the muscular arm that was aligned in his direction. This, however, failed to prevent the general from taking the initiative.

"Colonel Conran. At last we meet."

The scar on his face was as, if not more, noticeable than the lioness' fur that added to the colonel's diminutive height.

"You are a very elusive man, General, and now I know why; quite a convenient way of navigating around, via the ventilation ducts. I should have informed pest control to flush the vents, to clear out the *rats*!".

"Needs must, Colonel," replied the general, a vicious glare emanating from his blue eyes.

The colonel stepped out from the doorway into the corridor, his weapon firmly trained on the helpless general. Even from his vantage point several yards away, the general was given the impression that he towered above the colonel.

"I find it rather convenient that you should be in this sector, very shortly after my meeting with Governor Phillipoussis. Out of uniform I may add. We have been looking for you, General!"

"This is madness, Conran. Do you honestly believe that this genocide is the right destiny for the human race?"

"It is a better alternative than that which we have available now, General. Better that a few people die for the long-term benefit of the human race, than everyone dying for the fulfilment of primitive beliefs."

"I disagree. It was primitive beliefs that forced us to be rejected by Earth. All you are doing is returning the human race to the days of destructive chaos that ultimately cost us our home planet. Now it may cost the human race its very existence!"

"No, General…"A twisted smile crossed the colonel's face. "It will just cost *you* yours…"

There was a loud explosion accompanied by a flash, as the colonel tightened his grip upon the trigger. The general felt a massive impact that knocked the breath from his body. His vision blurred and almost instantly he became engulfed by a blinding light.

For what seemed like hours the dazzling whiteness obscured his vision, and then a vision came to him. He felt no pain as a familiar figure from his past materialised. It was to her that he turned his thoughts when he struggled to maintain his grip…

I see your perfect face. Those eyes that show me love in a world of pain… 'I do not need love.' But how can you say that when you have lived as long as I? Isolation shows you many things… What is love? It is appreciation of another… But you don't provide love. You appreciate the wonder of your creation… I am alive, but I am not alive. You say that everyone has their strengths. My strength is greater than any that you could hope for… As the agent of chaos… I take life and now I defy death…

Instantly he was returned to reality. The general was still staring at the smoking barrel of the blast pistol. Now he felt the pain… Despite strong urges to double over he maintained an upright posture and almost casually looked down, examining his body. There was a growing patch of blood around the point of impact in his stomach.

No pain…

Returning his gaze to the increasingly horrified visage of Colonel Conran, his own features assumed a twisted grin.

"I beg to differ," he replied….

Chapter 45

Accompanying the small pocket of resistance were three Beluga submersibles. Standing atop the cruising vehicles were the slender groups of thirty-two Alliance Space Troopers, armed with blast rifles.

Glen, Mike and Rhona stood amongst one of the three groups, gripping their HP-1 pistols tightly. Before, everything had happened so fast. Now, with a brief hiatus from activity their minds drifted.

Rhona had, for the most part, liked Danny. She had never approved of his womanising, and had often chastised him for his bad jokes, but with his absence the value of his friendship was given an uncomfortable clarity. Looking at Glen she could see the conflict in his mind. She knew the guilt that he was feeling over suggestions that Danny may have contributed to Governor Tasken's death. She felt it too… He had been as much a victim as the rest of them.

Glen tried to focus on something else. Automatically his thoughts turned to his living and breathing therapy – the sharks - but no matter how hard he tried, the expression of horror on Danny's face kept leaping out from the darkest corners of his mind.

On one side of them, the streamlined, muscular bodies of Kauhulu and Cleopatra cruised alongside the sub, with Poker Face and Astra patrolling the other. Cleopatra was now beginning to bulge with the unborn pups gestating inside her. They watched her graceful movements, silently feeling great concern for the survival prospects of the female Great White and her unborn young. As they looked at her, she returned their gaze with a large black eye.

Glen felt the depth of that stare. It made him feel as if he were under a spotlight, or worse still on the podium waiting for his judgement. He found that he couldn't look into that piercing orb for very long. Once again his shoulders became heavy with a burden far greater than the weight of his oxygen tanks. He thought of Danny, his friend's last moments of suffering indelibly branded upon his brain, as it must have been upon the minds of his friends. Their silence spoke a thousand words. The recollection of those all too recent harrowing events brought the return of the nausea, churning waves that danced painfully around inside his stomach. He tried very hard to think of something else, but in this harsh environment it was proving to be more than challenging.

"Officer Davis?"

The voice brought him back to his senses, but it wasn't one familiar to him.

He felt a tug on his safety line, and awkwardly he glanced around, hoping to trace the cause of the disturbance.

One of the troops waved to get his attention.

"Amazing creatures, aren't they?"

"Yes, they certainly are," replied Glen.

"I can see why they are so renowned in human folklore…"

Glen smiled. It always gave him goose pimples, when people exhibited admiration towards the sharks, hearts melting in their mouths. Given time, fear always collapsed under the rising spirit of admiration for these predators.

"Believe me, you haven't seen any creature as good at hunting as these beasts. They are amazing, but this is the real beauty, right now, watching a shark glide along when it is at peace, when there is no frenzy for food. In many ways sharks are a living paradox of themselves… Beauty and the beast. You should feel privileged to see this, Private!"

"Lieutenant, Sir," replied the soldier, "I'm glad they're on our side. I wouldn't like to rub one of these fish up the wrong way…"

"Okay, cut the chatter. We're approaching the host organism. Stay fresh."

The voice was Sergeant Scott's, stern and abrupt.

"Science Officer Davis, I want your team to head to the seabed when we execute the plan. It will leave you less exposed than floating in the open ocean. The Carcinomas will have one angle less to attack from. Two of my troops will accompany you for added protection. From there, you can orchestrate your sharks and create a suitable distraction!"

"Acknowledged," replied Glen, anxiety taking hold of his body.

If only they had found the seabed before the first attack that took Danny's life, perhaps they would not be mourning the loss of a friend at this moment. Casting cursory glances in the direction of Mike and Rhona, they nodded their agreement.

"Team One will approach the organism and lay the charges in the designated areas. Teams Two and Three will secure the perimeter of the field. Do I have everyones' agreement?" yelled the sergeant through his helmet.

"Yes, Sir!" was the response.

The birthplace of chaos emerged, the pink pods hanging in the water, drifting with the flow of the ocean's steady current. Almost immediately, the sharks had gone.

It would be a miracle if they survived the confrontation, and at the very least were not killed in crossfire. Upon further reflection, they decided that it would be a miracle if any of them survived this conflict. They were only a few metres away from the nearest pod. As far as they could see along the vertical stem of the organism, hatched pods were visible; hollow shells exploded from the inside out.

How many? Thirty, forty, maybe more!

The logic of the plan became clear. With the vast majority of the Carcinomas unborn, destroying the host organism was the best way of hurting these beasts. Worse would be to come if the unborn were not eliminated while the opportunity presented itself. The survivors could be picked off after the explosion.

Glen, Mike and Rhona were escorted to a small outcrop of rocks, from where they had good visibility of the host organism and the surrounding area. As they touched down, particles of silt were kicked up from the terrain beneath their temporarily finless boots. Their sonar scanners beeped incessantly, as the signals of the three minisubs hovering several meters above them registered on their instrumentation.

While two of the vehicles circled patiently, one dropped to the seabed, near the base of the organism, searchlights wandering, probing the depths. With a precision that emulated from disciplined training, the divers detached themselves, and finned to the monstrous base of the organism. They began expertly placing the charges.

It became apparent to Glen that the divers descended to a position below that of his small entourage. It was only then that he realised that they were perched in the concave basin of a meteorite crash site. Upon their descent he had failed to notice it. As he looked to discover why, one of troops accompanying them dropped his weapon. Upon contact with the floor a brown cloud erupted from beneath the weapon. As the soldier fumbled to regain the rifle, inadvertently making the cloud worse, Glen realised why. The covering of sand particles in the crater was extremely thick. This concerned Glen, and once the disorientating cloud had dispersed, he raised this with the clumsy trooper.

"Soldier, what if in all likely probability, the silt should get kicked up in the confrontation. How the hell will we see where to shoot?"

"Officer Davis, we have checked the whole area. The terrain is exactly the same throughout this proximity. At least from this vantage point, we have some cover from the rocks!"

Glen had to concede that the soldier had a point, and a period of silent observation followed, while the divers around the base of the host organism continued to work feverishly.

"I don't like this," said Rhona. "Where are they? They should be breathing right down our necks right now."

"Maybe they are not here at all. Maybe they are attacking the settlement, and they don't know that we are here," proposed Mike.

"I doubt that," replied Glen. "I expect that we have been spotted. With our searchlights, we stand out like ink on paper."

"Maybe the sharks are distracting them."

Their words caressed the environment like a kiss of death…

"*Movement!*"

Suddenly, everyones' senses were alerted, as dozens of sinister forms burst into the proximity of the host organism, their skins rapidly changing colours in a bizarre, stroboscopic effect.

Another living paradox… Beauty belying death!

No one needed an invitation. Suddenly the sea was illuminated with bright flashes as the soldiers created their own stroboscopic effect, as they opened fire…

For what felt like an age, the creatures threatened menacingly and were silenced by the judgement of blast rifle fire. Still they attacked with ferocity, unperturbed by the mounting death toll of their own kind.

From his vantage point, Glen spotted a strange sense of hierarchy in the nauseating beasts. The bigger the specimen, the more openly and ferociously it attacked, unperturbed by the smell of blood from its own kind.

Frighteningly quick, and unbelievably manoeuvrable, the abhorrent beasts appeared to toy with their prey before tearing the soldiers to pieces with one of the many cruel weapons in their arsenal. Glen was accustomed to the presence of violent predators, but he had never witnessed any creature that seemed so chaotic, frenzied, and willing to inflict pain and misery on its victims. Now, above any other time, it was clear that these horrific monsters would not hesitate in exacting suffering on anything that might resist their dominance of the ocean.

As one Carcinoma was killed another hatched to resume its place, as if rolled off a production line of killing machines. Like their predecessors they fled their wombs unwittingly into the sights of death-dealing weaponry.

The sharks patrolled around the perimeter of the battle area picking off Carcinomas that were unfortunate enough to think that survival lay beyond the battlefield. It was imperative that they stayed out of the range of the divers' weapons. Human judgement could easily be impaired at these depths, and in the chaos, one oceanic predator could appear as threatening as another, especially in the expanding clouds of spilt alien and human blood…

For a time it appeared as if the small band of troops would turn the tide, despite their dwindling numbers, before an event occurred that cast a dark shadow upon their cause. From their rocky shelter the Elasmobranch scientists assisted the battle, shooting the strays that emerged from the barrage of blast rifle fire above them.

With his limited peripheral vision, Glen spotted movement in the pink sphere directly above the soldiers who carried on laying the explosive charges. They were oblivious to the stirring motion that began the birth process of the Carcinoma.

"Team One, look ou-"

The pod exploded in a haze of fluid. Within seconds, the group working on the charges were mangled in a spasmodic whirlpool of torment, and the troops offering covering fire were unable to react in time. Blood and silt clouded the area. Instantly Glen repeatedly fired blindly into the cloud. The shells from his HP-1 pistol struck home, sending the newly born creature into convulsions. Never before had Glen seen a creature so equipped to kill from birth, as these beasts. He had seen the footage of unborn sharks munching on the undeveloped embryos of their brothers and sisters, but nothing as bloodthirsty and savage as this. The convulsions ceased and Glen picked his moment.

"Rhona, cover me!"

In a flash, without waiting for a response, he headed for the cloud of dissipating blood. Panicked, she fumbled with her keypad as Glen disappeared into the red haze…

"Where are you going?"

It was close… Team One had been a single press of a button away from priming the explosive charges. The 'armed' button winked enticingly at Glen like a flashing beacon in the fog, as he journeyed into the cloud of bodily fluids.

He pressed it.

Chapter 45

It ceased winking.

"Glen, *look out!*" Rhona's voice screamed in his ear.

Glen whirled around - as quickly as the water density would allow - only to be greeted by the gaping jaws of a Carcinoma heading towards him. It was too late to react. By the time he redrew his pistol it would be all over.

So this is how it ends…

He shut his eyes. It was said that imminent death gave rise to rapid flashbacks through a human memory. Glen had no such release from the present. His mind was filled with images of the uncompromising jaws tearing him into pieces, the vile tongue caressing his shredded flesh, feeding demonically from his torture. The impact never arrived…

Something large flew past his side, disturbing the water, and knocking him cleanly off his feet. When he dared to reopen his eyes, Kauhulu had a firm grip on the alien beast and began methodically tearing it apart, pulverising the soft underbelly. Lying helpless in the sand, he watched mesmerised, adrenalin racing through his body. Just feet away the mighty fish's large tail thrashed wildly from side to side as the ferocious shaking of his head brought an unpleasant demise to the Carcinoma, its snapping beak and armoured hide unable to reply to the efficiency of a natural killer.

Suddenly, Glen was plunged into blackness as a huge cloud of silt kicked up from the sand engulfed him. The displacement of water caused by the violent attack hit Glen like a train, and he was launched into the stalk of the host organism. The breathing apparatus responded to the shock by automatically readjusting the mixture of oxygen that circulated around his domed helmet, allowing him to regain his breath. Suddenly, he felt a pressure around his waist that once again squeezed the air out of his body. He was cleanly snatched from the seabed and emerging from the cloud, he found himself being propelled through the water at tremendous speed. Helpless to see the identity of his attacker, he could easily guess the nature of the predator. Momentarily his heart stopped.

I'm finished… Please make it be over quickly…

Then the pressure was gone and he descended slowly once again in the close proximity of another of the divers… Rhona! There was no blood, no pain, not even a leak within his pressurised diving suit. Looking back, he saw the retreating form that he recognised all too well, surging towards another target. A chunk was missing from her dorsal fin. Astra!

Rhona left the cover of the rocks and helped Glen into an upright position.

"Are you all right?"

"I think so," replied Glen, shaken.

Mike Cullen maintained his position of relative safety behind the rocks, picking off alien targets as they swam past. Briefly, he had seen the Carcinoma attack Glen, and the mighty shark intervene. His concern rose sharply for the safety of his friend, and the distraction to his own personal safety was one that he could ill afford at this dangerous time.

One of the Carcinomas spotted him, and began powering past him in a kaleidoscope of colour. It darted around unpredictably, avoiding the shots of Mike and the troops that supported him. He fired repeatedly, the spent ammunition of his pistol accompanying the covering fire of the two troopers. It was almost surreal how such a weapon-laden creature could deploy itself in such a malleable manner, almost at ease with the death surrounding it.

"I need to reload," said one of the troops.

"Well, be quick," replied his compatriot.

Quick was not quick enough…

Mike saw Glen and Rhona returning towards their position amongst the rocks.

"Mike, *behind you!*"

He turned, visually picturing the sight before he saw it. It was not too dissimilar from his prediction. The ruse had been almost perfect in its conception… Mike's heart furiously pounded in his suit, seemingly aware of the fate that awaited it. The two beasts were regarding him with huge, yellow eyes, floating two feet away.

The momentary, icy calmness of the Carcinomas was unsettling in the extreme. This kind of terrorism was their natural state… Instantly their skin colour changed from the greyish hue of the rocks into a flaming blood red. By then he knew what his advancing friends also knew. He numbly accepted the truth.

One moment of distraction had cost him his life. It was too late…

How much pain must we suffer before this conflict can be ended?

The inanimate bodies sank like discarded blankets over the rocks, human and alien flesh forever entwined. The act of barbarous cruelty had been the end of the two Carcinomas.

The battle that had furiously raged around them now paled compared to the rush of emotions that wracked Glen's body, as he clung limply to the torn remains of his friend… Sinking to his knees and casting a wayward glance in Rhona's direction, his tear-laden eyes managed to distinguish her paralysis at the loss of another friend.

Glen yelled into his voice piece.

"Sergeant Scott. Your explosives are *armed*. Why are we still here?"

"Team One didn't respond. I saw the commotion, and believed you all to be dead."

There was a pause.

"All troops prepare to retreat."

The remains of dead alien and human floated aimlessly through the water. The creatures' numbers had been vastly reduced, so much so that they were now limited to surprise attacks. Sergeant Scott's voice resounded in Glen and Rhona's hearing aids.

"Officer Davis, get your team and your fish out of here! We will cover your retreat."

It was an order that they were not going to quarrel with. Calling the sharks to return, Glen and Rhona made a hasty retreat, hitching a ride on the dorsal fins of Kauhulu and Astra. Needing no second invitation they headed towards the settlement limits, scything through the ocean, leaving the clumsy metal forms of the battling submersibles trailing far behind…

The sharks dropped them safely just outside of the settlement limits. Glen and Rhona checked their oxygen levels.

"Should have enough to get back," Rhona exclaimed, through tear-stained features.

"Me too," replied Glen.

Suddenly, Glen was aware of something drastically wrong, as Cleopatra emerged closely behind them.

"Where's Poker Face?"

Glen looked concerned, a gesture that was echoed by Rhona.

"I don't know, he didn't return with the others."

Glen was about to type a message on his keypad, when a message flashed up on the VDU display.

POKER FACE GONE!

The words thundered home… Numbness came over the divers. Yet another life had been consumed by this chaos…

Glen felt a gentle nudge in his back. He turned to see Kauhulu hanging in the water. He was covered in cuts around the nose and mouth, but nothing that wouldn't heal. Glen stroked the shark's nose and checked one side of his body for further injuries, while Rhona examined the other. Once he was satisfied that the mighty beast was not in a bad state, he began the same process for Cleopatra and Astra, calling to each of them in turn. They were relatively unharmed, apart from some surface scratches.

Life was full of contradictions – paradoxes. In order to defend a belief that the Carcinoma had threatened, to show compassion for other forms of life, they had contradicted that very belief in destroying the population of Carcinomas as another form of life on the planet. As a result, their friends had perished.

To be free of the bloodshed brought no relief to the scientists as they waited for the explosion that would mark the end of the existence of Carcinomas on Coleshia…

Only one of the vehicles returned, with ten, battle-weary troops riding atop its metal alloy hide.

As planned, the charges exploded, and sent tremendous shock waves through the ocean, that tormented the sensitive organs of the Great White sharks. Agitated, they burst away, and it took Glen and Rhona several minutes to calm the frightened creatures down. Sergeant Scott reminded them that their air supplies were limited. Their own survival was still an issue.

Glen and Rhona sent the mighty fish away to feed. It may have proven to be a permanent farewell, but at least the Elasmobranch Team had succeeded in giving every species in their inventory a chance of survival. They would have to travel some miles before finding anything in their diet, but being oceanic predators, Glen and Rhona knew that they would overcome prolonged periods without food. They were now, also equipped to deal with any of the remaining Carcinomas that lurked in the depths.

A new chapter had begun in the colourful history of the Great White shark...

The submersible made its slow progress towards the Coleshian settlement. Glen tried very hard not to think too much. His gloved hand clutched tightly around Rhona's, as they both tried to gain some comfort from the conflict.

Locked in their own thoughts, they were closer now than they had ever been, the loss of their friends repeatedly slamming home in the aftermath, like waves against rocks. What was to come? Now that they had survived the confrontation, how would their return to the settlement be received?

Glen found small comfort in all of the chaos, staring at the beautiful face that hid under the domed helmet next to him:

Rhona... She saved my life and she is still here with me now. If ever I needed a sign of trust, surely this is it? And yet, by her being here, she must trust me too! Who gives a damn for the opinions of the Coleshian authorities? My friends believed in me... My friends... Why should anything else matter, regardless of the consequences I may suffer? Now, at least the sharks are free...

Chapter 46

First there was joy; an overwhelming relief that their mission had been a success. In the docking bay, the surviving troops embraced, thankful that they had survived the nightmarish encounter. Then there were tears as sadness became prevalent at the loss of comrades and friends. As they exited the water and climbed out of their cumbersome diving gear, military troopers and science officers congratulated one another.

To Glen, the victory was hollow. He had wrestled with his emotions already, and he knew why he had done what he did. The loss of two of his closest friends left him with a futile anger that lacked direction, and was heavily in need of guidance. Allowing his diving gear to crash to the floor, the awful truth that the beaming features of Danny and the reassuring sincerity of his closest friend would no longer greet him as he left the water, rocked him on his feet.

As he held Rhona, the tightness of her embrace made the need for words unnecessary. Nevertheless, he could not help feeling that there was a level of hypocrisy in their actions. The very reasons that the shark had become endangered in the past had been the downfall of the Carcinomas as well… The risk had been great, the cost was heavy, but the Coleshian settlement was safe, for now at least. The precarious situation of Colonel Conran remained a mystery to them.

Docking bay maintenance staff gathered around the group, asking of their success.

"What is the latest news on the negotiations?" asked Sergeant Scott.

"No change," replied an engineer, who wore an apologetic expression on his face.

Before any more questions could be asked, the sounds of heavy footsteps resounded in the large room, drawing the attention of the entourage. Heavily armed troops filled the docking bay, blast rifles extended in their direction.

"Sergeant Scott, your troops and the Elasmobranch Team are required to speak before the Coleshian High Council. They demand an explanation for your actions."

"Are we under arrest?" retorted Glen, anger trying to disguise itself in his voice.

The soldier did not make eye contact with him.

"We have been instructed to use force if necessary. Please co-operate, and this will be resolved peacefully."

Glen and Rhona stared at one another. This was what they had been expecting. Phillipoussis had made true his threats. Relief and sadness were no longer on the minds of the two science officers. Their fate was no longer in their hands…

The huge cylindrical conference hall was a hive of activity, and chattering voices. The warriors of the deep entered the room, and the chatter ceased. The Alliance Troopers, led by Sergeant Scott, and Science Officers Glen Davis and Rhona Skallen, had not been granted any time to prepare for this encounter. They were still wearing their dry suits that left small puddles of water behind every step, as well as providing uncomfortable squelching sounds to the many ears in the room.

High above them, the figure of Governor Phillipoussis gazed down upon them in a pompously dignified manner. He was sitting in the ornately decorated head speaker's chair, located on an elevated podium. The troops and the two science officers stood tall, awaiting their fate.

The Governor spoke:

"You have been brought before the Coleshian High Council to explain your actions. You have all been accused of directly disobeying High Council orders, in carrying out the assault on the Carcinomas, a course of action that has thrown the entire Coleshian settlement, and possibly the fate of the human race, into jeopardy. Your actions have angered Colonel Conran, and, as a result, the Utopia could be on its way to meeting the same fate as the Elysium. If he destroys the Utopia, how will our settlement continue to function? You have shown great ignorance of the facts, and have put many lives at risk. On behalf of the Coleshian High Council and the citizens of this planet, I demand an explanation, in particular, from you, Mr Davis. Against my specific concerns and direct orders, you engaged the alien life form in battle. It was reckless, selfish and ignorant to our plight. Please provide me with a satisfactory excuse for your behaviour."

Glen had to think quickly. He was tired, emotional and somewhat disorientated from his violent excursion. There was no thought spared for the troops who had given their lives in the battle. That sickened him, and he felt ashamed for being a member of the human race. Self-preservation could be so ugly. Now, he was being subjected to humiliation like a trapped animal, exposed and threatened, but like all creatures in this situation, he would do what was necessary to survive.

"Governor Phillipoussis, and members of the High Council, if an explanation is what you require, then that is what I shall provide. Like many people in this room, I am a first generation Coleshian. I have been raised into the hierarchy of the Ark Project. My father and his forbears gave their lives to this aim, as did many of *your* blood relatives. I need not remind you that one of the primary directives of the Eden Treaty was to preserve and show compassion for our fellow life forms. I have devoted my life to this aim, working to restore elements of such life into a new home; life that has been nurtured, wrapped in cotton wool. …May I remind you that before Colonel Conran made his presence known, the Coleshian people were facing a massive threat from the Carcinomas! Not only would these creatures have destroyed the ecosystem, but eventually, they would have turned on the settlement, possibly before anyone could arrive at a suitable outcome to Colonel Conran's demands. The attack on the monorail is testament to that fact. I believe that it was necessary to take this action, because as a Coleshian citizen, I felt obliged to act in accordance with the directives set out in the Eden Treaty. Despite the current climate, and until a change has been established, we still operate within these directives."

The assembled High Command absorbed this information in silence. Once again, Glen felt the full force of Governor Phillipoussis' powerful stare, the stare of judgement bearing down upon him. Silently determined, he resolved to make sure that the governor received no hint at his growing feeling of inadequacy in front of this audience.

Once again, the governor spoke, his voice booming around the large acoustically sound room.

"And what of the cost? As the head of Aquatic Science Team 107, you must be aware that responsibility lies with you, with regard to the personal safety of your team. I see that only you and Miss Skallen have returned. Does that not show a gross negligence of your responsibilities, Mr Davis? Perhaps this is a similar degree of aptitude that you exhibited in dealing with the late Governor Tasken's horrific demise... Not to mention the lack of consideration you exhibited towards the Coleshian people in this delicate time. I have spent hours trying to convince Colonel Conran that you acted independently from our instruction, so that he would refrain from blowing the Utopia to pieces!"

This was the heart of the matter. Two of his team had died because of a decision that he had made, and many more lives were at risk. Try as he might, Glen knew that he could not ignore these facts.

"Governor, weeks ago the High Council was rallying behind the Elasmobranch Team and the mission we were embarking upon. We were declared as shining examples of citizens of the Ark Project. Now, where do we stand?

A small army of terrorists threaten untold damage to our planet if we fail to compromise our beliefs, and because we are too afraid to defy them, the High Council chooses to denounce the Elasmobranch Team as traitors. I find the level of unquestioned hypocrisy disturbing."

The pain in his voice was evident, as was his sincerity, and now emotion was pouring anger into the cocktail.

"I stand before you now, not because you feel it is my duty to explain my actions as a Coleshian citizen, but because I believe that we were right in our actions… I will not apologise for any consequences of what I have done, and if the Coleshian High Council deems it fit to hold me responsible for acting with negligence, then so be it!"

There was a burst of laughter from the governor's chair.

"Your stubbornness to accept the truth really is amusing, Mr Davis. You have lost two of your colleagues…"

"No they were friends, and there were three casualties, not two!"

Watching on, Rhona's mind flashed back to her friends' helpless movements, as the lethal beaks tore into their helpless bodies.

"Three?"

"Yes, three. It would appear that one of the sharks was lost in the confrontation as well."

Phillipoussis looked incredulous:

"You place the life of a fish in the same category as those of your colleagues?"

"Yes, that is why I am an Elasmobranch scientist. I view sharks as being far more than simple-minded fish. The relationship that my colleagues, and myself, built with them was of a strong nature. And our actions were hurried on the basis that judgments made from observing Colonel Conran's *curious* dress sense suggested that his compassion towards other forms of life was very limited. As a result, we decided to release the sharks. We could not guarantee their safe release without tackling the issue of the Carcinomas."

Rhona watched helplessly as the debate unfolded. Glen was being boxed into a corner. In that moment she realised what made Glen different from the few men that she had been closely involved with. She realised that he had faced some of the most difficult decisions of his entire life in recent weeks and he had faced them with courage. Now he was being made to look like an incompetent, irresponsible figure, with a complete disregard for life. Yet despite the way that the situation appeared through the manipulated words of the High Council, he refused to bow down… Now more than ever, it was clear to Rhona why Glen had appealed to her so much. The greater the tide of misfortune pushed him in one direction, the greater his effort was to swim against it. It served only to strengthen her adoration for him.

"Governor, she interrupted, "he speaks the truth – none of the team took part in anything that they perceived to be morally questionable…"

"*Silence, Miss Skallen.*" Phillipoussis' voice echoed around the conference hall like a clap of thunder. "May I remind you that in this Conference Hall, you may only speak when you are personally being addressed."

Glen turned to Rhona and grabbed her hand. Tears were beginning to well up in her eyes at the painfully obvious prospect of what was to follow. When he had faced certain death in the deep beyond the settlement limits, he feared the loss of the most pleasant feeling he had ever known, Rhona's company. Although he had not been able to verbally articulate his feelings to her, he realised that his courage had come from her support and belief in his actions. She had saved his life out there. In this time of conflicting emotions, one of particular clarity emerged from the swirling haze of feelings.

I love this woman…

"It's all right, Rhona," he said soothingly, smiling weakly at her, carefully stroking his index finger down her soft face to catch the tears that threatened to blemish the rosy texture of her cheeks.

It amazed him that even after they had been through hell, she remained a picture of natural beauty…

"Mr Davis!" Governor Phillipoussis boomed at him. "It would seem to me that your impulsive behaviour has needlessly cost lives. In disobeying orders, you attempted to take large-scale action at your own will. As a result, people died."

Turning to the assembled committee, the latest Coleshian governor addressed them.

"I propose that the High Council set a hearing for a later date to discuss Mr Davis' capabilities to operate as an active officer within

Coleshian society."

Glen realised the severity of his situation. It would be easy for the authorities to accuse him of gross negligence with regard to Governor Tasken's death now. He had made *himself* a scapegoat!

Governor Phillipoussis now turned his attention to Sergeant Scott, who had watched the proceedings in silence. He had given no emotion away through his expression, adopting a clinical visage in true military fashion.

"And how do you fit into all this, Sergeant? As a highly decorated soldier in the Coleshian Military Forces, I must express my disappointment at your contradiction of Coleshian High Council orders," said the governor, sighing.

"Governor, I *was* acting upon orders."

"*Orders!* From *whom?*"

"General Miller, Sir!"

Chapter 47

It had to be more than just coincidence. As soon as the sergeant had mentioned his superior officer's name, the giant entrance to the left of the governor's chair slid back, allowing a modest procession of soldiers to file into the room. They were wearing the military uniforms of Penusia, and their hands were placed across the backs of their heads.

Conran's troops!

These were followed by a large procession of Alliance Space Troopers, armed with blast rifles that were aimed at the line of defeated soldiers. At the back of the procession, two troopers walked in front of and behind what looked like a stretcher. It floated in between them, as they firmly held the handles in a vice-like grip. A white sheet was draped over a bulky shape that lay on the stretcher, hiding the identity of the mass.

Gasps of astonishment went around the room.

"*What is the meaning of this?*" yelled Phillipoussis, rising from his chair. "Explain yourselves."

"We are acting upon orders, Governor."

"From whom?"

"From *me!*"

A figure entered the room, walking slowly, and with tactful, carefully considered steps that were not the natural gait of a man his size. He wore the red uniform of an engineer, which failed to disguise the blood soaked area around his stomach. The reason for his unusual stance became clear to several astonished eyes, as blood began to drip from the wound onto the floor. His wound was highlighted by scorch marks on the red fabric. The sheer fact that he was still standing left every member of the hall dumbstruck and frozen...

In life, timing is the most crucial factor... Not if, but when... Especially when it comes to dealing in truths...

"*General Miller!*" said the governor, incredulously.

The look on his face had changed from one of the cat playing with the mouse to one of someone who had just seen a ghost. Glen and Rhona watched the scene unfold, unable to peel their eyes from the man who seemingly defied death. Somehow, they both shared a very strong feeling that a lot of mysteries would now be resolved, and giant leaps would be made towards the truth...

Despite the fact that he was bleeding heavily, the general still had the air of someone who commanded authority and respect from those around him. He showed no sign of pain.

"General, what is the meaning of this?" repeated the stunned governor, in parrot fashion to his earlier question.

"Governor Phillipoussis, I wish to be given permission to address the High Council. I have important information regarding the future of the Coleshian settlement."

"General, you have interrupted an important meeting. In case you failed to notice, you are bleeding. You should be receiving treatment for that injury, man, not standing here."

Briefly, the general almost allowed the faint trace of a smile to crease the corners of his dried lips.

"I'll live," he replied.

Governor Phillipoussis' annoyance at the interruption gave way to feigned concern for the general's condition.

"If indeed that is true, which on current evidence I find very hard to believe, I suggest that you speak before you bleed to death. How on Coleshia did you end up like that anyway?"

"If you will permit me, Governor, I shall explain the whole situation before the witnesses in this room."

Looking somewhat bemused, the Governor replied:

"Well then, I suggest that you leave this gathering in suspense no longer."

The general strode to the centre of the hall, signalling for the condemned divers to be seated. They obliged. In doing so Glen noticed that Sergeant Scott's stern features had changed from blankness to extreme concern for his superior officer. It was obvious that the sergeant was resisting a strong urge to run to the general's assistance.

"In recent days, a number of disturbing discoveries have come to my attention. I need remind no one of the delicate situation that the Coleshian people have been placed in, held to ransom for their beliefs. Before I disclose any more information, I will put your minds at rest... The threat is no more. Colonel Conran's rebellion is over!"

At this statement, the whole hall erupted in an explosion of voices.

"*Please*," yelled the general over the noise, "allow me to explain."

"Nonsense, General. Conran is in the guest accommodation awaiting the completion of the negotiations," interjected Governor Phillipoussis. "We are to leave the settlement to search for a new home planet. We have no choice!"

"I'm afraid not, Governor," replied the general, turning to face Phillipoussis.

He motioned to the men carrying the stretcher. They placed it on the floor, and one of them removed the sheet. Beneath was the inert form of Colonel Conran, now without the grotesque decoration of the dead lioness. Even in death, the colonel's harsh features did little to give his face any sign of having found peace in the uncharted territory of the afterlife...

"The colonel and myself did not see eye to eye on things..."

A gasp resounded throughout the large hall.

"General," said the governor, fear rocking his voice, "it was stated that any attempt on the Colonel's life would be met with the destruction of the Utopia. You have condemned us all by your actions. We are doomed."

"I'm afraid that is no longer the case either, Governor. Any attempt to contact her will be met with silence, but not because she is destroyed. At this stage the Utopia is unharmed in Coleshia's orbit. She is depressurised and all her inhabitants have been killed, including Conran's army!"

"How is this possible?" cried the governor.

He now appeared very pale, and his wrists tightly gripped the arms of his chair.

"Allow me to explain. When the Elysium exploded, I took the liberty of travelling to Penusia to see the extent of the damage. As will become evident, this will explain the reason for my absence. I witnessed destruction on a mass scale, but I also witnessed pure barbarism. Conran's troops were not performing a salvage operation, they were recruiting... Anyone who refused to denounce the Ark Project they murdered in cold blood. This order was executed to the very peak of Penusia's hierarchy, resulting in the mass slaughter of the Penusian High Council, and Governors Astran and Varden.

Unknown to them I tailed them to the Utopia, where I saw my own troops inhumanely slaughtered, but the worst truth of all is hidden in this mutiny. As perhaps a few of you suspected, the Elysium *was* deliberately destroyed and Colonel Conran instigated her destruction!"

"But why? Such loss is senseless," replied Governor Phillipoussis.

General Miller turned from the seated audience to coldly regard the official.

"Governor, I was hoping that you could tell me. You see, Conran was not working alone...The human race has been deceived by a conspiracy on the most unbelievable scale! Governor Phillipoussis, I put it to you that you were in allegiance with Colonel Conran. You co-conspired with Conran to ensure that Penusia buckled by destroying the Elysium!"

Once again, the audience erupted into a melee of shouts and jeers, while the governor bore the look of having just been shot, and not quite recovering from the shock of it...

"*Preposterous*. It is a heavily punishable crime to accuse a council member of such an offence. You had better have evidence to back up your claims, General."

"I can assure you, Governor, I do. You see, I was always one step ahead of you… I have been aware of a fact that no individual alive today could possibly know, even the most devilish. You see, at the Ark Project's inception, steps were taken to ensure that such human behaviour would be countered during our voyage of discovery. The World Council of Earth and the military forces of the time co-operated in a highly classified operation. Its name was MACU…"

"MACU… What the hell does that mean?" replied the governor angrily, seriously beginning to lose the fragile grip on his calm persona.

"MACU. is an abbreviation for Military Automated Cybernetic Unit."

"Rubbish… Never in recorded history have we had the ability to produce cybernetic technology. This is pure science fiction, General."

"I'm afraid not. The MACU Project, I can assure you was very real and it resulted in the development of one functioning unit, called LB–42, whose priority was simple… To protect the Ark Project, and its directives, set out in the Eden Treaty, to protect the long-term interests of humankind, and those of the accompanying life forms on the mission to the Quaker solar system. To install balance where humanity has created chaos…"

"This is all very interesting, General, but you have to prove all this."

"I am coming to this. You see there can be one reason why I know this…"

Once again the injured general stared around the huge hall.

"I am LB-42!"

His announcement was met with looks of shock and disbelief…

"Allow me to demonstrate this, and in doing so, I will also dispel any of the discrepancies in my discovery of the conspiracy to overthrow the Ark Project. If this were not true, I can assure you that I would not be standing before you now. Use your good sense… This wound would prove to be fatal to any normal human being."

The general moved towards a portable computer terminal, while he continued to speak.

"That is where, both yourself and Colonel Conran made a critical mistake. You were right to view my absence as a threat, and this resulted in his attempt to kill me."

The general undid the right sleeve to his suit and rolled it up, before taking hold of his wrist with his left hand, and twisting it hard, in a clockwise direction. There was a sickening click that shattered the brief silence and made everyone within earshot wince. The general, with a face set in stone then proceeded to remove his right hand, blood pouring onto the floor.

"Do not be alarmed. This hurts less than it appears."

Placing his hand on the terminal monitor, he fumbled inside his right wrist, which now revealed electronic circuitry, and he removed a small cylindrical object that brilliantly reflected the light - a memory disk!

All around the room, people struggled to gain a better view of this technological and rather gut churning wizardry.

Holding the shining disk up to the congregation, he continued his explanation.

"You see, when I was developed, it was with a consideration to the technology that was relevant at the time. This of course, was the technology that was incorporated into the systems of the star cruisers that brought us to the Quaker solar system, and bought us enough time to create a new home here. As predicted, the rate of technological evolution slowed dramatically following our departure from Earth, due to a lack of resources. Look around you now. Much of our existing technology is based upon the systems developed for deep space travel nearly three hundred years ago. In the time when the human race used to inhabit the planet Earth, technological progress used to double on average every two years. In technological terms on the same scale, our current situation represents stagnant progress. It is this factor that allows me to bring you this information now."

With that the general inserted the disk into the terminal's hard drive. The curved wall to the immediate right of the governor's chair suddenly flickered into life.

The audience watched…

The assembled group witnessed the unfolding of the conspiracy, images of Conran's rebellion destroying the Penusian High Council and flashes of blast rifle fire igniting the windows of the administration building. They watched as the image drew closer to the besieged building and infiltrated its very heart. The image jolted slightly with every footstep that they now realised had to be those of the cyborg – General Miller.

When it felt as if they could bear no more death, the picture disappeared down a plushly decorated corridor, and to one door with the nameplate scratched away. The scratches had been an attempt at removing the words that had adorned its surface before. Now the scratches formed the words: GOVERNOR VARDEN. Upon entry into the room the audience were shocked to see two, lifeless charred bodies sprawled on the smouldering bed. In horror, the shocked Coleshian Council realised they had just seen the recently murdered remains of Governor Varden and his partner…

Despite the gruesome nature of these images, the general continued to stand inert, by the terminal, as if he were in a state of trance. His meditative state remained as the images changed to the interior of the Utopia; Conran's merciless order to slaughter her resident band of troops… then, the horrific sight of the distorted bodies that had suffered the effects of a space vacuum, floating aimlessly in the images. As the images ceased as abruptly as they began the final pieces were placed into this twisted jigsaw puzzle by the trance-like cyborg…

"Upon anonymously returning from the Utopia, I was aware of Conran's arrival in the Coleshian settlement. My priority became to find him and trace his movements. Once again, I used the ventilation shafts in the complex to move around. The 'negotiations' proved to be the missing link."

The images started once again, this time from behind the grilled maintenance hatch of the ventilation shaft in the governor's office.

"So, Legion 2, at last we are close."

The mocking voice was that of Governor Phillipoussis.

"Yes, Legion 1, soon the human race will abandon the Ark Project," replied Colonel Conran.

The truth was told…

For a moment there was silence.

The assembled group struggled to come to terms with what they had just seen. No one looked more shocked than Governor Phillipoussis, and no one felt more aggrieved than Glen Davis.

"Because of your lust for power, millions of people have died. You tried to use my team as a scapegoat for Governor Tasken's death, when *you* sabotaged his PAD device, and *you* murdered him. I understand now. You were protecting the governor's equipment before he died. I saw you! You used emotional blackmail against me, because I was so close to the truth. There *was* a conspiracy on a higher level, and I was right. It was all about power! When the Coleshian authorities eventually discovered sabotage, you were going to point the finger at me as an unstable individual. You had it all worked out."

Governor Phillipoussis just stared back at him, lost for words, with a look that would be more suitable for someone who was staring down the barrel of a gun.

Glen continued the onslaught.

"Before you left for Penusia you visited our laboratory. It wasn't an official visit at all was it? You were trying to gauge our likelihood of success, to see how much of a threat we posed to your plan for the human race… If the Carcinomas were eliminated, beyond Conran's regime there would be no need for us to leave Coleshia. You told me that being humane would not ensure our survival or that of the ecosystem. You weren't referring to me at all. You were referring to *yourself!* You never believed in the Ark Project, did you? You share the same antiquated beliefs as our ancestors. Conran's assault gave you an excuse to ignore Coleshia's problems; to hold back on our offensive. Predicting that we would contradict your wishes, you let us leave, assuming that at the very least we would be killed without military assistance, thus neutralising the opposition to your plan. But that went wrong because Sergeant Scott and his troops turned up, under specific orders from General Mill… LB…him! I failed to realise how the sharks created such an obstacle for you to overcome, and in response, you managed to kill two birds with one stone… Eliminating Governor Tasken by using the sharks, and at the same time discrediting our operation completely! Tell me, Governor, was the demonstration really Governor Tasken's idea… or was it yours?"

Once again, the cyborg interrupted.

"That's enough, Mr Davis. I can appreciate your feelings, and I believe you are correct. Today is a very sad day in the history of the human race, and we must use it as a reminder of the dark times that we thought we had left behind. It seems that selfish human emotions are still prevalent within our society, and we have not evolved as much as we initially believed. Let this be the turning point in the Ark Project."

LB-42 motioned to two of the troops.

"Governor Phillipoussis, you are under arrest, for the murder of Governor Tasken, conspiracy to the murder of the Penusian race as well as conspiracy to overthrow the Ark Project."

In the past, the lack of emotion in the general's speech had been attributed to a military discipline, mere moments ago the temperament of an artificial intelligence, and right now the expression of someone who had seen so much, and could not be shocked by anything! The dumbstruck governor, however, could be, but he was determined to express the thoughts that were on his mind…

It should just about buy me enough time…

"Do you honestly think that this was purely the crusade of mad men? How pathetic, how *primitive*… We didn't do this because of power. You still don't see, do you? All that the human race has done is prolong its suffering. In time we shall be forced to leave this system in search of a new home, and once again we will have our backs to the wall, as we did all those centuries ago on the planet Earth. We have been told to suppress our own instincts of self-preservation for the sake of the precious wildlife. It will be our end…"

"No, Governor," replied the cyborg. "It was the inability of the human race to ensure its own survival that forced us into leaving our home planet in the first place…"

The cyborg motioned with his working hand. The troops moved forward with menacing purpose.

"*You fools,*" cried Phillipoussis.

He stood up from his chair and produced an object from his robe. A blast pistol!

Panic erupted, and in the split seconds that followed, the congregation dived for cover, while the troops raised their weapons. Although quick, the reaction was ill-fated…

Governor Phillipoussis pulled the trigger. In a second his head had dissolved, and a scorch mark adorned the fabric on the headrest of his chair. The wound cauterised almost instantly. His decapitated body fell from the podium, and landed with a soggy thump on the floor… With his life, went the final trace of opposition to the Ark Project…

Chapter 48

Project Date: Day 53 of Year 0405

Once again, the dreams returned - vivid nightmares that recounted the horror. The violence… The deaths…
He relived those moments of extreme anguish and memory, imagination leaked into the messy pool of his mind as he witnessed their suffering at the furious attacks of aquiline beaks.

When he finally awoke from his tormented slumber, Glen felt no relief from finding himself in the present. Whereas most nightmares ceased when the individual afflicted by them awoke, his continued in the real world.

Feelings of guilt plagued him, like an unpleasant odour that he couldn't shake off…

But at least I am not alone any more!

Glen stared at the beautiful form sleeping peacefully next to him. Rhona too had been experiencing nightmares, experiencing a great sense of loss, similar to his own. At night her thoughts blurred into a brutal collage of her friends dying, pleading with her to free them from mercilessly slashing jaws… She had spoken of how Mike and Danny slowly transformed with each blow into the monsters that had so violently ended their lives…Before launching themselves at her. This sleep however, brought her some welcome hours of solace.

Since the confrontation with the Carcinomas, neither of them had even contemplated re-entering the water.

The hearing assessing the competency of the Elasmobranch Team had not materialised after Governor Phillipoussis' death. They had not been reinstated as Officers. With the release of the apex predators into the ocean they had fulfilled the release schedule of their inventory, if somewhat controversially…

Glen was beginning to assume that this state of limbo that they found themselves in was perhaps the closest that they would ever come to recognition for their efforts in saving the settlement. It wasn't reward that he craved, but an acknowledgement of the sacrifices that his friends had made. Yet, at the same time, Glen almost felt gratitude for the fact that he still had a home to return to… It was down to one individual that he could find this contemplative state in his own accommodation, lying next to the most important person in his life…

As his eyes caressed Rhona's perfect curves with far more than carnal adoration, his thoughts went to the saviour of the human race…

With the knowledge that I have, I still see him as a human being…

When Glen and Rhona were eating breakfast, they received a request to attend an appointment in the new governor's quarters. Since the pandemonium following Governor Tasken's death, Phillipoussis had never appointed a senator - had probably never intended to - and, as a result, a huge gap had been left in Coleshia's administrative hierarchy that needed to be quickly filled. It had been a short list for suitable candidates for the position of governor, and no one raised any objections to the nominated appointee…

Later that morning Glen and Rhona travelled to the main settlement via one of the transport submersibles. The monorail repairs were yet to begin, and transport between the Aquatic Science Centre and the main complex was still manually controlled. They travelled in silence, each locked in thought regarding the pending meeting. They drew comfort from each other's presence, and their hands joined.

From her position next to the viewing port in the vehicle's alloy body Rhona stared out into the depths. The sea did not hold the same magic for her now. She had believed that she had witnessed the most frightening terror that the ocean had to offer when she joined

Elasmobranch Team several years before. How wrong she had been…
A shiver went down her spine.

Suddenly, a spark lit up the water around the viewing port. It ceased momentarily before igniting again. From the dim light that it created Rhona spotted movement in a number of locations. As the submersible passed over the area of activity she realised the reason for it, as the monorail line appeared in her view. Beneath the rail hung a carriage surrounded by teams of divers brandishing a variety of cutting and welding tools…

"You must be wondering why I have summoned you here?" said the figure seated in the governor's chair.

"The thought had crossed our minds," replied Rhona.

The figure laughed slightly, and stood up; the purple folds in his robe disappeared as gravity took charge of the large garment.

"Let me ask you, Officer Davis, Officer Skallen, how do you feel about the eradication of the Carcinomas from this planet?"

Glen and Rhona looked at each other. Rhona answered for both of them. It was obvious that there was a lot of pain masked in her voice.

"Numb…"

A brief interval elapsed as the figure absorbed this information before speaking a considered response.

"An interesting assertion, considering the cost to yourselves, and the unfortunate consequences that would have befallen the Coleshian settlement had you not acted as you did. Why do you feel this way?"

"We are scientists who work to preserve life, and now we have been responsible for inflicting suffering. There is no satisfaction to be gained from watching friends suffer a painful death."

Blue eyes regarded them from a chiselled featured face that was touched by the formation of a smile, articulated in a manner suggesting that this was still an emotional reaction under a high degree of practice. Despite this, the intention of the sentiment did not go unnoticed by the couple sitting opposite him.

Glen struggled to picture the man in anything other than the perfectly pressed military uniform of the Alliance Military Forces.

"It is a troublesome dilemma that you must find yourselves in right now," said Governor Miller perceptively.

Glen nodded. Somehow the cyborg seemed far more articulate now in the position of governor than he ever did as a military leader. Who really knew the extent of his secrets and his skills?

He continued his perceptive judgement of their emotions.

"You struggle to see the good in what you achieved. You look at the loss of your friends and you feel that you betrayed all that you have worked to protect for so long. You must see the bigger picture. The action that you took was the right choice. Due to your efforts, a major threat to the Coleshian settlement was eliminated, albeit at an unpleasantly large cost of those close to you. The sacrifice that they made has not gone unnoticed, believe me, and you should feel proud of their courage, and your own."

"At the moment grief makes it is very difficult to see it that way," replied Glen, forlornly.

Governor Miller definitely had a different air about him. He was no longer a blunt Military General; he had a level of charisma and emotion to his behaviour.

Rhona wondered how many times his personality must have changed over the years.

If only they could see him now... The saviour of the human race and now the light that guides all of us... He seems so human and yet he has survived for centuries... How has he survived for all these years?

It was a question that played on the tip of her tongue, and yet she felt unable to speak it. Somehow it seemed inappropriate to satisfy her curiosity at his expense. She sensed that deep down this survivor battled his own demons in ways that they would probably never know... The irony was strong. Human treachery had become so bad, as to now place humanity's destiny in the hands of one of its creations...

The fact is that we are not responsible enough to govern our own destiny...

"When Conran was aboard the Utopia, and I had to make a decision, sentencing those troops to death was not easy... At the time it felt like it was the most evil thing that I could have done, and yet more people would have suffered had I not done it. We may have played on opposite sides of the border, Mr Davis, but our actions and motives were not too dissimilar!"

"I can see that, but all the time, you had your directives to guide you. In addition you did not lose anyone close to you either," replied Glen.

"Rather a rash judgement, don't you think, of someone who was alive centuries before you were born? I have emotions, just like you, Mr Davis... In the eyes of the Ark Project we have committed no crime because we worked towards the greater good."

The new governor was pierced by Glen's words as his thoughts drifted back to someone whom he had cared for... Time had not diminished his feelings. She was the one person who had showed him true kindness in his infancy, his mental retreat in times of difficulty.

Dr McAllister, when you created me, did you envisage that I would create so much destruction on the Utopia, and be appointed leader of this confused race as a result of that action? You told me once of how I would have to learn about the contradictions of humanity and life... This is one of them... I am a saviour and a murderer, how can that be?

"I have been given this opportunity to do everything I can in the interests of the..."

Momentarily, the governor paused. The words 'Ark Project' and 'Eden Treaty' were waiting to be spoken as they had been in solitary mutterings of self-assurance thousands of times in the past. On this occasion, however, they remained unspoken.

"... in the interests of the *human race*... I am blessed with the knowledge that others do not have, because my body contains technology, which even today is compatible with the systems that support the human race. In the past my compatibility, if you like, with the databases of the star vessels allowed me to continually reinvent myself in various guises, for the benefit of identity records, as and when necessity required it... Hopping between the cruisers every generation, it was easy to remain inconspicuous, but it broadened my understanding of the journey out... That is all I have done now, although somewhat more conspicuously! During my years aboard the star cruisers, I witnessed, first hand, the struggle and suffering that the human race had to endure on the journey from planet Earth..."

Glen nodded.

"Did you ever see our home planet?"

Governor Miller wryly smiled at him before responding.

"Mr Davis, you are the first Coleshian who has had the courage to ask me that question. On a couple of occasions I did, but from the stars!"

"What did it look like?"

"Beautiful... When I was... born... Earth was a volatile planet, considered far too dangerous for me to see from her surface. The storms were extremely violent, swirling cloud formations, highly intense conditions that beat humanity into submission... No one on the surface could escape easily, and no one among the stars could visit her safely!"

Hinting at a smile, the governor continued:

"But that was the past... With the future comes the obligation to uphold the responsibilities of our past. That is what the Elasmobranch Team did, and your companions shall be remembered for it."

"Wait one minute, Governor," replied Glen. "There are still things that we do not understand!"

"Well, let me enlighten you."

"Okay... If you knew that the Elasmobranch Team were acting in a correct manner, why did you stand in opposition to the idea of implicating the sharks in the eradication of the Carcinomas?"

"I was wondering when we would get to this... I did not wish to see your initiative fail. I know many things, Mr Davis, but shark psychology is not among those areas of expertise. I had to be sure that you had considered all the possibilities of your suggestion. That, you must surely understand? If I was opposed to your plan, then I would not have gone against the Coleshian administration and ordered military support for your operation, would I?"

Glen listened, judging the answer to be sincere. Then he launched his next assault.

"Fair enough, but we are also forgetting a major issue in all this."

"There are several, Mr Davis. To which one are you referring?"

"Well, let's try Governor Tasken's death. I have sat here and listened to you sing our praises, but you seem to forget that there was an investigation taking place, in which I was a chief suspect. I already know *whom* was responsible, but I have not been made aware of *how* the sabotage was put into motion!"

Governor Miller returned to his seat, and looked squarely at the two science officers.

"Well, you are certainly entitled to an explanation... I received the report on the PAD device this morning. The means of sabotage was simple. A sub-standard battery was inserted into the device after Officer McCormick carried out his checks. If you recall, Governor Tasken's gear was guarded by Phillipoussis on the day that the demonstration took place. Obvious really... The plan was executed on the basis that no one would consider a member of the High Council to be unscrupulous enough to commit such a foul deed. The plan worked very effectively, fooling everyone including the unfortunate governor..."

"If Phillipoussis were still alive today and you had failed, do you think that the truth would ever have come to light?" enquired Glen.

"What you were facing, Mr Davis, was a duel; your word against his. Phillipoussis was well respected amongst the Coleshian hierarchy, and you would effectively have been standing against the entire High Council. He would have been able to use the undisputed facts of the investigation – the nature of the sabotage to any end that he saw fit."

"You mean he set me up?"

"Not just you... He would have discredited the entire team because everything that you stood for opposed the 'new order' that he was trying to effect."

A period of thought transpired before the new governor spoke again.

"Now that Alliance Military Troops have been dispatched to salvage what they can from Penusia, there remains one challenge… Coleshia has a large ecosystem beyond the settlement limits, one that has been severely damaged…. I would like Miss Skallen and yourself to lead the operation to re-address the balance of the ecosystem again, working with the other ASC Release Teams."

For a moment Glen and Rhona looked astounded. Words escaped them.

"The Coleshian High Council seems to have changed its tune," said Glen, somewhat cautiously.

Governor Miller smiled.

"We all know that many agendas were being considered a short time ago, several of which were less than amiable. During this difficult time you acted in the best interests of the Eden Treaty and the human race, not to your own agenda! The Ark Project needs individuals like yourselves, who can deal with responsibility, and you have proven your expertise in this field."

"After we contradicted the High Council's orders I thought that we would never be allowed into the ocean again," stated Rhona.

"Miss Skallen, your reaction to the extinction of a species that took the lives of your friends only serves to reassure me further that your level of compassion for all life demands that you are presented with this opportunity. We both know that Phillipoussis was giving orders that did not have the sanctity of life as their motivation. There will be a whole new generation of wildlife requiring Brainchips and careful study in the time to come."

"And what of the Carcinomas?" asked Glen. "Our operation did not destroy all of them. There are bound to be survivors."

"All the more reason to restore the ecosystem to its natural beauty as soon as humanly possible. As we speak, patrol teams are sweeping the ocean searching for Carcinomas, and assessing the damage. They will soon pick off any remaining specimens… So I would be most interested in your reaction."

Centuries of isolation have taught me that the importance of my exist-

ence is to be humane, not human...

As an agent of chaos, I was pretending to be an embodiment of life that I am clearly not, fulfilling the desires of those long gone...

Momentarily Glen and Rhona were witness to the cyborg's brief interlude into his past, as he silently stared at the wall behind them.

"Governor?"

Dr McAllister, so much of what you taught me was a lie... You were not my mother; I am not human, for if I was I should have died centuries ago... Conran should have killed me, had I truly been alive, had I truly been human... No longer do I have to pretend. I have done what you have asked of me. Now I exist to fulfil myself!

Glen and Rhona stared at one another, wonder on their faces, giving way to broad smiles. Glen turned back to the new Coleshian governor, an answer hanging on his lips...

Governor Miller, you are more human than you will probably ever realise...

Chapter 49

Project date: Day 105 of Year 0405

The yellow submersible bobbed up and down on the ocean waves. In the distance an island broke the symmetry of the horizon. The vehicle had surfaced a respectful distance from the island, so as not to disturb its inhabitants. Despite an interval of nearly two kilometres, the huge size of the man-made land mass did not go unnoticed to the inhabitants of the brightly coloured vehicle.

An access hatch opened on the topside of the craft and Glen Davis emerged, taking in the fresh sea air and the breeze that created the gentle swell of the ocean. It was a beautiful day, and the sun shone brightly in a clear blue sky. It's awesome power reflected dazzlingly upon the waves, and his eyes struggled to adjust to the clarity of the view around him.

As he turned his attention to the inhabitants of the island, a gust of wind brought distinct sounds to his attention that disrupted the gentle hypnotic slapping of the waves against the hull of the submersible. At least there was one species that was easy to track down... He listened with interest to the grunting and hollering of one thousand chattering voices.

Through his telescopic lenses Glen could see the island more clearly. There was no vegetation upon its surface, but there were several inclined surfaces on each face of the structure. It was not particularly pretty to look at, but it served a purpose. Increasing the magnification on his lenses he picked out a bustling community of movement.

Zooming in further, he saw the creatures, many of which were basking in the sun on the island's flat plains.

On the slopes leading to the water's edge, cumbersome, plump bodies moved to and from the water, awkwardly propelling themselves along with swift rippled body movements. They traversed the angled slopes with difficulty, but it was for the sea that they were evolved, and it was in the sea that they fed.

Atop one of the curved artificial rockeries lay the proud form of a bull seal. He was nearly twelve feet long, with powerful head muscles and a streamlined body. Behind one of his eyes a small protrusion appeared from his flesh – his Brainchip! He bathed in Coleshia's sun, his large eyes watching his kin to check that they were safe. Lazily he rolled to one side, his large black nostrils flaring as he breathed in and out.

Glen scanned the landscape, looking for the telltale signs of another presence in the area. Carefully, he examined each of the seals that waddled past the line of sight of his binoculars. At last, he found what he had been looking for… One seal bore a set of scars from a deep laceration. The wound appeared to be healing, but it was relatively fresh. The seal had been lucky. The wound had obviously been received from the jaws of a predator…

"Rhona, I've found one!"

She appeared in the open hatch next to him.

"Can I see?"

Glen handed her the lenses.

"There must be hundreds of them now. Where am I looking? Oh yes, I see it… They were here, Glen!"

"I know, I think that they must be adapting well. Let's check the sensors, maybe they are here now."

Glen disappeared into the cockpit of the submersible. Fiddling with the craft's intricate controls, he checked various visual displays. Rhona rejoined him.

"If they are here, we will detect them through their Brainchips."

"Yes, look, there's one a few miles away. Quick, get the diving gear."

With no hesitation and frantic with excitement they climbed into their dry suits. A red light blinked in a rhythmic sequence on each of the garments - PAD devices! Since accepting Governor Miller's offer, they had both longed for this day on countless occasions. This would be their first encounter with the Great White sharks since the confrontation with the Carcinomas.

After a seemingly painful lengthy preparation of the equipment, Glen and Rhona felt the same nervous exhilaration that had always appealed to them before entering the huge pool in the Animal Release Zone…

Glen fixed his helmet and checked his Bodywave keypad.

"The Implant Team is on its way."

"That's good news," replied Rhona. "There are a lot of seal pups out there that need Brainchips."

"Yes, they will certainly have their work cut out for the day."

The two divers climbed to the edge of the submersible, and jumped, feet first into the water. Air bubbles surrounded their descent. They remained near the surface, and decided to move away from the stationary vehicle.

What they had noticed since beginning their study was that the wildlife was beginning to filter back to the areas of the ocean that had, until recently, been derelict and abandoned. The ecosystem was balancing out very well, and fortunately enough, the haste of the response to the alien threat had been sufficient to perturb permanent damage. The healthy state of the seal colony was testament to this fact, but only time would tell whether this was to remain the case. Now it was time to check on the progress of the apex predators…

Glen looked at Rhona. She grinned back at him.

Once again, Glen typed the familiar words into his miniature keypad that was strapped to his left wrist.

FRIEND.

Time passed… No response… He retyped the call.

For some time it appeared as if no response was forthcoming; and then…

FRIEND.

From the deep blue haze below the surface, a familiar body shape emerged from the murk. The Great White shark moved closer, but the divers found it difficult to identify the individual. As the magnificent beast cruised past, the realisation dawned upon them as more movement appeared in the water. It was Cleopatra!

Suddenly Rhona cried:

"Glen, look, she's given birth!"

Behind the huge body of its mother, cruised the form of an infant Great White shark. It swam by, inquisitively, almost fearful of the newcomers. Natural selection had not been kind to the mother. Only one of her pups had survived the infant stages of life… It must have been no more than two feet long. Tiny claspers emerged from its sexual glands, identifying it as a male. Its teeth were pointed, not triangular. Nature carefully included this feature so that the young shark could catch small fish, until it was of a size when it could handle larger prey. From a certain age the familiar triangular points that aided the adults so well would replace the infant teeth.

"My God, Rhona. This is incredible. I never thought that I would ever see this."

"Look how she protects him. It's amazing how maternal her behaviour is," she replied.

Unable to tear their eyes away, Glen and Rhona continued to watch mother and offspring glide gracefully by.

Now there would be a new addition to the inventory of the Implant Team. Eventually, Cleopatra and her pup disappeared once more into their domain.

Glen and Rhona returned to the surface in the close proximity of the submersible. Just as they were about to shed their gear a large triangulated fin broke the water's surface some fifty yards away. Quickly, the two divers hit the water again, and upon the creature's next pass, they identified the individual - Kauhulu!

The worthiest king of them all…

The sight of the mighty fish almost brought tears of relief to Glen's eyes, as he swam in an uninhibited manner past the two divers, allowing them to stroke his tough skin. He bore some deep scars from his encounters with the Carcinomas, but they were not enough to quell his strength and skill as an oceanic predator.

Suddenly, almost as quickly as he had appeared, he was gone. Glen reached an outstretched gloved hand as the shark disappeared once more into the deep. A message appeared on their keypads:

FRIEND…

It was a difficult fact to accept, but Glen knew that this was the last time that he would be able to think of Kauhulu as an ally – a friend. Now he was a top predator establishing his territory in the ocean of Coleshia, and Glen was a scientist ensuring that the transition to his new home took strong effect. For the benefit of that transition, minimal human contact with the sharks had to be respected from now on. It was painful to take, but somehow Glen felt that this was not the last time that he would see the magnificent fish…

When they had relieved themselves of their diving gear they embraced, overjoyed that the sharks appeared to be winning their struggle for survival. Their encounter with the Great Whites had a far more profound effect on them than simple joy. In that brief glimpse of beauty and predatory grace, Glen and Rhona had rediscovered their love of the ocean.

Suddenly, the communicator in the submersible crackled into life. Standing in the access hatch they glanced around. In the distance, two brightly coloured objects emerged on the surface, catching the dazzling beauty of the sun as they rocked on the waves. The Implant Team had arrived. Now they had a lot of work to get through.

"What would you prefer, implanting some rather sensitive and aggressive seals, or sitting in the drink with a friendly Great White shark?" asked Glen.

Looking towards the island with an expression of foreboding Rhona replied:

"I'd take the Great White, any day in a Coleshian month!"

"So would I… Never underestimate the strength of a shark, Officer Skallen."

The flirtatious tones in Rhona's response sent Glen's pulse racing.

"And never forget the strength of the people who respect them, Officer Davis!"

Glen looked to the future. He felt the past falling away, a stream of bad memories disappearing into the chaos that had randomly dumped them where they now found themselves. Somewhere, Astra would be finding her own territory… They looked forward to finding her in her new home.

Glen looked forward to building his life with the woman he loved, and now held in a tight embrace. Where in the past there lay fog, the future promised sunshine… He kissed Rhona, and allowed his consciousness to drift into her dazzling dark eyes, which extended affection towards him.

For the first time in his life Glen Davis took a step back and allowed himself to feel happy and contented…

EPILOGUE

Hunger…! At this stage it was the one factor driving the beast on. The sinister creature cruised stealthily in between the rocks, its vividly acute eyesight watching for signs of danger, or possible meals. The Carcinoma changed the colour of its skin, mimicking the dark shades of the rocks that concealed it in its silent vigil. It had been some time since it had seen another of its own kind. Once they had been numerous. Now, the creature felt the solitude and exposure of the elements. It felt vulnerable!

As it cruised near the seabed it began to run out of oxygen. Pressure was building up in its air sacks, and it felt the need to return to the surface to breathe. The surrounding area looked empty. Perhaps now was the best opportunity to gather some strength. Instinctively the Carcinoma steeply inclined towards the surface, powering its armoured body into the shallower depths.

Fear had made the beast apprehensive. Now, in full adult life, it was aware of the new dangers of its environment. To some species it was an instinct born later than others, in this case too late. There was a new form of life in the ocean that had destroyed its fellow beings, hunting with a tenacity that the creature had never before encountered.

Its yellow eyes watched the surrounding water for signs of danger. It was near the surface now. A long period of time had transpired since it had last fed, and now fatigue had weakened its body, slowed its reflexes. When the creature hit the surface it expelled its air supply, a fountain of spray erupting from the surface. Breathing in, it felt a tremendous pressure around its stomach, and suddenly it was launched from the sea.

The creature returned to the waves with an almighty dispersal of water. The pressure was gone, but now pain replaced it. A haze of its own blood surrounded the beast, as it struggled to reach the surface for air, in a pink haze. The Carcinoma's highly tuned eyesight picked out the form of its attacker. It was one of the hunters!

How long had it been tracking its movements? It was as if the hunter knew of its presence without seeing it. The creature realised its fate, mortally injured, and paralysed from the numbing pain in its stomach. The hunter circled the helpless creature, menacingly. Then another movement caught the Carcinoma's attention. It was far smaller than its attacker, but it looked like a miniature version of the hunter. Where the larger hunter swam, the smaller one followed.

The creature began to feel numb, all feeling leaving its body. Lack of food and the force of the attack had taken its toll. The Carcinoma had become a helpless target. As it began to lose consciousness it was aware of a number of things. The large black eyes that spoke a million intentions, none of which it was capable of deciphering. The beautiful streamlined body that effortlessly circumnavigated its helpless form. The rows of sharp, triangular teeth that had decided the creature's fate, and the triangular point that emerged sharply from the hunter's back. Unlike others of its kind, a large chunk was missing from this protrusion. This was the price to be paid for straying into the territory of another.

The hunter closed in for the final attack…

As mother and infant departed, the body of the dead Carcinoma sank into the depths, leaving a trail of pink blood.

The mother regarded the infant with one of her black orbs, and in a language alien to other species she said:

One day you will hunt and defend your territory with the pride of your ancestors…

To obtain further copies of the book, or feedback your thoughts on the book please contact the author, Neil Clift, at:

Neil.Clift@btopenworld.com

Thank You